PRAISE FOR

Beautiful Disaster

"Can this really be a debut novel? In *Beautiful Disaster*, Laura Spinella weaves the past into the present with a sure hand as she tests the boundary between love and obsession. With its evocative Southern setting and finely drawn characters, *Beautiful Disaster* confronts the reader head-on with this question: What would you risk for a love you know is right and true?"

—Diane Chamberlain, author of *The Shadow Wife*

"*Beautiful Disaster* is a beautifully crafted romance set against a Southern backdrop. A powerful tale about the power of love. A wonderful read."

—Wendy Wax, national bestselling author of
The Accidental Bestseller

"Who can resist a dangerous man with a complicated past and a sweet side that exists for only one woman? Laura Spinella takes the fabric of this familiar scenario and twists it into unexpected knots just for fun. I loved following Mia and Flynn through their passionate beginnings and into their uncertain present. *Beautiful Disaster* is a lovely, sexy, soulful debut."

—Jean Reynolds Page, author of *Leaving Before It's Over* and
The Last Summer of Her Other Life

Beautiful Disaster

LAURA SPINELLA

BERKLEY BOOKS, NEW YORK

THE BERKLEY PUBLISHING GROUP
Published by the Penguin Group
Penguin Group (USA) Inc.
375 Hudson Street, New York, New York 10014, USA
Penguin Group (Canada), 90 Eglinton Avenue East, Suite 700, Toronto, Ontario M4P 2Y3, Canada
(a division of Pearson Penguin Canada Inc.)
Penguin Books Ltd., 80 Strand, London WC2R 0RL, England
Penguin Group Ireland, 25 St. Stephen's Green, Dublin 2, Ireland (a division of Penguin Books Ltd.)
Penguin Group (Australia), 250 Camberwell Road, Camberwell, Victoria 3124, Australia
(a division of Pearson Australia Group Pty. Ltd.)
Penguin Books India Pvt. Ltd., 11 Community Centre, Panchsheel Park, New Delhi—110 017, India
Penguin Group (NZ), 67 Apollo Drive, Rosedale, North Shore 0632, New Zealand
(a division of Pearson New Zealand Ltd.)
Penguin Books (South Africa) (Pty.) Ltd., 24 Sturdee Avenue, Rosebank, Johannesburg 2196,
South Africa

Penguin Books Ltd., Registered Offices: 80 Strand, London WC2R 0RL, England

This is an original publication of The Berkley Publishing Group.

This is a work of fiction. Names, characters, places, and incidents either are the product of the author's imagination or are used fictitiously, and any resemblance to actual persons, living or dead, business establishments, events, or locales is entirely coincidental. The publisher does not have any control over and does not assume any responsibility for author or third-party websites or their content.

PRINTING HISTORY
Berkley trade paperback edition / January 2011

Library of Congress Cataloging-in-Publication Data

Spinella, Laura.
    Beautiful disaster / Laura Spinella.—Berkley trade pbk. ed.
        p.   cm.
    ISBN 978-0-425-23860-8
    1. Women interior decorators—Fiction. 2. Triangles (Interpersonal relations)—Fiction. I. Title.
    PS3619.P5635B43   2011
    813'.6—dc22   2010037206

PRINTED IN THE UNITED STATES OF AMERICA

10   9   8   7   6   5   4   3   2   1

For Matt,
who never questioned, never hesitated,
who let me do this unconditionally

ACKNOWLEDGMENTS

Writing may be a solitary act, but it is never a solitary effort. First and foremost, thank you to Susan Ginsburg, the extraordinary agent who knew the way. Thank you also to Bethany Strout; the opportunity to be a part of Writers House amazes me every day. Thank you to Berkley Publishing and my editor, Leis Pederson. Her steadfast enthusiasm and flawless guidance are the perfect complement to this book.

My sincere gratitude to my first reader, Cathy Jensen, and my in-between readers: Kimberly Hixson, Jeannine Jamieson, Christine Lemp, and Annette Scannapieco. My profound appreciation to Melisa Holmes, who read this manuscript more times than one human being should be asked, who will answer the phone and seemingly insane questions at all hours, and whose friendship has accompanied me from Athens to Boston and all points in between.

Several people shared their area of expertise, providing the threads that helped me weave this story. Thank you to Staff Sergeant Matt Zeiszler, USMC; Judy Connelly, RN, MS, CNRN; Laura Catanzaro, LEED® AP; Master Bruno Souza; and Miss Bryna Starling.

Finally, thank you to my family—extended and near, my parents especially. Thank you to Matt and Megan, who often picked up my slack, and to Grant for asking every day how the writing went. To Jamie: *Go Dawgs!* I hope you have as much fun as your mother did.

Beautiful Disaster

Chapter 1

MARYLAND

You wouldn't think that the smell of bourbon could derail a business dinner. Yet as Aaron Hough was served another drink, Mia wondered if holding her breath was a viable option. Time had a clumsy clutch on her arm, the thick aroma of distilled grain grabbing like an embrace—or maybe just a noose around her neck. *Focus, focus, focus . . . You've worked twelve years for these two hours.* She sipped her wine and tried to fill her nose with the benign bouquet of house chardonnay. It really didn't help. It wasn't really the bourbon. The smell was a trigger for banished thoughts and discarded dreams—things that no longer had a place in her life. But as the millionaire investor turned to his PDA, Mia seized the opportunity and slid the glass of bourbon toward him.

He caught her.

"Is there a problem, Mia?"

"Problem?" She blinked, doe-eyed, her fingernails tapping against his glass. "No . . . no problem." Tipping it, she examined the tea-colored liquid. The contents of the glass—or her head—

caused Mia's toes to curl up tight inside her pumps. "Ice," she insisted, forcing a smile. "It didn't look like there was enough ice."

"I drink it neat," he said, gliding a toast toward her before
drawing a long sip.

"Bourbon's kinda meant to be sipped, not slung. Like this . . ."

The words in her head were old, though the voice was crystal clear. And it invaded like always, like a vagrant crashing a
country club. Pursing her lips, Mia focused on the silver-haired
businessman seated across from her. Seeing this man hold a glass
of bourbon was a stark contrast. While Aaron Hough could be
described as dashing, he hardly matched the untamed image
that bourbon conjured up. Mia cleared her throat, dismissing
the inappropriate thought.

"Yes, of course, Aaron. Sorry. As I was saying, I think you'll
be impressed with the final presentation for the mock office. Eco-
friendly interiors have made terrific progress. But holistic design—
not everybody appreciates the difference. The success of this
project could lead to revolutionary changes in the common office—
comparable to Xerox machines and computers. The concept is real.
And I have to say, your interest has been . . . exceptional."

"Well, I didn't make millions—okay, billions," he corrected,
raising a brow, "without taking a few risks. And I know you've
had a difficult time securing a backer. Holistic design, it's an
atypical investment for me, I won't kid you. But, damn it," he
said, smacking a fist onto the table hard enough to make her
jump, "I thought it was time to take action, set an example for
my peers. You know how it is. Bullheaded, filthy rich moguls;
we're skiing in the Italian Alps one week, on a mission to save
the planet the next."

He rolled into a hearty laugh and Mia followed his cue. It
was their third meeting and she never could pin down his eccentric humor. She supposed it was part of the whole millionaire—

billionaire—mogul motif: long-winded jags on the life and times of Aaron Hough, laced with unfunny bits of self-deprecating humor. He finished the drink and Mia settled into her seat, prepared to be engaged as he filled her in on his post-Yale years, which was where he'd left off at their last meeting. With a breath of surrender Mia reminded herself how hard she'd worked for the potential contract, even passing on conventional projects that were a sure thing. Eventually he'd concede the conversation, allowing Mia the chance to talk about the future of her designs. Then she could get into the details, the innovative plans she had for Hough's portfolio of commercial properties. It was only a matter of keeping her focus—the telltale aroma of bourbon notwithstanding. Rallying appropriate interest, Hough caught her off guard with an unexpected change of topic.

"It's a shame your husband couldn't join us. I feel as if I already know Michael, or should I say the man behind the creative force of Montgomery Interiors. Out of town, is he?"

The laborious breath halted and Mia teetered on the edge of a white lie. "Well . . ." she began, deciding to err in favor of the truth. "To be honest, Aaron, Michael had tickets to a rock concert—the one downtown." She laughed, hoping he'd follow her cue. "It was a once-in-a-lifetime, backstage pass kind of thing. An old college buddy invited him. But he was sorry to miss—"

"No need to explain," he said, waving her off. "Imagine the fantastic trouble he'll get into! I believe I'm damn jealous. Nothing like a night of youthful insanity."

"I don't know if I'd categorize anything Michael does as insane. It's more"—she paused, scrunching her brow—"more like a calculated departure from the world of finance and a corner office. As for trou—"

"You know," he said, and her mouth clamped shut. "I once

arranged an entire business junket around a leg of Madonna's European tour. Front-row seat at every venue." Mia smiled, praying there wouldn't be an explicit recollection involving Aaron Hough and the Material Girl's leg. "I don't want to brag, but by my third trip backstage . . . Well, let's just say I was intimate with the inner circle."

Mia kept a poised expression, hiding a merciful sigh when her phone rang. The words *Good Samaritan Hospital* popped up. This time she caved, giving in to the white lie. She knew it was Roxanne. A doctor at Good Sam, and a friend since college, the culinarily challenged physician was probably looking for a hot meal. But Aaron Hough didn't know that. "Oh gosh, I'm so sorry," she said. "I need to get this, it's the hospital."

He stopped cold. "Of course, I hope it's not serious." He rose from his seat as Mia excused herself and hurried toward the restaurant's vestibule.

She laughed as she answered the phone, thinking what little patience Roxanne would have for Hough's self-indulgent humor—direct, no-nonsense, and opinionated, she surely would have interrupted to ask how he'd managed to squeeze his head through the restaurant's door. "What's up, Rox? If you're hungry, something tells me I'm going to have a doggie—"

The Southern drawl was expected but the voice eerily tense. "Mia, be quiet and listen to me. I only have a minute. Then I have to get back to him, back to the emergency room . . ."

* *

Rushing to the table moments later, Mia barely gathered enough composure to make her excuses. "I have to go. It's, um . . . it's an emergency," she eked out. "There was an accident. Roxanne—she's a doctor, a good friend of mine. She said there was a horrible wreck, an intersection near the downtown arena.

Roxanne said he—" She couldn't finish the thought; it was too unbelievable.

"How terrible. Let me drive you, I insist."

Mia hardly heard him. On a mad shuffle through her purse, she tossed a lipstick and a pack of gum onto the floor, finally coming up with her keys. They dropped from her hand and Aaron retrieved them. "Drive me?" Mia said, a glassy gaze meeting his. "No—you can't. I mean, that's very kind of you, but it's not necessary. I know a lot of back roads to the hospital. It'll be quicker if I drive. I'll be fine." Moving fast toward the exit Mia spoke over her shoulder. "I'm sorry about dinner."

"Nonsense, it's not important. I hope . . . I do hope Michael is all right," he called after her.

Pivoting on high heels, Mia almost lost her balance. With her mouth agape, her arms slapped aimlessly through the air. "Thank you." It was all she could manage, running for the parking lot.

* *

Every time the emergency room doors swung open, Mia's heart leapt from her chest. A nurse had showed her to the waiting room—hours ago. She had grabbed Mia by the arm and told her to sit, calm down. Hyperventilating like that could lead to serious consequences. In turn, Mia wanted to grab her by the throat and demand to see him right then and there. After a dozen inquiries to the charge nurse, she managed to stay in the chair, connecting with the part of her brain that knew how to cope with catastrophe.

The conversation with Roxanne had been brief. Life-altering discussions should take longer, or so Mia thought. There was shouting in the background. A nurse, maybe an intern, calling out, "His stats are dropping again, Dr. Burke. Do you want to intubate?" Roxanne answered in some warrior doctor dialect, like a translator at the UN. Mia could have sworn she was speaking in tongues. The only part she understood was a demand for four units O neg and that someone open all his IVs—stat.

Mia forced her eyes away from the emergency room doors, scrubbing a hand over her face. "Damn, I should have told her, B positive. He's B positive." But it all happened so fast. It was one of those everyday things, misplaced—like your winter gloves. As she waited, Mia tried stitching together the scattered information. There wasn't much to go on. Roxanne had spoken in short, jerky phrases, saying that she didn't think he'd make it. That if Mia wanted to see him . . . see him before he . . . *died*, she'd have to hurry. She said something about owing her as much before she hung up. Mia drove like a madwoman through Silver Spring rush-hour traffic. She would have driven straight through hell if it meant getting there in time. But they were already in surgery when she arrived.

For the past two hours and forty-seven—forty-eight—minutes, everyday things had kept Mia company. They surfaced at random, like friends at a reunion. It had been some time since she thought about coffee so strong the smell could spark a case of the jitters. As the first hour came and went, it was soft cotton T-shirts worn so hard Mia could see the shape of his body as the shirt fell to the floor. And crossword puzzles. She still had no patience for the one in the back of the *TV Guide*. He once did the *New York Times Best Of* collection—in ink. Mia bent forward, hands pressed to her head. It was a lame attempt to silence his voice, a penetrating timbre that played best in bed on dark rainy nights. At the moment she couldn't take it. Mia closed her eyes, thinking that when she opened them it would be a dream. He was always in her dreams—maybe this was just a bad one. After she married Michael, when he was there every night, Mia guessed that would put an end to them. It wasn't the case. The doors opened again and rainbow patterned scrubs headed straight for her.

"Mia Wells. You are Mrs. Wells, right?"

Her words were out of sync, like in a movie when the dialogue doesn't match the actor's lips. Mia nodded, curious if it was still the right answer.

"Dr. Burke is out of surgery. She asked me to bring you up to the ICU."

Life pulled Mia to her feet. "Then he . . . he's still alive?" *The morgue, the morgue is where they take you to identify a body.* "If you're taking me to the ICU then he can't be dead, right?"

"Yes, he made it through surgery. Won't you come this way, please?"

But she could tell it wasn't good. The nurse's tone didn't offer anything beyond *not dead*. Mia followed her to the elevator, trying to keep comfort with those everyday things. As they waited, as the floors clicked by, she eventually got back around to Aaron Hough's bourbon. It was an everyday thing turned ominous, and the timing wasn't lost on her. She stepped from the elevator, understanding that the short ride to the sixth floor was going to change everything. It didn't matter. It wasn't like she had a choice.

Double doors swung wide and Roxanne appeared. Mia stopped midstride.

She was anticipating a pressed white lab coat, her name neatly embroidered above the pocket, everything in order, every blond hair in place. What she saw put the moment in context—bloody scrubs, hair stuffed tight under a cap, a band of sweat circling it. And the look on her face . . . The only thing to which Mia could relate it was the time she'd accidentally slammed Roxanne's hand in a car door. This was worse. Seeing her, Roxanne's pace slowed.

"I . . . I was going to change," she said from a distance. "I didn't want you to see me like—"

"Rox, are you . . . ? God, there's so much blood," she said, shuffling a few steps closer. She gulped hard and forced her stare onto Roxanne's face. "He's alive? He's in there?" she asked, pointing.

Roxanne nodded. But her gaze kept flicking past Mia's head, like she was looking for someone. "Listen, I don't know if I did the right thing. Michael, he—"

"Michael's at a concert clear across town," she said. "You know that." Then, in a smaller voice, "I . . . I can't think about that right now." Mia closed the remaining space, ready to push right past Roxanne and go see for herself. And she would have if she could just get her mind around it, get her feet to move. Stepping off the end of the earth would require less mental preparation. For twelve years she had wondered. Gotten up and gone to bed with the same question. Thought maybe she'd dreamed him up, thought he was dead. She thought he'd be better off that way if she ever caught up with him. More than anything, Mia thought that this was the moment that came after insanity. "Answer me, Roxanne. Are you sure it's Flynn?"

Chapter 2

A motorcycle eased through three lanes of backed-up traffic. Some drivers leaned on their horns in frustration, while others honked to cheer on the rider, pumping their fists at the highway-turned-parking lot. Twelve miles later he finally saw the problem: two automobiles involved in what had to be a fatal crash.

Emergency vehicles were scattered across the interstate, dispatched to mend the situation. In the distance, fire trucks dotted a cloudless sky. The intense June Georgia sun caught their flashing lights, absorbing the ruins of shiny metal objects fanning out into a sparkling kaleidoscope of carnage. A ninety-degree day had to break one hundred on that scorched pavement. Even breathing required effort. Wavy fumes of heat seemed to be the only things moving with urgency, while the humid air stood unmotivated, hanging around like a disinterested bystander.

Only a few yards away, the rider eased over to the breakdown lane as a tow truck prepared to move the first vehicle. The mangled minivan looked as though it had been delivered there from the jaws of a vehicle compactor. The second car sat in the median. It hadn't fared much better, with a smashed windshield and the driver's door crushed through to the passenger side. The bike idled and the rider took off his helmet, shaking out a sweaty mane of hair. With the eye of a seasoned rider he surveyed the parts strewn across the sweltering blacktop. Surrounding him were the remnants of a motorcycle. It was in more pieces than it ever had been in on the assembly line. The rear sprocket and drive, the primary chain cover, a speedometer crunched inside its shell, the ignition coil, and a mangled front fender skirt. Unique to the Harley Davidson and no bigger than his fist was a black motor housing. Aside from the tires, it was the largest piece left. The drama played out further when the tow truck pulled away and revealed the worst of the tragedy—a body covered with a bloodied sheet. Behind mirrored sunglasses, the rider's pale, careful eyes reconstructed the accident. On second thought, the two cars didn't look so bad. At least the parts wouldn't have to be collected in a bucket with a pair of tweezers.

He looked over the car in the median, noted its proximity to the body and the point of impact. "Jesus," he mumbled. The biker had been the meat in the collision, the two vehicles sandwiching him in between. He gave a dry swallow and offered up a token prayer for the deceased.

A grim-faced state trooper began to redirect traffic around the site. The biker looked over the scene once more, realizing that something was missing. He revved the engine and took his place in line. "Stupid bastard," he whispered as he passed. "Wasn't even wearing a helmet."

The bike rumbled up to the curb in downtown Athens, announcing his arrival like a lion advancing on new territory. Goddamn, but it was hot. He was used to hot places. Not that he had ever learned to like them. Rural Indiana, where he grew up; Parris Island; the bottom of hell—he always ended up in places where sweat was part of the dress code. The sidewalk was thick with college kids; they kept the place going, from what he had heard. College towns were a handy place to hang for a while. Nobody asked too many questions. If anything, people encouraged a come-as-you-are attitude. The casualness appealed to him. Conforming would never work out—ask any Marine.

An eternity on the bike coupled by hours in a traffic jam had left his long legs cramped and a little wobbly. Food would be a good idea. He tugged at the sweaty jeans that were seared to his skin and pulled a red bandana from his pocket, blotting his grimy brow. Stepping to the curb, he attempted to blend in with the crowds of backpacks and portable CD players. He felt the staring eyes as he moved among them. Girls mostly. Girls always looked at him. He wasn't the typical fare, with hair as long as theirs and the scruffy beard. On most days it led to the Jesus remark before lunch. He didn't care, but sometimes he wanted to lean in toward their probing, dewy eyes and whisper, "Yeah, just think what your old man would do if you brought me home." He liked college towns, but he wasn't interested in college girls. Despite their glances, they weren't really looking for a guy like him either.

Even with his sunglasses on, he had to squint past scalding rays to read the sign for Mike's Burgers. From the look of it, he wondered if grease came à la carte on the menu. Hell, it was air-conditioned, there was food, and he was hungry. Forty-five minutes later he had downed the last of Mike's famous cheddar burger, a double order of fries, a beer, and two ice waters. All the while he watched a group of young men joke and carry on, betting their afternoon beers on a game of darts. He crunched down on the ice, curious if at their age he would have enjoyed spending daddy's money quite so much. He couldn't relate, but it sure did seem like fun. Finished with the water, he dunked the end of the bandana into the glass, then rubbed it along the back of his neck. The rolling tide of sweat had subsided, leaving what felt like a gritty coat of pavement over damp, dirty skin. In between the sailing darts, his mind wandered back to the accident. He couldn't shake it. Motorcycles could be dangerous things. You had to take care, follow the rules. Even a rogue like him understood that. He paid the tab and decided to walk the town. The hottest part of the day had passed; his jeans had relented their stranglehold on his thighs. At the door he caught the dart-playing boys gawking—okay, sometimes guys looked too.

The accident hung with him, provoking a sense of loneliness, maybe a whisper of fear. Who would have given a damn if he had been the dead rider? He cleared his throat as if to dislodge the thought. Vulnerability was a luxury, not an instinct—and he couldn't afford it. It didn't mesh well with a life that ran like some feral animal in search of its next warm hole and raw piece of meat.

A few doors away from the restaurant he dropped onto a sidewalk bench. He felt only marginally out of place, sitting next to an overflowing urn of potted petunias meant to beautify the downtown. He removed his sunglasses and cleaned them on his sweat-dampened T-shirt, then propped them on his head. The waning sun dipped behind the foliage of a curbside maple offering welcome shade. He tapped a Marlboro Light from its pack and lit it, further alienating himself from the picturesque scene. Taking up the length of the bench, he stretched out the achy, locked muscles of his arms. Three straight days through the Deep South had taken its toll. A cheap motel with a decent bed and a shower, that's what he should be thinking about, not death's random grasp, or mattering to someone.

He was ready to head back to his bike when a group of college girls drew his attention. They were a giggling lot, crowded

around the window of a small boutique across the street. He
had noticed the shop earlier. The window was filled with delicate bobbles and trinkets—girl stuff, for sure. He imagined the
clerk's startled expression if a guy like him were to wander into
a place like that. There would be an internal struggle: Should
she offer assistance or go straight for the can of mace? He found
himself laughing aloud at the mental picture as the girls walked
away. They moved in one simultaneous cloud of honey blond
hair, perfumed bodies, and sensual drawls. All except one. She
stepped in the opposite direction, calling out, "Save me a seat,
Rox. I'll be there in a few."

"Don't be too long, Mia. We'll get ahead of you," one of the
blondes answered. Mia waved to her friends and headed toward
him.

He stopped laughing, but the smile widened and now he
wasn't looking, he was staring. It was impossible not to; she was
beautiful. A brunette, an odd sight in this sweet cavity of the
South, a place where blond belles were more abundant than
magnolia leaves. She passed by, smiling at him or smiling from
before—he wasn't sure which. But he grabbed the chance to get
a closer look. Beautiful was a pedestrian description. She was
astonishing, stunning, hot . . . all of them. Huge wide-set eyes;
even from the distance he could see them sparkle—not green,
not blue, but something in between. Wispy bangs framed her
face with hair longer than his, falling midway down her back.
She wore it down. Heat tolerant, he thought. Impressive. And
the smile, it was probably more invitation than she intended.
His body rotated around, taking in the rear view. No words, just
a hollow gulp and a grin that turned a little sly. He untwisted his
body and looked back at the empty sidewalk. "Ah, shit, what the
hell," he murmured, tossing the cigarette into the urn of petu-

nias and popping up from the bench. He had seen death today. Might as well see what life had to offer. His long, eager strides easily caught up to her. "Um, miss, excuse me."

She turned, clearly looking for the other girl he must be talking to. Mia's eyes settled on him and the smile faded to uneasiness. "Who, me? You're talking to me?"

"Ah, yeah." He stepped back, giving her plenty of space, his hands shoved in his back pockets. Still, she took a step of her own. "I was wondering . . . Well, I saw you with your friends over there. I just got into town." *Maybe this wasn't such a great idea. She looks ready to scream.* "Could I buy you a beer?"

"A beer?" she questioned, as if alcohol were unheard of, as if there wasn't a bar on every corner.

"Yeah, a beer," he said, rubbing a hand over his bearded chin. "It's hot. I was thirsty. Thought maybe you'd like to join me . . ."

"You? You want me to have a beer with you?" she repeated, her hand darting back and forth between the two of them in a nervous fit.

"Yeah. Are we not speaking the same language here? It's not that difficult of a question." *That went well. Not only did I scare her, I insulted her too.* Doll's eyes. That's what they were, tremendous doll's eyes, crystal clear hazel in the middle, gray around the edges, and if they opened any wider they'd probably pop right out of her head. "I mean, if you're not doing anything, that is." His voice trailed away, his Adam's apple bobbing with faded enthusiasm.

Mia pointed in the direction of the friends who had long disappeared, raking a hand through her hair. "I . . . Well, it's very nice of you to ask, but I have to, um . . ."

She was struggling for politeness. Unbelievable. Good manners even when accosted by long-haired strangers. He had the sudden urge to ask her what was the matter with her. Didn't her mother warn her not to talk to strangers, especially ones who looked like him? "Hey, that's okay," he said. "It was just a spur-of-the-moment idea. And probably not a very smart one."

"Oh, no, like I said, it's nice of you to offer." But her head was nodding in agreement. "It's just that I'm meeting my friends."

"Right, your friends." Friends. She probably had dozens, and boyfriends too.

"Well, maybe some other time." Feeling as if he'd somehow violated her with the conversation, he turned to walk away. To his amazement, she called after him.

"Hey, um, what's your name? You know, in case I see you around town."

He turned, but kept walking backward. She probably wanted to know should she need to file a police report anytime soon. He hesitated, his eyes streaming over her figure. God, but she had incredible legs. Ah, what could it hurt? He'd probably never see her again. "Flynn. Name's Flynn." He never missed a stride, spinning back around.

"I'm Mia," she replied, as if surprised that he was retreating.

He spun on the heels of his weathered black boots once more. "Yeah, I know." He turned and disappeared around the corner.

Chapter 3

"Hey, Mia. What took you so long?" asked a well-decorated blonde whose wary glance darted toward her. She scooted over in the booth to make room and Mia sat. "Walking the streets alone isn't safe. They found another girl at Alabama today," she said, plucking skewered cherries from a plastic sword. "This one beaten senseless and drowned in the bathtub."

"Did they really? How awful," Mia said, putting a hand to her mouth. "That's nothing to be flip about and you know it." Roxanne Burke finding sarcasm in serial killings—for her it was a natural train of thought.

"I'm not," she insisted. "But I heard it was some random guy she picked up at a party—invited him back to her place. How often have I said," she cautioned, pointing the sword at the table of girls, "it's what that kind of behavior will get you?"

"So how many girls does that make?" asked another blonde, this one bleached platinum and also attractive, though not in Roxanne's league.

"Six, I think. And Roxanne wasn't being flip," offered a third blonde. "She's just ridiculously paranoid. 'Bama's like a zillion miles from here." Roxanne frowned as Sara blathered on, chasing her beer with a clear shot of something that certainly wasn't water. "Hey, Lanie, what do you call a pretty girl at 'Bama anyway?"

"Dead, apparently," Roxanne mumbled, sipping her fruity concoction.

"A visitor," Lanie offered, gulping her beer. "Come on, Sara, that joke is older than the Arch," she said, referring to the centuries-old University of Georgia entrance.

"I know, but it's so true," Sara said with a shrug.

The four girls broke into instantaneous giggles. With the first pitcher nearly empty, Mia ordered a beer from the passing waitress. The Odyssey was one of those offbeat college haunts where the floor was terminally sticky and the beer sometimes warm. But it was a short walk back to campus and the refreshments were dirt cheap.

"So did you find the paintbrush you were looking for?" asked Roxanne before she tossed popcorn into her mouth, taking meticulous care not to smudge her lipstick.

Roxanne Burke was the true debutante of the group and an utter contradiction. Plantation raised and cotillion bound, she was so beautiful it dripped off her like sweet icing over warm sticky buns. Heavenly blue eyes, beauty-contestant legs, and a face that had surely been kissed by the angels made Roxanne's looks her cross to bear, at least outwardly. She was actually more brilliant than beautiful—a fact that simply wasn't the first thing that struck most people. It amazed Mia, the assumptions people made about a girl who looked like that and sounded like that. And from what she had witnessed, it never dulled. Roxanne, on the other hand, couldn't be bothered—which wasn't to say it didn't bother her at all. But her focus was elsewhere, letting speculation roll on by like water over a stone.

"Mia, are you listening? Hello? The paintbrush? A half hour ago a number nine feather edge was a life-or-death matter," she said, snapping open a compact and applying a fresh coat of powder. Roxanne would never venture beyond the mailbox without a proper face. It was an integral part of the contradiction.

"The brush? Oh, right, the art store. No, I suppose I didn't. I got distracted." She was going to explain, but she didn't know what to say about her encounter with the denim-clad, long-haired stranger. Mia wasn't sure what she thought about him. Only that he *was* distracting, causing her to get halfway down the street, no longer interested in where she was going. Any explanation and Roxanne would arrive at a firm opinion that would quickly become her own.

"You're hopeless." Roxanne laughed, poking her with the plastic sword. "Can't even send you off down the street without a note reminding you where you're going."

The laughter and chatty banter rolled on and eventually a group of young men joined their small party. Lanie and Sara knew two of them, frat boys with a reputation for snagging the date of their choice. They naturally gravitated to Roxanne. She paid them no more attention than a pesky insect, plucking off their post-adolescent wings because, well, what else would she do with them? The night wore on and the boys soon tired of trying to impress the beautiful but socially awkward Roxanne. They took turns dancing with the other girls while she watched.

Mia stumbled back to her seat, having surpassed her usual cutoff point of three beers. It was a rule she and Roxanne invoked after a near-disastrous freshman year. College life and its no-holds-barred shot of freedom was a challenge to most freshmen, but more so for Mia, a girl who had a knack for being attracted to the wrong choice, like the tide to the moon.

Her father had been a prominent district attorney who'd

measured himself by the number of criminals he convicted. He died during Mia's last year of high school, leaving her a sizable trust and a landslide of free will, which turned out to be more enticing than the cash. While the money provided the means, it was the opportunity to make choices that motivated Mia most. It was a big learning curve for a girl who had been happy making art her focus, and whose father was happier still making all the decisions. Consumed by her social calendar—a way of life that Mia never could appreciate—her mother, Clarice Montgomery, wasn't much help. Actually, she seemed rather accepting, if not downright pleased, when her Bohemian-edged, artsy daughter took her father's last known advice and attended his alma mater—six hundred miles from home. This would make it difficult for Mia to stumble in on one of her mother's cocktail parties—one she'd been forewarned about—barefoot, wearing paint-splattered jeans, and eating cold pizza.

It was fine. Since her father's death, home was more a word than a place. As mother and daughter they were more about opposing lifestyles than matching ideals. Lincoln Montgomery had been the buffer, able to relate to both the women in his life who couldn't relate to each other at all. He adored being on the fringe of Mia's art, observing but never indulging. It pressed the boundaries of a man who was dedicated to symmetry and a cause. He was firm but kind. Until he died, it worked for a girl who had trouble finding her footing within the boundaries of standard procedure. Mia's first inkling of real life choices came not long after she arrived in Athens, discovering that a six-figure trust came with more responsibility than balancing a checkbook.

She had partied and played with her newfound wealth and independence until her grade point average was circling the drain, with her trust fund not far behind. A new car was quickly followed by a DUI and a few panicky hours in the Athens police station until Roxanne bailed her out. Sitting in the grungy cell, Mia could only imagine her father's disgust. He'd been gone less than a year, and here was his daughter staring at the very bars he had put criminals behind. It was a sobering humiliation, being associated with something so tainted. But Mia also recalled a wave of resentment. Lincoln Montgomery wasn't supposed to be dead; he was supposed to fix things like this—or better still, keep them from happening in the first place. The incident was a caution and a warning, but not quite enough to stop her.

Mia almost lost control of her life while she did lose her virginity to a seemingly nice boy from Alpharetta whose name she could not recall the next morning. They hadn't even used a condom. Fortunately, Roxanne was there in the aftermath, keeping it all together. And for that, Mia was grateful. There was somebody willing to pick up the slack that her father had left behind. It was Roxanne who held Mia's hand while she bit her fingernails to the nub, hoping that one regrettable mistake didn't result in another. The explosive sigh of relief could be heard across campus when Mia's STD and pregnancy tests came back negative.

From there Roxanne launched into a much-needed lecture on safe sex, responsible drinking, and not blowing an entire trust fund in a calendar year. It was good advice from someone who lived with the understanding that protecting yourself was paramount to risky desires. And Mia had grown accustomed to taking her social cues, if not daily direction, from her roommate and friend.

It had been nearly three years since the incident with the boy from Alpharetta. Mia had proven herself a worthy pupil, mastering tipsy but never again stone-cold drunk, only dating one other boy seriously, and curbing her spending habits. She'd grown up a lot in the last couple of years, but not enough to satisfy Roxanne, who still viewed herself as the adult in charge.

Tonight, though, Mia wasn't feeling all that responsible, content to let Roxanne play her part. The untamed man on the street, with his rough-and-tumble looks and bold invitation, tugged at what had become a predictable life. It made her wish for just a moment of insanity. She sighed at the thought and plopped down next to her best friend, ordering another pitcher. It was a small sign, something she wouldn't ordinarily do.

"Hey, thirsty tonight, aren't we?" questioned Roxanne as she raised a motherly eyebrow at Mia. She never missed a thing.

"Oh, come on, the guys will drink most of it anyway. I promise, last one. You're being more reserved than usual," Mia said, trying to change the subject. Her smoky eyes pulsed wide as she cast a teasing smile over Roxanne, who had difficulty finding a guy who met her standards. In fact, on a city-size campus, Mia could only think of one: Michael Wells. He was a good-looking grad student who, like Roxanne, took advanced calculus for the fun of it, living and breathing academic success. But to Mia's surprise nothing had sparked beyond their competitive tendencies. She shrugged, thinking she should encourage Roxanne to give him a call. "Odyssey crowd," Mia continued, gazing over the tipsy college clientele. It wasn't even a baseline for Roxanne. "You'd have to lower your standards for them to find your feet."

"No doubt," she said, turning a bright smile onto Mia. "Stepping over their drunken, prone bodies. That's as close to my feet—or any other part of me—as they'll get." Acerbic humor delivered with the perkiness of a homecoming queen. That was Roxanne. And nothing made Mia laugh more.

"I don't know what I'm going to do when you go off to medical school and leave me behind with my token textiles degree. I'm *sooo* glad you decided to stay for the summer semester," Mia gushed, throwing an arm around her.

"And I'm so glad I talked you out of majoring in papier-mâché and to put that artsy ability toward earning a real living."

Mia rolled her eyes at Roxanne. "I was only minoring in papier-mâché," she joked. "And I could have done something with an art degree."

"You'll do more with interior decorating, like feed yourself for the next twenty years. Besides, after I graduate from medical school, I expect to hire you. You'll have all the kinks worked out by then, and you'll certainly have given up those crazy bare-bones designs."

"They're not so crazy," Mia defended. "Recycled cardboard is a huge untapped resource. You watch; someday there will be a line of people waiting for corrugated furniture."

"Naturally." Roxanne smirked. "They'll be afraid to sit on it. And think of the perks. If you get fired, you can pack your office up in your furniture. How handy is that?" Mia huffed, concentrating on what was left of her beer. "Listen, keep designing those *Veranda* magazine covers: upscale, elegant—they're gorgeous," she marveled. "Things like silk drapes, not recycled furniture. That's what people want from their decorator."

"Interior designer," she corrected. "But I suppose you're right," Mia admitted, knowing several professors had echoed the same sentiment. "Besides, it's what I'm living for, the chance to decorate the distinguished *Dr. Burke's* tower office." The twosome laughed as Mia downed one more gulp. "So, Rox, if you're not drinking and you're not interested in flirting with any of these fine Southern boys, what are you doing sitting over here all by yourself?"

Roxanne's chin tipped higher. "I'm watching him," she confessed, pointing a perfectly buffed nail across the bar. Mia cocked her dizzy head to one side and followed Roxanne's steady finger to the far side of the bar. "I'm watching Jesus polish off his second bourbon, straight up, no ice."

A stunted "oh" was the only thing Mia could manage as her gaze came to rest on Flynn, sitting alone, trying hard to blend into his side of the bar.

"He's been here for a while. Seemed to be looking at you at first. But I figured that had to be a mistake. I mean"—her eyes flicked over Mia's striking but innocent features—"my guess is you're not his type."

"What makes you say that?" Mia asked, intrigued by the instant secret she now harbored from the all-knowing Roxanne. "Not pretty enough for him?"

"Pretty? No, I doubt *pretty* is on his to-do list. He's probably into things like leather thongs and pierced body parts that don't include your ears. All of which, I believe, puts you out of the running."

"Hmm. For a girl who's been pigeonholed as a dumb blonde her whole life, you're a pretty quick judge of character." Roxanne bristled at the remark, tightening her already straight-spine posture. "You really think he's that wild? I think maybe he's just . . ." The words slurred as she leaned into her friend. "Undomesticated." Mia popped back up in her seat, pulling away. "I bet I could get him to buy me a drink."

Roxanne looked her over, her brow gathering in disbelief. "You? You think you can get that"—she motioned toward him—"to buy you a drink? For a lap dance, maybe. But solely based on your, uh, sweet but tame charms?" She frowned at Mia. "You'd stand a better chance of selling him that cardboard chair, assuming it came with a whip. Come on, let's go home." Roxanne tugged at her arm, ready to make her exit.

Mia jerked it back. "I'm serious, and I'm not that drunk. I'm more versatile than you know. What? You think the only guys I can attract are collared-shirt, close-cropped preps who've had the same condom in their wallet since the ninth grade? I'll bet you my chem lab—yours to finish—if I can get him to buy me a drink in"—she glanced dramatically at her watch—"under two minutes."

Roxanne's eyes brightened as she suppressed a telling smile. "All right, Mia, but what do I get when you lose?"

"Well, that's how sure I am that I'll win. But just to make it fair, if I lose I'll wash your car this weekend."

"And wax, a coat of wax too," Roxanne wagered, her blue eyes narrowing cynically, like a bookie on to a sure thing. The bet was on; Roxanne abhorred anything that could be construed as manual labor. Mia took a deep breath and rose from her seat, fussing a moment with her skirt, finger combing her hair. "Don't bother, unless of course you *are* wearing a leather thong under that thing." Roxanne playfully peeked under the edge of the skirt as Mia slapped her hand away then smoothed it again. She settled back into the booth, arms folded. "Well, what are you waiting for? Second thoughts on that bet? Don't worry, I'll be right here watching. And I promise not to laugh when he bolts for the exit." Mia threw her a cutting glance as she started out across the bar.

Chapter 4

Flynn wrinkled his gritty brow and swiped his mouth with the back of his hand. He had discreetly observed the animated exchange between Mia and her friend and figured it might have something to do with him. Finger pointing and whispers were not uncommon. But now she was coming toward him, probably a warning to get lost before her boyfriend, the football star, showed up. He'd go quietly; he didn't need any trouble. Surprisingly, there was no hesitation in her step and she confidently took the seat next to him as if they were old buddies.

"Hi, Flynn. I didn't see you over here." Her smile was bright and anxious; she didn't appear to be on the verge of telling him off.

"Hey there, Mia," he said softly. "I didn't expect to find you here. I mean, I didn't follow you, if that's what you're thinking."

"It never occurred to me. I was wondering if that drink offer was still good?"

"Um, sure. Can I get you that beer?" The shyness she'd exhibited earlier seemed to have vanished, no doubt with some encouragement from the alcohol he could smell on her breath.

She glanced past his arm, eyeing his drink. "You know, I think I'm ready to up my game. I'll have whatever you're having. Bourbon, is it? Straight up, no ice, right?"

This was startling. He would have guessed she was a cautious social drinker with a three-beer max. "Whatever you want, sweetheart." He smiled, unsure of what to make of the burst of brazenness, and flagged the barmaid. Once the drink was delivered, he asked, "So I take it you go to school here?"

"Yes, just starting my senior year. Cheers!" she said, throwing back a hideously large gulp.

He could have sworn he saw tears well up in her eyes as she stifled a cough. "You okay?"

"Ah, yeah, sure. It's just that bourbon, um, is not my usual."

"Is that right? Well, you might fare a little better with it if you don't treat it like a shot. Bourbon's kinda meant to be sipped, not slung. Like this," he said, demonstrating.

"Of course, I see." She followed his lead.

He observed her, drawing in a shallow breath as her pouty pink lips made delicate contact with the glass. She caught his stare and the earlier shyness edged back. Mia put the drink down and steadied herself against the bar with arched fingertips, swiveling in the seat. She looked like a kid at a candy counter. Flynn guessed she didn't frequent too many barstools.

Smiling at him, she dove headlong into conversation. "So what brings you to Athens? Are you from Georgia?"

"No, Indiana. I do a lot of traveling on my motorcycle, you know, see-the-country kind of thing. I've been in Alabama the past few weeks. A guy I know mentioned Athens, said it was pretty country. Just thought I'd check it out. It's way prettier than I imagined."

"Mmm, I thought so too." The compliment registered a moment later and her gaze fell to the floor, hiding a warm blush. "I mean, I'm from Maryland. Not from here either."

Flynn couldn't remember the last time he'd actually seen a girl blush. This was the girl he'd noticed earlier, the one whose unassuming manner made her the center of attention. "I see. You're a ways from home then too?"

"I guess Athens is kind of home now. Since my father passed away, my mother and I aren't particularly close. I don't have any brothers or sisters."

Families, not a favorite subject. "Um, sorry about your dad. What kind of degree are they sending you back with?"

"Textile Applications."

"Pardon?" he asked, wondering what else the real world had invented while he wasn't paying attention.

"It's a business degree really. I'm going to be an interior designer. I thought it would be more lucrative than papier-mâché." She laughed and his brow furrowed. "It'll be fun, kind of like decorating at Christmas, only year-round. Instead of ornaments and mistletoe, it'll be paint chips and window treatments . . . that sort of stuff."

"Right, of course," he said, expressing the same vagueness she did over the bourbon. "What the hell is a window treatment?"

"A fancy way of saying I'm going to charge you two thousand dollars for these silly silk drapes."

"Oh, makes sense." A mutual smile passed between them and he brought the glass to his lips again. She did too, although Flynn was sure she was holding her breath with every sip.

"How long will you stay in Athens? Don't you have a job or a family?"

"I find work—construction, somebody's always looking for a mechanic, whatever's paying. I don't usually spend more than

a month in one place. I like to keep moving. My mom's in Indiana, a brother out west, and my sister, Julia, lives in Texas.
They're there if I need them, but that doesn't happen too often."
He leaned back, appalled at himself. She was a goddamn dose of
truth serum. Things were falling out of his mouth as though his
ability to censor had short-circuited.

"Isn't that lonely? Maybe even a little scary? What would you
do if you got sick or hurt? Don't you need anybody?"

It wasn't the response he was expecting, and was way too
close to that queasy feeling of vulnerability he'd fought off earlier. "I guess it's not something I consider on a daily basis. What
made you think of it?" he asked, turning the question back on
her.

"That's easy. I'm horrible at being on my own. I wouldn't last
five minutes by myself. I don't know what I'd do without my
friends," she said, pointing at the girls. "To tell you the truth,
before my father died, the only thing I remember deciding for
myself is what to get him for his birthday, and even then he
left a detailed list. I probably couldn't decide what to have for
breakfast without six different opinions." She laughed. But he
suspected there was something decidedly unfunny about it.

"Nothing wrong with having a support system. Just didn't
work out for me, that's all." He spied her nearly empty glass,
flagged the barmaid, and asked for two ice waters instead.

"What have you been doing, crisscrossing the country on
your motorcycle since high school? There's never been anyone or
anything you've belonged to?"

Damn, how did the conversation end up here? Shifting on
the barstool, Flynn finished his last gulp of bourbon, matching
the one she took. The gap of time in his past—he didn't know
how to account for it, couldn't explain it. In minutes she had
managed to wriggle under his skin, past the grime and sweat,

brushing against things that mattered. Gathering a breath, he was forced to say something. "I was . . . I was in the service for several years." It wasn't that much of a lie.

"Really? What kind? I mean, which branch?" she asked with an innocence that made him melt.

"The Marines . . . I was a Marine." He tried to say it in a finite tone, as if there was nothing more to know, but he could tell she expected him to go on. That wasn't going to happen. Maybe a flash of coldness would end it. "What's the look for, Mia? Can't picture me with the haircut?" And suddenly she looked hurt. *Damn.*

"No, no . . . it's not that. The Marines, that's huge. Were you stationed overseas?"

Again, his brain short-circuited from his mouth. "I did some maneuvers overseas, but I wasn't there for long."

"You were stateside, then. How long was your tour?" she asked proudly, having nailed the appropriate noun.

"My tour? Um, long enough. Hey listen, it's really not something I enjoy talking about. Not a lot of great memories, you know?"

"Not one nice memory? I'm sorry . . . that's awful."

Her fingertips grazed his arm and their eyes caught. Flynn felt at a disadvantage without his sunglasses. God, she was looking right into him. The small remark was so sincere and unsettling it caused him to turn his head away. He concentrated on the barmaid, a woman with a tattoo that dipped into fleshy cleavage and hair that was a bottled shade of red. He never worried about the kind of conversation he'd have with a woman like that. Silence settled between them as Flynn searched the busy bar for a place to hide his vulnerability. He rubbed his palms over his denim-covered thighs, realizing his hands were sweaty. The noise kept filtering in and out. The attraction, like the tide to the moon, kept pulling the two of them toward each other. Mia finally rescued him with a mutual distraction.

"So, is Flynn your first name or last?"

"Both, I guess. It's all I've gone by for years."

"You mean kinda like Madonna or Cher?"

A gilded smile returned and he relaxed. "More like Judas or—"

"Or just plain Lucifer," came a voice from behind them.

"Roxanne." Mia sighed without turning. "What's the matter, Rox, did you get lonely? I suppose you thought I'd be right back, but here I am, enjoying my drink." She spun around, raising her glass, greeting her with a look of triumph. "I'll need that chem lab by Monday."

Flynn turned to get a closer look. He'd noticed her before. Hell, blind men would notice her. Roxanne was something beyond a vision. Watching her glide primly toward them, he figured somewhere there had to be a tag on her that read BEAUTY QUEEN—DELUXE MODEL. But even from across the bar he sensed that the assumption was too simple. She was too engaged, concentrating on her surroundings as if she were on the front line. He didn't care for the type, always on the defensive. "Well, hello there, beautiful," he said, grinning sweetly, positive it would irk her. "Guess you caught my name, but, hell, call me Beelzebub, Prince of Darkness. Whatever turns you on. Buy you a drink, babe?" He winked, smoothly delving into the part.

In incremental, deliberate tics, Roxanne's head rotated toward Flynn, responding to the remark like she'd heard fingernails on a blackboard. "Well, the devil's spawn does take many forms," she replied coolly, looking Flynn over as if he were in need of an exorcism. "And no thanks, *babe*. The drinks are safer on the other side of the bar."

Flynn peered over to find the two frat boys making out

with Mia's friends. One had his hand halfway up the platinum blonde's shirt; the second looked as if his tongue were scraping the other girl's tonsils. His focus turned straight back to Roxanne. "Hmm, yeah, looks like a church social. What time's the prayer meeting?"

"Why? Does the Antichrist want to give the invocation?" she shot back. "Bet you do a mean imitation. Mia, I'm going to the restroom and then we're going home. You've made your point."

Flynn leaned back and folded his arms, curious to see how Mia would handle the ultimatum.

"Oh, well, Flynn and I, we were just talking."

Roxanne's brow pulled tighter, corralling her authority. "Right, but it's late, so say good night and let's get going."

Flynn watched, sure that he saw the heat in Mia's face rise.

"No, Rox, I'm not ready. But you go ahead if you want. I'll come home with Lanie and Sara in a little while."

"And leave you here with him? I wouldn't dare. Lord have mercy, what in the world have you been drinking?" Roxanne snatched her glass and gave it a hard sniff. "Great, Mia, beer then liquor, never sicker. You'll be in fine shape tomorrow. Probably throw up in my shower bucket again. Honestly . . ."

"Roxanne, you're being incredibly rude," Mia snapped, the anger in her eyes palpable. "What's the big deal? I'm fine, we're just talking."

During the entire exchange, Roxanne and Flynn had barely looked away from one another, a standoff of wills. He didn't offer an opinion; anything he said would just have been fuel for her fire.

Roxanne's fists rested firmly on her narrow hips, her soft painted mouth now in a tight, unwavering line. She forfeited the staring contest, her gaze finally shooting to Mia. "Like I said, I'll be right back, so finish the drink and your intellectual exchange on religious heretics and let's go." Mia didn't move and he watched a sharp swallow swim through Roxanne's delicate throat. "Besides, I need to get a jump on that lab." She turned, stalking off in the direction of the ladies' room.

Mia jumped up from the barstool, practically knocking Flynn's drink from his hand. "Do you believe her? I mean, who does she think she is?"

"Apparently she thinks she's in charge." He shrugged, feeling a little let down. Apparently Roxanne was going to prevail. Finishing his ice water, he pulled a tight roll of bills from his pocket. "Listen, Mia, it was really nice talking to you, but I don't want to cause a problem."

"You're not! She is!" Mia turned toward Flynn, watching him settle the tab. "You're going?"

He thought he heard disappointment. "Yeah, I still have to find a room, and I'm pretty tired." Flynn gave a lazy stretch, and he caught her eyes traveling his body. He considered for a moment what he'd like to do with hers. His thoughts dusted over the shapely legs that disappeared beneath a sexy, white skirt. It was short but not tight, sashaying along with her when she walked. She wore a sleeveless summer blouse, cut just low enough to attract the eye, revealing the tiniest bit of bare stomach. It was both sexy and sweet, made of some delicate pink fabric. But it was the fine strap of something silky beneath that drew his attention. Flynn admired it all for a second longer, then shook it off, thinking it was a dangerous game in which to indulge. Chatty, innocent, and way too easily influenced. "It's been a long day. Even Satan has to rest up for tomorrow's souls."

She licked her lips and glanced nervously around the bar, those doll's eyes sparkling wide. "Take me with you!"

"What?"

"I said I want to go with you. At least I can show you where the decent hotels are. Then you can give me a ride home," she added, making it clear that it was an act of defiance and not an invitation. "Come on, before she comes back." She tugged at his arm and her voice was almost pleading. She was surreal.

Perhaps he'd made a hasty judgment; maybe she had more resolve than he'd given her credit for. Flynn looked around a bar that was brimming with inebriated college kids. There were worse things to be had right there. It could be fun for a few hours. Then he would return her home, before she mistook him for anything but a brief walk on the wild side. "All right, Mia, but you have to at least tell your other friends that you're leaving." The protective urge he had when he first saw her on the street crept back. Part of him wanted to warn her not to do this. What did she know about him? Roxanne, for all her bossiness, was right. He could be any one of a hundred things, none of them good. Mia did as he asked, then grabbed his hand as she led him out the door.

Chapter 5

"That's right, you ride a motorcycle," Mia said, her confidence fading as she surveyed the ominous black bike glistening under the street lamps. It seemed to beckon to him, matching him so completely.

"Yeah, remember, I told you. Bike, cross-country—part of the whole devil image. Hey, listen, if you don't want to go, that's okay. I'm sure I can find a room with no problem. I've had plenty of practice. Besides, you've probably already given Roxanne a heart attack."

Guilt rose in his voice, but Mia quickly reaffirmed her decision—especially since Roxanne seemed so sure about hers. "No, it's fine. I want to go with you. I haven't been on a bike in years . . ." She caught his skeptical expression. "Okay, so I've never been on a motorcycle in my life. I'm riding it, not driving it. How hard can it be?"

"That depends. How drunk are you really? Do you think you can hang on?"

"Do you want me to walk a straight line for you? Count fingers? I'm okay. Promise."

He took a long look into her eyes and a measured breath as if calculating the possible hazards. Flynn's arm softly brushed against her stomach as he reached past Mia, causing her to break out in a rush of goose bumps. She wasn't sure if it was novelty or curiosity, but there was something that made him wickedly desirable. Before her tipsy mind could wander toward a quixotic thought, something heavy crunched down on her head, his hands tightening a strap around her chin. "Oh . . ." she said softly, reaching up to touch the helmet she now wore.

"You ride, you wear. Motorcycles are dangerous. Now, it's not gonna fall off, is it?" he asked, his eyes looking hard into hers. "That's as tight as I can get the strap. Listen, whatever you do, don't lean. Look over my shoulder and hang on."

She nodded yes, the helmet bobbing back and forth on her head. Mia was glad there were instructions. She could work with that. "But what about you? Isn't that dangerous?"

He only shrugged. "Nah, we're not going far. I'll be fine." Without another word he slung a leg over and cranked the motor with the obvious ease of a veteran rider. She hesitated, really absorbing him for the first time. The bike fit the long line of his body well, the lean muscle in his forearm tensing, connecting with the handlebars as if they were an extension of him. He stood for a moment, straddling the bike, reaching deep into his pocket. Even with the long hair, Mia could not recall ever seeing anything quite so masculine. He was as hard and streamlined as the machine he rode. She watched with fascination as a hair elastic appeared. Flynn expertly trapped the wild waves of his chestnut locks into a ponytail. Looking at her awestruck face, he shrugged again, remarking over the roar of the motor,

"It's hell to get the knots out otherwise." He edged forward and jerked a shoulder at her. Laughter erupted from her throat and she scrambled onto the bike, ready to ride.

Moments later they were winding through Athens's main thoroughfare, climbing the hilly streets, dipping deftly into the pocket of the next one. It was a fun city in a car, but exhilarating from this perspective. Instinctively her hands clasped around Flynn's waist. She found herself pressing hard into his back to block the wind, peering boldly over his shoulder at familiar terrain that had taken a precarious turn. She pointed out upcoming lefts and rights, guiding him down sorority row where big mansions housed throngs of old Southern alliances. They were as historic as the campus itself. Riding so free, Mia couldn't help but think that their rules and structure seemed confining. The air was fragrant and intense. She welcomed the sticky breeze, even if it was only man-made, motorcycle induced. It felt good.

When Flynn stopped for a light, he peered over his shoulder. "Doin' okay back there?"

"Oh yes! It's really so much fun!" She could see a smile creep onto his bearded face; he was probably amused by her giddy, schoolgirl answer.

"Hang on," he warned, quickly squeezing his hand tight over hers. A shiver of excitement pulsated through her body; her breath caught as the bike took off. Maybe it wasn't just the ride.

Mia directed him down a winding lane, thick with trees, the streetlights now gone. The only thing she could see was a narrow stream of pavement, lit from the bike's headlamp. "There's a big old house down this road. They rent rooms. It's a little hard to find in the dark, maybe a mile or so farther, on the left." The bike was moving slower now, the wave of exhilaration gone. An antsy feeling took root and she started to wonder about the dark road, rethinking her strategy—not that she had one to begin with. Mia let go of his waist and rubbed her hands on her bare thighs, realizing the skirt she wore was bunched up between her legs; not the smartest choice for motorcycle riding. Regardless, there she was, on a dark road with a near total stranger, slightly drunk. And she'd brought him there. Another swell decision. Roxanne's bossy demand suddenly seemed reasonable, and Mia wished she were there. Of course, Roxanne would never be so careless as to put herself in a position like this. "Here, turn here." She pointed to a dirt driveway, which she would not have spotted without the two shiny reflectors that flanked it. He cut the engine and she hopped off before the bunched skirt became an enticement. Quickly unbuckling the helmet, she thrust it back at him as if it were a game of hot potato. Thankfully she could make out a man at the front desk, the light of a television flickering brightly behind him. "Well, here we are," she said, trying to keep her voice steady. She was a dead giveaway when it came to nerves; Roxanne always said so. Her voice sounded like a bird tangled in a live wire when she was nervous. He seemed to sense it, stepping away from her, just as he had on the street.

"Yeah, looks like a nice place. How did you ever find it?"

Great, he probably thinks this is where I bring all the men I pick up in bars. "I didn't find it. I was here with someone. I mean I've never been here before, except twice . . . Somebody I picked up." Mia's eyes squeezed shut tight as his bugged wide. "I mean, to pick somebody up, not like that. A friend, she works here on the weekends. She says it's clean and cheap. Reasonable, I meant reasonable." She blew out a deep breath, thinking that was better. He probably didn't think she was a slut anymore, just an idiot.

"No, cheap is fine," he said, nodding at her rambling, edging toward the door. "I guess I'll go check in."

She followed, hoping she could use the phone and call someone to retrieve her, or at least make her presence known to the clerk. *That way he can help identify him in a lineup. Or worse, maybe he can just identify my body. Oh God, what am I thinking? What am I doing here?*

A less-than-congenial clerk, engrossed in a box of candy bars, took Flynn's money and shoved a room key at him, all the while cramming a Zagnut bar into his mouth. " 'Round back, private entrance. No smoking. Checkout's at eleven sharp." He licked coconut-covered peanut butter from his fingers and turned back to the television.

Flynn leaned over to Mia and whispered, "Clean and cheap; guess she never said anything about friendly, huh? I'm going to drop off my stuff and then I'll take you home, okay?"

She nodded as he walked out, feeling badly about her sudden ax-murderer judgment. Just the same, she'd save him the trouble and call a friend. "Excuse me, could I make a call from here? It's local. And a restroom; is there a bathroom I could use?" The sudden onset of nerves plus the beer made the need for a bathroom immediate.

"No calls from the desk. Your room's got a phone in it. Use that one," he grumbled, flipping from *The X-Files* to a Braves game, unwrapping another Zagnut.

"Well, what about the bathroom?" Even if she couldn't use the phone, there was no way she was going to make it all the way back to town without a potty break.

"Hey, you know, we got all the modern conveniences here. Your room's got a toilet too. This one's broken," he said, pointing his candy bar at a sign that stated as much.

"You don't understand. You see, we're not together. I mean, the room is for him, but I'm not staying with him."

With his jaw chomping away at the chewy center, the clerk flung his chubby head back as if Mia was keeping him from savoring the best part of the candy bar. "Look, lady, it's simple. If you want to use a phone or a toilet, you have two choices: Either use the ones in your room or rent another room."

I can't use the one in the room because I've brought this total stranger, who lives on a motorcycle and has half a name, down this desolate road and now I need to call someone to come and get me. Plus I have to pee like a racehorse, you ignorant ass! But no such words would come. She couldn't find the wherewithal to admit her foolishness or to confront this latest stranger who was hell-bent on redirecting her life. She tried once more to persuade him. "Listen, you don't seem to realize—"

"Lady, what the hell do you want from me!" he yelled, throwing the rest of the candy bar onto the desk.

A deep and equally loud voice broke from the doorway. "Mia, are you all right? What's going on?"

She turned to find Flynn staring down the clerk, looking as if he might leap across the counter. Signs and signals crossed in her head. He seemed so ready to come to her aid. "Nothing. There's nothing wrong." She gulped, watching his pale blue eyes sear a hole through the clerk's chewy center.

"She needs to take a piss and she doesn't seem to want to use the toilet in your room. Could you help her out?" he groused, sneering at them.

Flynn took two huge steps across the lobby and stood inches from the clerk's pudgy face, which suddenly went marshmallow white. "Excuse me? Who the hell do you think you're talking to? Did you eat your manners along with that box of candy bars?"

"Flynn," she said calmly, taking him by the arm. "It's okay. Really," she coaxed, giving him a gentle tug. "Let's just go."

Flynn looked at her and then back toward the clerk, whose petrified face pleaded for him to take Mia's advice. A hissing sigh escaped his throat as he turned and walked out.

"Sorry. I'm sorry I lost my temper, but he shouldn't have been rude to you. There's no excuse to talk to a girl like you . . . like that," he said, his hand gesturing toward the door. "And you shouldn't do that either," he added, turning his attention to her.

"Do what?" she asked, wondering if she was next in line for a tongue lashing. But his voice had calmed, and he now spoke firmly.

"Let anybody talk to you like that. It's important to stand your ground—especially when the other person is so obviously out of line." She nodded, considering the advice. "Come on, I'll take you home now."

Mia realized she was still holding his arm. His skin pulsated with heat and she could feel the residual quiver of a muscle. The encounter had upset him more than her.

"Oh, that's right, you need to use the bathroom. Tell you what. I'll wait outside. You go ahead," he said, holding out the key. "And lock the door."

Her fear vanished, instantly replaced by profound guilt. She wanted to crawl under the closest rock. She struggled for something to smooth it over. "Um, listen, Flynn. It's hot, I'm thirsty. Can I buy you a beer?"

His remaining anger faded and his face softened. "Me? You're talking to me? You want to have a beer with me?"

"Yeah, are we not speaking the same language? It's not that difficult of a question . . ."

* *

There was no beer available, but there was a soda machine on the side of the house. He insisted she take the key and use the bathroom. Although Mia had made the offer, he bought two Cokes. A rickety picnic table sat under a grove of Georgia pines, the area well lit by a security lamp. Flynn settled on top of the table, figuring she'd be relieved, not only to have used the facilities but to find him making use of the outdoor amenities, such as they were.

"Hey, there," he greeted as she made her way toward him. "You look more comfortable. Hop up, it's a great view. There's some heat lightning to the west," he said, offering her the can of soda.

"Thanks. Oh, look at that . . . it's like the Fourth of July," she marveled, gazing at the natural spectacle that did dress the night sky in a festive mood.

He grinned, wondering if she equated everything to a holiday. Surrounded by a pool of light, Flynn could see a relaxed smile on her face. He reached up and brushed back a strand of hair. "You do pretty well for June heat and a helmet." It surprised him when she didn't flinch, only a quizzical look. "Your hair. Most people would be a mess after a ride in the heat like that, but look at you . . . you're beautiful." He spoke casually, as if commenting on the weather, reaching around for the knapsack he'd retrieved from his bike. "It's a little late for straight soda. Mind if I freshen up mine?" She shrugged and he felt her curious stare on him as he took out a flask-size bottle of Jack Daniel's. Having emptied half the can he skillfully poured about a third as much bourbon into it.

"No sense in drinking alone." Mia held out her can, waiting for her share.

"No way. I'm afraid it's straight soda for you. I'm just going to have this one for the road, then I'm taking you home."

"Well, that seems unfair; you're the one who's driving, not me."

He hesitated, then nodded. "You're right," he said, putting the can aside. "Besides, I've seen what a few drinks do to you. Maybe Roxanne was right to be concerned." But the bottle of Jack Daniel's stayed in his hand. He was thinking that getting her really drunk would be a fast ticket to every smarmy fantasy that was rolling through his head and over her. But his mind kept curving all the way around, full circle, envisioning the way she'd look at him later.

"Mmm, I suppose I've given her reason in the past. I've made my share of bad choices."

"Who hasn't?"

Mia didn't hesitate. "Roxanne, for one." The smile went away.

"Yeah? What the hell brought you to that conclusion?" He laughed but stopped short, suddenly tangled in her serious expression, wanting to know why Roxanne got to pass on human error.

"Not everybody gets Roxanne, that's for sure. You can't. Not unless you know the whole story."

"The whole story," Flynn parroted, sure that any story about Roxanne centered on a scarring, unsuccessful bid for prom queen, or maybe a bad hair day.

"Roxanne may come off as bossy and abrasive—"

"*May* come off . . . ?" he said, cocking a brow. "I've known drill sergeants who were less tightly wound."

Mia laughed. "Well, I wouldn't know anything about that. But trust me," she said, "Roxanne's attitude isn't without reason." She stopped, looking him over. "Let me ask you something. Are you exactly what you appear, for the reasons people assume?"

And there she was, right under his skin again. But having been the one to pursue the topic, Flynn felt obligated to answer. "Um, no," he said softly, "I suppose not. It's more about getting from one day to the next—the assumptions just aren't worth my time."

"Funny, I could say the same thing about Roxanne." A curious glance rocked between them, and Mia smiled. "Circumstance elevated life to a whole different level for her. Every day is about succeeding, protecting the people around her. That's a tough job," Mia said. "No margin for error."

And that much he could relate to. Considering his own margin for error, Flynn picked up his drink and forced a single gulp down his throat. But it was the seriousness in Mia's voice that spurred him on. "So what happened to taint somebody so young and—admittedly—beautiful?"

"It didn't happen to Roxanne. Well, not directly," Mia said, taking the flask, pouring some into her can before he could protest. "Her older sister . . . Rory." He watched as Mia's thumb rolled through the condensation, hesitating, maybe deciding if he was worthy of her confidence. Drawing in a shallow breath, she sipped the drink, her gaze panning the night sky. Mia turned and looked at him. "It's a very long story," she said, "and not really mine to tell." Clear code for it was none of his business; clearer still was her loyalty to a friend. "Let's just say because of Rory, watching for the train wreck is what Roxanne does."

"I see," Flynn said, guessing Rory must have slammed headlong into it. "So I suppose that makes me your train wreck." The sound of soft, throaty laughter surprised him, gliding through the steamy night air. Mia shook her head, her long hair swaying back and forth as her eyes fluttered over him. It made his breath tremble and his insides go gooey in some way he hadn't thought about since the eighth grade.

"I don't know, Flynn. So far, you're just a guy who wanted to have a drink. It's not a crime; it's hardly cause for concern. Roxanne overreacted—I get that. Actually, the two of you are rather straightforward. It's my motivation that's less clear. I bet her that I could get you to buy me that drink . . . knowing of course you would. I brought you here, put myself in this position, and can't figure out for the life of me why I did any of it. Well, other than to step away from an average existence. And that, I think you'll agree, is not a great reason to take off with a stranger on his motorcycle." She tipped her chin to the moonlight, turning her concentration to smaller things, like the universe. "You want the truth? If you kissed me right now, I wouldn't be the least bit offended. Oh, I might slap your face—good posturing, you know? But I really wouldn't mind."

His mouth turned down slightly. Flynn wasn't sure what to make of her declaration, but he was fairly certain he didn't want to get slapped. "That's a lot to think about. But right now, I'll let you finish your drink. I'm more sweaty pavement than skin. I'm going to take a quick shower." He hopped down off the table and went inside, leaving the door open, leaving Mia to make her own choice.

* *

Mia sipped the drink. The bourbon slid down much easier when sugared up with a can of Coca-Cola. Her bulleted reasons for going with him didn't include everything. Yes, it may have been reckless, a knee-jerk reaction to Roxanne's control, but it wasn't all impulse. She was drawn to him in a way that didn't seem normal, but all the same felt quite natural. It struck her even before he approached, when she crossed the street downtown. She had smiled at him but wasn't sure he'd noticed. There were all the obvious signs: the dangerous look, the hard liquor, the hard life—which he hadn't mentioned yet, but Mia was certain it was there. It was a rare, combustible attraction, disturbing and beautiful, like that unexpected heat lightning illuminating a black, cloudless sky. At the time she thought that was all there was to it. The risky stranger on the bench, he hardly fit within the guidelines of her safe existence. But Mia felt a need to dig in when Roxanne balked; it wasn't her choice to make.

Before Mia realized she'd been thinking and walking, she

was back inside his room. Her heart was the only muscle left moving; the rest of her stood there, wide-eyed and frozen, knowing it was somewhere she shouldn't be. As Mia noted on her first trip through, the room was what she expected: cheap furniture, two double beds, no air-conditioning. She wondered what drove him to such a rogue existence, to spend day after endless day riding cross-country only to end up in a place like this. Timidly, she peeked toward the bathroom, where the water had just stopped running. She closed the door, but not quite all the way, in case there was need for a fast getaway. Of course, where would she go? No doubt the desk clerk had lapsed into a sugar-induced coma by now, as if he was any use in the first place. Mia molded her body tight to the wall, thinking maybe he wouldn't even notice her and she could observe him, the proverbial fly on the wall. She took another gulp of her drink. Fine thing about whiskey, it always came with a shot of courage. *Or stupidity.*

A waft of steam was the first thing out of the bathroom, followed by Flynn, wearing a pair of fresh jeans, towel drying a thick wavy mane that grazed the edge of his shoulders. She never really thought about long hair on a guy, not in that way. On him it was fascinating.

"Well, if you aren't the last person I expected to find in here." He glanced at her, continuing to go about his business. "I would have figured on our friendly desk clerk puttin' a chocolate on my pillow before you showed up."

"Yeah, funny, I was just thinking about him too." Her eyes followed Flynn across the room, staring hard, as if he'd just invented nakedness. He was a mesmerizing mix of bathwater and clean sweat; a window fan blew a steady, hot breeze at him. There was no boy in him—he was decidedly different from what she was used to seeing around campus, not a thing left to fill out or grow into . . . all man. Flynn draped the thin white towel around his neck, hanging on to either end, his lanky muscles flexing the expected tattoo on his upper arm. It distracted her momentarily. Mia tilted her head, trying to place the shape. Some military emblem, she guessed. An angry looking scar zig-zagged across his left shoulder, and she wondered, bar brawl or jilted lover? Her eyes gravitated to his bare chest and she caught herself staring just as he caught her looking. The heat rose in her face and her focus flicked away. *He just took a shower. It's a hundred degrees. What did you expect, long johns?* Flynn reached for a black leather saddlebag. Mia's breath was on hold, and she sighed louder than she meant to when a benign white T-shirt emerged and he slipped it over his head.

"Would you like to search it?" he asked, making contact with her stark eyes, tipping the bag in her direction.

"Search it?"

"Yeah, are we having a language problem again?"

"Language . . . Oh, I . . . No, I don't want to search it." *Yes, I do, but that would be rude.* "Besides, you were a Marine, right? You can probably hurt somebody just as easily with your bare hands."

The remark was intended to ease the tension, but his face went dark and distant. With a glare of agitation, far different from the one he'd used with the desk clerk, Flynn came toward her. Mia's breath halted halfway between in and out, making it impossible to speak . . . or scream. His hands hit with a thud against the knotty paneling on either side of her head. Escaping through the solid wall seemed more likely than getting past him. She was trapped. It appeared the train wreck was imminent. Soft blue eyes turned steely as they met with hers, and she blinked hard at him. But the sound of his voice was quiet and sure.

"I would never *ever* hurt another human being like that.

Know that much." His hands dropped from the wall, and he sulked across the room, picking up his drink. He stood with his back to her, finally speaking over his shoulder. "If you're ready, which I'm sure you are, I'll take you home now."

Mia peeled herself from the wall and tried to speak, but nothing would come. Instead she walked over and lightly pressed her palm to his broad back. His body grew rigid as her hand made contact and his head snapped to attention. "Flynn . . . I'm sorry about whatever happened to . . . Well, I'm sorry."

This time the shaky breath was his. As he turned, his fingers reached up and traced the outline of her cheekbone. His hands, they were the opposite of her skin, uncared for and rough. But his touch was gentle, like butterfly wings, and oddly Mia found herself at ease. *What is that? In his face, his eyes, something I can see . . . but don't understand.* Something completely removed from her average existence. Mia fought a rush of involuntary tears—relief that evidently he wasn't going to kill her, compassion for what she saw in his face. He started to say something. Mia leaned in, poised to listen, but instead found herself drawn into a long, sensuous kiss, and her average existence was over.

Chapter 6

Violent pounding erupted over the pre-dawn silence, vibrating through the flimsy walls, knocking a Kmart watercolor to the floor. Flynn leapt from the bed, a shockwave pulsing through him that he hadn't felt since that drill sergeant blew a whistle in his ear at two a.m. He dove at the door, flinging it open, ready to pounce on whomever or whatever was on the other side. But he was forced to check his anger as his wild-man expression met with a stone-faced sheriff's deputy.

"That's him! Where is she? Where's Mia?" demanded a voice that was stuck in his head like gum on a shoe.

"Hold on, Rox. I'll handle this. Sir, would you step outside please?" Even though he was bare-chested, and the top button on his jeans was undone, Flynn obeyed, pulling the door shut behind him. "We have reason to believe that you were the last person seen with a young woman, Mia Montgomery. Do you know where she is?"

"Maybe. What's this all about? Did she do something wrong?"

"Did she do something wrong? Would you listen to him?"

Roxanne ranted, flailing a fist in his direction, so close he had to duck back. She looked damn angry; well, as angry as anyone who looked like her could. Roxanne took a hostile step closer, and the deputy held out an arm to stop her.

"I'm just wondering, is this an official investigation?" He yawned, still trying to shake off the six a.m. revelry.

"Would you like it to be? We're just trying to locate Miss Montgomery. An official missing persons report can't be filed for forty-eight hours."

"Missing persons? Wow, you do go right for the panic button, don't you?" he remarked, squinting at Roxanne through the early morning light. "She's in there." He nudged a bare shoulder toward the door and stepped aside. Roxanne plowed past them into the room. Flynn pushed the door open all the way, inviting the officer inside as well. Then he stood at the end of the bed, his hands shoved in his pockets, marginally concerned about being arrested.

"Mia, thank God. Are you okay? What did he do to you? What happened?" Roxanne yelled, jostling her a bit, hovering over a body tucked securely under the covers.

A raspy voice finally croaked from beneath. "Mmm, what's going on? Roxanne?" Lying facedown, Mia pushed up to her elbows, not comprehending the unfolding scene.

"Your clothes, Mia. For God's sake, where are your clothes?" she demanded.

Mia bent her head forward, fumbling at her chest. She finally flipped over in the bed and pushed the covers back. "On me," she stated, blinking with wide-eyed confusion. "Roxanne, what are you doing here?"

"What am *I* doing here?"

"Man, for a college town they sure have a lot of language issues," Flynn said to the deputy, a small smile crossing his lips.

"Oh, shut up! The fact that her clothes are on proves nothing!

Mia, you didn't call, you didn't come home. You disappeared with a stranger who looks like a card-carrying member of the Manson family. I called the police. What did you expect me to do?"

"The police?" Mia questioned, noticing the deputy. "Oh, you mean your cousin. Hi, Bobby." She waved to him, a yawn spilling out before she could stifle it. The deputy returned the gesture, losing much of his threatening posture in the process. "And I did call you, Rox. Didn't you get my message?"

"No, what time did you call?"

"Late . . . Maybe around two, I guess. When you didn't pick up I figured you had turned the phone off and went to bed. Flynn and I were talking. It got so late. I guess I fell asleep." Mia rubbed a hand across her sleepy eyes, finally focusing on him. A terrific smile broke across her face. "Hi."

"Hi, yourself. Do you usually draw such a large crowd before breakfast?"

"Enough!" Roxanne shouted, shooting sharp stares at both of them. "I want to know what happened here."

"Mia's fine. And not that it's any of your business, but I slept in the other bed," he said, motioning toward a second set of rumpled sheets. "I wasn't aware that Mia had to have your permission to—" Flynn started in, but Mia held up a hand to stop him.

"Like he said, nothing happened. Isn't that obvious? I'm sorry you were so worried." Mia pushed the covers back farther and pivoted her legs around. She started to get up, but her head seemed to weigh her down. She drew her hands up to her temples, massaging vigorously. "Do you think we could finish this conversation later? Like maybe after I've had a bottle of aspirin and remove the lint from my mouth?"

Roxanne stood in the center of the room, her arms folded tight across her chest, looking as if she might implode. "Fine.

Get yourself together and let's go." Her eyes darted to Flynn, who was attempting to remain a silent observer. Realizing the situation would not require a crime scene investigation, Roxanne's sharp tongue took over. "At the very least, Mia, you should have had him vet checked before spending the night." She opened the door and looked back at Flynn. "Tell me, exactly what is it you're doing in Athens?"

He returned the stare, but couldn't stop the edgy bob of a deep swallow. "I'm auditing a class," he answered deadpan, stone-faced. "International Relations and Comparative Trade Issues."

Roxanne snickered, opening the door wider, waiting for Mia to follow.

"Flynn, I . . ." Mia started.

"Mia, it's okay, go ahead." Flynn's eyes and body moved toward his sleeping beauty, blocking out Roxanne and the thunder of unrest she brought. It had been so serene, those hours before. The less said, the better; she was making it ugly enough. The strap of Mia's camisole slipped off her shoulder. He reached for it, adjusting what he could.

"Will I . . . Will I see you again?" she asked in a whisper, as if they were a fragile secret.

"I don't know. We'll see."

"But last night you said . . ."

"I know, but last night was before this morning. We'll see. You'd better go." He tipped his chin toward Roxanne and cousin Bobby. Mia's glassy doll's eyes were full of disappointment, but not nearly as much as his heart.

* *

Mia ducked into the backseat of the police cruiser, feeling every bit the criminal. She could imagine Roxanne's panic—albeit a few hours too late, and she never meant to cause such a problem.

But there was no point in discussing it, at least not right now. Roxanne was too angry to speak. Mia could tell from the way she sat, stiff in the front seat, thrumming her nails against the console. The last time she was that mad she'd lost a twenty-dollar bet with Henry Wong over who could recite the periodic table of elements faster.

Mia rested her throbbing forehead against the cool glass of the window. The camisole strap slipped from her shoulder again. She tugged it back into place, realizing that she missed him already. Nothing had happened and everything had happened. It was something she could never explain. Coolheaded, real-world Roxanne wouldn't understand.

That one explosive kiss—she felt it everywhere, from the parts of her body that were drawn to him like bees to nectar, melting over the core of her brain, invading a place where logic and reason had been programmed to reject him. At that moment she would have gladly gone further, given him whatever he wanted. He wouldn't consider it. "You don't want to do this, Mia. Not here, not with me," he had said in a husky, restless voice, stroking her cheek. She'd told him yes, in a throaty whisper she didn't recognize. Didn't he want her? He laughed, touching her face again with those rough gentle fingers, then backing away, telling her she had no idea how much. Flynn's blue eyes had stroked her body the way she wished his hands would. It had made her skin hunger for more; it still did. "Not tonight, sweetheart," he'd said quietly. "You regretted coming here with me. Think how sorry you'd be tomorrow. I don't want that." His voice had been filled with the temptation he struggled against. A dismal rewind of the boy from Alpharetta ran through her mind. There were all kinds of internal signs that this was different, but she couldn't prove it. Not to herself, or him.

They started talking, him sitting on the floor, her perched in the center of the bed, trying to ignore a desire that traveled down a road far different from want. It required a level of self-control Mia did not know she possessed. He seemed able to tap into all kinds of underlying behavior. He also found plenty of other reasons for her to stay. Flynn was an aggressive conversationalist, a trait one didn't expect at first glance. He drew her into talk about her college life, her friends, her past. The most mundane details seemed to fascinate him: the color of her childhood bedroom, the name of her dog, how winning first prize at the junior high art fair sparked a passion. She shrugged, noting that her parents weren't quite as enthusiastic, art being something her father marveled over, like a magic trick, and something her mother merely tolerated. "I suppose they saw it as a talent, but they didn't take it seriously. That made it a hobby until I realized my entire college curriculum was nothing but art. So I hung a quick left into interior design."

He appeared so immersed that Mia found herself confiding things she'd never said out loud. "I'm not too sure how good I'll be at it. To be honest, deciding color schemes and special ordering Italian leather chaises doesn't really excite me." Flynn had made a quiet observation, something about patience and real passion needing more inspiration than a four-year degree.

Darker subjects followed, as Mia explained in vivid detail about her father's passing. How, in what seemed like seconds, a sudden cancer took down a man she'd looked up to her whole life. She described the even more abrupt feeling of abandonment when she realized how little help her mother would be and that life was now hers to negotiate. "His death was so impossible. I still think if I pick up the phone, he'll be on the other end. I miss that. He always knew what to do. My father was never one to second-guess himself—ever." She hesitated. "It either was or it wasn't, like the cases he tried. There was no such thing as 'sort of guilty.' I suppose that's why he had one of the highest conviction rates in the state of Maryland."

"Your dad, he was a lawyer, a prosecutor?"

Mia reluctantly nodded, thinking she'd just painted her father as some merciless steamroller of justice. "Well, yes, but he had a whole other side, legally speaking," she offered in his defense. "Murderers and thieves weren't the only type of criminals that he was devoted to convicting."

"People don't come much viler than that," he said, shifting his position.

"To him they did. He did tons of pro bono work, taking on big corporations with bad habits—like dumping toxic waste into rivers, burying chemicals in landfills. Environmental terrorists," she said, smiling. "That's what he called them. But sometimes I'm sorry he was so adamant, such a champion for the cause."

"Because of the time it took away from you?"

She shook her head. "Because it's what killed him. His cancer was caused by exposure, the hours spent at chemical landfills learning what he needed in order to prepare his cases. He believed in what he was doing to the point where nothing else mattered. I know it's selfish for me to think that way."

Flynn reached for a cigarette. "I don't think it's selfish." He stared at it for a moment and put it back. "I think it's human."

"Still, it was important. I shouldn't be angry at his dedication to a cause. I should be angry there was a cause that killed him." She sighed. "It's a tough point of view to get your mind around—I'm still working on it."

"Yeah, I know how that goes . . . And your mother," he'd asked, switching gears, "was that her passion too?"

It had made Mia laugh. "My mother? No, not quite. Not unless you want to hold a black-tie dinner at the Sierra Club. She tolerated it the same way she viewed my art . . . or me."

"I can't believe she's that disinterested. I mean, just look at you."

There was an unexpected flutter in her chest, the kind that came with somebody thinking more of you than you thought of yourself. "Oh, sure, if something awful were to happen, if I got in a car wreck or broke a major bone, she'd send flowers." Mia smiled at his appalled expression. "Okay, I'm sure she'd do the motherly thing and come running. But day to day, we're just not on the same page, never have been. I don't know, it kind of all comes back to my father. Ever since I was a little girl I had the feeling I was more my mother's rival than her daughter, always vying for his attention. It wasn't her fault or mine, just the finite hours in a day. I assume it's the reason I don't have any brothers or sisters. My mother didn't want the competition."

He nodded, remarking thoughtfully, "I always figured it was the reason I do have younger siblings. My mother was trying to get it right."

Hours later the conversation had moved on. Flynn grinned, tossing out a dare, asking about her first kiss. And they were back to where they started. He'd skipped her answer about the kiss, mumbling something about needing a smoke, disappearing outside. She had tried to get him to talk about himself. It proved futile. Flynn wasn't offering much more than what she already knew, constantly turning the question back on her. After calling Roxanne, Mia had stretched out on the bed, her eyelids growing heavy. It was the only time he came near, sitting on the side of the bed, pulling a thin blanket around her. "I'm *soo* sleepy," she mumbled. "You said you stay. Sometimes a month." The words were groggy and faint. "Will you stay here?" The cover was tucked high around her chin and she felt the bangs that tickled her forehead mysteriously brush aside.

"Yeah, I just might have to."

It was the last thing she heard as sleep won out.

Chapter 7

In the machine-run inner sanctum of the ICU, Roxanne walked a few paces ahead. Mia hesitated. Coming here *was* going to change everything. This tragedy, the memory of that first kiss, it all sucked her breath away, making her behave as though she'd been oxygen deprived. Mia shook her head. "Damn you, damn you, damn you, Flynn," she whispered. Hearing her, Roxanne turned, nearly pushing her backward.

"It's not too late, Mia. You can get on that elevator and go home—no one will think any less of you. Calling you like that—I should have thought it through. I reacted to the shock. You don't have to do this."

Don't have to do this? How can I not do this? I haven't stopped loving him for a second. Not when he left me, not when I fell in love with someone else, not even when he confessed murder in my ear. Mia squeezed her brain shut. It was too much to think about on top of everything else. She ignored Roxanne and any pending moral debate. "You haven't answered me. Are you sure—?"

"Yes, I'm sure it's Flynn. There was no ID. But I knew it was him before they got the blood off his face. The ER team is probably still trying to figure out what made me jump like I'd seen a ghost."

Mia gathered her arms around herself. "I see," she said tightly. "Which room?"

"On the left, six B," she said, pointing a clipboard down a shiny white corridor that looked as if it might lead right to heaven.

The two women rounded the corner to a room that was mostly glass walls. The need for privacy was a moot point on this floor. Mia's fingers flew up over her mouth, an audible gasp gushing forward. There were more tubes and wires than body. Everything beeped and chirped; a blood pressure machine kept vigil, and a heart monitor thankfully showed some sign of life. Mia's eyes fixated on the respirator, watching it rise and fall, and soon her own breath was in step with the rhythm. Her nose filled with the smell of blood and dirt and the lingering hint of death. Through it all there was no mistake—it was Flynn. The tears were coming fast, big puddling ones that Roxanne didn't need to see. "Can I . . . can I have a minute? Then you can tell me everything."

"Yes, of course. I'll get cleaned up, change my clothes." She took a step back, but her hand reached out to Mia's shoulder. "You're going to be all right if I leave you here?"

Mia's hand shot up, grasping Roxanne's fingertips. "I'll be okay."

"You know that's all I've ever wanted. Since the day Flynn arrived—and the one after he left." There was a simultaneous sigh, two people breathing in and out the effect of one man. "Here," she said, poking a small envelope over Mia's shoulder. "Like I said, there was no ID, no personal effects. Nothing on him except this. If, um, if you did come, I thought you'd like to have it."

Mia absently took the envelope. "Can he . . . can he hear me?"

Before leaving she replied, "Uh, it's hard to know. Sometimes, if they recover, patients recollect people talking. I don't . . . I don't want to give you any false hope, Mia. His situation, it isn't good."

"Never has been," she murmured, edging up to the bed. Mia surveyed his body, taking stock through glassy, frightened eyes. Smeared blood caked over the scar and part of the tattoo. It didn't matter; she knew how deep the scar went, where every line in the tattoo led, how it changed when the muscle flexed and contracted, the way it looked now, relaxed. Long lashes. He had the most exquisite long eyelashes. When he slept, she'd watch them flutter against that road-weathered skin. They were the antithesis of him. Mia sharply reminded herself that he wasn't asleep; he was comatose. Greedily, she wanted more. She wanted to see his smile, feel that smolder of anticipation—the moment his eyes would lock with hers. Mia would have given up forever right then to hear Flynn call her name. To have him reach for her the way he always did, as though he could never get enough.

Like salve to a wound her fingers gripped his, but she couldn't move his arm. A Velcro strap held it securely to the bed. Gashes were stitched everywhere, making it seem as though he were zippered shut. There was a rainbow of bruises, so many they almost connected; a cervical collar firmly held his neck in place. Mia worried that he was cold. A hospital gown was the only thing covering him, loosely draped around his body. She wanted to ask someone for a blanket, but she couldn't find the door. Her eyes were stubbornly fixated on him.

He appeared to have a terrific sunburn, something she'd heard Roxanne refer to in the past as "road rash," when a person's face skidded along the pavement. His shoulder was tightly bandaged and she'd overheard a nurse saying something about a fractured pelvis and ribs. Everything in the room was making a sucking sound and it looked as if there was a small garden hose coming out of his chest. His hair also bore its share of trauma, thickly matted with dried blood. Even so, there was a tremendous sense of relief when she touched him. This moment was the answer to one of those life-affirming questions, like, does God exist? Why was I born? Will I ever see him again? Questions like that.

"Hey, Flynn, it's me," she managed in a tiny voice. "I don't know if you can hear me. God, I don't even know if you want me here, but I had to come. You had to know I would." Mia smiled, reaching for comforting, obvious thoughts. "You know how I am about signs . . . Well, earlier . . . before, I almost drowned in the smell of Jack Daniel's. And just this morning, I heard your song on the car radio. Can you believe that? You remember— that old Gregg Allman song. I don't hear it too often. If it does come on I can't listen. I have to change the station." She glanced down at their joined fingers and ignored the surroundings, absorbed in a conversation she'd waited twelve years to have. "Used to be when I heard it, I could picture you in the room. That got a little weird so I had to stop." She let go, brushing tears from her face, running her fingertips over the deep scratches on his cheek. The smile dissipated. The scratches were raw and hard to look at. It was astonishing when he didn't writhe in pain as she touched them. There was a startled gasp, but Mia realized a hopeful second later that it came from her own throat.

This was agony. The coma set free words that might otherwise have been restrained. They were measured and absolute. "You don't know how long I've walked through airports and shopping malls, tourist traps and crowded sidewalks, searched miles of highway looking twice at every man on a motorcycle, wishing for it to be you. But here, in this place . . . I never wanted to see you like this."

Tears dripped off her chin, splashing down on the fingers that she had linked again with his. The envelope she held crunched in her hand and she let go long enough to tear it open. A broken chain and a silver cross tumbled into her lap. Mia pursed her lips tight as her mouth turned down and her shoulders jerked at the fierce pain that rode through her. The past exploded with the velocity of a bullet aimed right at the present. Yet Flynn didn't move. He didn't respond. The heart monitor didn't break into an erratic pattern of lost love found.

* *

Roxanne, dressed in a pressed lab coat, brought her a cup of coffee and the two sat down in a small conference room. Mia looked around at the stark furnishings: a table with three chairs, a diagram of the skeletal system on the wall, a second one of the inner workings of the brain, and two boxes of Kleenex. This was where they brought you to hear bad news. "Just say it, Rox. Just tell me what you know."

While it turned out that Roxanne was a brilliant physician, her bedside manner had failed to thrive. The emergency room was a good fit; it required lightning-fast reflexes, a sharp mind, and brief personal encounters. It was also a chance to save people as they came through the door.

"He was unconscious when they brought him in. According to witnesses, his head pretty much bounced off the windshield of an SUV." Her fingers tapped at the foam cup, as if deliberating her thoughts. "He, um, he wasn't wearing a helmet." Her glance rose to Mia's. "Even I might have guessed he had better sense than that," she whispered. "As far as injuries—the repairable ones—he has a nasty fracture to his pelvis, three cracked ribs, and a dislocated shoulder. Enough deep gashes that he kept two interns well into the next shift before they got him sewed up. Worse, he has a collapsed lung and a lacerated liver. That required emergency surgery, which I assisted with." She rattled it off, orderly and sedate, as if it was her grocery list from the Food Giant. "The external stuff, the bruises and gashes, that will all heal."

"And what won't heal?" Mia asked, her gaze locking on folded hands.

"We just don't know. We're mostly concerned with his head injury. He's already had a CAT scan plus a full body X-ray. There was some initial swelling in the brain and a small bleed."

Mia drew a deep breath. She'd heard Roxanne talk enough over the years. Swelling was bad; bleeding couldn't be much better.

"They'll do another scan first thing tomorrow. Head injuries are unpredictable. On the upside, he's very strong. He never stopped breathing on his own. We've got him on a vent to protect his airway, to make it easier for him. His spinal films were all negative. That's a good thing, Mia," she said, mustering encouraging words. "If he were to wake up, he probably won't suffer any permanent paralysis." Mia responded with a wide-eyed blink as she tallied the grim outcomes. "He's being monitored for increased cranial pressure and we've got him on meds to decrease the swelling and prevent seizures."

"What about the pain? He just looks so broken. God, it has to hurt."

"We've also got him on a morphine drip, but we don't want to overmedicate him. It makes it that much harder to wake up. That could happen tomorrow, next week, or most likely—" There was an eerie pause. "Mia, I'm only saying this because I want you to be prepared—most likely, never." Roxanne hesitated, letting it sink in. "We'll just have to take it one day at a time—an hour at a time for now."

Mia nodded at each bit of information, thinking that along with the laundry list of dismal facts, Roxanne should have just handed her the Yellow Pages, open to Undertakers.

"It's not all bad. I could have sent you straight to the morgue instead of the ICU. When he came in they had already tagged him as an organ donor. Motorcycle wrecks like that—I've seen plenty. It never ends well. He's alive for now. It's a gift, Mia. It's that chance you've always wanted to say good-bye." She stopped, looking over his chart. "Does, um, does Michael know you're here?"

"No, of course not. Flynn . . . he's not something we discuss—ever."

Leaning back in her chair, she stared at Mia. "Well, I suppose that makes three of us. But being as the pink elephant is decidedly in the room, what's your plan?"

She looked at Roxanne, whose pursed lips were pulled into a tight frown. "I . . . I'm not sure. It's not a conversation I've ever thought about. Bringing Flynn up in any context seems bizarre. I'd call Michael and say what? 'By the way, hon, I've ditched the most important meeting of my career so I could rush over to the hospital and see my ex-lover.'" *You know, Michael, the man who stands in between us. The reason I can't love you the way you love me. The man I still think about when . . . Oh, God, I'm a horrible person.* "It's too complicated for a voice mail, don't you think?"

"Not if you want to give him a stroke," Roxanne said, arms folded on the tabletop. "I can't even think where you'd begin . . . 'Gosh, Michael, remember the guy you used to see me around campus with—rogue, rough, and ready? He rode into Athens on a motorcycle, hung around for a year—just long enough to devastate me, and left.'"

Mia shook her head, snickering at Roxanne's slanted point of view. "He doesn't even know that much. Michael was a grad student, more your friend than mine. Athens is a big, busy place. Back then he barely knew I existed."

"Don't be so sure, Mia. Maybe the details about Flynn were more than he wanted to know." She hesitated, shifting in her seat. "Regardless, I should think you'd like to skip ahead. You know, to the parts of Flynn's existence that are most disturbing—I mean, beyond devastating you."

For a moment she only stared, amazed that Roxanne was still beating a twelve-year-old drum. "You're not seriously going to start with that again?"

"Mia, I haven't mentioned Flynn since the day I swore not to. But don't think I've forgotten. I have a good mind to call the authorities. Surely there's some sort of DNA test they can run. Nothing's ever been solved; it's still an open case."

Mia's body tensed as an old anger sparked. It was a subject that had nearly ended their friendship. "Same rules as last time, Roxanne. Nothing's changed. You pursue this conversation— DNA, or any other CSI scenario, and I'll never forgive you." Mia spoke with more conviction than she had on most any occasion, including the day she married Michael Wells. She had to; Flynn was sacred ground. "It's a wild theory you've concocted about a man you hate, tying him to a series of despicable acts. It's insane."

"Maybe *he's* insane," Roxanne said, sounding like she was still offering a medical opinion. "Let me run the facts by you one more time. Six college girls die, broken into more pieces than a box of winter kindling. From New Mexico to Texas, Arkansas, Iowa, and Minnesota," she said, beating a finger into the tabletop. "They die all the way from Albuquerque to Birmingham, Alabama—places he admitted to traveling through," she offered as if it were evidence. "Flynn has no ties, no life, no explanation for his existence. Then he gets sidetracked, thinks he's found absolution while sleeping with you. Surely, after everything, you've reconsidered the timeline. What are the odds that someone else was in those same states, on those same campuses?"

"What are the odds that I'm going sit here and listen to this crap again?" Mia challenged. She rose from the chair, tapping into a strength Flynn had instilled. It was one of many intangible things he did leave behind. "Let me be clear, Rox. We're not going to do this. Flynn is two doors away, fighting for his life, and all you want to do is color outside the lines of your overactive imagination."

"Imagination has nothing to do with it," she said, her face more serious than the last heart attack she'd sent up to the ICU. The pause was palpable, a terrific standoff of opinions. "Horrible, *unimaginable* things do happen, Mia."

Years later and it was still an impossible point to argue. "True. But they didn't happen to me," Mia said, holding out her arms as if to demonstrate her well-being. "And Flynn isn't what you think; he certainly had nothing to do with those murdered girls."

Roxanne sucked in a breath, gathering a chart tighter in her arms. "I'm sorry; I shouldn't have brought it up. Flynn's one thing we'll never agree on." Mia nodded. Now that she thought about it, she'd be more amazed if Roxanne had given up on her conclusions about Flynn. "It's my theory and I'll keep it to myself," she said, repeating an old understanding. She firmed up her stance, segueing to facts she could prove. "But regardless of anything else, Mia, I do know what Flynn did to you when he walked out on you. And I don't want to see history repeat. I . . . I don't think I could stand it."

Me either . . . Eyes wide, a shaky breath blew out of Mia, that feeling of abandonment regrouping like an offshore storm. "I know, Rox," she said softly. "It's like you said before. You just want me to be okay, twelve years ago and now."

"More than okay, Mia."

"More than okay," she agreed, forcing a smile. "This is, um . . ." Mia's arms swung even wider, shaking her head. "This is all a bit unexpected," she confessed, a tear pushing forward. "It's been so many years. I never thought he'd . . ." She stopped; it was a thought better kept to herself. But she saw Roxanne nod, as if reading her mind. As much as they disagreed about the man in the bed, Roxanne was the only person who could understand how unexpected it was. "I, um, I know it wasn't easy for you to call me, that it went against instinct." There was a hard hum from Roxanne's throat. "Listen," Mia said, her voice softer. "I'm going to sit with him. When you have time, I'd like to know what else they plan on doing for him, any tests they plan on running, any changes. If there's anything he's not getting because of his . . . his status, with no obvious insurance, arrange it. I'll pay for it."

"I'll take care of it," Roxanne said as Mia walked toward the door.

She stopped, turning back around. "There, um, there was one more thing." Roxanne looked up from the chart she was studying. "You said when you called that you 'owed me that much.' I'd like to know exactly what you meant."

* *

Rattling off words about mending past transgressions, Roxanne eluded the question with a timely beeper. As she watched her rush off, Mia made a mental note to revisit the remark. Roxanne didn't owe anybody a thing—at least not that she would ever admit to anyone. For now she let it go. Getting back to Flynn was all that mattered. Being in the same room was imperative for a million reasons, but mostly to assure herself that it wasn't a hallucination.

Before returning to the ICU, she stopped by her car, in part to quiet the memories Roxanne had ruffled and also to retrieve her portfolio. While the present situation couldn't be more surreal, the timing also couldn't have been worse. Deadline was fast approaching on Aaron Hough's design proposal. It was the most intense project she'd ever undertaken and the chance of a lifetime. Riding in the elevator, Mia choked back something between nervous energy and hysteria; the sentiment suddenly had multiple applications.

A nurse who appeared to be all business nodded as Mia passed by the desk and entered Flynn's room. He was still there. Her heart skipped a beat as monitors and medical equipment tended to his. For a long moment she just stared, the wake of twelve years bursting like a bad dream. Sitting in a chair, Mia pushed the portfolio aside. She didn't know what she was thinking toting it up there. She'd stand a better chance planting a kiss on Flynn, thus righting his comatose state, than she would have accomplishing any work. Contemplating the fairy tale remedy, Mia's gaze traveled his broken body. With a wish, a prayer, and her whole heart, she leaned over and brushed her lips on the only patch of unmarred cheek. Eyes shut tight, her nose pressed into Flynn, breathing him in. "I know better," she whispered. "You'd never let me get away with anything so easy."

The nurse who came in to check on him never inquired as to who Mia was. That was good, since she wasn't particularly sure of the answer. She scrutinized the nurse's every move, then Mia rose from the chair, inching closer each time the nurse touched him. She needed to make her presence clear. Someone was watching over him. "How . . . how is he doing?" she finally asked.

"He's stable, no changes." Though busy with her patient, she did glance at Mia's anxious face, at the hands wrung in a squirming knot. "Think of it this way—the human body has an incredible ability to heal itself. Right now, it's his sole focus. And that," she said, continuing her protocol, "will take time and a tremendous amount of patience." Mia nodded, curious if the instructions were getting through. Flynn could be wildly stubborn. "So you'd better find some."

Mia's gaze flicked to hers. "Oh, you mean me?" Wringing hands was nothing. She unknotted them, tried to unclench her body, then sat as the advice and a sense of uselessness sank in.

"Do you draw?" she asked, adjusting his IV.

"Draw?" The nurse pointed at the portfolio. "Oh, that. No . . . well, yes. I'm an interior designer. Offices. I specialize in commercial interiors, holistic design," Mia mumbled, wondering if anything could sound less relevant. Yet random thoughts continued. "I was at a dinner meeting, working on a big . . . huge project when this, um, happened."

"Always the way," she said, capturing Flynn's vitals on a monitor. "Interruption is an inherent part of catastrophe. I'm sure he wouldn't mind if you kept at it. In fact, it might even help."

"Help? How could it possibly help?" Mia asked, sure that the nurse was now patronizing her.

"I've handled my share of coma patients. He's more likely to respond to your presence than a room full of strangers." Finished with her tasks, she offered Mia her further insight. "Surrounding them with voices they know, conversations they're used to, people they love . . . It can facilitate the healing process, and it might just be the enticement he needs."

Mia nodded, consciously disregarding any *people* he might have encountered—never mind loved. She didn't want to think about any significant conversations Flynn may have had in the last twelve years. Fingering the edge of the black portfolio, she made the gutsy assumption that her voice was the one he'd want to hear. The nurse edged toward the door. "Your big project—he must have had input."

Mia's head snapped up as the nurse bull's-eyed a guarded secret. Flynn was her catalyst, the silent encouragement for every design risk. "You really think it could help?"

"He's in pretty bad shape—there's no guarantee." The raw observation caused Mia to pinch back another wave of tears. "But I do think the power of positive energy is limitless. For him, that can't happen soon enough." A second nurse appeared in the doorway.

"Margaret, if you have a minute, I could use a hand across the hall."

Mia's eyes fluttered over Flynn and she turned quickly to the exiting nurse. "Thank you . . . Margaret."

She sat for a while longer, assessing relevant topics and trying to find a starting point. In the end she went with instinct. With Flynn, it was all you had to go on. She pulled over the tray table, then unzipped the portfolio and turned on her laptop. The small room wasn't conducive to big ideas or sketch paper; sample materials and pages of gathered data fell around the two of them. A newspaper clipping wafted onto the bed. "Oh, this will explain a lot." She smiled, picking it up. "And you'll probably get a kick out of it." Mia held it up as though he might read the headline aloud.

"Okay, so you see it's me," she offered, rolling her eyes at a photograph of herself and a silver-haired businessman poised over an array of atypical furniture. " 'Office Ideas that are All Trash,' " she read. "Cute, huh? 'Local commercial designer Mia Wells pitches holistic eco-friendly office to developer Aaron Hough . . .' He's this mega-billionaire investor, Hough Development. I'm not so sure what you'd think of him," she said, furrowing her brow. "Okay—maybe I do." She walked to an empty corkboard and tacked up the clipping. "Anyway, you always said I'd . . . Well, I believe the words were 'knock the design world on its collective ass.' And here we are—maybe," she added with crossed fingers. "It's taken me years to put all the pieces together. To understand how the environment, space, and holistic design impact each other."

She paused, thinking back. "I'm getting a little ahead. Remember the cardboard furniture? Countless recyclable uses, but spill a cup of coffee and, well, let's just say wet cardboard has its issues. But look here," she said, holding up a finished drawing. "This suite is designed to house a hundred employees. Eighty percent of the hard surfaces are made from recycled product. The cubicle dividers, flooring tile—reclaimed rubber with zero toxins!" Mia laughed. "Glamorous, I know. But it's safe for the user *and* benefits the environment. Believe me, that's a tough combination. People are just getting to that level of awareness, how the two things have to interconnect. And you were so right about the glass mosaics. They *are* more than pretty art." She reached into the portfolio and pulled out a brightly colored sample, not so different from the ones Flynn used to admire. "It was the relevance to the design that had to evolve. They reflect and absorb light, shift vibrational energy," she explained, referring back to the drawing. "I have piles of data proving the effect in the workplace, increasing energy and productivity." Realizing she'd been on a blind ramble to a captive audience, Mia paused. No, he'd want to hear every word; she was sure of it. She edged closer, hands full with the visions he'd inspired. "You have no idea how much of this is because of you. I never would have hung in there otherwise. You've been here, Flynn, every step of the way—from the beginning."

Chapter 8

ATHENS

For seven days after that one extraordinary night, Mia looked twice every time she came out of a building or drove in her car. She'd even gone to the Odyssey alone, sitting at the bar, hoping Flynn might wander in. The sound of a motorcycle engine caused her head to jerk in whatever direction, the rumbling motor sending her heart into a rhythm of anticipation. There was no sign of him. On the fifth day she called his motel, hanging up with a thud of disappointment when they said he'd checked out. By week's end she'd all but given up. After the scene with Roxanne, who could blame him? She should have been firmer, showed some backbone when Roxanne barged in, listened to instincts that said, *This is the guy, or at least let me find out if this is the guy.* But like so many other instances, she let Roxanne take control. It had been a rough week between the two, she and Roxanne not speaking for days. Mia tried, more than once, to smooth things over while making her point. She was met with a brick wall.

"Mia, it's absurd," she said, sitting in the middle of her bed, surrounded by a moat of textbooks. "There's nothing you can say to justify spending the night with a total stranger." Roxanne held up a hand, stifling Mia's argument. "Yes, nothing happened. I get that. But what guarantee did you have that that would be the outcome?"

"Flynn," she answered, aware of her lack of tangible proof. "I admit it, Rox; it was a risky choice—but it was mine to take. And all the terrible things you're thinking, they crossed my mind. But he's not like that—not even close."

"Humph!" she snorted. "Maybe not right then. Maybe not even right away. But eventually that kind of behavior, that kind of guy, leads to one thing—trouble. The kind that'll have you dialing 911, or maybe totally out of touch because you're locked in the trunk of his car."

"He rode a motorcycle," she said flatly. Roxanne sighed, returning to her schoolwork. It was at that point that Mia wanted to drag her to the closest mirror and say, "See, I'm not Rory. What happened to her isn't a blueprint for my life, or Lanie's, or Sara's, or yours." But as the week wore on, and with no sign of Flynn, she let it go. Besides, it would take something beyond her tactical know-how to alter Roxanne's thinking.

Slowly things began to edge back toward normal. After Mia insisted that she simply couldn't apologize again—at least not for scaring her into a bloodhound hunting panic, Roxanne backed off. She even brought home a peace offering, Mia's favorite: a double pepperoni pizza. The gesture seemed oddly generous. Roxanne hated pepperoni. She finally admitted that they'd gotten the order wrong. It was supposed to be *half* pepperoni. At least that made sense. They munched on the pizza, with Roxanne surgically removing every spicy round of meat while they exchanged mutual gossip and girl talk was restored. A short while later, Roxanne tossed her textbooks aside, suggesting a trip to the mall or to see the comedian who was appearing on campus that night. Mia declined, uninterested in the comfort of new shoes or the distraction of indulgent humor. She wanted to feel that fire again. That deep, intrinsic sense of being that she'd felt with Flynn. It seemed she couldn't get her mind to move past a man who ignited far more than risky behavior.

* *

It took three trips to the admissions office for Flynn to run into the right person, one who would be willing to give up Mia's schedule for a sad story about the long-lost sister he was intent on finding. Being a savvy conversationalist came in handy under the right circumstances. It always took people by surprise when the rough exterior, the one he used for everyday living, peeled away to reveal traits that went more naturally with a trendy haircut and a fifty-dollar shirt.

"And you won't breathe to a soul where it came from?" whispered an openly gay clerk, his eyes shifting from his coworkers to Flynn. He tucked a scrap of paper into the palm of his hand as if it were top-secret information.

"No, no, she'll never know how her big brother found her. Thanks, man. You woulda made our momma happy, God rest her soul."

"Just glad I could help. Family is so important." He spied the helmet Flynn carried and his fingertips fluttered across it. "Uh, tell me something. Do you always ride alone? I'd, um, love to ride with you some time."

Feeling his face go all kinds of red, Flynn dropped the piece of paper. He snatched it up and cleared his throat. "Yeah, well, I'll have to get back to you on that."

He carefully tucked the paper into his pocket; other things needed his attention before he saw her. He wanted to be smart about this. There were obstacles here. Big ones. He'd have to say all the right things in the right order. He'd have to get around Roxanne. Another guy wouldn't be too much of a problem; he could deal with that. But girlfriends hung around, sometimes for a lifetime, and Roxanne's influence would swoop in like a driving hurricane, tremendous and devastating. Hell, no doubt she'd already convinced Mia he *was* the devil's spawn. And worse, what argument could he offer that he wasn't? Everything about her told him she might understand—she made him feel human, the way her hazel gray eyes danced over his body, like he was worth something. It had been two years since he started this gritty cross-country trek, roaming through his life, from town to town. No other woman— not even the ones he took to bed, then rid himself of—made Flynn want to share anything more than a meaningless hour or two of raw flesh. He'd been a selfish prick with most of them—damn, all of them. It wasn't their fault; it was all him. There was no real way to go about the rest of his life. If he'd learned anything, it was that there was no road that led to absolution, no destination that let him forget about murder—except, just maybe, her.

A majestic oak stood in front of the building where Mia's business law class was about to let out. He'd waited there the day before, just watching. Like when he'd seen her on the street downtown, on campus she was surrounded by a group of chatty girls, all of them beautiful, Mia the standout. They were all clad in short shorts or micro minis with skimpy tops. She was the rebel, not caring for the trend, feeling no need to fight the heat, dressed in low-slung jeans, cheap flip-flops, and a gauzy shirt. The sheer fabric caressed her breasts and he forced his eyes elsewhere. One more fantasy about them and Flynn was sure he'd be meeting some baseline criteria for perversion. Her hair was longer than he recalled, a caramel shade of brown that, when soaked by the warm Georgia sun, radiated highlights

that glowed like a halo. A deep tan flattered her supple skin—
something natural or something she worked at, he wasn't sure.
But wondering where those tan lines ended had kept him up
several nights in a row. She was beautiful, sophisticated, and
almost too sexy until he recalled a sprinkle of freckles across that
delicate nose. To Flynn, they accentuated her innocence.

The tree's hulking branches were good cover yesterday and
he'd gone undetected. Flynn had waited and watched, feeling a
little ridiculous and somewhat ashamed. For God's sake, he was
practically stalking her. This was not his usual pattern. But he
wanted to make sure that the attraction was as strong, the impact as meaningful. Hell, he wanted to make sure she was real.
He'd gone to the Laundromat that same afternoon with all his
clothes. Today he waited in the hot sun, exposed to every element, in freshly washed jeans and a clean T-shirt. It would have
been difficult to wait in anything else—it was all he owned.
Looking nice and not smelling like hot tar and exhaust fumes
hadn't been an issue in some time.

Students began to pour out from various buildings, crowd-
ing the narrow sidewalks. A few moments ago he was the only
person standing there on the old north campus, his heart in his
hand. Now he felt like a big ugly slug in a swarm of honey bees,
boys and girls buzzing around him in every direction. It almost
made him turn and leave. He didn't realize that this was a good
thing. Not until he heard Mia's voice. It was like cool rain on hot
pavement, washing over him.

"I'll be sure to give it to her. Really, I don't mind."

"I'm glad I ran into you, Mia." Flynn didn't move, observing
from the sidelines a man who looked more like an instructor
than a student. He shadowed Mia's slim frame, clearly hanging
on to the stack of papers he was trying to hand her. "It was a
nice surprise."

"Michael Wells hanging out in the art building—imagine that," Mia said. "Roxanne's never set foot inside."

"I like to check out the paintings. Besides, Roxanne has no time. She's too busy trying to one up me in calc. Give her that," he said, finally relinquishing the papers. "It's the converging series problem that I just solved using Taylor's theorem—she'll be crushed."

"Okay." Mia laughed, stuffing the papers into her backpack. "Tell me something, Michael. Do you ever take a break?"

He retreated, smiling at her. "The second after I rule the world."

"Have at it," Flynn mumbled, watching.

"See you, Mia."

"See—" But as she turned toward Flynn, Mia never finished the sentence.

He could see it. Her prior conversation vanished into nothingness, books, papers, and lessons learned fading fast as Mia's eyes met his.

* *

"Flynn," she said, her voice smoky, softer than in the moments before. Mia clasped her hands to her chest, guessing he might see her heart pounding through it. "How did you . . . ?" *Not find me; maybe he's not looking for me.* "What are you doing here? I . . . I thought you left." She watched him take a big gulp of air. He almost looked nervous. The dark brown waves of hair were pulled neatly into a loose ponytail, accentuating those prominent cheekbones. It looked as though the beard had been trimmed. Too warm in the intense summer heat, she guessed. He pulled sunglasses from the bridge of a nose that clearly wasn't as straight as God intended. Flynn's gaze rested on her. His eyes were a buoyant shade of blue that didn't match his image. Mia remembered thinking that was why he hid behind the sunglasses. His eyes gave him away. She stepped closer and touched his forearm. It was sticky from the rising humidity. Nevertheless, skin never felt so inviting.

"I didn't leave. I just had some things to do before . . . before I could see you again. I . . . I mean, if that's okay. You . . . You look just beautiful, Mia."

The way he said it, the words struck her as if they were his most private thoughts tumbling out, uninhibited and pure. Mia's face broke into an instant smile. She was wearing only a hint of mascara, yesterday's jeans, and a black eyelet blouse that had seen better days.

"I meant, if seeing me is anything close to what you want. If you don't want me to go."

"Go?" It was all Mia could say, shaking her head in disbelief. *Want you to go? Is this possible? Could you have had the same aching, out-of-body experience I've had for the last eight days?*

"Hmm, language problems again." He wiped the broad palm of his hand over his bearded mouth, then folded his arms. His straight stance widened at the leg, almost at ease. "Look, I'm just going to be blunt. I thought a lot about fancy, lyrical things I could say, but it all sounded like bullshit to me. I don't want anything like that between us. I don't do this that often."

"Do what?" It was a natural question, but frankly, Mia could not have cared less what the answer was. Her senses had already dismissed the world around her, forgotten where she was, where she was going. Flynn was the only thing she saw. Whatever he wanted to do was fine by her.

"This," he murmured, pulling her toward him. His lips kissed hers with an ease that said they'd been doing it forever. Her backpack slid to the ground and her hands moved willingly around his shoulders. He held her tighter than he did in the motel room, as if to say he wasn't letting go this time. Mia's entire body curved into his; she could feel his belt buckle dig into her stomach. She could also feel the answer to any lingering question about his desire for her. It caught her by surprise and she pushed away slightly, sheepishly glancing at her toes curled up tight in her flip-flops. A nervous giggle escaped before she could squelch it, the words *Reader's Digest* exiting her mouth.

"Excuse me?"

Her eyes didn't budge from her feet. "When I was twelve I read in *Reader's Digest* that curled toes were a sign of heightened sexual arousal. I'm thinking that's true." She laughed, wiggling her toes.

"Sweetheart, your toes ain't seen nothin' yet."

Flynn tipped her chin up, his lips gliding over hers again, smooth and anxious, her mouth opening wider for him, wanting more. He tasted like a burst of crisp, fresh air, his soft beard tickling her face. She wanted to know what the rest of him tasted like, and it occurred to Mia that she'd never entertained such a thought in her life. His hand slid from her back to her bottom and she leaned harder into him. The kisses were deeper now, his tongue penetrating her entire mouth. Lord, but he could kiss. Everywhere he touched tingled with expectation. The prospect of aroused toes faded as other parts of her body began to clamor for his attention. The girl who lived a civil, three-beer-maximum life suddenly interrupted. Mia reluctantly pulled away, her hot forehead pressed against his chest, her peripheral vision catching the unwanted stares of passing students.

"We're, um, we're making out in the middle of campus. We're making a scene," she murmured, wondering why she even cared.

"Mmm, I see that." He tucked her head under his chin, rocking her in his arms. "Maybe we should go somewhere else, if you want. But don't you have an art class next?"

"Uh-huh. Art. Abstracts. We're doing abstracts," she said, caught somewhere between reality and a salacious dream. "Good art takes time. It can wait. We probably shouldn't go to my apartment. Roxanne will be there. But she's going home for the weekend. We could wait until . . ."

"Don't even say it. Being with you isn't going to hinge on her schedule. It's fine, I've got it covered."

"But you checked out of your motel," Mia said, realizing that each was oddly privy to the other's whereabouts.

"Yeah, my new place is better. Air-conditioning," he mumbled, as preoccupied as she was. "The front desk clerk is friendly, diabetic. No candy."

"Oh, I see." Mia realized that her hands were clenched, gripping a fistful of his white cotton T-shirt. It was unlike her, and unnerving. She let go, smoothing the fabric back into place, feeling his hard chest beneath her palms. She gave up, resting her splayed hands there. It remained a wrinkled reminder of the heat between them. "I need to know something, Flynn. I'll be honest, I don't think it matters what the answer is. I think you know I'm going with you either way. Could you just tell me, is this going to be a one-time thing? Will you disappear as mysteriously as you showed up?" *Like a wild brush fire out of nowhere, destroying everything in its path.* "As long as I know, I think it will be okay." It was a lie, but Mia thought she needed to sound casual about casual sex. She looked up from the T-shirt where she had directed the question, and into his face. It wasn't sitting well with him.

"I suppose this is where I feed you some line about living for the moment or offer you halfhearted assurances about my intentions. You deserve an honest answer, so I'll try to give you one." Mia gave a small nod, unsure if she was going to like this explanation. "I've done things in the last week that I've never thought about doing in my life, including flirting with a guy named Chip." Uncertainty crept onto her face. "Ah, he was cute," he said, a wry smile sneaking across the beard, "but no competition for you. Anyway, staying, going, they aren't rules I adhere to. Unless"—he hesitated—"unless somebody has locked the door. And that probably has a lot to do with how I ended up like this." It was a hint, but he wasn't about to elaborate. "The way I live, it's not like the way most people live. It's not how you live, that's for sure. How about this?" he offered, stroking the long line of her throat with the edge of his fingertips. "I won't just vanish. I promise. You'll know what I'm thinking all the way. Is that enough?"

What made you like this, Flynn? So intense and remote at the same time. I want to know. Mia looked past his shoulder, breaking eye contact, trying to let reality and clear thinking guide her. They were both out to lunch. "All right, Flynn. For now it's enough." *Well, didn't I make that super easy. I just told him I'd sleep with him no matter what!* She sounded like she was giving in. Roxanne would be appalled. No, Roxanne would slap her silly and drag her home. She sharply reminded herself that Roxanne had no place in this conversation. Mia picked up her backpack, and Flynn automatically took it from her. "So, where's your new place?"

Chapter 9

His bike was parked just outside the historic arch, the black iron symbol that welcomed all onto the campus. She saw two helmets hanging from the motorcycle. It was a huge sign. "For me?" she asked, taking the shiny black helmet a size smaller than his.

He smiled, dismissing it. "Well, I sure as hell didn't buy it for Roxanne. Riding without—that's how you end up as roadkill. Motorcycles are dangerous. You have to be safe when you ride. No games."

"So, why do you ride one?"

"Hmm, good question. When I . . . got out, there wasn't much fate left to tempt. It seemed like the logical thing to do." He helped her put the helmet on and adjusted the strap, the careful gesture saying more than words.

They breezed out of the city limits to the next town over. The college lifestyle, a pace that dictated everything, faded. Thoroughbred horses dappled grassy hills as scores of didactic brick buildings trickled down to a few, all of it slipping away on the waning horizon. Kudzu overtook everything roadside. The lush vine fascinated Mia. Nothing like it existed in the coastal Maryland town where she grew up. It was really no more than a weed, strangling the otherwise pristine landscape, climbing on telephone polls, trees, and houses. Even so, she loved the green, the effervescent life it seemed to bring to all it touched. The air intensified in the wide-open space. Mia breathed in summer heat, renewed from this different perspective.

A few miles later, Flynn pulled into a place called Annabelle's, where tidy cottages sat in a row behind the main building. "It's perfect. How did you ever find it?" she asked, trying to remove her helmet with some semblance of know-how.

"I'm just a natural at spotting perfect." He grinned, the compliment hitting on the beat this time. "There's a bike shop about two miles farther down. I got a job there. The guy who hired me recommended it."

She stopped in her tracks, a cloud of dusty gravel swirling up around them. Mia gently grasped his arm. "You got a job? Why didn't you tell me?"

"Didn't think it was that important," he said, walking a few feet, turning back toward her. "It's not like it's my life's passion. Guy's got to eat, pay the rent." He motioned toward the cottage. "Come on and see. It's not the Ritz, but it's clean and it's common ground. There's even a pond out back."

She hadn't given any thought to his financial situation. He gave the distinct impression that he could live off air. Mia walked a few steps behind, glancing at the helmet that swung from his hand. She had no idea what something like that cost, but it couldn't have been cheap. Her eyes traveled his lean body. Was it that way because he could only afford to eat once a day? She tried to remember back to when he paid for the drinks. Was it a roll of cash or just a few bills? A twenty. He'd put a twenty on the bar, but left a five-dollar tip. At the motel he had paid cash too. Mia looked at Flynn's back pockets, admiring the fit. *No hardship there.* No outline either. For such well-worn jeans, the imprint of a wallet would surely be there. No wallet probably meant no driver's license. No name. No attachment to anything except the here and now. That was the way he wanted it. Her stomach lapsed into an uneasy flutter as Flynn turned the key in the lock.

* *

Once she was inside the room, Flynn wasn't exactly sure of the protocol. Tossing her on the bed and tearing off her clothes, although tempting, didn't seem to be the right move. He could always sense fear, and Mia's was no exception. There was conversation; they'd done well with that the other night, as long as it was about her. She fascinated him—everything in life was in front of her. No doubt she'd start asking questions about him, and that's when things generally went sour. He watched her survey the room, her eyes going grateful when she saw the sitting area with an undersized sofa, the TV facing it. It told him something. As much as she might want this, she wasn't ready. *Don't let me blow this. She isn't the kind of girl you just fuck. Who am I kidding? This isn't even the kind of girl you have an affair with. This is the kind of girl you have a life with.* And, damn it, a life was the last thing he deserved.

"Mia, can I get you a soda or a beer?" he asked, motioning to a small refrigerator.

"Sure, sounds good. Whatever you're having."

"Well, you know I'm not much of a straight soda drinker . . ."

"Then the beer's fine," she cut him off.

The tough attempt not to appear intimidated wasn't lost on him. He opened one and handed it to her, their fingers mingling over the icy sweat that rolled down the side of the beer.

As the cold can made contact with her lips, Flynn's concentration rested solely on her mouth—just like the other night. He wanted to kiss her again. She caught him and mistook his stare for something far more dangerous.

"Don't worry, it's just one beer. It won't make me do crazy things. Or maybe that's not the right answer." She sat on the edge of the dresser, her eyes glossing over him, as if trying to read his thoughts. "Is that what you want, for me to lose control? Would it make it easier?"

"Make what easier?" He didn't like the sound of her voice. It had gone from soft and vulnerable to accusatory. "I'm not trying to make anything happen here." Oddly, he found that he meant it.

"That's a lie."

He shook his head. "I don't lie, Mia. Where's this coming from?"

Her eyes darted away, focusing on his small pile of belongings—all bags, like any homeless person: saddle, sleeping, and duffel. He could see her forehead crinkle beneath a layer of wispy bangs. She bit her fingernail, glancing pensively between him and the pile. Then, from nowhere, she bolted.

"Whoa, Mia, wait. Where are you going? What's happening? What did I do wrong?" In one quick step he blocked her exit and snatched her wrists up, holding her captive. Her eyes went wild at the implication. He released her immediately, his arms flying up like he was under arrest, but it was too late. She nearly catapulted to the door, clawing at the lock in a panic-stricken frenzy. His big hands came from behind and calmly snapped the bolt over, opening it slightly. Mia held on to the knob, debating which way to run or perhaps whether to stop and tell him off first. To his amazement, she turned and leaned her weight back against the door, but the feral look remained on her face.

"It's not fair. I would tell you anything you want to know, all you have to do is ask. I don't understand anything about this. I don't do things like this. It's insane; I want this more than I want to breathe. But I can't. Flynn's law, I'm not allowed to know anything. Not even a real name, a whole name. Nothing." Mia wiped her nose with the back of her hand, blinking back fear.

"You're right."

"I am?" she asked, as if she'd never been before.

"Tell you what. Forget sex exists, in this room or anywhere on the planet, for that matter."

"Fat chance," she mumbled, her eyes swimming over his body.

"Seriously. Talk to me, Mia. What do you want to know?" He'd probably be the one bolting for the door in the end. Flynn braced for the poking and prodding, the tedious dissection. He would rather face a firing squad. He was expecting a demand for zip codes and blood types, dates of interest, ex-lovers and names that appeared on birth certificates, but nothing like that came.

"What's your favorite food?"

It was blunt and cold, but decidedly answerable. "Fried chicken and mashed potatoes."

She nodded; he seemed to have earned a point. Her head came forward off the door. "Favorite band?"

"All-time or recent?" If it was recent, he was already in trouble.

She threw him a bone. "Definitely all-time."

"Rolling Stones."

"Mmm, an alien from another planet could have come up with that answer." She was unimpressed.

"When I was a kid I loved the Allman Brothers. I had a cassette tape I used to hide under the covers and listen to at night. I listened to it so much it finally wore out, snapped right in two."

"Better." Her hand released the knob; her shoulder blades inched away from the door. "And in school, what was your best subject?"

He didn't hesitate. "Trouble."

"I believe you." She took a small, cautious step forward, still closer to the exit than to him. "And your birthday—just the month."

"April," he said with one deep breath. Then he smiled. "Eighteenth."

She smiled back. "Ah, going for bonus points. Okay, your mother, what's her first name?" A challenge question.

"Lynette," he said softly as Mia teetered on the edge of a precipice that led to all things bad. His body tensed, preparing for the next round; his throat went dry. "Do I get a question?"

"I suppose," Mia said with a shrug. The fear seemed to be giving way, and she was enjoying the dominant role she was playing.

"Can I get my beer?"

"I'll allow it," she said. He took two sidesteps and snatched it off the dresser. "What about your father?" Flynn stopped mid-swallow. "What does he do?"

"Screw up." She narrowed her eyes at the evasive answer. Flynn took a breath and guzzled a fair amount more. "He's career Navy. Thirty-odd years in."

"Ha, and you're from Indiana? Not a big port of call."

"Only tells you how often we saw him."

"Oh, I . . . It wasn't good when you did? See him, that is." The game intensified. Mia tucked a piece of hair behind her ear, looked down at her feet, and took a bold step forward. It was a dare.

"No, it wasn't." He hoped it would be enough. She took a tiny step back. Flynn rolled his head in a sweeping gesture of unease, compelled to go on by pure desire. "He used to beat on my mother—and on me, if he was in the mood. Ah, they were both screwups. Even so, she didn't deserve that. Once, he came home after being gone for three months and found her in bed with another guy. It was quite intentional on her part." Mia's eyes grew wider, her expression easy to read. It was the kind of story she'd heard tell about, but never directly. Hell, he'd gone this far. "Torment was the only thing they had in common, and us kids, sort of."

She seemed to have forgotten about the game, taking another step in his direction. It was different from the others, uncalculated and sympathetic. "I'm sorry, Flynn. That's an awful way to grow up."

"Doesn't matter. It's got nothin' to do with . . ." He stopped. It was too much information. Let her think a rotten childhood had made him this way, give her a way to explain his rogue existence. It was what she was looking for. He cleared his throat to go on, truth serum again. "Anyway, he blew back into town when I was seventeen; we hadn't seen him for almost a year. My mother actually had some guy livin' with us by then. You can imagine the war that set off." She nodded, keeping very silent, moving yet another step closer. "But this time it took a wrong turn."

"How so?"

"My sister, Julia, she walked into the middle of it. The three of us, we usually made ourselves scarce when stuff like that went down. I'd sneak them into the school, Julia and Alec. We'd sleep on the gym mats. It . . . it was safe. My mother always seemed a little disappointed when we came back the next day." He exhaled a shaky breath; it wasn't something he'd ever said aloud. "Julia, she decided she was going to confront the bastard this time. He started whaling on her worse than anything he'd ever done to my mother or me. I couldn't . . . couldn't allow that. I didn't realize until that moment that I was bigger than him, and apparently stronger."

"What did you do?"

He knew where Mia's mind had gone, to the other night when he went slightly crazy over her remark about hurting someone with his hands. *God, sell it to her. She'll think that's all the evil in me, think she's got it all figured out. Then we can end it. She'll never have to know the things I'm capable of.* "What do you think I did? I beat the living shit out of him. I wasn't going to let him do that to my sister, to Julia. So I guess that does make me a bit of a liar. The beating, it was quite intentional." He put the beer on the dresser, folding his arms tight. "Bloodied him up so good he ended up in the hospital." It was a casual explanation with all the emotional depth of a mud puddle. *So, Mia, are you glad you asked? Do you like my family portrait? This ugly story? The trash I come from? And you still don't know a goddamn thing.* "Afterward, Social Services got involved. My mom took his side—but they didn't. Julia and Alec ended up with my grandparents; I ended up on a bus to Parris Island. It was my choice. I took off, joined the Marines. Figured that would burn my old man good, you know? A career Navy guy with a son in the Marines. It was the best insult I could come up with. Joke was on me. My parents couldn't sign off fast enough." Flynn realized he'd said the last part with his eyes closed. When he opened them he was startled to find Mia two steps from his face. What the hell was she doing there, so close to him? She was so goddamn beautiful, and this . . . This showed all the signs of a beautiful disaster. *Damn, I shoulda just fucked her when I had the chance.*

Chapter 10

If Flynn's body were any more rigid to her touch, he would have snapped in two. Her hands reached up and grasped his biceps, his arms stiffly folded as if he were ready to be entombed. Mia's arms slid around Flynn, embracing him with all the gentleness his life lacked. Her lips delicately grazed his cheek, nuzzling into the crook of his neck, and she whispered, "I understand you hated every minute of that. I'm sorry, but I'm glad you told me." Finally, she felt the ground grow a little firmer beneath her feet, leveling off between them. Flynn didn't respond. She reached around and worked his hair free. It fell around his shoulders like thick, musky woods. She wanted to get lost in it. His skin smelled of soapy detergent and desire. His hair brushed against her face and neck.

"Mia, be careful." His eyes were closed tight again. "I will call your bluff. What is it you want?"

"And here I thought my seduction technique was so smooth. I want you."

His sinewy arms unfurled, then gathered around her body

like a cocoon. Their lips came together in one of those explosive kisses that apparently was going to define them. Smaller, tender kisses floated over her throat as he reached for the buttons of her eyelet blouse. Mia pushed his hand away and hastily obliged him, yanking it over her head. Clothing suddenly seemed highly inappropriate, buttons a terrific waste of time. But she wanted equal footing. She grabbed the edge of his T-shirt and ran her hands up underneath until he pulled it off. A few wisps of hair were scattered over a taut chest. Mia moved her fingers over them and down his flat stomach to where a thicker trail of hair disappeared inside the waistband of his jeans.

She felt powerful and intoxicated as his mouth dusted over her shoulders, breathing those uninhibited feelings into her. The floor was gone. Flynn lifted her entire body in one fluid motion, depositing them both onto the bed. He loomed over her, his eyes ahead of his body, already making love to her. She touched his face and ran her fingers over the broad line of his cheek bone, rustling through the thick mat of his beard, assuring herself that he was real.

He asked, although he had to know the answer, "Are you sure, Mia? Because another second and I'm not going to be able to stop." An achy laugh rumbled from his throat. "At least not without causing myself a considerable amount of pain."

Between the soft, lingering kisses with which she swathed his hard body, Mia answered, "When I first passed you on the bench . . . You remember?"

"I remember."

"This, right here, is what went through my mind. Like a sign. I couldn't even remember where I was going. It was the best thirty-second fantasy of my life."

"Thirty seconds? Damn, I hope I can make it last a little longer than that."

They both fell into a moment of breathless laughter before things went quiet. They stared willfully at one another. With his legs straddled on either side of her, Flynn reached over and grabbed a pillow, gently tucking it under her head. This was going to take some time. He eyed the front closure of her bra and deftly snapped it open with one finger. The black satin cups slid away and she watched his face go soft, a silent gulp pass through his throat.

"Look at you, Mia. My imagination needs work. You're incredible." The words went beyond lusty adulation; they were more of that empowerment that he seemed to vicariously pass on to her. She reached for his hands and pulled them toward her. His lips moved hard over her mouth, then like velvet down her neck, his teeth nipping against the silky skin of her shoulder. Mia's eyes widened at the quick hint of pain, stirring an emotion that definitely wasn't fear. The tender touch returned as fast and his mouth discovered what it seemed to be searching for, lightly suckling her breasts at first, then more hungrily, aggressively. Her hands tousled in the locks of hair, brushing it back, urging him on.

With each stroke of his tongue and lips, Mia wanted more. She wanted it to last all night and she wanted it instantly. Her eyes were half closed, indulging in the glowing warmth his touch ignited. The kisses slowed again, and she opened her eyes, daring herself to engage in more than the feeling he brought to her. Looking past her breasts, Mia was startled, never having seen her nipples quite that erect, begging for more on their own. But Flynn had moved on, tiny little kisses now barely touching her skin, his tongue swirling around her navel, his fingers unsnapping her jeans. She began to wiggle out of them with his help, but stopped abruptly, putting her hand on his arm. It wasn't a sign to stop, more like a guarded pause. Mia's mind flashed to the late start she'd gotten that morning, the hand that had jammed into a nearly empty underwear drawer. "Oh, I forgot," she murmured in a panting giggle.

"Forgot what?"

Mia didn't reply; she just nudged at his arm, signaling him to keep going. He glanced up at her face to make sure he understood and then finished stripping away the jeans. "Oh, Mia, tell me you have one in every color for every day of the week. I would have never guessed." His finger hooked around the lacy edge of a microscopic black thong, tugging at it not so gently.

Her hands flew up around her face, stifling more girlish giggles. "Well, you have no idea how wrong you'd be. I'm a little behind on my laundry. It was the only thing left in the drawer. A birthday joke from Lanie and Sara. I never put it on before today."

"Well, if that's not a sign," he said, still examining the provocative lingerie. "Stand up. I want the full view, spinning included."

Her hand dropped from her face and she blinked at him, somewhat startled, completely intrigued. "Now? You want me to stand up?"

"Yeah, well, I can tell you that five minutes from now I'll be looking at it on the floor. It probably won't have the same effect."

He lay across the bed, propped up on an elbow, waiting for her to comply. From any other man it would have been a demand; from Flynn it was a come-as-you-are invitation. Instead of sliding to the floor, Mia stood right up on the bed, placed her pearly painted toes on his chest, and pushed him down. "I want you to have the best possible angle," she said, raising an eyebrow at him. Determined to give him the show he seemed so eager to watch, Mia gathered her hair in her hands and piled it up on her head. She arched her back and did a leisurely full turn, her taut breasts jutting out in front of her, the thong doing its part. She dropped the hair, and with her hands riding over her bare cheeks, she turned on the balls of her feet once more. Somehow Flynn leveled inhibitions she would have fought in the privacy of her own bedroom. Mia looked down into his captivated face and fell to her knees. "Enough show?"

"Enough," he whispered, slipping his hand around the hollow of her neck, pulling her close and kissing her hard. Mia's knees went to rubber, quickly giving way. He stood up and pulled off his own jeans. Mia sensed the smolder in her eyes as she gazed over him. She wasn't feeling the slightest bit shy about what she saw. Flynn was more than she imagined, and in the last eight days she'd imagined quite a lot. Clothes were an insult to his firm, sinewy body. He was one hard muscle of lean definition. Nothing on him was wasted. Mia reached out, instinctively pulling Flynn to her. There was no hesitation as he took her in his arms and laid her on the bed. She shuddered in anxious relief when he picked up where he'd left off, knowing that she needed more, that she wanted his mouth on her breasts, on her stomach.

"Mia." He stopped, waiting for her to make eye contact, playfully tugging on the thong with his teeth.

That deep, soothing voice, it was as sensual as his kiss lapping over her, heightening every sensation. "Hmm, yes?" was all she could manage, completely lost to him.

"I want . . . I want to make love to you. But first, first I want to take you somewhere else."

For a moment she didn't follow. Surely he didn't expect her to move, to get out of this bed? But his meaning was swiftly realized. His hands took the place of his teeth, casting the thong to the floor as promised. Flynn's hands slid between her legs, gently pushing them apart. Suddenly his hot mouth was on the inside of her thighs, kissing them with as much finesse as he'd shown the rest of her body. His fingers expertly delved past warm, wet ringlets, deep inside, to places that made her automatically clench up tight around him. With a shuddering gasp, Mia's back arched. She had no control, her muscles tightening and melting at the same time. His fingers swirled outside, cleverly finding just the right spot, so delicate and pleasing she thought that surely his hands were made for just this.

Flynn glanced up at her and smiled. "God, you are so ready for this, Mia. I've barely touched you, and look, you're already right on the edge."

She tried to respond, but only a groaning sound of approval would vibrate from her throat. As his mouth took the place of his fingers, she squirmed slightly and pushed away. Or was she pushing toward him? The feeling was too much for one person to handle. He didn't ease up, holding tight, a growl of satisfaction emanating from within him. Flynn wouldn't allow her a moment to regain control. She gave in to the fiery stroke of his tongue, falling to sweet surrender, her fingertips sweeping across the top of his head. Muscles she was unaware of ached with expectation as wild uncharted sensations claimed her body.

Moments later, a wave of passion crashed over her, carrying her away to some incredible vista, a place she'd never before encountered. It lasted longer than she thought possible, then delivered her safely right back to him. She gasped for a much-needed breath, but he never stopped. His mouth and hands moved fluidly across her skin, taking care to caress any place he might have missed on the way down. Then Flynn's body was suddenly up over hers, the weight of it reining her in. The look on her face must have startled him as he finally offered a moment's pause.

"Mia, you still with me? Are you okay? You, um, you look a

little lost," he whispered, his mouth sucking on her earlobe, the feel of his tongue causing a tremor of aftershock.

She nodded at first, unable to form words, her hand now shyly covering her eyes. "You were right. I did go someplace else," she said breathlessly, reaching her arms around his neck, although she wasn't terribly sure she could hold on. She blinked once, twice. Focusing seemed far too much trouble, but it was a pleased look on his face that came to her clearly. He kissed her again, her taste all over his breath. It was oddly exciting, and she returned his kisses, wondering if it would be like that every time, eager to find out. Her hips began to involuntarily rub against his body, quite like the way a wild animal would tempt its mate. "Flynn, please. Make love to me. I can't wait anymore. Besides, I'm starting to feel a little guilty, like this is all for me."

He grinned and reached over to the nightstand, and a condom appeared out of nowhere. "In a minute," he said, laying it on the pillow next to them, as if he could wait all day. "I want to know something first. And don't worry, sweetheart, this all goes toward my turn."

"What? What could you possibly want to know at this particular moment?" Frustration colored her voice. Whatever enduring force of nature he was working with plainly wasn't available to her. She bucked under him, her body serving him with fervent temptation.

Flynn swung a muscular leg over hers, pinning it tight to the bed, ending the advance. "How many lovers have you had?"

"What?" she asked, pulling her head as high off the pillow as it would come. "Why? Whether it's two or ten, will it make a difference? Is this some sort of test I have to pass?"

"Yeah, like I'd be the one to invoke that criteria." He laughed. His humorous tone started to irritate her. She wanted the passionate Flynn back. If he wanted to talk, fine; but let it be dirty little words of encouragement.

"It's just a question. You can tell me it's none of my business—which is probably true—or you can trust me and answer me."

She searched his eyes, trying to figure out if it was a game or a serious inquiry. He was giving nothing away. In fact, he was painfully patient for a guy whose hard-on was pressing against her like a throbbing dam wall. She narrowed her eyes. Mia didn't want to answer, not because it wasn't his business, but because she didn't want to think about any other man in that way; not with him. As if leisurely killing time, he tapped the sealed condom against the pillow, looking at her, just waiting. "All right," she said with a breath of surrender, "I'll tell you." His leg relaxed, allowing her to move freely again. "Two. I've had exactly two . . . well, I don't know if you'd call them lovers. I mean, technically I had sex with them, but never like this. Well, technically I haven't had sex with you," she said, trying to rectify that fact, her entire body pulsating against him, almost begging.

"And . . ." he prodded, clearly wanting more story.

She rolled her head around on the pillow, unable to convey the intensity of distress she was feeling. "And what?" She could tell he wasn't going to budge, and wondered if he was this stubborn about everything. An exasperated sigh rose from her belly. He could get her to talk about anything. "The second one was Billy Banes. We went together for about five months last fall. We only did it, like, maybe five or six times. My personal opinion, I think he's gay."

Flynn tried to muffle a laugh as Mia jokingly slapped at his chest. "I'm sorry. And the first guy? Tell me it was better than that?"

Mia felt her expression go flat, the smile disappearing. She briefly entertained the idea of making something up, something exotic and delicious. But she couldn't lie to him, not even to repay these moments of torture. "Mmm, the first. No, actually, it was worse."

Flynn crinkled his brow, the playfulness gone from his eyes. "How was it worse?" The inquiry had turned on him. The question was suddenly worth every moment to drown in that penetrating look of concern, wrapping around her like a protective fortress.

"No, nothing horrible like that." A thousand-pound weight lifted from his expression. "Just a major mistake. He . . . I gave it away to nobody, for no particular reason. The short story: very drunk, very stupid, very regrettable. It's part of why Roxanne got so mad the other night."

"Oh, God, now I am sorry I asked. We have to make a rule, right here and now. No *R* word, never ever when you're in bed with me. Got it? She makes me want to take a vow of celibacy."

She shivered a little at what he implied, that there would be a next time. "Well, you're the one who brought it up. Good, does that mean we're done with this sad exploration of my past?" He didn't answer with any words, only sank deeply into her lips. She was nearly carried away, his passionate kisses taking her back to that idyllic place to which only he knew the way. Mia almost let the question slide. "Why, Flynn? Why did you want to know that?" she asked between panting gasps, meeting his roving mouth every so often. "Is it some sort of guy ritual? Is there a macho scale of virility you need to rank yourself on?"

He stopped, the look in his eyes sincere and doubtless. "I didn't need to know. I just wanted you to remember who was before me. Because now, Mia, you know who's last." She didn't question it; she didn't ponder it. But the words caused a feeling to pulse through her more intensely than the vista he'd brought her to earlier. "Now, hand me that condom," he instructed.

Her mind was awash with dreamlike thoughts that hadn't even been a possibility that morning. She watched intently, silently, as he tore the packet open with his teeth, quickly sheathing himself. The thought of how many lovers he may have had did race through her head, but she pushed it away. No doubt the number climbed well into double digits, or worse.

Flynn eased into her with an expertise that said as much, slowly stroking her, teasing until she was ready. Her legs locked around him, coaxing him on. Only for a moment did he ever appear to be in anything other than complete control.

"You're so fucking tight." He groaned, swallowing hard, his eyes squeezed shut. She couldn't tell from the language, his expression, or her own experiences whether that was good or bad. Without ever having looked at her, he answered, "Yeah, that's a good thing, sweetheart. A very nice thing. But you've got me so hot it's requiring a whole other level of willpower."

"But I didn't do anything," she innocently replied.

In the midst of his controlled passion, he laughed, his head falling to the pillow next to her, a slight whimper of frustration seeping from his gut. "Mia, sweetheart, have you ever looked in a mirror?"

They flowed into a liquid chasm of like-minds and heated bodies. It was beyond anything she had imagined, read about, or witnessed in the soft-porn movie the girls had once rented. It certainly cast a shameful light on the bedroom skills of Billy Banes and the boy from Alpharetta. Flynn was simultaneously powerful and sweet, never letting her be anything but the center of his attention.

Once they'd made rhythmic peace with the crushing thunder of passion that possessed them, once he seemed sure she was able to handle everything he had, Flynn began again, taking her back to that much anticipated place. Mia had always been under the impression that this particular part belonged to the man, but evidently he hadn't heard the same rumor. The thrusting crested to a violent threshold as the chintzy headboard smacked hard against the wall and a lamp vibrated off the nightstand. All the while his strong voice whispered through the air, asking if she liked it, if she needed him to slow down. At first there was only a timid nod as Mia replied with throaty rumbles of encouragement. She found her voice at the end, coming right before him, begging him for all he had to give. It was more electric than before, more satisfying because it led him to the same place.

In the moments afterward, the only sound was their exhausted gasps for air. Mia reached to her cheek, thinking the sweat between their bodies was pouring down her face. What a lovely picture that must be, she thought, sharply brushing the drops away, realizing they were tears. For all his bravado, Flynn was quieter than she expected, leaving her to wonder if he'd enjoyed it as much as she did. She found the strength to open her eyes. Flynn's head was crooked in her shoulder, his body still heaving with deep breaths into a pillow.

"Flynn, say something. Please? You're, um, making me nervous."

"Can't," came the deadpan reply that she thought was an octave higher than his usual deep voice.

Oh my God, I was so awful he can't look at me. He can't even speak. "Why . . . why won't you talk to me?" Her body wanted to brace for the answer, but all her muscles ceased cooperating after the last orgasmic explosion ruptured her.

A long arm flew up in the air, hitting the mattress with a thud. Still, his body didn't make a move. "Destroyed," came the muffled reply.

"Huh?"

Finally he wrenched his face from the pillow, his eyelids fluttering open then closed. For the first time she noticed his beautiful long lashes. Why hadn't she seen them before?

Flynn struggled to push himself up, as if someone had zapped all the strength from his body. Words dragged from his mouth. "You. Destroy. Me." His forehead bumped against hers, his hair creating a wall of privacy around them. Flynn softly brushed his lips over hers.

It gave her a smidgen of hope, but no confidence. "Flynn, talk to me in sentences."

He must have caught the pleading tone in her voice, because his head popped up, his face returning to that protective look of concern. "It means, Mia, that every sex cliché you've ever heard just happened, to me anyway." She blinked, crinkling her brow. He pushed his hair back so she could see his face clearly. "Let's see. The earth did in fact move, I've now touched the face of God, my world did indeed rock, and if you'd like I'll cap it off with a cigarette in bed. Now, do you follow?"

A glorious if not conquering smile beamed across her face. She nuzzled against him and buried her head in his shoulder. "I follow."

Chapter 11

Mia awoke in the middle of the night, a river of contentment lapping over her until she realized she was alone. His arm had been there before, curled around her very much like it belonged. She sat straight up in bed, reaching for the lamp. It was still on the floor. Her legs hit the ground in a panic, only a crease of light from the heavy drape illuminating her path. She fumbled toward the bathroom where the door was wide open and flipped on the light. He was gone. Her fingers raked through her hair, grabbing the long locks that still smelled of his whole body. "No, he promised! He said he wouldn't do this!" Her heart pounded so hard she thought it would burst into a million pieces. This feeling was going to tear her apart, so vacant and opposed to everything she'd felt earlier.

Through stinging tears Mia spied his T-shirt on the edge of the bed. *Maybe a little forget-me-not for idiots who'll believe anything.* She told herself to shut up and snatched the shirt, pulling it over her head. It wasn't possible; she couldn't have been that wrong about him. Her toe snagged the thong and she skimmed it up over her shaking legs. Anger and panic were driving her so forcefully that Mia didn't bother to look around for his belongings. She plunged her feet into her flip-flops and threw open the door. The night air wasn't much cooler than the day, and it hit her like a choking veil of steam. If he was gone, she hoped it would choke her to death. The distant parking lot was just globs of hard, dark shadows, making it impossible to discern if the motorcycle was still there.

Then she thought about the pond he'd mentioned. The moonlight cast a decent path and she headed to the back. She wanted to call out, but it seemed ludicrous if he was gone and desperate if he wasn't. Her fast stride lapsed into a panicked run, her head pivoting from side to side, searching. Nothing. Nothing but lightning bugs, crickets, and heat. A security lamp launched a clear circle of light near a dock. She stopped, scanning its circumference. The breeze picked up, rustling a cluster of trees, drawing her attention. Mia whipped around, nearly knocking herself off balance. There, barely visible in the dim light, was a man crouched on the ground. Her heart wanted to melt with relief, but an icy warning from her brain held it back. Something wasn't right. Calm steps, Mia told herself. *Get the panic out of your voice. Don't say anything stupid. Say something like, I noticed you were up and I thought we could take a walk in the moonlight. Yeah, because that's what I always do in my thong in the middle of the night.* A moment later and it didn't matter. She was twenty feet away when a gasp rose from her throat and she ran the remaining steps. "Flynn, what's the matter? What are you doing sitting out in a field—stark naked?" His knees were dug into the ground, hands tight by his sides, clenching tufts of grass. His long hair was the only thing touching his shivering body; his eyes were closed. There was no recognition, no sign that he knew she was there.

Whatever was happening to him—this was what she had seen in his eyes that first night. This was the something distant and scary. But that was before. Now, whatever the problem, Mia felt it was just as much hers as his. Cautiously she knelt by his side. His body was one steady convulsive twitch, the sweat catching in the moonlight, shimmering on his stony face. Mia wished she knew more, had paid better attention in sociology, psychology—one of those -ologies that might have given her a clue what to do next. She wished she were as smart as Roxanne. Instinct would have to drive the plan of action. That thought made her stomach a little sick. What if she made it worse? Pensive, she pulled her hand back, then reached out again. Mia gathered her nerve and touched his arm. "Flynn, can you hear me?" There was a screech from his throat, an inhuman sound. He looked at her, squirrelly-eyed and disoriented. "Oh, God, I'm sorry!" she cried, still not sure if he was hearing her. "I didn't know what else to do. I . . ."

His hand reached for her face; it was all he could do to make contact. The tremors worsened if he moved. "Here . . . You're still here . . ." he managed in some crazed voice that didn't belong to him.

At least he recognized her; that was something. "Of course I'm still here. If you'd stayed inside, I would have been a lot handier. Tell me what's happening. Why are you out here?"

"Don't ask now . . . Do some . . . thing . . . for me."

"What? Just tell me . . ."

"Inside, the duffel. Small . . ." He gagged on the jumpy, scattered phrases as if they were suffocating him. "Zip . . . per. Bring me the bag."

She nodded. The fear in her face told him she'd do exactly as he asked. Mia raced back to the cottage and tore into the black duffel. There was nothing. Socks, T-shirts—a few tangible things that assured her he was a part of earth. Then she saw an outside zipper. She slipped her hand inside and withdrew a clear plastic bag. She bit hard into her lip, feeling used and disgusted. It was filled with joints, nine or ten neatly rolled maryjanes, looking party ready. "Damn it! Drugs? He's about nothing but drugs. Damn him!" She almost threw it down and left. Instead, she held the bag up, staring, as if expecting it to explain. What Mia did know about hard drugs was scary and real, a vicarious lesson learned courtesy of Rory Burke. It was the kind of stuff that would make you turn and run. And she probably would have, but that underused instinct intervened. *It's a bag of pot. It's not the same thing.* Grabbing the duffel bag, disregarding his privacy, Mia rooted around, searching for something worse. It wasn't there. The hope that she wasn't that wrong about him, curiosity, an irrational bond—she wasn't sure which one made her take the lighter she also found in the pocket. But as Mia headed toward the door, only one thought guided her: She couldn't leave him there, alone in a field, naked and shivering.

She was wary on her return, keeping her empathy in check. There was no need to give any more of herself to him. Not until she got some answers. "Here," she said, standing over the coiled mass of shivering flesh, thrusting the bag at him. He tried to reach out, but his hands were shaking so violently there was no way he could take the bag from her, no less light a joint. She tapped her flip-flop into the ground, knowing the choice was hers. "This is just pot, right?" He nodded. Believe him, or don't. Mia drew the plastic bag back to her and grabbed a joint from the batch, tossing the rest aside. She put it between her lips, flicked the lighter, and drew several hard drags. The air began to fill with the murky aroma that defined college parties and courted inane laughter. At the moment, she couldn't think of anything less amusing than this. Realizing she'd have to finish the job, she knelt next to him, holding it up to his quivering lips. He drew it in and she watched as he took grateful drag upon drag, thinking there had to be more to this.

It took almost an hour for him to calm down—or come down—enough to get him back inside. She said nothing, just brief pertinent bits of conversation like, "Can you get up? The cottage is this way. Watch your step." *Do you see the landmine over there? I've already fallen into it.*

Strategically bypassing the bed, Mia helped him into a chair, her fantasy of waking up beside this unbelievable, inspiring man shattered. She tried to ignore the rawness, the empty promise that gnawed at her gut; tried to take responsibility. No one had forced her. She was more than willing to get into bed with a man she knew practically nothing about, whose past indicated something other than pleasant family dinners and warm holiday reunions.

Mia not so nicely threw his jeans at him. "Can you put them on?" she snapped, turning her back while he struggled into them. He hadn't said a word since asking for his party favors, and his silence baited her anger. "Then you've got about ten seconds to start talking if you don't want me to walk out of here." It was a bold move for Mia; she didn't often take charge. Even in this condition he managed to unearth her emotions, although the ones from before were decidedly more pleasant. Silence answered back and her heart broke a little more. Her head nodded. This was what he wanted. Still wearing nothing but her thong and his T-shirt, Mia reached for her clothes. She kept her back to him as big, stupid tears rolled down her cheeks. Flynn didn't deserve to see how much this hurt. With her clothes in hand, she headed for the bathroom, shrouded by what she guessed was her poorest choice yet.

"I don't know how," came a raspy voice, barely audible.

"Don't know how to do what?" Mia whipped around, and her eyes scalded him with a sharp demand for answers.

"Explain it." Flynn bent forward in the chair as if his stomach were in a wrenching knot.

Mia fought a wave of sympathy; he was such a mess on the outside. She wondered what might hurt that she couldn't see. It was impossible to make out any expression through the mass of tangled hair. "Try," she hissed in a tiny whisper.

"You don't want to mess with this, Mia. It's better if you just keep thinking what you're thinking and go."

"And how do you know what I'm thinking?"

His head tilted back as his gaze dragged up from the floor. His face was a ruin of despair and humiliation. "You think that was me rip-roaring high on something. Maybe a little PCP or meth."

"I'm hoping to God not."

He leaned back, managing solid eye contact. "It wasn't, I swear." Mia let her jeans slip back onto the bed as she stood, pressed against the mattress edge. "Believe me, I didn't want to ask you to get my stuff, but it was the only way down."

Like she had during yesterday's game, she took two tiny steps in his direction, no hint of her disposition. Her face had gone solemn and sad. "Down from what then? And why should I believe you?"

"You shouldn't. That's what I've wanted to say to you from the moment I saw you on the sidewalk. You shouldn't let strangers buy you drinks, or ride on their motorcycles, Mia. You shouldn't kiss them when you come out of class and you most definitely shouldn't let strangers take you to bed, no matter how fucking incredible it is," Flynn said, finding the nerve to leer at her body.

There was an unexpected flush of excitement. "I think you stopped being a stranger somewhere between oral sex and the second mind-bending orga—" Mia's hand clamped over her mouth; they were very naked words and she wasn't used to them. *What the hell is the matter with me? I sound like a guest on* Jerry Springer. Mia forced the subject back around, unsure if he was telling the truth about the drugs or if she only wished he was. "I have a cousin who was messed up on crack. They put him in a treatment program and he did really well . . ."

"I don't have a drug problem," he insisted. "If I did, for you I'd check myself into the thirty-day rehab at county general and detox until I pissed pure gold."

"I'm flattered," she said, unable to keep from smiling at his bluntness. "Then what, Flynn? What made you want to get out of that bed, away from me?"

"Don't think like that. I didn't do it to get away from you. It was to protect you."

"From what?"

"From me."

"Oh, for God's sake, the next thing you're going to tell me is that you sprout fur and bay at the full moon. I'm not that gullible." *At least, I don't think I am.* His hands still trembled. Mia sensed that he was doing everything he could to hold it together. "Maybe they have coffee at the front desk. Do you want me to see?" He nodded weakly. "I'll be back. Think it over. You're going to have to come up with the right answer if you want me to stay." She wrenched on her jeans and walked to the door, still wearing his shirt. "And I'm bringing you decaf."

* *

Decaf with a side of hemlock, Flynn hoped. He had to think fast; the truth was out of the question. She was freaked out enough over last night's episode. Anything smelling of the rancid truth would be suicide. How the hell did he get here? He'd done so well, answering to no one. Mia was an astonishing, unexpected complication, but worth every damn risk. Unless her safety was in jeopardy. That was unacceptable. But he also promised he wouldn't leave, wouldn't just bolt. What a jackass. What an unfathomable fucking corner he'd painted himself into. He couldn't stay or leave, couldn't tell the truth or lie. He was a terrible liar. It was the reason he lived like he did. Loners didn't have anyone to lie to. Half-truths. Half-truths were better than nothing. Maybe he could buy some time with a carefully worded dissection of the whole fucking mess. But how much, and which parts? Before he could figure it out, she was back.

"Lucky you, they had decaf and donuts. I didn't know which kind you like, so I brought all of them. Though I don't know if a sugar high is the best thing for you." She was trying hard to be cold and stern with him, but that trip wire of lusty warmth, the one he kept stumbling on, seemed to be derailing her plan as well. "I don't know how you take your coffee either," she said, poised over the foam cups, sugar packets in one hand, creamer in the other. "I don't know how you like it, or why you sit naked and shivering in a field, in the pitch dark, like some POW." Mia stopped, her stare shooting him like a bull's-eye. "What happened to you in the Marines?"

Holy Christ, there goes the first half-truth. He was careful not to react to her conjecture. He would have to slow it down, no starting from places he had no intention of going. "Will you sit? And black, I take it black."

"Of course you do," she said, shoving the cup at him, falling into the small sofa. "Let me guess: plain donut, no frosting, no sprinkles. How uncomplicated, just like you."

He let her have the sarcasm. Maybe it would burn off some anger. "What'd ya do, Mia, steal the entire box?" he asked, reaching for the naked donut in the pile.

"Hmm, right, like I'd have to. I know how to flirt for what I want. Friendly, like you said. The front desk clerk was happy to hand over whatever I wanted."

Flynn grabbed her wrist, pulling a chocolate glazed donut away from her mouth mid-bite. "Don't do that, Mia. Don't fuck with me right now. It's not going to get you the response you're looking for." He let go, not caring for a second what she thought, not caring if it sent her screaming into the parking lot. "You're smarter than that kind of behavior."

"What behavior? I'm not—"

"Using sex as a means to an end. It's not a good idea."

The donut dropped back into the box. "Sorry, I— You're right, sorry."

They sipped tepid coffee in silence for a time, letting the tension level off. Flynn nervously edged back into the chair, somewhat confident that she wasn't going to bolt, not sure if his legs were steady enough to stop her if she did. Making deep eye contact with his empty cup, Flynn spoke in a careful voice. "Peyton. My first name is Peyton."

"Ohh," she murmured in a drawn-out breath as if she'd just been made privy to one of the secrets of the universe. She leaned in, anticipating more. "Then Flynn is your . . ."

"Middle. Flynn's my middle name. But it's all everyone has ever called me—almost everyone. It's my mother's maiden name. Peyton Flynn McDermott, the whole name I left behind along with the rest of my life."

She curled up on the sofa as if settling in for a fireside chat, resting her chin on her hand. "And what happened to Peyton Flynn McDermott that makes him run . . . from people, from life, from warm beds?"

"The bed part is easier to answer. I'll start there." He felt like he was slicing into a vein. Whether she knew it or not, he was about to bleed all over her. "It starts with a nightmare, always the same one." She didn't ask for details; he didn't offer any. "I wake up, or at least I think I'm awake, in a cold sweat, a panic. I can't breathe and I know it's coming."

"Did this happen last night, the nightmare?"

"Yeah, you were sleeping so peacefully—it was beautiful. I hoped for a second it might help me hold on, calm down. But really, it only made it worse. I didn't want you to see me like that."

She was adamantly shaking her head. "You should have woken me up, given me the chance. Maybe if I'd been awake I could have helped."

"Hey, I've been doing this for a while, Mia. I'm not experimenting on you. Anyway, when the panic sets in, rooms are small places. I've trashed quite a few. That's why I have the sleeping bag; outside's better if the weather's good. Trashed rooms get expensive. I couldn't believe it—I'd gone from total ecstasy to sheer terror. I've never been on such a downward spiral."

"I know what you mean." Mia rolled her eyes, exhaling the breath that she seemed to have been holding.

"How's that?"

"When I woke up and you were gone, well, I thought you'd left. You said . . ."

"I didn't say. I promised. Promised you I wouldn't do that." She was blinking back tears. He felt the guilt and responsibility begin to mount. It had been a long time since that feeling was attached to anything new. He hadn't thought about how she came to find him outside. Flynn reached over, gingerly pulling her hands. Mia's body floated along until she was in his lap. The salvation that silken skin offered revived his strength. Flynn was suddenly fighting the urge to carry her to the bed.

"Will you tell me the rest? I want to understand what happened to you."

It jerked him back to the explanation he owed her. Like a wild animal fresh from the hunt, he knew he was about to drag this beautiful creature into this deep black hole of his. Flynn drew a breath. If he wanted her to stay, he had no choice. "It's kinda like if you were to wake up in a coffin and find the lid nailed shut." Mia squirmed a little, a low groan of acknowledgment coming from her throat. "You'd do anything to get out, right? You'd scratch, claw, scream—take down whatever was in your way."

"That's what being inside a room feels like when this happens?"

"No." His head shook, the beard, the mouth turning down into a hard frown. "That's what being in my body feels like when it happens. Rooms are just an unfortunate recipient of my attempts to escape. Anyway, it was coming, the panic. It's like I stand on a razor-thin edge between reality and madness. I'm fighting to keep from falling into it, going back there. You see why I left? I couldn't put you in the middle of that." He raked a hand through his hair, his neck resting back against the chair. "God, I must sound like some kind of fucked-up head case to you . . ."

"Don't say that. That's not what I'm thinking. How often does this happen?"

"I can go a few weeks, a month sometimes, but it always comes back."

"When did it all start?"

"It's, um . . . it's been a long time. At first it was just the nightmare. The panic and not being able to control it, that happened over time. It's gotten worse the last couple of years."

Mia's fingertips delicately brushed along the outline of his face, as if trying to feel what was underneath. "What happened to you? What did they do to you so you'd end up like this? You said there were no nice memories from your time in the military. I can only imagine . . ."

"No, no, you can't imagine, so don't try." Her hand dropped, tracing the outline of the scar on his shoulder, and he pushed it away. "Mia, this is where it's going to get dicey. It's not a matter of won't or can't tell you—I don't know how to tell you. It doesn't translate." *It's not a story human beings can understand.* He searched her eyes, waiting for some hint of which way she was leaning. Beneath that wispy layer of bangs, she crinkled her brow in serious debate.

"What about the pot?"

"The pot, well, that's really part of the cure, not the danger. About a year ago, I was traveling with some bikers in the Midwest. We got to drinkin' one night and I must have said something about the nightmares. The next day, this guy asked me if I ever tried meditating when it happens. He told me about this whole colony of guru types in Iowa that study TM—Transcendental Meditation. Said his brother suffered from the same thing and learned how to transfer the energy into a meditative state. I was willing to try anything so I headed up that way, hooked into some outcasts from the inner TM circle. They did teach me the basics, but they were throwbacks. You know, hippie types. There was this older guy, caught somewhere between meditation and methadone. Anyway, when he finally understood what I was up against, he suggested the pot, a calming energy by way of inhalation," he offered with a raised eyebrow. "Between that and the meditation, I'm able to talk myself down. Eventually. That's what I was trying to do when you found me. It's a hell of a mind game. I don't always win." He waited, watching her contemplative face, thinking it would be best if she just said she couldn't handle it and left.

Her tenacity surprised him.

"All of this," she said, circling her arm in the air, "isn't it some kind of post-traumatic stress? Isn't the military responsible for helping you with something like that? I've heard about people who've been in wars, the effect. They can get you help . . ."

"Look, Mia, I wasn't in a war. They're not responsible. I don't want anything to do with the goddamn Marines. I did my time—and then some. I'm done with it." His hands fell away from her sides, letting her know she was free to go.

"But you won't tell me. Wait," she corrected herself, "you don't know how to tell me what happened to cause all of this? You'd rather just let my imagination draw the conclusion, knowing it could be worse than the truth?"

Swinging her legs around, Flynn popped Mia to her feet, struggling to pull himself out of the chair. He scrubbed his hands over his exhausted face and moved away from her. "Draw whatever conclusions you need to, sweetheart. I'm very sorry you got caught in this. I'm not a damn bit sorry about what happened there," he said, gesturing to the bed. "It's a fucking dilemma either way. If I had any sense, if I wasn't really a selfish prick, I'd make the decision for you." He lit a cigarette and took a hard drag, retreating back to the place where demon handling was a one-man sideshow. Mia gave a small nod to the ultimatum, her eyes puffy and red. The disaster his presence would bring to that beauty and innocence. Mia approached and he braced for the slap she had threatened him with days ago. Instead she reached up and plucked the cigarette from his mouth.

"I don't like cigarette smoke—it's bad for you, it's bad for the environment. Can you deal with that much?" He took it back from her and snuffed it out. She bit her lip and carefully looked him over. "Marijuana smoke when necessary, that's another story." Her hand came up, smoothing his wild mane of hair; her head tilted to the side. "Two more things. Your shirt," she said, tugging at the sleeve. "Can I keep it? And if I were to ask you for the truth from the here and now, will you give it to me?"

"Whatever you want to know, Mia. From the here and now."

"Tell me what you want right now, more than anything. A drink? A shower? The open road?"

"For you to take that shirt off. I'll gift wrap it for you."

Chapter 12

MARYLAND

The value of a clock in an ICU is purely medicinal. It delivers the cue for lifesaving rituals performed on the hour: administering meds, monitoring IVs, taking readings, changing bandages. For everything else it's just a reminder of the minutes lost. It seemed a little silly at first; for heaven's sake, they'd already lost years. But as hours turned to days, each ticking moment became a steady drip, a torturous claim of whatever might be left. So it was that, and a sense of union that had never waned, that bolstered Mia's resolve to help him. She was determined to find a way to bring Flynn back. What happened after that . . . well, Mia knew it was a lie to say it didn't matter.

Reclaiming her role as Flynn's champion was like slipping into a comfy old sweater. Having leapt blindly to his aid years before, this time confidence was Mia's guide; she even implemented a few savvy business maneuvers on his behalf. She delved into research on coma victims and learned that massage often brought about good results. That was a no-brainer. Last winter she'd designed a totally green Zen massage studio outside

D.C. It took one phone call. Having been so impressed with her work, the masseur couldn't come to Mia's aid fast enough, insisting that he take on Flynn's therapy pro bono. Other tasks, simpler by definition, were more emotional by nature. It took every ounce of professional calm she had when Mia walked in on a nurse poised over Flynn's head with a razor in hand. "Too matted," she groused. "This will be easier." Fighting her gut instinct—which was to wrestle the nurse to the ground and turn the buzzing shears on her—Mia stuck to practiced negotiation. If it posed a medical problem, she understood. Otherwise, they could take the time to wash it; she'd gladly help. Three bottles of diluted peroxide later, they managed to chip away at the layers of dried blood, reviving Flynn's chestnut waves.

A second-year neurology resident had been assigned to his case. Mia took an instant dislike to him, finding him condescending and rude. She smiled, thinking Flynn would approve of her methods. He never could stand for anyone to talk down to her. Surely, the head of neurology was a much better choice. But that was unheard of, the staff insisted. Dr. Logan wasn't taking new patients, and certainly not one that qualified for indigent care. When an initial call went unanswered, Mia was undeterred. She suspected that a request from Dr. Burke might do the trick. Though getting Roxanne on board with that plan would be the long way around; Flynn didn't have that kind of time. There was another option. With a spot-on Southern drawl and some attitude, which was ingrained, she left a second message posing as the esteemed Dr. Burke. He responded immediately. Mia did wonder, as she waited for Dr. Logan, if there was any man Roxanne couldn't intimidate. Raising a brow, she smiled at Flynn's slumbering body. There was one. When Dr. Logan arrived, a lengthy consultation ensued where Mia did most of the talking. The man was exceptionally qualified and genuinely compassionate. It only took a bit of gentle persuasion for him to agree to take the case. The busy doctor even took time to inquire about Mia's drawings, which had become as permanent as the medical equipment in Flynn's room. Dr. Logan appeared as interested in them as he did his new patient. Mia explained, in detail, the benefits of a green environment. After completing a fresh round of tests, the chest tube and ventilator were removed. Flynn was breathing fine on his own. Mia thought it was a sign, but Dr. Logan insisted that it didn't reflect on the coma.

Mercifully, Roxanne had switched to the night shift. Three solid weeks of a grueling schedule had kept her at bay. When the rotation ended there would be fallout. Mia was ready for as much. What she was less prepared for was Michael's reaction. There would be fallout there too, undoubtedly followed by an utter explosion. But as the moments eked forward, with weeks instead of days dedicated to Flynn, how or when that might happen seemed less apparent. Michael's nonstop schedule facilitated the situation. His dealings as an investment banker took him out of town some weeks, out of the country on occasion. When he was home, moments beyond the ICU ticked by in an awkward stutter, making it difficult to focus, never mind confess life-altering situations. His absence left time and space, and Mia used it to complete her designs while watching over Flynn.

At first it seemed like fair justification. Even long after he'd vanished, Flynn encouraged concepts that almost everyone else labeled eccentric, her husband included. Having witnessed her past successes, Michael was far more impressed with Mia's everyday designs. She understood; he was proud of her accomplishments and reluctant for Mia to take unnecessary risks. But his inability to appreciate her passion was a needling reminder of things they didn't share. The deal with Hough was the first time Michael had shown real interest in her eco-friendly, holistic mission. And Mia had hoped it was a positive sign in a passive marriage. So with logistics and reason working to her advantage, she could only assume that culpability was causing the ulcer-like burn in her stomach.

Flynn's return *was* unexpected. The feelings attached to him—not so much. Over time, before Michael, Mia had managed to compartmentalize. Flynn was gone. There would be no substitute. It was like learning to live without a limb, and she thought she'd done a decent job. While concentrating on her career, Mia expended emotional energy elsewhere, choosing to invest in someone other than herself. She made a hesitant call to the local Big Sisters program, landing a role she didn't get to play in real life: mentoring someone who didn't have all the advantages. It was something Mia might never have considered without having heard a tale or two about how unforgiving a childhood could be. It took effort, but proved to be good medicine and an even better reward. Still, it didn't fill every void. There were inconsolable moments, empty nights that Mia thought wouldn't end, an ache with which she never made peace. She liked to think that she lived with measurable fulfillment. Life didn't have to be about a man, particularly if you couldn't have the one you wanted.

Men became vague reference points, like constellations: permanent entities, difficult to pinpoint, a map to incalculable emptiness. There was an occasional date, two if the guy thrived on a challenge—which, in part, explained how Mia ended up married to Michael. After years of being mentored by Gisele DeVrie—interior design's Dalai Lama—Mia ventured out on her own. Hoping to cultivate a clientele, she convinced Roxanne to accompany her to a college alumni event. *Dr. Burke* had groused about going, having to forfeit a Saturday night in the ER where, according to her, mangled bodies were in good supply. However, after running headlong into Michael Wells, Roxanne changed her tune. She also didn't waste any time baiting her hook and casting him in Mia's direction. She could still recall their conversation in the ladies' room, not having seen Roxanne that enthused since beating the national MCAT scores by a mile. "Can you believe Michael Wells is here?" she gasped, reapplying lip gloss that was still a direct contrast to her persona. "He, um, he asked about you right away."

"Me?" Mia had said, busy determining the number of business cards she'd handed out. "What would he want with me?"

"He remembered you, wanted to know if you were here alone."

She shrugged, looking into Roxanne's reflection. "I'm not, I'm here with you."

"That's not what he meant," she said, rolling her eyes. "I think he'd like to ask you out."

A well worn stone wall went up. "Oh, well, tell him I'm absorbed in starting my own business. I don't have time to date—him or anyone else."

"Tell him yourself," Roxanne said, turning to face her. "Mia, it's been six years. Maybe it's time to take a chance." There was a noisy pause as an unspoken past rumbled by the two of them. "And I can't think of a better prospect than Michael Wells. He's an incredibly nice man, handsome, successful. If you ask me, he's perfect for you. I doubt any woman would view a date with him as a hardship."

"If you think he's that fantastic why don't you go out with him?"

"Michael?" she asked, looking as if Mia had suggested swimming with sharks. "Let's see, two self-professed overachievers with a competitive streak that would rival an Olympic team. I'm thinking he requires somebody with a softer edge."

"Mmm, I suppose you have a point," Mia said, recalling their college days, Michael serving as a formidable studying partner for Roxanne but little else. "I'll think about it," she said, merely to appease Roxanne.

Michael, it seemed, had another plan. As they exited the ladies' room he was standing nearby, flanked by two women who looked more than willing to take him on—or take him home. From the moment he excused himself and approached, Roxanne appointed herself team captain. It helped launch a courtship that she championed all the way to the altar. "Mia," he'd said, extending a hand, clasping hers firmly, "I don't know if you remember me, Michael Wells." He was as handsome as she recalled, as successful as he'd intended. "Roxanne and I had some classes together at UGA . . ."

Mia was polite but straightforward, telling him exactly what she'd said to Roxanne. That while she appreciated the invitation to dinner . . . the theater . . . an alumni gathering to watch a football game—all of which he offered during the next few weeks, she couldn't possibly accept. Her sole focus was getting a fragile and fledgling business off the ground. She didn't hear from him for a month or so, not until he turned up at her brownstone basement studio, claiming a decorating emergency. Sure that he could afford a more prestigious design house than hers, which was a blip on the map, Mia offered him Gisele DeVrie's personal number. She also figured it would snuff out any lingering interest. But Michael was undeterred, asking how any entrepreneur could afford to turn down a sure thing. He had a point. After designing his office—a corner suite with a fabulous D.C. view—Michael contracted her to redo his home office. Admittedly, Mia was flattered by the attention, professional and personal. To celebrate the project's end, Michael surprised her with a catered lunch on his veranda. The midday bottle of French wine and the personal chef were poised to impress anyone, even someone who was unaffected by the sheen of a lifestyle.

In the year that followed, a friendship flourished. And from what Mia had heard it was a sure path to lasting romance. She allowed the theory to have enough nourishment to take root, eventually taking Michael up on his offers. They took weekend drives to the Eastern Shore, and met for lunchtime picnics on the National Mall. He remembered her birthday, showing up with an appropriate gift—nothing that she could read too much into—and offered her business advice if asked. He was focused and suave, doing what Michael Wells did best. The two of them visited his family's home in Virginia where a warm and inviting crowd made it easy for Mia to blend, easier still to come back. While Mia managed to avoid labeling their relationship, she'd grown curious about his family's perceptions. On their way back to the city, sitting in a bottleneck of Sunday traffic, she peppered him with questions. "Michael, is there any chance your family thinks you're gay?"

He turned toward her, an incredulous look on his face. "Um, no . . . I don't think so."

Mia said nothing else for a moment, staring at the snaking glow of taillights. "Well, do they think I am?"

Looking at her, Michael's eyes pulsed wide, and he had to slam on the brakes or hit the car in front of them. But his answer was sedate. "I'd have to say no to that too. Especially after my cousin Stan, the degenerate, dragged me out to the garage. He wanted to know what kind of naughty lingerie you own."

"Oh, I don't believe that! Your cousin Stan is so sweet."

"Ha! Give me a break," Michael said, inching into the left lane. "Ask him some time exactly why he was suspended for two weeks in the tenth grade. Though according to him, they never did find all the peepholes in the girls' locker room."

Mia offered a sideways glance, the conversation edging toward things they'd made a pattern of ignoring. "So what do you tell them about us?" Mia pressed, surprised by her need to know.

His shoulders shrugged, creeping back into the right lane. "That we're friends. We get along great, enjoy each other's company," he said, eyes focused on the rearview mirror. "Have dinner together once or twice a week."

"And they don't think that's strange? They don't wonder why we're not . . . not a couple?"

It was a good thing they were in a sports car, Mia thought. The nimble vehicle moved like lightning, shooting from the center lane, through a clogged fast lane, and into the emergency lane where Michael thrust it into park. "Why? Do you think it's strange?" She swallowed hard; she'd never heard Michael raise his voice. Mia stared into dark eyes so filled with desire that it made her breath rattle. "Yeah, Mia, they think it's strange. And don't, for a second, think that it's not humiliating to stand in my father's garage and tell Stan, the family pervert, that what's none of his goddamn business isn't mine either!" It was the breaking point. Mia was overwhelmed by emotion—mostly his, enough of hers. Michael's desire boiled over, and he grasped Mia's shoulders, kissing her hard. He kept kissing her, and she let him. She kissed him back. Finally Michael inched away, Mia's mouth stinging from the roughness of his beard, maybe the shock of the connection.

"I, um . . . I don't really own any naughty lingerie." She gasped, tears in her eyes.

Still, it took time. Three years later, and on the third proposal, friendship captured romance. While dancing the first dance at their wedding reception—a regal affair that she might never have imagined—Mia held on to Michael for dear life. She never did care for being the center of attention. "I have to confess," he said, his warm cheek pressed to hers—still she shivered a bit. "I never thought this day would come," he said, gliding smoothly to the music. "Happy?" he asked.

"Of course," Mia said, closing her eyes . . . drifting, popping them open fast and wide.

"Good," he said, holding her tighter. "Because I'm so goddamn happy I hate to think anyone isn't feeling exactly the same way—especially the bride."

It caused Mia to inch back and look at him, realizing that he was joking. "Michael, how much champagne have you had?"

He laughed. "Not a drop," he said, kissing her. "This isn't the kind of thing I'd take a chance on forgetting."

Life began again. And why not; she'd married a wonderful man who wanted more than anything to be married to her. She did love him. Michael was patient and kind, loyal and trustworthy—not surprisingly a former Eagle Scout—passionate and giving. Mia followed through, touched by the flowers he sent because it was a Tuesday, returning the sentiment by showing up to bed in the kind of nightwear she'd learned that Michael favored. White, simple, and expensive—undoubtedly a thorough disappointment to Cousin Stan. Mia's eyes would remain focused on her husband as the nightgown slipped to the floor, her body giving in to his. But her mind would stay up late, as if petitioning the act, hours after he'd drifted into a satisfied slumber. Mia would leave the bedroom and wander aimlessly through the house, sometimes ending up on the front lawn. There she'd stand, shivering . . . freezing, waiting for physical pain to override the ache. Looking up into a clear cold sky, Mia guessed that constellations, no matter how substantial, couldn't outshine a single brilliant star.

An affair of the heart was one laden with guilt. That wasn't so new. It had been there for the nearly two years they'd been married—like an ugly wedding gift she didn't have the heart to return. As three weeks passed at Flynn's side, Mia contemplated telling Michael, starting the sentence at least once a day. She toyed with a generic explanation, but it would only exacerbate an unintentional lie. In the beginning of their relationship, Michael had asked about Flynn, and Mia's answers were decidedly vague. He seemed content to let it go, and Mia was relieved. It was a time that had come and gone years before Michael mattered, and she saw no benefit in disturbing a tender past. Mia never considered, not once, that someday she'd have to come clean. Michael would be hurt, furious, and rightfully so. No, it was better this way. If Flynn died, maybe she'd tell him years from now when they were old and it didn't matter so much. If Flynn lived, well, if he lived . . . Sitting at his bedside, Mia's head fell, cradling into her hands, praying. *God, he has to live. I'm burning in hell either way. Please let him live.*

Somewhere in between contemplating the yawning jaws of hell and sidestepping her husband, Mia managed to keep a firm hold on her work in progress. She had to. It was the only thing keeping a firm hold on her sanity. No matter what the outcome, at least the Hough proposal was finite. Either he'd be a pioneer and invest in her designs or he wouldn't. And after the work she'd put in . . . Well, she didn't want to fathom that disappointment. She dried a tear and looked toward Flynn. Other matters, she guessed, weren't as clear-cut.

This particular morning Mia couldn't get comfortable. She adjusted his bed linens a half dozen times, started and stopped as many sketches. A summer rain pounded at Flynn's window, as if the dark clouds were calling for him. It was a distracting tangle of guilt, a looming deadline, and bleak weather. Nothing seemed right. Days before Michael left for a conference in Vegas, the two of them arguing when Mia refused an invitation to join him. She hated Las Vegas, the gambling and glitz, a fact that he never could remember. Of course Michael had called, minutes after his plane landed. "It's me. I'm . . . I'm sorry about the way I left. I forgot. You hate Vegas. You know, it's a quick flight to Tahoe. You could meet me there this weekend. Let me know." Mia had listened, dialing and hanging up—almost throwing the cell phone across the room. A change in venue wasn't going to solve the problem.

Twice the nurse had been in at Mia's insistence, assuring her that Flynn was fine. Yet something was amiss. His comatose state, while unremarkable, had certain markers that she tallied each day. It wasn't anything a medical device might gauge, just an energy they shared. This morning Flynn seemed different. His skin was clammy and there was a subtle shift in his breathing. No doubt he was absorbing the negative vibe Mia was generating. Surely it oozed like lava from those earmarked for hell. Maybe, for the moment, he'd be better off without her standing guard.

* *

With the last pieces to Hough's mock office due to arrive, Mia decided to see to the delivery. Along with her proposal, Hough had advanced her the cash for a prototype. She'd never had a client offer money for a maybe; it underscored his interest. While most of the building—a downtown vintage brick rehab—was under reconstruction, the crew had completed five hundred square feet for Mia's design. The middle-management office was about to get the royal treatment—albeit totally holistic and green. She hadn't been there since the floors were installed, a gleaming bamboo. Even on the gloomiest of days they sparkled with promise.

"These look terrific, Sam! And with all the work you guys

have to do," she marveled to the foreman, shaking rain from an umbrella.

"Not a problem, Ms. Wells," he said, glancing up from a computer screen and papers, which were spread out over a make-shift desk. "But you'd better take care not to get them wet."

"That's definitely not a problem—they're tough as steel," she said, banging the tip of the umbrella into the floor for good measure.

"Yeah . . . yeah, I remember, that's what you told the guys," he said absently, continuing to punch at a calculator. He gave up, tossing down what looked to be a pile of receipts in apparent aggravation.

"Something wrong?" Mia asked the generally pleasant fore-man.

"It's the books, not really my thing. Hough's people will have my hide if I can't get the accounts payable to balance." He glanced at her, a look of chagrin anchored to his face. "I'm 19,999.63 bucks in the hole. Hough's gonna think I'm pocket-ing his cash."

"Oooh, that is a lot of money." She cringed. But she knew Sam Kramer fairly well, enough to know that wasn't the case. "Can I help? Numbers aren't really my thing either, but I've got-ten pretty good at profit and loss. Work with eco-friendly design long enough and you learn the long way around to a profit."

"Nah," he said, closing the computer screen. "Thanks, though. Hey, about your design. I wanted to tell you, every-thing you're doing, you got my boys plenty fired up. Especially the part about sustainable resources: 'a hundred years to grow a forest of oak trees versus five to replace the same amount of bamboo.' You're very convincing, Ms. Wells. I don't suppose you could offer a few inspirational words about tape and spackle?"

Mia laughed, feeling slightly less bound for hell. "I'll see what I can come up with." She peeled open a carton and dove in, unpacking an array of sculpted desk accessories, which appeared to be more decorative art than ecologically savvy. No one would ever guess that the brightly colored pieces were made from outdated phone wire. Part of the intent was to sell the idea that upscale commercial design and environmentally sound materials could cohabitate. While holistic-based interiors had made progress, there was still a gap between form and function. That's where Mia felt her designs had an edge—even over other holistic designers—combining art with what was good for you and the environment. And Aaron Hough had made clear his penchant for stylish amenities. "Listen, Sam, your crew really outdid themselves. Would they accept a case of beer for their effort?"

"Delivered by you personally?" he said, raising a brow. "That would be more than nice; I'm sure they'd appreciate it. And don't worry, we'll recycle the empties. But honestly, what you're doing here, it made an impression."

"That's good to hear. You know, somebody once told me I'd find a way to do it all, combine pretty *and* save the world."

"You've got the pretty part down, that's for sure," he said with a wink.

Feeling her cheeks flush, Mia looked away. "Um, not me, I meant the design aspect. And he was an unusually big believer."

"Hey, don't sell yourself short. For a white collar gig this looks like comfy digs to me," he said, surveying the room. "But what I don't get is the space, how you've got it divvied up."

"Well," she said, looking at a disbursement of office space that didn't follow traditional methodology. "Holistic design begins with the footprint, the most efficient use of materials, space, energy—things like air quality. Do you have any idea the number of illnesses that can be linked to unchallenged office air?" He shook his head, glancing worriedly around the space.

"Anyway, rehabbing this building is a big part of that transition, using what's already here and making it beneficial. As for the interior, it's the way light travels through the room, vibrational energy and intangible elements combined with physical goods. It's based on low-impact, highly recycled materials that aren't only advantageous to the earth but to the user. It's the element that separates holistic design from the common eco-friendly measures we see a lot of nowadays. And," she added, positioning a stunning glass divider, "it also includes an artistic component that is scientifically proven to heighten the healthy effects."

"No kiddin'?" he said, reaching into the box, retrieving a festive-looking wastebasket with a rainbow of hues highlighting its woven design.

"Trash receptacles," she said, taking it from him, "are the exclamation point on my work. It's a pet project my father would have loved, seeing this kind of progress. It's also made out of the earth's worst enemies—potato chip bags and candy wrappers."

"Okay, so you toss your Doritos discards into something sweeter than a standard metal round file. How's that benefit Mother Earth?"

She shook her head, smiling. "No, the cans are *made* from recycled food wrappers. If things like this were manufactured on a large scale they'd be cost effective, and the long-term impact would be incredible. Holistic and eco-friendly design has so much to offer—if you can break down the barriers and embrace change. That's tougher than you'd think."

"I get it. That's where somebody like Hough comes in."

"More or less. I'd love to sell the design for a single office building that's floor-to-ceiling holistic and sustainable, but that's just the hook. Aaron Hough holds the keys, literally, to a lot of other commercial real estate. If I can convince him, it could be the springboard to thousands of offices just like it. I've sold plenty of holistic designs in ones and twos, mostly to people who were bigger environmentalists than me. But never to someone with an ability or desire to mainstream it."

"Well, I really hope that works out for you," he said, placing the wastebasket next to a workstation. "If not, you can always give it the standard decorator treatment. Not so eco-friendly but a sure thing."

"Well, I could. But that's not what Hough hired me to do. It's what makes this project so special. Knowing that someone with clout is taking my work seriously . . . It's"—she took a breath—"it's what I've been working toward for years. Standard design pays the bills, but it's not my passion."

"Yeah, but your regular designs, they're top-shelf, right? I mean, this is nice and all, but if it doesn't fly you can—" He stopped, perhaps guessing that he'd said the wrong thing. "Listen, I've got to get back to crunching these numbers," he said, reopening the computer. "There's got to be an obvious glitch somewhere. A $19,999.63 error should kind of jump out at you."

Mia nodded, slightly deflated. People were often impressed with holistic design, the personal benefits and earthly advantages, but true believers were rare. He meant well. "Sam," she said, as he busied himself with the calculator. "How do you know my everyday designs are any good? You've never seen them."

"Um, I guess, just by looking at this," he said, swinging his arms wide. "Besides, I heard Hough say as much. He was by a few days ago, had some suit with him. They were talkin' you up, saying what a terrific job you did on those ritzy law offices over on Broad Street."

Mia crinkled her brow, glancing around her project in progress. "He said that?" The Broad Street project, while remarkably high-end, was textbook design—standard materials, zero eco-interest. It was apples and oranges, comparing a Hummer to the next generation gasless engine. It was curious phrasing from a man who'd sought Mia out based on her holistic design philosophies.

"Yeah, you must have done some work for the guy that was with Hough. He looked like a numbers guy, and he was running a blue streak about how you designed his off—"

"Wait!" Her phone rang and Mia's hand shot up, her heart jumping. It was the ring tone dedicated to the hospital—the ICU.

Chapter 13

ATHENS

The entire apartment smelled like a Baptist church basement after Sunday services—the aroma of fried chicken, heavenly temptation. The cozy dining table was set for three with an actual tablecloth, matching silverware, and linen napkins. Mia had bought them for the occasion, thinking there wasn't enough she could do to force this meal into submission. She fussed with them now, refolding the birdlike creatures she'd painstakingly arranged, wondering exactly how cloth napkins were going to improve her chances of this night succeeding.

For two months Mia Montgomery had lived a perfect secret. Happiness caught her by surprise, a feeling of contentment, a well of fire she'd never imagined when Flynn asked, would she stay? One astonishing night, minus the naked midnight stroll, mirrored by another. In the heartbeat of a moment, it seemed like it had always been just that way. Mia ignored the disturbing flutter of relief; the one that came with a sense of powerlessness when he actually followed through, when he didn't simply vanish. Lunch-hour dates soon became habit. Mia would smile and try not to let her apprehension show as he'd roll out of bed, heading back to the motorcycle shop. Flynn would kiss her good-bye, always saying, "See you later, sweetheart," leaving her to wonder if she really would. It did fade as trust grew over time. Flynn appeared equally mesmerized by her, and why not? After all, had she not "destroyed him"? Mia invented clever excuses to steal away from the apartment she shared with Roxanne. She was having a terrible time in chemistry, had to hire a tutor. Not once, but twice a week. Her grades were that bad, or so she said. It wasn't a complete fib. For a guy who blew into town on a motorcycle, with an arguably vague past, he was amazingly well versed in most subjects. Romance occasionally smoldered on the sidelines as Flynn happily assisted with any schoolwork that was troubling her.

Mia had no qualms about her secret, the little lies she had to tell to be with Flynn. There was only the two of them, no family or friends. It was private, intense, and she didn't want to let anyone else in. It could have gone on that way forever if it weren't for a comment Flynn made after a particularly torrid rendezvous that neither of them wanted to end. He was still breathing heavily, lacing up his boots, already five minutes late for the brake job that was next in line for his attention. Less motivated than him to dress, Mia fussed with the sheets and straightened the bedspread. Flynn looked up from the boots and drew a metaphor over the action, laughing at her need to "cover up their sordid affair." Mia laughed too, but her pillow-fluffing enthusiasm faded. Had he said it out of humor, or maybe as a subtle hint? Did he want more than this? Mia knew more about Flynn than any other human being, of that she was sure. But there were dark places and many things he didn't share. If he wanted more than this, he would never say. It was up to her. Mia began to take down the barriers between

Flynn and the rest of her world, thrilled, excited, and terrified when he didn't object.

She began with the biggest brick: Roxanne. She decided there would be no sugarcoating of facts. Preparedness was everything when approaching Roxanne with unpleasant news. Mia ran the impending conversation through her head a dozen times. Did she remember Flynn? Roxanne would toss her a motherly look of concern, followed with an expletive and a remark like, "What would possess you to bring him up?" "Well, as it turns out, Rox, he never did leave town. In fact, we've been seeing each other for weeks. Okay, months." There would be upset and objection, hurt feelings when Roxanne realized Mia had been keeping it a secret, and then, naturally, every attempt to dissuade her. Mia planned a simple defense: "I think I'm incredibly, hopelessly in love with him." Mia knew Roxanne well and the actual conversation did go much like she imagined, except for a few extra expletives.

Finishing with the napkins, Mia ducked back into the kitchen to check on the chicken. She hoped he was hungry, she hoped the gravy wasn't lumpy, she hoped the two of them didn't kill one another before dessert. Mia sipped another cold mouthful of wine, her third glass. It hadn't done a thing to settle the butterflies in her stomach. The doorbell rang and Roxanne blew past from the bedroom, insisting she answer it. Her hair in a sexy upsweep, she wore dangly earrings, spiked heels, and shiny lips. It was a unique rendering. Mia wanted to title it "Beauty Queen Dressed for Inquisition." *Stop it. Roxanne agreed to try, for me. She said she'd be nice. Flynn promised not to agitate her by calling her "babe," or just plain old "bitch" to her face. This was going to be a disaster.*

When Mia came out from the kitchen, Flynn was standing in the living room holding a colorful bouquet of summer flowers wrapped in pink tissue. She smiled at him. Jeans, T-shirt—he dressed for no one. She guessed the flowers were more for Roxanne's benefit than hers. "They're beautiful," Mia gushed, taking them. "Aren't they beautiful, Rox?" There was a spark of hope. He was trying. Flynn swooped down, gathering Mia into a firm kiss, obviously staking his territory. On the other hand, perhaps he was only willing to meet her halfway.

He raised an eyebrow, smiling at Roxanne. "I hope you're not allergic."

Mia recognized the smile that was returned. *Careful, Flynn, watch your fingers.*

Roxanne caught a stray strand of hair that had escaped from the up-do and tucked it back into place, batting feathery lashes in his direction. The drawl was on fire. "It's no problem, but I had no idea the highways were so full with flowers this time of year."

Score one point for Roxanne.

"Roxanne," he began, but hesitated. "Uh, nice earrings." Mia was impressed; he was working hard to keep his cool. Fortunately the chicken jumped in to assist.

"Mia, you didn't . . . That's not fried chicken I smell, is it?"

She beamed a smile of domestic satisfaction, the butterflies easing up. "Uh huh, and mashed potatoes. You said something about it being a favorite . . ."

"Taking a quiz. At the cottage, was it? I believe I passed."

"Did you ever." Mia cleared her throat, recalling that Roxanne was in the room. She wasn't used to this, conversations with Flynn that included other people. "Dinner will be ready soon. Do you want something to drink?"

"Yeah, sure," Flynn said, hands stuffed in his pockets, looking equally put off by the demands of a third person. His gaze wandered, unable to find the comfort zone he enjoyed when it was just the two of them. "Hey, you didn't tell me you got this back." He crossed the room, brushing by Roxanne to a design board busy with swatches, sketches, detailed notes, and a giant red C-. He unclipped the paper marked with furious scribble and the letter grade. "You got a C minus?" Mia rolled her eyes, fighting a wave of embarrassment. She meant to put away her Interiors Concepts final project—or, better yet, just throw it out. "How the hell did you get a C minus?"

"Finally," Roxanne said, "something we agree on. She's capable of such beautiful work. Between Mia's artistry and what has to be some inbred sense of style that she totally disregards . . . Why she keeps pursuing these left-of-center designs is beyond me. I told her it was a nutty idea—recycled furniture, even the blinds, concrete floors—I mean, yuck. We all might as well get a cell at the state penitentiary."

Flynn started to reply but stopped. Instead he focused on Mia, glancing at the graded paper. "I know how hard you worked on that. It was an A project and then some. You even researched the chemical compositions to come up with nontoxic dyes."

"Well, not exactly." Mia folded into the hug he offered. "Let's be honest, you came up with the compounds. And for that," she said, pointing to the paper, "the professor noted 'stellar achievement.'"

"You helped with this?" Roxanne said. "I should have known; those compounds were a wee bit complex. Wait," she said, eyeing Flynn. "How would you know—? Whatever. The grade speaks for itself. Next time she'll know better."

"Next time she'll know going in that the professor's an ass," Flynn said, glaring at Roxanne. "What else did he say?"

Mia read from the paper, "'Project shows a curious passion, fanciful imagination . . .'"

"That doesn't sound so bad—" Mia held up a hand, stopping him.

" 'It also demonstrates narrow applications, zero client appeal or reasonable marketability. While imagination inspires design, Ms. Montgomery, it must first and foremost have purpose.' I didn't think I went that wrong. I just wanted to design something that appealed to more than magazine aesthetics—something that mattered."

"It's exactly what I said," Roxanne groused, shooting a look at Flynn. "You might stumble on one nut held up in a tree house who's interested in recycling his manifesto into a tablecloth. But as for the masses, nobody wants to spend their time wallowing in salvaged junk. People with a nine-to-five existence need to be surrounded by ambience and high-tech. Not reminded that the earth's going to hell by way of global heating. That's like a bazillion years away. Who cares?"

"Warming. It's global warming, Rox," Mia quietly corrected.

"Whatever." She shrugged. "You have a huge natural talent, Mia. Go with that. Any one of your regular designs would have been an easy A. This is nonsense and you're wasting your time." She sulked into the kitchen, giving her blond hair an irritated toss.

It was a mile walk across the room, reattaching the graded paper to her project. A quiet moment later Mia felt Flynn behind her, hands on her shoulders, mouth pressed to her head. "Don't listen to her," he whispered. "She doesn't have a clue. It was a great design, Mia, full of smart ideas, way ahead of the curve."

"Maybe so, but my professor pretty much agreed with her."

"No, he said it showed passion and imagination." Turning her in his arms, he smiled. "It's not your fault he couldn't see around the curve."

Swallowing down the lump in her throat, she smiled back. "Thanks, I needed to hear that. As for this," Mia said, poking at the project, "I guess it's back to the drawing board—or just the Dumpster."

"Don't you dare," he said with something more than cursory comfort. "There might be a thousand more steps to turning that into what it can be. But if you give up, you'll never get there."

She nodded, not quite feeling his enthusiasm. "Hey, I'll get you that beer."

"Okay," he said, still looking over the design board. "I'll plan conversation for her highness's return."

"It couldn't hurt." She dropped a quick kiss on his lips before heading into the kitchen.

"Hey, Mia . . ."

"Yeah?" she said, walking backward.

"If I forget to tell you later, dinner was terrific. And someday, you're going to knock the design world on its collective ass." Their smiles connected as she disappeared inside.

"Roxanne, come on. Company's in the living room. You promised."

"I know, I'm coming. Just grabbing a glass of wine. I was stirring your gravy."

"You don't drink wine and I'd be amazed if you could identify gravy without a lab analysis. Now go."

"All right, I'm going already. Just do me one favor. See if you can keep the mouth-to-mouth to a minimum. He makes me want to floss." She gave an exaggerated shiver, poking a wooden spoon in the gravy.

"We'll try." Mia shooed her away, handing her a beer. "For Flynn."

"Is there anyone else?" she purred sweetly, pushing through the swinging door.

The conversation trudged forward, design talk put aside, as Mia managed to get dinner on the table. Both of them dove in to help, desperate to get away from each other. Flynn seemed glad for the distraction of food, busily filling his plate. "Mia, this is fantastic," he said, wolfing down gulps of a crispy breast. "I had no idea you could cook like this."

Roxanne delicately popped a cherry tomato into her mouth, eyeing the opening. "Oh, Mia's a fantastic cook when she has the right tools."

There's the windup.

"But it's probably hard to demonstrate when you only have a hot plate for cooking."

And the pitch.

Flynn swallowed hard and blotted his mouth with a napkin, taking a dramatic pause before flexing to knock it out of the park.

"Flynn, did you know," Mia interrupted, loud enough to grab their attention, "when Roxanne was in high school she was the homecoming, prom, Strawberry Pageant, and Watermelon Festival queen?"

"Is that right?" he said with inflated enthusiasm. "So what, they just didn't have the Ice Princess competition that year?" He never looked up, stabbing a leg with his fork.

Roxanne's electric blue eyes pulsed wide, and her back went erect against the chair. It was war. "No, no, Flynn. There's never an 'Ice Princess' competition in high school, sugar." Her head cocked to one side, the drawl going gooey, sweeter than honey. "But maybe you needed to have attended one to know that."

"Oh, I went to high school, Roxanne. In fact, I was voted most likely to rob a convenience store. But I'm so glad *you* didn't go to high school with Deidre Zeller."

"Oh, and why's that? Did she find you more irritating than I do?"

"Nah, we voted her biggest bitch. Woulda broke her heart to lose to somebody pretty as you." He never stopped eating, picking up his beer, saluting her before guzzling a long mouthful. As they continued to lob insults at one another, Mia was suddenly glad she didn't prepare anything that necessitated steak knives.

Roxanne's beautiful face went flush with anger. "Listen, you Lynyrd Skynyrd throwback, I don't know what Mia sees in you. Maybe every girl has to have one, the guy you use as a lifelong reference for mistakes not to be repeated. Though in your case, it would be a remarkably low threshold. She'll probably have to start dating drug dealers just to get an upgrade!"

"Yeah, well, if the same holds true for girlfriends, she'll have to join a witches' coven for the upgrade there. You know, Roxanne, you ought to—"

The earsplitting sound of metal hitting glass interrupted them as Mia's utensils slammed into her plate and she bolted for the kitchen. Roxanne and Flynn were silenced, left staring at the dinner plate, cracked right down the middle.

A few moments later, the two of them sulked into the kitchen. Mia had her back turned and was scrubbing a frying pan with violent strokes as dishwater sloshed every which way.

"We're, um, sorry," Roxanne mumbled. "Really, we are . . . sorry." Apologies were not what she did best.

Flynn spoke louder, over the rush of running water. "Yeah, Mia, I . . . we both behaved badly. I'm sorry. Would you come back to the table? We promise, no more fighting. Please?"

It was the "please," that got her. There was little Mia found she could deny Flynn, even when he acted like a complete jerk. She shut the water off, and threw her head back. "I just . . . I just wanted the two of you to get along. You don't have to be best friends. You don't even have to like each other much. But I was hoping you'd realize that you do have one thing in common." She turned to face them. "Me. I'm not going to hang around just to dodge the splatter from your bloodbath." Like scolded schoolchildren, they both offered a submissive nod.

"Fine," she said, throwing the dishrag on the counter, "if the two of you think you can manage a civil conversation then, Roxanne, you can clear the table. I'll get dessert." Inwardly Mia had huge reservations about giving it another try. They were two of the most stubborn, acerbic people she'd ever known. Their chances of finding common ground were practically nil. Then she realized that was the entire problem. She was the common ground. Plunging a knife into an ice cream cake she honestly wondered if there was enough of her to go around.

Mia flipped on the television, thinking a spin through the channels might be the right counterweight. Maybe they'd discover a mutual interest. Maybe on some remote cable channel she'd find an ex-beauty queen demonstrating how to change motor oil. She settled for Animal Planet. It was an unfortunate choice. She exhaled a wheezy breath as two lions tore furiously at the bloody carcass of an antelope.

"You don't look so good. Are you all right?" Flynn asked, easing in next to her.

"Huh? Oh, fine," she murmured, tossing her uneaten cake on the coffee table. Moving on, she stopped at the evening news. Current events—that could work. A reporter was coming in live from Birmingham, Alabama.

"And that's all authorities are willing to say at this point, Jim. Students are holding another candlelight vigil, as this would have been Marissa Middleton's twenty-first birthday. There are no leads in the murder of the University of Alabama coed. It's been over two months since she was found, badly beaten, drowned in a bathtub. All leads appear to have grown cold. Police are theorizing, however, that this murder is linked to a string of cross-country coed killings that have taken place over the past two years. All the victims were brunette, attractive, and by friends' accounts, friendly and outgoing. Colleges around the country are braced for the possibility that their campus could be next. Back to you in the studio," he reported with a morbid grin of satisfaction.

"Damn," Flynn said, rubbing a hand over his mouth, "ice cream cake is cold." Mia changed the channel once again. The spinning, chiming whirl of *Wheel of Fortune* filled the room. "Mia, did you seriously want to go to that concert in Atlanta next week? If you do, I don't think it's too late to get tickets."

She smiled, flattered that he would remember a small remark about an offbeat bluegrass band she followed. "I really hadn't thought about it. If you want to go, I'll drive. I love your bike, Flynn, but I'm not sure I want to ride all the way to Atlanta on it." She took his plate from him and snuggled into the crook of his arm.

"Um, would you be interested in going too, Roxanne?" Flynn asked, delivering the civility he'd just promised. "I can probably get three tickets."

Roxanne blinked, clearly lost in thought. "What? Ah, no thanks. Funny, Mia and I don't share the same taste in music, either." They both shot her a warning glance. "So, tell me something, Flynn." Roxanne slipped from a chair to a giant floor pillow. She shyly tucked her legs beneath her and struck an unassuming pose. "Have you been traveling a long time on your bike? I mean, don't you have a home anywhere?" Mia's attention was drawn away from the TV, listening carefully, but she didn't pick her head up off of Flynn's shoulder.

"Yeah, there's some family. My sister lives in Texas and I have a brother in the Southwest."

"The Southwest? That's an interesting part of the country. Do you visit much? I mean, that's an awfully long way, from there to here. Mia tells me you came here from Alabama. Were you there long? Isn't it tiring, all that riding?"

What are you up to, Roxanne? This isn't just polite conversation.

"It has its moments. But you get used to it, the riding. I like open spaces."

"Mia mentioned that you were in the Marines. What was that like? Did you enjoy it?"

"It was the Marines, not a Caribbean holiday. Enjoyment wasn't really one of their goals." Mia felt Flynn's body tense up against hers. Her hand automatically rose to his chest, and she gently stroked her fingers across the soft cotton fabric. He fought it, then relaxed a bit.

"I see. Well, what about your travels? Do you have family scattered around the country? That's really interesting, because I don't have a single relative outside the state of Georgia. I could visit them all in a day. What about yours?"

"Well, I went to see my brother when I first got out. That's when I bought the bike, a couple of years ago. Eventually I ended up at my sister's, hung out awhile. Texas took some time, it's big country. After that I just started state hopping, a long shot up through the middle of the map. Saw my mom for a day in Indiana. That was probably the worst of the ride. Missouri, Kansas, Arkansas, really nothing to see." He stopped, leaning forward, scraping his fork through a puddle of ice cream, avoiding Roxanne's intense stare. The silence seemed to force him to go on. "Um, it does get monotonous, so I take breaks. One of the advantages of traveling like that, you can stop anywhere. I took a construction job in Little Rock for a while."

"Oh, but that didn't make you want to stay, maybe put down some roots?"

"Ah, no. No, it didn't. I moved on to Iowa. Had some, uh, business, I guess you could say. One winter in Iowa is enough for anybody," he said, glancing up. "I headed south again, but decided to make a slingshot trip through Canada, back through the upper Midwest last fall. Since then, I've been working my way southeast."

"Canada, upper Midwest, huh? That's off the beaten path."

As he rambled, Mia's head slowly inched up from his body. Flynn talking about himself, that was generally a nonevent, but now he was babbling to Roxanne like she was long-lost kin. When he finished speaking, Mia was upright on the sofa, blinking at him in utter disbelief.

"What?" His eyes jutted to her, then to the television. "*Mission Impossible*," he loudly announced, a clear attempt to end the discussion.

"Huh?" the girls replied in unison. Flynn pointed to the television, where Vanna had revealed the letters *m*, *l*, and *n*. A few turns later and it was game-show bedlam as a contestant reached the same conclusion.

"How in the world did you figure that out from three consonants?" Mia said, her stare shuffling between him and the game of hangman.

"Lucky guess," he said, shrugging.

Roxanne, who also seemed distracted, gazed at the television then back toward Flynn. She mumbled just loud enough for Mia to hear, "Yeah, it's amazing what you can deduce from a limited amount of information."

Chapter 14

Three pairs of jeans lay stretched out across Mia's bed, each matched to a different shirt, the ensembles creating various statements. She jerked a lavender tank top away from the middle pair and replaced it with a slinky, low-cut black blouse. It was a bold deviation from a wardrobe that consisted mostly of jeans and comfortable cotton shirts. Roxanne wandered in from the hall. She passed by Mia and snatched up the blouse, examining the price tag.

"Hmm, why didn't you get the matching skirt? Then your outfit could be worth more than he makes in a year." She tossed it back onto the bed and flopped into a chair.

"Ah, sharpening your claws again, Rox? Careful, I wouldn't want you to snag one on my new outfit. For your information, I did get the skirt. It's over there," Mia said, motioning toward a skimpy, thrill-seeking skirt that hung from the doorknob. "I was thinking it's too dressy for an outdoor concert, but maybe I will wear it. I think Flynn would love it."

Roxanne snickered, rolling her eyes. "Right, like you need to dress to impress him. Like he's not getting it all for the asking anyway."

Mia held a hand up in protest before there was some analogy about purchasing cows and getting milk for free. "Roxanne, I'm in too good of a mood. Don't start. I've been looking forward to this all week. Listen, can I borrow that silver necklace of yours? You know, the one with the onyx stone. It's exactly what this needs. I promise, I won't let Flynn hock it," she said, smiling sweetly.

"Fine, it's on my desk."

Mia scooted across the hall, shuffling through a desktop filled with Roxanne's busy schedule notebooks, medical school correspondence, textbooks, and a map. *A map?* When she turned, Roxanne was standing in the middle of the room, reeking of nervousness.

"I was just coming to help. There's so much stuff in there. Let me look, you'll never find it."

"Don't bother, I found everything. What is this?" demanded Mia, holding the map covered with scraps of sticky notes.

"Nothing. It's nothing. Give it to me." Roxanne sprang across the room, grabbing for it as if Mia might burn herself on it.

"Don't give me that." Mia held the map tight to her chest, walking back to her room. "Why do you have a map of the country covered with sticky notes, and why does the one in New Mexico say 'Flynn starts here'?" They stood in a momentary face-off. It was generally Mia's job to cave, to give in to whatever Roxanne wanted: what was for dinner, the movie on TV, plain versus pepperoni. While Mia viewed the tiny controls as insignificant, Roxanne's need to dominate larger issues, like Flynn, was fast becoming an irritation.

Roxanne backed away, oddly agreeing to acquiesce. "All right, Mia, I'll tell you. But you're not going to like it."

"I already hate it. Start talking."

"Right now it's only a theory. I didn't want to tell you yet because it would be my word against . . . Well, just give me the map and I'll explain." Mia held out the map and Roxanne spread it out over the boudoir fashion show. "I want you to be openminded about what I'm going to show you." Mia cocked her head to one side, reading the notes that began in Albuquerque, New Mexico, and trailed across two dozen states, ending in Athens, Georgia. "Flynn said he started out riding cross-country two years ago starting from his brother's, who lives in the 'Southwest.' Do we agree on that much?"

"I suppose, but I don't know where exactly. He's never said." *What in the world are you up to, Roxanne? Why do I suddenly feel like I'm in the middle of a Nancy Drew mystery?*

"Well, for argument's sake, let's say it was around here," she said, pointing to the sticky farthest left. "Albuquerque, near the university. From there we know he went to Texas to visit his sister. 'Hung out awhile'—those were his words, right?"

"That's what he said . . . I guess," she said, following Roxanne's finger across the map.

"We know that from there Flynn says he stopped in Indiana to see his mother. We also know he worked a construction site in Little Rock, Arkansas." Roxanne's banter was heating up. She was plowing toward something that Mia was positive she didn't want to hear. "He spent some of that winter in Iowa; remember he said how cold it was? Said he had some 'business'? Him, what *business* would he have in Iowa? Now that grabbed my attention."

"Good Lord, Roxanne, I thought you only took copious notes in organic chemistry. He was talking so fast I don't see how you could recall any of this," Mia protested, clearly recalling the "business" to which he'd been attending. For a moment

Mia considered telling Roxanne about the nightmares . . . how he dealt with them, the pot. She passed; it would only feed her fire.

"Well, I probably would have tuned him out completely, if it hadn't been for the news report we were listening to before that. Do you remember?"

Mia shook her head, studying the map, then Roxanne. "No, I don't, but I'm guessing that all of this doesn't tie into a segment on cross-country travels on the back of a motorcycle."

"Hardly." A paper clip was fastened to the edge of the map, and behind it were copies of news stories printed from the Internet. Mia felt her expression shift from confused to concerned as she began to leaf through them. "I know you're going to think it's an incredible leap, but for one minute forget about how you feel and listen to the facts. When I started looking, it was no more than a wild hunch. To be honest, I wasn't really expecting to find anything—but look," she said, fanning the news stories out. "Look at these stories and the places Flynn said he traveled to. Most important, Mia, look at the timeline."

She focused on the first headline, reading aloud, " 'UNM Grad Student Murdered,' " glancing over the date. She didn't bother with the story, moving on to the next one. " 'University of Texas Coed Slain.' " Mia's head began to involuntarily nod. "The Case of the College Killer" became evident as she continued with similarly worded stories, Arkansas on to Iowa. The fifth headline belonged to a girl from Minnesota State, a grisly discovery made by her roommates after they left her alone for the weekend. At the bottom was the last printout, Marissa Middleton, the girl from Alabama, beaten and drowned in a bathtub. Mia bit her lip hard and held the pages tightly, studying them, then the map. "I see what you're getting at, Roxanne."

"Look at the dates. They're awfully close. From what Flynn

told us the other night, he was somewhere near each one of those murder scenes during that time frame. You at least have to agree that it looks suspicious."

Mia crinkled her forehead, her gaze darting between the map and the news stories. She closed her eyes, blocking it all out, thinking only about Flynn and an instinct that told her this was nothing more than Roxanne's overprotectiveness, her own past interfering with Mia's present. Mia's grip eased, and her expression went flat. She refused to feed it. Placing the papers on the bed, she began to put away the map.

"Mia, what are you doing? Look at the map, look at the trail Flynn admitted to. You can't just dismiss this."

"Dismiss it? Oh, I wouldn't dream of dismissing it, after all the keen detective work you've done. Tell you what, Nan. You give the Hardy Boys a ring and when they get here we'll all put our heads together. I bet we can not only solve these murders, but maybe we can get Flynn to admit to being Jack the Ripper too." She finished refolding the map with pinpoint precision, and reattached the news headlines. Mia moved them aside and continued to fuss over the outfits on the bed.

Roxanne grabbed her arm, pulling Mia's body around to face her. "I'm not doing this to hurt you. I'm doing this because I care what happens to you."

Mia jerked away. "You're doing this because you don't believe any man is trustworthy, particularly one who doesn't meet with your preapproved notion of good versus evil."

"It's not a bad standard, Mia. If Rory had given even a little consideration to the kind of man—"

"And there we go," she said, an arm sweeping past Roxanne. "I figured the comparison wasn't too far behind. You have to stop this, Rox. What happened to Rory isn't going to happen to me."

Roxanne shook her head, her sky blue eyes clouding with concern. "Probably not," she said with a shrug, the drawl deadpan. "But what are the odds that it would have happened to Rory? My fear is that something worse will happen to you. There's a chance, Mia, that Flynn is more dangerous than Rob Valente ever was."

Hearing Roxanne say the name of Rory's ex-boyfriend aloud, it was beyond taboo. Mia swallowed hard, staring, wanting to make clear the world of difference between someone like him and Flynn. "Roxanne," she said, slow and steady, the way you'd give a speech into the bathroom mirror, "you're my best friend and one of the smartest people I know. You've been there through some really crappy stuff, bad decisions on my part. But about Flynn—what you've conjured up here," she said, pointing to the map, "you couldn't be more wrong. He's not a drug dealer, he's not a serial killer, he's not dangerous." Roxanne tried to interject, but Mia held firm. "Drop it. I mean it, Roxanne. You're pushing toward a conversation I'm not sure either of us wants to have. Now, if you don't mind, I'd like to get dressed. I told Flynn I'd pick him up at four."

"Maybe you could look at this from my perspective. What do you want me to do, Mia? Sit around and wait for you to turn up dead? What would you do if this whole situation were reversed?"

Mia looked hard into Roxanne's face, truly considering the scenario. For one outrageous moment she considered Roxanne and Flynn. She shook it off. Worlds colliding and little green people made more sense. She chose softer words than the ones she was considering. "I think I would trust what my friend had to say about the man she loves. I'd believe that she knows him better than me. I'd give her credit for having some speck of common sense that would tell her if she were sleeping with a killer.

Then I would mind my own business." Mia turned back to arranging her wardrobe.

Roxanne's chin tipped upward, her posture beyond stiff. "All right, Mia. I can't force you to listen. And even if it's all just a wild theory, even if it turns out that Flynn spent the last two years building houses for the homeless, donating his paycheck to the poor, there's one thing I'm not wrong about."

"What's that, Rox?" she said, folding her arms. "Not like I could stop you."

"He's going to end up hurting you—badly. Whatever he is, he's not wired to deliver happily ever after. And that, Mia, is what you want more than anything." She didn't wait for a reply, closing the door as she left.

Mia unfolded her arms, her steely resolve crumpling along with her body onto the bed. One hand reached out, fingering the silky blouse. The other brushed against the edge of the map. Mia pulled herself upright and reopened it. *It's not possible. There is no way Flynn is responsible for this. It's true; there are things I don't know about him. Whatever he's keeping from me, he has his reasons. But I swear, I trust him with my life. Doesn't that go against Roxanne's entire argument?* She thrust the map away and grabbed the blouse. It was far easier to paint Roxanne as controlling—resolute, if not rabid, about making sure that no one she loved ended up like Rory. A brilliant and beautiful second-year med student, Rory was a lot like her younger sister. And she would have had everything if it weren't for Rob Valente. He got her hooked on prescription meds and ecstasy, moving on to riskier drugs that ultimately cost Rory everything. Now it was permanent history, altering both Rory's and Roxanne's views of the world. Roxanne's tainted point of view was enough, Mia reasoned, to dismiss such an outrageous idea like Flynn and murder.

* *

A short time later, Mia found Roxanne in the living room, engrossed in a thick textbook—some cold topic that, for her, provided the warmth of a security blanket. Roxanne's eyes shifted up from the book. "Ah, I see you decided to go with the skirt and blouse. Good choice. Dressed like that, you can always sell your body for a ride home."

"Oooh, clever, but I'm driving, remember?" Her voice dropped to a hushed tone. "Unless, of course, Flynn decides to steal my car. Grand theft auto probably comes before serial killer. I guess Flynn's qualified."

"Excuse me for worrying. But I happen to care a great deal whether you end up in a ditch or just emotionally traumatized for the rest of your life."

"Flynn isn't going to do either of those things to me. I know you don't believe that." Her tone softened, weakened by Roxanne's overblown concern. "Listen, we'll be back early tomorrow. Try not to dwell on this. Try not to spend the entire night turning Flynn into some kind of homicidal maniac. Try using that stellar brain to channel positive karma."

"Fine, fine, you don't have to say any more. Like you said, you know him better than I do." She flipped the book closed and tossed it aside. "Mia?"

"Yeah?" she said, tucking a pair of flip-flops into the pocket of her overnight bag.

"I'm sorry I can't see what you see in Flynn. I'm sorry if I seem . . . overbearing," she said, raising a brow, Mia returning the gesture. "But the kind of man who'll deserve you—I mean the forever guy. Well, ask anybody, Lanie or Sara . . . It doesn't conjure up someone like Flynn."

She nodded, seeing Roxanne's vision. "Ah, the Prince Charming model, glass slipper, footman, glint on his tooth when he smiles."

"Okay, sure. In addition to anchored, safe, and a permanent address."

There was a pang of appreciation. Her father was gone, her mother *disconnected* at the very least. It was comforting to know that someone cared so much. Even so, Mia responded with the truth. "Maybe so, but anchored is predictable, safe is relative, and castles are drafty."

"Maybe," Roxanne agreed, not sounding terribly convinced. "Well, have a good time."

"We will," she said, heading out the door.

"And Mia . . ." She stopped and turned. "Be careful," Roxanne said, wishing more than safe travels.

Chapter 15

The folksy twang of the Chatter Blues Band filled the twilight sky, making concertgoers forget about sticky temperatures and the buggy blankets on which they sat. It made Mia forget the disconcerting conversation she'd had with Roxanne hours before. Her face was a perfect smile, looking down at Flynn, whose head rested peacefully in her lap, her tan legs lazily stretched out before her. A wavy thread of hair had strayed from the captured chestnut locks and she brushed it back, thinking he couldn't possibly look more content. He seemed so happy, just to be there with her. It was reassuring, making Roxanne's theory look as if it bordered on complete lunacy. Mia's gaze drifted helplessly from the band back to Flynn. He grinned, catching her fingers in his.

"Hey, you want another beer?" He sat up, kissing her before she could answer.

"No, thanks, I'm driving. But you go ahead if you want." Mia ran her fingers over his lips, erasing a smudge of lipstick, glancing toward the band as they left the stage for intermission.

"Okay, I think I will. Line looks pretty long," he said, squinting into the distance, back at her. "It's so hot, don't you want anything?"

Mia shook her head, giving his hand a squeeze as he stood. "I've got everything I need."

He stretched the stiffness from his body and bent forward to kiss her again, hesitating as he glanced over her outfit, looking as if he wanted to say something, smiling instead. "I'll be right back."

"Flynn?"

"Yeah?"

"The, um, lipstick," she said with a giggle. He wiped his mouth, laughing as he walked away.

Mia watched until the mane of hair and the sinewy body faded, the crowd thickening around him. It was bursting with clean-shaven men in pressed Dockers shorts and sockless loafers, and women vainly trying to fight off the last decade, momentarily removed from their suburban existence. It was no argument that Flynn stood out; the long-haired wild child sprouting in a field of ordinary people with nine-to-five jobs and pedestrian biographies. She couldn't help but notice how women looked at him. Always the odd glance at first, then the double take. He was the dare they never took, the kind of handsome the eye needed time to absorb. Flynn was a perplexing mix of all-American good looks camouflaged by a veil of irreverent, untamed features. Mia would watch them stare, reading their unsolicited thoughts. They saw him as a project. Take him home, clean him up, give him a haircut and a collared shirt.

She laughed softly to herself, knowing it would be like trying to tie down clouds or sitting a lion at the dining room table. He wasn't about the kind of things to which you might pin a daydream or tuck into a hope chest. Maybe he couldn't deliver picket fences or Sunday afternoon barbecues, but Mia was beginning to wonder if happily ever after was about something else entirely. Besides, those sounded more like her mother's ideals than hers. Still, if she was being honest, there was something attractive about tradition. The idea caused a nervous shiver to run up her spine, so at odds with the heat. Mia reminded herself that he had never said a word about staying. He certainly never spoke in the future tense. It had been an implicit part of his terms since the beginning and she accepted it. Flynn vanishing—the idea edged its way back into her consciousness. Mia's heart broke the agreement, fluttering a bit as she wrenched her neck to see if she could find him again.

A droning voice, sharp in her ear, interrupted her thoughts. "Hey, aren't you Mia Montgomery, from business law? Don't you look super hot in that pretty little outfit?" he said, wiping the back of his hand across a damp brow.

"Huh? What?" Immersed in thought, she hadn't noticed the guy who had taken Flynn's place on the blanket. Her focus was forced onto a red-faced young man she vaguely recognized. He was that clean-cut, suburban definition of handsome, a jokester from the back row of her business law class where he passed the time with a bunch of his fraternity brothers. "Oh, yeah. I'm Mia. How do you know . . .? I'm sorry, I don't know your name."

One of his fraternity brothers leaned in and poked him hard in the shoulder. "I told you that was her, Justin. She goes from plain hot to sizzlin' when she takes off her jeans." He laughed, feigning a punch to the boy next to him. "This here's Justin Tremont. Justin's been wanting to meet you."

"Ah, hell, he'd like to do a lot more than that," noted the third fraternity brother, looking Mia over as if she were the three-for-a-dollar raffle prize. "Your ass, well, your ass in your jeans, it's basically the reason he's flunking the class. But in that outfit, you've just given him a whole new reason to fail."

Mia felt her face go red as she stiffened on the blanket. Past experience said someone else should handle this. But it was Flynn's advice that led Mia down a different path, determined to stick up for herself. "Excuse me? Did you leave your manners at home? I really don't appreciate your comments—"

"That right?" he said, playfully grinning. "Let me work on that. I'm sure there's something I can do that you'd appreciate. Have a beer with me—or whatever."

Her mind flashed to a similar invitation made by a much different man. If his breath had been any thicker with alcohol, she would have passed out from the stench, his sweaty body now a leering threat. Mia leaned back at a sharp angle just to clear the personal space he was rapidly invading. "Listen, I'm here with someone. He'll be back any second and you might want to be gone by then." She looked past his eager face, searching for Flynn. Even self-defense could use a little backup. While Flynn was strikingly passive, she figured his presence might be deterrent enough. But the boy's grin didn't ease, as if she were only playing hard to get.

The two buddies stood at the edge of the blanket, intentionally or not, blocking her path. Justin's stare was like a dirty book, all heat and anticipation, and, she realized, not on her face. Mia glanced down. The sexy blouse meant for Flynn exposed more than cleavage. Her position didn't help, her back arched, arms splayed wide behind her. Mia hastily tried to correct it, jerking forward. At the same time she attempted to push the boy away. He took the physical contact as a sign of encouragement. Inches from his face, the boy's breath hung on her neck like a filthy, wet rag. "Back off," she said through gritted teeth.

He laughed. "Hmm, feisty too. I saw your date. You go for the wild type, huh? Does he always dress you like this for public display?" Sticky fingers reached up and plucked at the blouse, stroking her arm. His hands continued on the uninvited scratch-and-sniff, tangling in her hair. "Bet it gets him off real good."

"Get the hell away from me!" she yelled in a voice she realized was lost in the buzz of people around her—not one person paid attention to her plight. Mia attempted to jump to her feet, but her heel caught on the hem of her skirt, tossing her hard onto her behind. It left her at a perplexing disadvantage.

"Come on, Mia, I know what girls like you want. Something a little crazy, maybe a little rough. I've been watching you all semester. You could do a hell of a lot better than him." Angry and humiliated, she tried once more to escape, but he nearly had her pinned to the blanket. "Give me a chance. I'll show you a little bit of crazy like you've never seen."

A sucker's bet, too much alcohol, frat boys egging one another on, no doubt an unfortunate combination of all three. Mia froze, horrified at the boy's audacity, his friends tightly shrouding him. The boy rose up over her, a hand groping her nearly exposed breast.

A lightning second later, cold beer splashed everywhere. Before Mia could regain enough composure to shove him away, his body flew up over her head like a Frisbee, landing hard on the empty blanket next to them. Gut-wrenching expletives escaped his mouth as he curled into a tight fetal position. Mia scrambled to her feet and her eyes locked with Flynn's. A red-hot anger was anchored to his usually calm face and, she thought, not just directed at the intruders.

Frat boys traveled in packs, always leaping to one another's aid. The two standing jumped Flynn from behind, one locking an arm around Flynn's throat, the other plowing into him waist high. His stance never wavered from the impact. Mia could swear he stared at her for one fiery second before bothering to react. The hesitation passed and his body became an effortless wave of precise movement. He detached himself from their collective clutch as if they posed no more threat than a swarm of pesky gnats. Flynn's arm flew back, responding with a grab to the second boy's groin, agilely flipping him overhead and drawing a woeful gasp from the gathering crowd. He lay there, stunned, as though Flynn had cut him in two.

The third frat boy was undeterred. He exploded with a cache of high school wrestling maneuvers, a futile attempt to plow Flynn under. Punishment was swift. Flynn delivered a sharp elbow to the top of his head, then turned and dispensed a knee to his chest. More agitated than injured, the boy staggered a few steps back before retaliating. Mia winced. Terror spiked in every nerve as the glinting blade of something more than a pocketknife materialized in the boy's hand. He hovered, eyes wild. Flynn's head cocked to one side and his stare went glassy. Mia thought she saw the smallest hint of a coaxing smile.

The boy paused, assuming he had the upper hand, maybe waiting for Flynn to back down. With an eagerness that was adrenaline pumped, booze inspired, the boy licked his sweaty lips, eyeballing his target. When Flynn didn't retreat, the boy's hold on the knife transformed from hostile to fatal. Gripping it hard, he lunged with lethal force, the heavy thrust bearing every intention of serious harm. Flynn was waiting. There was no detectable fear, as though the boy were coming at him with a Fourth of July sparkler. Practiced precision clearly took control of the knife-wielding arm. He twisted the boy around, and the two stood back-to-back as Flynn hyperextended the boy's arm over his own shoulder. With the muscle strained to its limit, the hand was automatically forced open. The weapon broke free, landing with a thud on a grassy patch in between the blankets. The boy dove, but Flynn was steps ahead. In one fluid motion he grabbed up the knife, cutting back with his elbow into the boy's oncoming jaw. His head bobbed like a jack-in-the-box as he stumbled over his own feet, dazed but not disabled. Flynn's entire body spun around, almost a graceful dance, until the heel of his boot made hard contact with the boy's stomach, ending any notion of another advance. He flopped around on the ground, struggling like a caught mackerel. Flynn pressed a dirty boot to his chest. "You will lose. Don't be an asshole, don't move."

"Flynn, look out!" Mia yelled as the second boy grabbed a lawn chair, swinging wildly for Flynn's head. Never releasing his prisoner, Flynn blocked hard with an arm and the chair took flight into the crowd. Before the boy could retreat, Flynn had him by the wrist, twisting until he dropped to his knees, screaming obscenities. Bizarre wails of humiliation and agony were the only sound as all else fell eerily silent.

Mia looked around, taking in the carnage, her heart beating so fast her breath had no hope of catching up. The instigator was on his hands and knees, spitting blood onto someone else's blanket. The two others remained captive, each moaning in varying decibels of pain. Mia focused on the gawking crowd, staring in arrested amazement. Then she looked at Flynn. He was unaffected, his breath unlabored. Only the flexed muscles of his arms showed the slightest hint of tension, leaving her to wonder what he might not be impervious to: kryptonite, silver bullets?

"What . . . what should I do now?"

The question doused any superhero image. It was so disjointed, so out of place from what she had just witnessed, Mia felt compelled to help him out. "What do you usually do?"

"Turn them over to security command." An answer shot directly out of the past.

"Oh, well, in this case, I think we should just run."

The knife was still tight in his fist. The boys lay around him in a writhing triangle of pain. Flynn jackknifed the weapon into the ground, where it landed sharply between their heads. Only then did he look startled, as if he suddenly recalled where he was. "Yeah, I think you're right." Flynn released both boys. In the same movement he grabbed Mia's hand; they took off in a full charge toward the parking lot. Trying to keep up with his lanky stride, Mia hurried along. But her legs weren't moving half as fast as her mind, guessing she'd just witnessed a huge piece of his secret past.

Chapter 16

MARYLAND

Nurse Margaret had been vague on the phone, only saying that Mia needed to come back to the hospital. She didn't take it as a good sign. She left the mock office in a mad rush to the ICU, running two lights and screeching to a stop in the ambulance bay. Inside, a languishing thirty-second wait for the elevator was too much and she charged up the stairs. Panicked and short of breath, she added startled to raw fear, finding Roxanne poised at the double doors of the ICU. Every hard line that defined Roxanne, from her pressed lab coat to her rigid posture to the humorless bend of her mouth, was even more pronounced as she waited, arms folded tightly. Whatever the news, Mia didn't want to hear it. If it was the end, if he was dead, she especially didn't want to hear it from Roxanne. "Just move," she said, ready to push past her.

"Dr. Martinez is with him."

"Who's he? Where's Dr. Logan?"

"He's a cardiologist. There was an irregularity in his heart rhythm—it's nothing. Lord have mercy," she said, glancing at her watch. "You must have broken the sound barrier to get here. I'm amazed you didn't end up arriving by ambulance. Paging Dr. Martinez was a precaution; he's fine."

"He's not fine!" Mia insisted, trying to squeeze between Roxanne and the door. "I told the nurse two hours ago that something wasn't right. Move, please."

Instead of allowing Mia to pass, Roxanne's hand closed around her arm. "Would you calm down, catch your breath? You can't go in right now. Just let Dr. Martinez examine him. Mia, this is out of control. We need to talk."

"What for? I'm well aware of your opinion on the subject," she barked, drawing the stares of waiting visitors. "Not now!"

"Yes, right now. There's nothing you can do for him. But I am curious as to how long you can keep this up. This isn't right—it isn't you! Michael is going to find out and the whole thing will explode in your face. I don't want that."

"Why? Because it would destroy Michael or hurt me?"

"Both, of course," she answered, sounding genuinely offended. "I've always had your best interest at heart. Please tell me you believe that much?"

While she did, a pat on the back wasn't her focus at the moment. Mia craned her neck, looking past Roxanne's shoulder. "I have to get in there."

"Five minutes. Just give me five minutes to talk to you."

Glancing through the glassed portion of the door, she caught Nurse Margaret's eye. There was a flurry of medical personnel going in and out of Flynn's room. Mia would just be in the way. Sucking in a sigh of surrender, Mia pointed to a small conference room. Roxanne followed and started to close the door. "Leave it open," she said, "so they can find me." Offering a curt nod, Roxanne sat on the edge of the table, holding tight to a thin folder. There was an exchange of uneasy stares. Roxanne wore dark-rimmed spectacles that clashed with a layer of beauty queen she was still trying to disown. There was a judgmental scan as Roxanne took in Mia's appearance. She drew a deep breath, shaking a head full of damp, untidy hair. Raising her arms, they slapped against her wet raincoat, a spray of water hitting Roxanne. Mia knew how everything looked—a mess. It didn't matter. "Let me save you the trouble, Rox. I'm not leaving him. I have every intention of explaining things to Michael just as soon as—"

"Soon as what? Just as soon as Flynn wakes up so he can add his two cents? It's not a bad plan, Mia. Screwing up your life is what he does best."

"Oh, for the—" Mia edged toward the door. Agreeing to the conversation was a mistake. "You don't know what you're talking about."

"Don't I? Just because I've been on the night shift doesn't mean I haven't been around. I've been up to his room at three a.m. I know the kind of time you've spent here, seen the sweater you left behind, the discarded lunch. Cheese fries and a double soy latte. Who eats that besides you? The pages of sketches tacked to his walls. Anything for close collaboration, huh? Tell me, is it as good as it used to be?"

Mia's gaze, which had been fixated on a coffeemaker, jerked to Roxanne, assuming they weren't discussing interior design. "You can't even imagine," she said dryly.

"Mmm, thanks, but I'll pass. He's an addiction, Mia—like any drug . . . nothing more. He crashes back into your life and you can't tell up from down, right from wrong. He skews everything. Or did I miss the part when you took your vows: 'til death do us part or Flynn rolls back into town'?"

"That's not fair. You have no idea what this is doing to me. It's not like I chose this situation, Roxanne. *I'm* not the one who abandoned Flynn in the middle of the night!" It was a colossal mistake. Admitting any wrong he might have done gave Roxanne the opening for which she'd been waiting. So it was something less than Mia expected when Roxanne didn't pounce. Instead, she pulled the glasses from her face, massaging the bridge of her nose and heaving a sigh.

"Yes, well, I hope you understand there's no way I could have anticipated this situation either." When Roxanne looked up, she was blinking back a tear. It accentuated the gravity of a weighty situation. "I'd forgotten the virility of the patient," she murmured. "So what are you telling me, Mia? You're just as in love with him now as you were twelve years ago?" Mia nodded. A verbal confession might taunt an undecided fate. "And if he wakes up tomorrow, what will you do? Just waltz out the door and say, 'Gee, thanks, Michael. It's been swell, but it's time to move on'?"

That stings, Roxanne.

"Destroy him to be with . . . with . . ."

Strange, she seemed to be struggling hard with words about Flynn that she would generally toss around like dirty laundry. It gave Mia time to put into sentences the jumbled thoughts that had been swirling around her head for weeks—maybe years. "I can honestly say I don't feel any different about Michael than I did before Flynn turned up. I just have better perspective. While I never would have chosen to leave Flynn, I did decide to marry Michael. I own that. No one is responsible but me." An eerie flash of lightning lit a dismal sky. When a crushing boom of thunder didn't follow through, destroying her, Mia dug in. "You know something else, Rox? There are about a million *ifs* in this conversation. And I'll be the first to admit that I don't have the answers. But since your type-A personality requires one . . . *If* Flynn did wake up, *if* I had the answers that are locked in his head . . ." *If he wasn't a wanted fugitive.* Mia swallowed that one down, knowing it was the biggest *if* of all. "*If* Flynn wanted me back, well—"

Roxanne couldn't take it, pounding her fingers against her temple. "Oh, Mia, think about what you're saying! What makes you think he even wants you? Regardless of Michael, or anything else, you're balancing an awful lot of your future on a shaky past. If you remember correctly, it didn't go so well in the end." Roxanne's cell rang. She yanked it from her waistband, glancing at the caller ID. "I have to take this." She stalked to the other side of the room, snapping instructions at whomever she was talking to.

Mia slumped onto the edge of the table. She shivered, her skin chilled from the rain. Or, more likely, the one memory she'd been trying to avoid.

* *

It was right before college graduation, the following spring. A year had passed in the swiftness of a heartbeat. June took her by surprise, actually having had the nerve to come around again. The weeks before had been bumpy. Change was in the air. Mia had kept a positive spin on their unspoken future, feeding Flynn hints about possible plans: *There's a design house in Atlanta . . . pass the salt . . . an entry level position . . . would you grab the mail . . . not my dream job, but a start . . . come back to bed . . . it's everything if you'll come with me.* She had kept all his secrets, understood his nightmares, and loved Flynn for exactly who he was. Would he do this for her? He hadn't answered.

It began oddly, Flynn spending the night at her apartment even after they had argued. Flynn rarely slept when he stayed, and he didn't stay often. But with Roxanne gone until Monday morning, he'd agreed. Thinking back, she was the only one arguing, saying something ugly about the way he lived his life before turning her back, burying her head in a pillow. He was his usual noncombative self, unwilling to engage her effort to goad him into an all-out fight. All night he seemed more restless than usual. She had dozed on and off, catching glimpses of him, knowing that he didn't want company. Mia worried that she was holding on too tight, had made too many demands. You couldn't do that with Flynn. Closed spaces, smothering arms—they didn't work. He was there at one, staring out the window into blackness. Mia rolled over at three, half awake, thinking he might have come to bed. It was only the pillow. She forced her eyes around the room. Flynn's back was to the wall. He was sitting, writing something. Even in the dim light from her desk, she could see his intense focus. She thought he might be doing a crossword puzzle. And the last time she opened an eye, right before five, he was on the floor, eyes closed as if deep in meditation. Not long after that, Mia felt his fingers brush across her forehead as he softly kissed her cheek, whispering something she still couldn't recall. The rumpled covers smoothed tight around her and she felt better, drifting into a sound sleep.

Silence woke Mia later that morning, her senses detecting the signs. She ignored them. Her fingertips reached out, anticipating the warmth of his body, meeting instead with the cool cotton sheet. Her nose didn't fill with the aroma of brewing coffee, coming on strong like an ardent admirer. A man who rarely slept often had a cup by five a.m. Even the bedroom seemed awkward, overly bright with sunshine. Awareness piqued. Mia padded into the living room. The coffeemaker sat cold, the apartment empty. She threw open the front door. His motorcycle was gone. The roar of the engine should have woken her. She fought the omen, tried to reason that he'd gone back to the cottage, maybe to the bike shop. She was humoring herself.

Hanging on to a breath of hope, she went to the cottage. Her heart officially snapped in two when the desk clerk told her that he'd paid up and checked out the previous day. He had been planning it. Flynn left, vanished just like he promised he wouldn't. Peculiarities from the night before made stinging sense, his disinterest in arguing with her. Why fight with a woman you planned on leaving in a few hours? It was so final. There was no telling which way he'd continue on down that broken road, no way to find him. Mia went back to the apartment and got into bed. She figured she'd wait there for the rest, for the breathing part of life to be over.

She lay motionless, not crying, just listening—meticulously absorbing the details before they vanished too. Mia could hear the sound of his voice through the rain that fell that night, feel his hands brush along her arm as the sheet pulled around her, his steady breath against her as she held the pillow tight. Days later the sun made an unwelcome attempt to alter her reality and Mia heard the bedroom door open. She didn't allow a moment of expectation. "Is it . . . Is it Monday, Rox?" she asked without looking.

"Yes, of course it's Monday. My organic chemistry final is in a half hour. I just got back. Isn't your final design project due today? Why isn't there any coffee? Is something wrong, Mia? Are you sick?"

"Sick? No." She still didn't move, the first flood of tears finally pushing past the desolation.

"What's the matter?" she whispered. "Oh my God, he's gone."

The conversation had gone something like that. It was hard to remember; her mind had been caught in a looping rerun of the past year, convinced that she had driven Flynn away. Too many demands, too tight of a grip—obviously she had loved him too much in all the wrong ways.

* *

The cell phone clicked off and it took Mia a moment to refocus on Roxanne. "Be reasonable, Mia. Think about the possibilities." Her eyes lit as she strode back across the room. "Flynn . . . he could be married. Did that occur to you? He could have a wife and a bunch of kids, a double-wide, all waiting for him in a premier mobile home community. Perhaps, right now, there's some poor woman dragging around a lot of sniveling brats just hoping to find their daddy!"

"Stop it, Roxanne." Mia rose from the table's edge, turning away. It was preposterous; she couldn't even put the picture together in her head. He belonged with her. "Just stop, he wouldn't . . . there just isn't . . ." But like so many instances, there was nothing tangible that she could offer in his defense.

"Good, Mia, keep denying it. Why not? It's worked so far. And while my theory about those girls might be a late-night movie run amok, I do know that there never was and still isn't—even in his dreamy comatose state—anything too innocent about Sergeant Peyton Flynn McDermott."

"Sergeant Pey—" She stopped. His whole name. It was something she'd managed to keep hidden from Roxanne for thirteen years. "How do you know that?"

"I did what I had to, hospital policy. I gathered from our last conversation that you weren't going to offer much information. Aside from that, how would you know if anything he told you was the truth?" Roxanne said, gripping tighter to the folder she held. "As his admitting physician it was my responsibility to do everything I could to identify him and his next of kin."

Mia struggled for control. Roxanne couldn't know everything; the attitude wasn't nearly self-righteous enough. "So, that's what you were doing in his room at three a.m. Swabbing his mouth. Roxanne, tell me you didn't—"

"Doesn't matter. If I hadn't done it, someone else would have.

Someone else also wouldn't give you the benefit of this conversation. At least I was discreet. There was a preliminary match to his DNA, and an initial ID." She stood, rounding the table as she spoke. "So let's compare notes, see if you really know anything about him. He wasn't discharged from the Marines, Mia. He was court-martialed." Roxanne stopped, her fingers squeezing hard into the back of a leather chair as she watched Mia's face. As if there were a gun to her head, Mia held painfully still. A change in breathing might tip her off. Roxanne was intuitive, if not plain clairvoyant at times. Dropping the folder onto the table, she flipped it open. "Peyton Flynn McDermott, United States Marine Corp. Elite Forces, first in his recon training class. Well," she said, glancing up, "that explains his brain. Rank, Sergeant. Arraignment, March 1991. Court-martial, July 1991. Subsequent proceedings, investigation, trial, and sentencing—classified. Trial and sentencing, Mia. As in prison. So how much of that comes as a surprise to you?"

Mia shrugged. "I didn't know about the first-in-his-class part," she said, feeling a swell of pride.

Roxanne returned the cool stare. "You might want to save the smug look. Serial killers often operate under misguided brilliance. As for the rest of the record, it's sealed, wrapped up in all kinds of military red tape." Her head cocked the opposite way, eyes narrowing. "No wonder my theory about those girls sends you into a panic attack. Give it up, Mia. What was he in for?"

She half-smiled, knowing a shot of truth serum couldn't drag it out of her. "It's no different than all those years ago. It wasn't your business then and it still isn't. Why would I tell you anything? You would have treated him like a crime scene waiting to happen. You did treat him that way. Adding a criminal record to your crazy theory—do you really think I was going to hand you that kind of information?"

"Oh, you mean that crazy theory of mine that just got a boost from reality? The DNA will come back. Whatever you're hiding, Mia, it will come out. You can't protect him forever; it's only a matter of time until you find out what he's really capable of. You know there will come a day when you appreciate my concern, when—"

"When what? I'll thank you?" *You're right, Roxanne, it is only a matter of time until you hear the details. When that happens you'll probably have Flynn shackled to the bed, comatose or not. He's still a fugitive. They'll come for him before he even wakes up.*

"Facts, Mia, are indisputable. You know, on my way up here, I was thinking of the irony, what a grand time a good prosecutor would have with him. Imagine what your father—"

"Leave my father out of this," she snapped. Having made peace with that very thought years ago, she wasn't about to let Roxanne dredge it up.

"Fine, but this is only another piece of an ugly puzzle." She closed the folder, pushing it toward Mia. "How can you keep doing this? You're a successful, smart woman who, need I remind you, married the right guy."

Mia's gaze darted guiltily around the room. *No need to go down that road, Rox. The truth is the right guy didn't ask . . .*

"You've moved miles beyond the college girl who took in Flynn like a stray dog. I just don't under—"

"Faith, Roxanne," Mia replied. "That girl had limitless faith; I have limitless faith. Look it up—it doesn't require a letter of reference, a testimonial, or your judgment. And believe it or not, it's still not something I have to prove to you."

Roxanne was poised to launch into another rebuttal when a lethal buzzing noise vibrated through the room. Morphing into some kind of automated doctor mode, she flew past Mia, plowing through the ICU's double doors. A crash cart went sailing by, nearly colliding with her. Seconds later, Mia realized that the buzz was echoing from Flynn's room. Medical personnel thundered past, Roxanne joining the stampede. Nurse Margaret's voice permeated all of it.

"Crash cart is on its way, stat! Flatline, code blue, six B!"

Mia fell to her knees.

Chapter 17

ATHENS

Neither Mia nor Flynn said a word on the way to the hotel, having narrowly escaped the frat boys. Flynn got out of the car first, slamming the door so violently the entire frame shook. He couldn't get away fast enough, two steps ahead of her all the way to the room. It wasn't that she didn't want to speak to him, only that she was at a complete loss as to what to say. *Wow, that was really cool, Flynn! Exactly how many guys can you beat the crap out of at once?* It didn't seem appropriate. Mia replayed the heart-stopping scene over and over in her mind. It was terrifying and fascinating. And for the first time she wanted to know how deep his secrets went. The precision skill, the detached calm demeanor—it gave her more insight than anything he'd confided in the months since they'd been together.

Once inside he disappeared into the bathroom, slamming its door too. Mia could hear the shower running. She sat on the corner of the bed, debating whether to pound on the door and demand some answers. But she couldn't decide which question to ask first. The water stopped after a time. Flynn emerged, shirtless, his hair soaking wet. He marched right over, catching her off guard. Mia leaned back, finding herself in the same position she was in on the blanket before all hell broke loose. She blinked up at him, briefly concerned about his state of mind. Was he aware of his surroundings and everything that had happened? He stood at the edge of the bed in between her splayed legs, so close that his hair dripped into the cleavage of her blouse. His arms hung straight at his sides, fists clenched. The expression on his face had not changed. Solitary, unflappable anger.

"That's what I get for being goddamned polite. I should have said something the second I saw you. I don't want to see this outfit on you again, ever."

"What? Don't tell me what I can or can't wear. You don't own me." Mia felt her own face go red over the domineering demand.

"Like hell," he hissed through gritted teeth. "If the way you're dressed is going to put me in that position, you can bet your sweet ass I'm going to have a say in your wardrobe."

"Well, I only did what you said." He narrowed his eyes, inching back. "Sticking up for myself, not letting some jerk insult me or whatever."

He sneered. "My mistake. Let me clarify. First, don't invite it. Second, don't take on three of them at once. And third, know when to walk away—or run, if need be."

"I tried to, but he—" Mia growled, turning her head away. She was flabbergasted. Not a soothing gesture, no comfort, not a question about how she had fared. Her head whipped back toward him. "I didn't do anything!" They were words she'd used before; her innocence had amused him then. This time they seemed to wildly agitate him.

He pulled her up off the bed and physically hauled her along, feet off the floor, across the room to a full-length mirror. Flynn dropped Mia in front of him, holding her there, forcing her to take in the complete reflection. Her flushed cheeks went well with the low-cut blouse and a skirt that had passed sexy two inches before. Her heeled sandals emphasized already long legs and her hair was a wild mass of heat-stricken waves. The outfit looked very different when it had lain benignly on her bed. Now, under these circumstances, it did border on licentious. Mia mentally conceded that she did not look like herself, that there could be a street corner in her future. His hand came up around her throat, cutting across her windpipe, lifting her hair up off her neck as his fingers roughly grazed her cheek. He made no effort to soften his touch. His voice was rougher than his fingers, hot in her ear. "Understand what they see."

Mia knew she should be intimidated, but anger inched toward arousal when his arms dropped from her face, brushing against the silky fabric and across her breasts. It occurred to her what he was implying, and Mia struggled to hang on to that anger. She gave herself a cursory once-over, unwilling to agree with his insinuation. "So you think that was my fault? The way I'm dressed was a come-fuck-me invitation?"

His hand tightened around her stomach, pushing the blouse up so his hot skin made contact with hers. "No, the come-fuck-me invitation was for me, I'm sure. But when you put this on, sweetheart"—his eyes were full of anger, his fingers tugging at the flimsy strap—"and stretch out on a blanket in ninety-degree heat, with a pair of legs that make a guy practically come in his pants, most men don't care who it's addressed to. That guy was an asshole. He got a taste of what he deserved—they all did. But you didn't help."

"Let me go. I don't like the way you're talking to me." Mia tried to wiggle free. His fingers pinched in, gripping harder around her waist. She wasn't going anywhere until he said so.

"Fine. But while we're on the subject of acting out, do I get an explanation for any of that back there? I mean, were you ever going to mention the ninja warrior routine or was it just another secret Flynn gets to keep from me?"

"Why, did you like it?"

She couldn't tell if it was sarcasm or survey. She also wasn't entirely sure where she arrived at the nerve to throw it right back at him. "Did you? Did you, Flynn, like the whole white knight thing, running to my rescue? From what I saw you'd better be damn careful about how you dole out the punishment. You're lucky you didn't kill one of them." Before her brain could register what was happening, Flynn spun her around. His hand squeezed her chin, assuring solid eye contact.

"I am nobody's white knight. Get that through your head. What you saw was reflex, nothing more. You get into a situation like that again and I will leave you to defend yourself."

The ugliness in his voice made her want to get away. But she wasn't particularly frightened, only hurt by his reaction. *Next time, be prepared to screw them all, Mia, because next time I'll sell tickets. What I feel for you isn't enough to want to protect you. You're on your own, sweetheart.* It was what she heard. Flynn's fury over having to defend her, when he so obviously could, was baffling. It didn't make sense.

Mia reined in her composure, determined not to be bullied by what she saw as a temper tantrum. "Maybe I'll just do that. Maybe next time I'll extend the come-fuck-me invitation to the entire frat house!" She hesitated, mentally swinging any jab to taunt him. "You can just wait outside while I screw every last one of them. At least then I'll know what I'm getting."

Her words singed through him. There was a visual standoff; blinking seemed unlikely. She'd hurt him. Good. He was fighting it. It was all over his face, in his eyes, always a dead giveaway.

Mia was surprised he didn't want to have the argument with his sunglasses on. Once more he spun her back toward the mirror. She went to speak, but his hand flew up over her mouth.

"Shut up, Mia. Don't talk. Don't say one more fucking word." From there he brushed her hair back from her face; not a gentle sweeping stroke, more like he was grooming her for something. "I didn't want this. God knows I wasn't looking for it, the way I feel when you look at me. Do you understand me, Mia? I don't fucking need this."

"Need what?" she spit out angrily.

"I said don't speak." Before she thought it was posturing. Now it was a direct order. "I can't afford to be in a position where things like tonight happen. So you need to understand something. Are you listening?"

She nodded. Mia's eyes were as wide as they had been the first time she saw him. Their faces were reflected in the glass of the mirror, his body pressed tight to hers. Every muscle pulsated against her and she wondered what he might do with all that anger.

"A long time ago I crossed a line that separates me from you, from the things you want, the way you live. I lost the right to all of it and I accept that. You, Mia, are an unneeded, unwanted fucking complication. Do you hear me?"

His stare was so intense against the glass she thought it might spark a fire. She nodded again, the words slicing into her, causing a pain so tremendous that it drove every other feeling from her body. He licked his dry lips and drew his head closer to hers, giving serious debate to something. His Adam's apple bobbed as he seemed to come to a decision.

"I wasn't in a war. I didn't spend years training recruits to turn on a dime or how to spit-polish their brass. I wasn't overseas defending this country. My ass was in a military disciplinary barrack because that's where they put you when you confess to murder. That's what I did in the Marines."

It was a million miles from anything she thought he might say. She looked into his reflection, his eyes. They almost repeated the admission, and Mia's forehead drew into tight contemplation. But the wide-eyed look of awe was gone. There wasn't the eruption of mortified shock he was probably expecting, only an illogical sense of relief. There it was: the explanation she'd been waiting for, a reason for the rogue existence, the nightmares, the distance he kept from the rest of the world. Flynn searched her face, looking for something—disgust, rage, fear. She assumed it was safe to speak, blurting out the first thing that popped into her head.

"Murder? You confessed to killing someone?"

"Murder—with my bare hands."

His anger toward her became clear, her assumption of a tantrum a moot point. The sexy outfit . . . drunken frat boys . . . her honor. She'd unknowingly put him in a horrible position, forcing him to return to a mind-set and a place he already couldn't cope with. She tried to twist around in his arms but he wouldn't let her budge. After a moment she stopped struggling and surrendered to his hold, leaning her head back against his shoulder. Mia wrapped her arms over his, keeping them tight, making sure he wouldn't let go. A trembling breath exited his body as they stared at one another in the mirror. "I hear you, Flynn. What you said, it doesn't matter, not to me. I love—"

"Don't. Don't say it, Mia." The words were sharp. He was uninterested in compassion or any other placating gesture. "You're so willing to accept what I just said, without the why or the details. How can you do that? It's just like when I first saw you." Their heads met with terse strokes of friction as he shook his head. "Don't take rides from strangers, Mia. Don't let them buy you drinks, and for God's sake, don't go to bed with them. Add another one to the list, sweetheart. Don't excuse murder like I just told you I robbed a penny candy store."

Mia held her head stiff. "So what is it you expect me to do? Do you want me to leave? If I tell you I never want to see you again, is that the correct response? Look at you. You're still angry with me, but you want *me* to punish you." She watched him take a hard gulp. He was furious about everything—having to defend her, her inability to hate him for his confession, the way his life turned out.

"You're right. I'm so fucking pissed off right now, I don't know what to do with it." He broke free from her hold and ran his hands the length of her torso, brushing over skin that was still too eager for his touch. "I take that back. I know exactly what I want to do."

"You're not scaring me. I'm not afraid of you, Flynn. You won't hurt me. I was more frightened by some jerk coming on to me in a crowded park than I ever could be alone with you."

"You think so? Another poor decision, Mia. Do you know what I want to do with this anger? How I want to get rid of it before it fucking eats me alive?" Flynn held her tight, shouting into the mirror. "Do you!" She shook her head. "I want to put some kind of mark on you that makes it crystal clear, that erases every breath that bastard put on you." He cupped her breast in the exact same spot the frat boy had. "And you won't like it."

She glared back, matching his defiant strength. "It's not working. You don't frighten me. You certainly can't make me hate you."

"Yes, Mia, yes, I can. Don't forget that. I've done worse. Hate is fairly low on my list of transgressions. Maybe that sweet little college-educated head of yours doesn't comprehend me. Language issues again, Mia. I don't want to make love to you. I don't want to have sex with you. I just want to fuck you, hard and mercifully uncomplicated. It won't be nice and sweet, the way you like it, what you're used to. It will be a man who spent years in prison. Lots of anger, baby. That guy tonight, I could have torn his head off. Do you understand what I'm saying?" He jerked her hard again. "Jesus Christ, that appeals to you?"

Mia looked boldly into his eyes. "No, but still, you won't hurt me." She even smiled, calmly gazing into his stare.

"What makes you so fucking sure?"

She replied with something more intimidating than his own threat. "I have more faith in you than you do. You see a single disaster when you look into that mirror. I see the whole beautiful man."

"Fine, then. With your permission, allow me to disprove your theory."

The lack of reply was as good as a green flag. Flynn grabbed a fistful of blouse. The sound of shredding fabric hit her ears before she grasped what he had done. He tore it from her body as if it were made of tissue paper. Mia stifled a gasp, holding her posture perfectly still. The culprit, the destroyed blouse, wafted to the floor and she realized he had wanted to do just that since they walked into the room. Her mind was working fast to keep up, wondering exactly what the difference was between making love, having sex, and just getting fucked. A shudder writhed through her body. He felt it and his breath jerked in, knowing he'd created doubt. He hesitated and she knew Flynn was questioning every action. Mia forced calm, her chin up slightly, blinking rapidly at her half-naked reflection. It was almost a poker game, a gamble on both their parts, and he upped the ante.

"Now, take off the skirt or we can just go the same route as the blouse, if you'd like."

It might very well have been the most reckless decision she had ever made—a wild leap of faith. But Mia was determined to prove him wrong the only way she knew how: by offering herself unconditionally. "If you don't mind, it was rather expensive."

He tipped his head to the side and gave her a small push forward. The idea that she wanted to salvage the forbidden skirt seemed to further fuel his rage. "I don't care how the fucking thing gets off you, just do it." Her fingers trembled as she tried to undo the zipper. She nervously glanced up at him. Flynn was staring as if she were a hooker who was taking too long—time was money. Add a lack of patience, Mia thought, to his list of tarnished virtues. As she kicked off the sandals, thankfully the zipper let go and the skirt fell to the floor. On tiptoe she stepped out of it, standing before him in nothing but a pair of lacy black underwear.

"Did I ever tell you, you have the nicest set of tits I've ever seen? Including the ones I've paid for."

That answers the hooker question.

"And this." He grabbed her around the waist, pushing the underwear aside, cupping his hand around her. "This slightly used—" He stopped, stumbling on the coarse word in her presence. "Well, you don't have a clue. I watch them, Mia. Every guy you pass has a fucking wet dream starring you. And you never notice. How naïve can you be? Christ, don't you think it was my first thought? You're just goddamn lucky the one thing you learn in prison is self-control."

A tiny gasp escaped her throat and she fought the urge to push his hand away. His voice had disintegrated into a raspy whisper, burning hot in her head. The attempt to exploit her vulnerability was making headway, but Mia refused to give in. She'd learned that much from him. He wanted her to beg him to stop, proving that he was nothing more than a vile animal. She didn't react, hanging on to a fine thread of composure. Mia held her voice steady. "Now what, Flynn? Shall I get on my knees and service you? You seem pretty attached to that mirror. Maybe you'd like to watch?" She met his steely gaze straight on. This wasn't what he was expecting. "Would that put you in the place you need to be?" For a moment she thought she had him and he would back down.

"That was my second choice. But if you insist." As he nudged her toward the floor, Mia recalled the promise he once made to call her bluff. "Have at it, sweetheart."

He didn't hesitate, unzipping his jeans, yanking them off. His penis, hard as a railroad spike, jutted at her stunned face. Mia froze, almost as stiff as him. She'd done this before, to his grateful satisfaction, but never from this position. The Flynn she knew wouldn't dream of asking. *But he didn't ask. I just offered. Another swell decision.* The hotel room carpet was rough and scratchy on her knees. She wondered how prostitutes compensated for that, or was it just a hazard of the trade?

Mia fought the degrading image of him throwing a twenty on the dresser, leaving her there afterward. Then she embraced it. *No, give him what he thinks he wants. Make it worth a fifty.* The only other choice was to crumble at his feet. She refused to give him the satisfaction. Rising tall on her knees, Mia gripped him tight at the hips, taking the full length of him in her other hand. Biting crossed her mind, nothing devastating, maybe just a nip to snap him out of it. But she quickly thought better of it. He was agitated enough. She took a deep breath, slowly taking him into her mouth. His weight immediately went back, bracing himself against the wall. A low growl radiated from within. For a guy who could beat the snot out of three strapping college boys, he suddenly seemed quite at her mercy. He shook off the vulnerability by grabbing a fistful of her hair, urging her on with a string of filthy expletives that she tried not to hear. Mia was almost relieved as he grew more rigid. In a moment it was all going to be over. Apparently Flynn drew the same conclusion, pulling Mia to her feet at the last possible second. She swiped her mouth with the back of her hand, positive of one thing: She shouldn't make the next suggestion.

"Nice try, sweetheart, but it's not gonna get me there."

Mia grappled for her resolve. She wanted to make eye contact, make him look at her to see what he was doing. He was wise to the tactic. Flynn's arms flew around her body and turned her so she couldn't see his face, hauling her to the other side of the room, bypassing the bed. Any hint of a game evaporated. She fought off the fear with memories: every tender touch he'd ever put on her, the way his eyes told her that he loved her. *He won't. I trusted him ten minutes ago. Trust him now. Prove to him that he's not what he thinks he is.* There were no signs or warnings; everything was moving wicked and fast. Mia sucked in a sharp breath. It was like being plunged into ice-cold water as he bent her over a table. She nearly screamed out for him to stop, biting deep into her lip, drawing blood to buy silence.

"Remember, I have your permission." With a fast jerk her underwear succumbed to the same fate as the blouse. "I assume you packed another pair."

"Flynn, I . . ." She struggled for something to make him wait, make him stop without directly telling him. "Don't you, um, don't you need a condom?" It was the only rational thought that spun out of the hysteria in her head.

A cynical laugh sputtered to the surface. "Make a mental note, Mia, safe sex doesn't enter into this act." He was always a step ahead, reading her thoughts. "Unless you want me to stop? In case you were a little vague on the definitions, this is getting fucked, sweetheart. There are no rules."

He stood still behind her, giving her the opportunity to get away and call it off. Mia didn't move. He was in some horrid place she barely understood, but Mia held firm to her belief that he wouldn't—couldn't hurt her. His hands ran up the length of her back, bumping over every vertebrae, the two of them at a truly awkward standoff.

Shit, this isn't good.

Mia could feel the deep gulps of air blow in and out of him. They were harder, more fear-filled than the panicked breaths she was trying to squelch. He sounded as if he'd been running a marathon. Mia sensed hesitation. She knew his eyes were on her bare body, how exposed and fragile she must look. Her gaze locked on a small tabletop sign that was shoved in her face: *Let us know how we can improve your stay!* She squeezed her eyes shut. There was no comfort from above or below, the smooth grain of the wood cold and hard. Tears seeped through her closed eyes, running sideways across her face.

Flynn's voice cut through the tension, something short of pleading. "Mia, tell me you want me to stop, goddamn it. Tell me you don't want this."

Find the courage. He will not hurt me. She wouldn't let him hear the fear, her voice steady and tight. "It's not my choice. I won't tell you to stop."

"Goddamn it! This is what you get for loving me."

His fingers gripped around her waist; she could feel his muscular thighs press against her legs. Mia forced herself silent, no noise, no clues to what she was thinking or feeling. She felt him pull back. Her fingers grasped onto the table, the hard edge digging into her hips and stomach. She could feel his breath, a low growl hissing out—almost a cry. "Why . . . how could you trust me this much?" Then it stopped. The fury she felt from him exited in one tremulous breath. Flynn's body came over hers, like a feather, his mouth softly kissing her shoulder. His cheek pressed against her back, and she could feel the dampness of a tear. Mia couldn't suppress a cry of relief. His lips hadn't touched her in hours. For all his violent posturing, Mia wanted him to kiss her again.

He stood up, pulling her body along with his, turning her in his arms. "I . . . I can't—I could never do this to you." His voice was broken and defeated.

Chapter 18

He took his first look at what he had done. The beautiful girl was gone. Runny mascara mingled with streaks of tears, dripping down her colorless face. She looked as if she had just witnessed some unbelievable, heinous act. Christ, she had. Her hair was a mass of sweaty tangles and the silky skin that he loved to touch was cold and clammy. The blood on her mouth made his stomach lurch. He wanted to wipe it away, but as his fingers went up Mia's head jerked back, repelling like she didn't recognize him. Flynn realized how hard she was shaking, realized that he was holding her up. He tried to pull her closer, tighter. She wouldn't relinquish the space. Every hateful thought he'd ever had about himself multiplied into some infinite number he couldn't comprehend. Standing over that broken, lifeless body didn't feel as horrid as this.

"Let me go," she said in a raspy whisper.

"I can't . . . You'll fall down."

His sudden concern for her well-being had no impact. "No, no . . . I'm okay, really. Just let go. Please." She wouldn't look him in the eye as she pushed away from his hold, stumbling to her overnight bag. A satiny summer robe slid over her body and Mia quickly covered herself, tying a snug knot. She went into the bathroom, emerging a few minutes later with a washcloth pressed to her mouth.

He'd grabbed his jeans in the meantime, thinking he should just leave. *There aren't too many ways I could have fucked this up worse. Yeah, there's one, you stupid bastard. Tell her the rest—finish it.* She said nothing, walking to a lamp and snapping it off. He guessed she could only face him in the dark. A stream of moonlight drew her out to the balcony. For one wild second he feared what she might do, the damage he had done, and he raced outside.

"It's cooler, feel that. There's even a little wind," she said, blotting her lip with the cloth.

It was the opposite of what he had anticipated, her demeanor strangely serene. Flynn waited. He wanted to see if it was some sort of gathering calm before she went nuts on him.

"So," she began with a long sigh, "it wasn't the most pleasant way to make a point, but I took you on. Hurting me isn't in you. You're not the mad, uncontrollable bastard you see in that mirror." She basked in her reflective mood, capturing balmy breezes and moonlight as if everything were going to be just fine. She said, almost smiling, "Will you admit that much to me? I think I earned it."

He wished to God he could tell her she was right. "I think you'd better hear it all before you draw that conclusion."

"I told you, it doesn't matter to me."

"Oh, so what you don't know can't hurt you. Is that your mind-set? Won't work, Mia. I've been trying to keep my ugly secrets from you for months. Every day it gets a little harder. You now know the most basic facts of a story that takes place a mile beyond hell. I can't let you think that's all there is. You're going to want to put it behind us and there are huge reasons you can't. You need to understand them."

Mia shook her head hard. "You don't have to bleed for me. I think I've proven how much I trust you."

"Hey, you just put yourself out there in a way I can't begin to understand. I don't think there's anything else I could ask of you." Flynn eased into a chair, turning the other toward her, hoping she would sit. He still didn't like the look of her perched on the edge of the balcony. "You deserve to hear this. And afterward, if you want to go, I'll hold the door, fuckin' applaud you for making a smart decision. That naïve streak you have, sweetheart, the one that keeps getting you in trouble with me, with other men, the one that makes you think you can fix this by loving me unconditionally—it's about to get blown to bits."

She sat down, responding boldly. "I get it, Flynn. There's a part of your past that maybe a lot of people couldn't accept. But without even hearing the details, I have no doubt there were circumstances, reasons . . ."

"Some might say. But I think you need to have lived it to truly understand my culpability. Responsibility has a different meaning to everyone—particularly different in the world I was in. I took my responsibility seriously—you might say too far. To this day, I say not far enough."

"There had to have been extenuating circumstances. If you went to jail for killing someone, how come they let you out?"

"Who said they let me out?" Her eyes did a double take. He nodded; she'd heard him right.

"So what are you telling me? You escaped?"

"That's right, sweetheart. You've been sleeping with a fugitive and convicted murderer. Proud of yourself? Bet it's not somethin' the other girls get to brag about, huh?" Light laughter rumbled from his throat. "Roxanne's starting to look right, isn't she? And you thought I only disliked her because she's a control freak."

"Anything Roxanne thinks is just . . . just the way she is. It has nothing to do with us," Mia snapped. "She doesn't know what she's talking about."

His brow furrowed. Why the hell was she suddenly so mad at Roxanne? "Anyway, there were a lot of reasons I escaped. The ones you'd figure, like the nightmares and, well, let's just say things I had no control over."

"What kinds of things?"

Flynn glanced at her, then into the distance. "Never mind, it's not important right now. One day everything just snapped into place. I got a miracle and a one-way ticket out. After years in a seven-by-ten cell . . ."

"The nightmares, God, you had them trapped in a cell. How . . . how could they do that to you?"

He shook his head, choking back more misplaced laughter. "I don't think my mental health was a big concern. The cell was bad, but solitary was worse. Bust up enough walls, can't follow the rules, can't keep quiet—that's where you end up, thirty days a pop." Any hint of humor evaporated. "There isn't a word for what those nightmares turned into in that hole. Got to a point where insanity looked like salvation. Trouble was, I could still make the distinction. I think I spent more time trying to climb out of my own skin, staring at my own vomit, than I did breathing." She'd been listening with her eyes forward, focusing on the dark. Flynn gently pulled her chin around so she would have to look at him. There was a second of comfort when she didn't pull away and he allowed himself to feel it. "Are you ready to go home yet?"

"Keep going. I'm still here." But her voice had changed, even if she didn't know it. The prospect of comfort vanished, the unconditional warmth gone.

"My first year in the Corp was, I don't know, average. But I did excel at certain things . . ."

"Things like I saw last night?"

He nodded. "That and a few more. About a year after basic, I was pulled out into what was described to me as advanced training, sent to Camp Lejuene. Recon Indoctrination Program. They spent eight weeks giving me all sorts of tests, mental and physical. It was tough stuff—made me want to fuckin' quit and scream uncle more than once. I dove through all their hoops. Ran twenty miles in hundred-degree weather, learned to tie every knot in their freakin' book and how to hold my breath underwater while I cut somebody's throat." He paused, catching her shocked expression. "Real person, rubber knife—at least in practice. Anyway, not everybody masters that one."

"But you did?" she asked, glancing at him out of the corner of her eye.

He hesitated; truth was truth. "Yeah, I did. I hung in there fairly well. Next thing I knew, I was in. Part of the very few. Elite Forces. I spent the next ten weeks in Little Creek, Virginia, with recon training. It's where I learned to excel at what you saw last night, where it became a reflex, not a skill. It's where I learned . . ." He stopped, looking away from her, toward nothing.

"Learned what, Flynn?"

"It's where I learned that compromise is not an option—that the mission can be worth more than a life. And make no mistake, Mia—I bought into the company line one hundred percent. We . . . I was trained to achieve an objective within a certain code, using whatever means necessary. And I was very good at it."

"I see," she said softly, making her own eye contact with the distance.

"There isn't anything after recon training, just the mission. First assignment went well. You would be amazed at what the United States government is responsible for containing, derailing, and destroying. We spent a month in the jungle in South America chasing down a band of drug smugglers. I couldn't figure it out at first—we were a little overqualified for drug trafficking. Months later, I found out that the money was being filtered through the office of our ambassador to that country. It was in the administration's best interest to make it go away quietly."

"In other words, you weren't exactly making the front page of *Stars and Stripes*. No glory or recognition." Flynn nodded in agreement. "Go on."

"Around that time things started to go a little sour in Northern Africa. We pulled a long-term assignment in a remote corner of Libya, bordering on the Sudan. It was the hottest, most desolate place—Christ, it was south of hell, that's for sure. Bands of rogue guerrilla forces used it for training camps, central supply. Our government was concerned about an uprising—these groups banding together, overthrowing the existing regime. As much as they disliked the government that was in place, at least they could exert control over it. Its proximity to other countries, its lack of rules, made it a hot spot for pirating activity. The guerrilla groups, they spent most of their time fighting for territory. Recon, that happens mostly at night. Our objective was to gather information first and dismantle the worst of them. I mean, there's no sense in taking the bastards down until you've bled them for every piece of usable intel. Understand, Mia, I used methods condoned by Special Forces—and ones you won't find in any government-sanctioned report." He paused, hoping the concept would sink in without the details. Flynn watched Mia's face grow sober, her breaths deepen.

"Elite Forces is a different team—very different from any

other part of the military. We didn't answer to anyone. And more important, they weren't responsible for us. Some guys rotated in and out, but there was a core group, eight of us that worked together. We were tight, a band of brothers. It takes a certain kind of person to work that detail . . . not all of it good." Flynn's eyes evaded hers, staring into the night. "Five months in, I made sergeant and they put me in charge. I was responsible for every single one of them—everything from making sure they didn't end up in front of a stray bullet to seeing that they didn't go into town without a pocketful of condoms. They relied on me for everything, combat to latrine. I set the tone for down time, engagement, and whatever was between. Those men acted on my orders, and only my orders. When you're put in that position, you're their leader, their sole judge of what's right and what's wrong."

"Wasn't there somebody higher up, in case you needed help?"

"That's a nice theory, sweetheart. But it doesn't work like that. As a unit we were very isolated. It's part of the challenge, part of the privilege, part of the risk you assume."

"I can see you, doing that. How they all must have looked up to you."

"Careful, Mia, don't wrap me in Old Glory just yet. When you fall from there, it's a long way down."

She crinkled her brow, nodding. "You . . . you couldn't have been much older than them."

"Actually, I was younger than some of them. It was a lot of responsibility for twenty-two—too much, in the end," he admitted. "There were guys in the unit who were married, had babies at home, wives . . . families who were counting on them. I think it's one reason I made sergeant so soon—I had nothing to lose. Anyway, sometimes we were assigned to run a security detail for a bureaucratic dog-and-pony show. Every so often politicians would feel the need to drop in on hell, just to make it look like the *good guys* were in control. It was our job to make sure guerrilla forces didn't get in the way—in other words, blow anybody up.

"Word came down from Central that a member of the British Parliament and a United States senator were planning that type of visit. I was particularly concerned about one of those guerrilla forces. It was run by a British National, Simon Goss. He was a Rhodes Scholar turned terrorist; thought he'd fight the system by engaging in guerrilla warfare and pirating. In the six months that I had been there, I'd made contacts, informants— one in particular who provided vital information. The word on the street was that Goss's group was planning to use this particular political visit. He wanted a media circus; they had plans to kidnap the senator and the Brit, maybe parade them around blindfolded before blowing their heads off. It was Goss's way of raising awareness, a telethon for the cause," Flynn explained. "It certainly would have put his warring faction on the national map."

"It sounds like a difficult situation not everyone could handle. Maybe you're being too hard on yourself."

"Just wait, Mia, the errors are coming. It was right around that time that I learned my informant, a Jordanian woman named Alena Wyle, was on both sides of the take—working for Goss and passing information to me. To say I was shocked would be an understatement."

"Why? Because she was a woman?"

He laughed a little, a gesture that still felt as misplaced as his emotions. "No, Alena was smarter than just about anyone I knew. It mostly whacked me right over the head because . . ." He hesitated, trying to find words to make it sound less dubious than it was. "Because I was sleeping with her." It was like

August heat hitting air, the way the memory dragged through his throat. "We were lovers, Mia. We were involved for some time—we . . . we even had plans. Alena was going to come back to the States with me."

"With you," she repeated, the surprise clear, her voice small and uneasy.

"Listen, if you don't want to hear it all . . . the details, I under—"

"No, I want to hear every word. I want . . ." Mia's stark gaze met his. "I want to know about this woman. Alena. What you feel . . . felt for her," she corrected, allowing herself the assumption that it was all in the past.

"You mean was I in love with her?"

"Yes," Mia whispered.

"Back then," he answered, "yes, I loved her very much." He stopped there. Until that moment it hadn't occurred to Flynn how what he felt for Mia differed. He looked at her, unable to move a breath in or out.

"Flynn?" she said, touching his arm.

He pulled it away. "When, um, when I discovered that Alena was working for Goss, well, my reaction was about what you'd expect. I was betrayed, hurt, angry . . . amazed that I could be so goddamn gullible. She tried to explain. Alena was working for Goss long before she ever hooked up with me. In that part of the world employment opportunities were, let's say, scarce for a woman like her—someone as smart as she was beautiful. Anyway, Alena insisted that things had changed, that she wanted out from Goss."

"Because you discovered her double cross or because she was in love with you?"

Flynn took a breath, silently contemplating the rest of the story. He'd never uttered it aloud. "At that point, I couldn't be sure of anything she was telling me. The only thing I did buy was the danger she was in. She assured me that if Goss found out that she was providing me with information . . . and sleeping with me—he'd kill her in a heartbeat."

"And what did you say to that?"

Flynn looked solidly at Mia. "I said that would be fucking fine with me—problem solved for both of us."

"And then?"

"What makes you think I said anything else? What makes you think I didn't send her back to Goss toe-tagged with a note telling that bastard exactly what she'd been up to?"

There was no hesitation. "Because you just told me that you loved this woman. You'd never do anything to hurt her."

A hard swallow rolled through Flynn's throat. He wished he shared Mia's assuredness. "After I cooled off, I told Alena that I'd help her find a way out. If Goss did learn that she was my informant, he wouldn't hesitate to kill her. That . . . that was unimaginable. The trouble was, I had to continue to trust her, believe that the information she was passing on to me was on the up-and-up. It was a huge risk that I had no business taking."

"Was it worth it?"

"She seemed to prove herself—passed a couple of tests. In-formation was certainly going my way. She managed to earn my trust again and I forgave her. Things, um, things between us, they picked up where we left off." He paused as Mia offered an uncomfortable nod. "According to Alena, Goss's group was moving ahead with their plan to kidnap the senator and the Brit. My only tactical choice was for our unit to take them out first. I devised a plan and put my men on the ground. My first mistake, I sent them in five to three."

"Five to three? I don't . . ."

"Oh, sorry, five men of ours to every three of theirs. It's standard op, page one in the rulebook—it should be straight double coverage. But there was a last-minute change in plan, a security breach in town. I had to send Ruiz and Jensen to follow up. It left me a man short, but I didn't have the time or resources to do anything different. The three of us, Ruiz, Jensen and me, we were going to follow as soon as they got back from town. The plan was to go in at night. Take out three guards and seize Goss's headquarters. A basic tag 'em and bag 'em. Alena insisted that there would only be three guards, and I took her at her word. Even so, I only sent in five men—Bradshaw, Kroeger, Jackson, Lopez, and Gilly."

"And did it work? Were they successful?"

"Two hours later I got a message back at patrol base, a ransom note of sorts, courtesy of Simon Goss. He'd taken my men hostage. I swear, Mia, I've never had a feeling like that since. It was like the earth swallowed me whole—or at least I wished it had. I'd sent five men right into the hands of the fucking enemy, a goddamn guerrilla welcoming committee."

Mia's hand covered her mouth as she tried to constrain an awestruck gasp. "Did Goss . . . did he kill them?"

"No, that would have been too polite. Goss and his men had captured Elite Forces. It's the top of the enemy food chain. There's nothing like torturing your biggest adversary. They were desert pirates, and that corner of the world was their ocean. Goss was going to make them suffer before he killed them— that was a given. I thought I understood what being responsible for my men meant. But I didn't, not really. Not until that moment." Flynn paused; maybe waiting to see if this time the world would just end it, swallow him whole. Closing his eyes, he began again. "Then, in the middle of everything, the phone rang—I'm thinking it's Goss with his demands. Maybe for weapons or intel I have a prayer of getting my guys back. And

I'm wondering what I'm going to say to keep them alive until I can get them out."

"Was it him? What did he want?" Mia asked, wide-eyed and slack-jawed, as if someone had yanked the blindfold off her in the middle of an action movie.

"It was a stateside call. Central Command would only patch something like that through if it were an emergency or something really important. Turned out that it was Jensen's wife—his goddamn wife, on the other end of the phone, telling me she just gave birth to twins—a boy and a girl! I could hear them crying in the background while she's crying into the fucking phone. It was surreal, Mia. Here I've got Ellie Jensen from Blue Meadow, Arkansas, gushing over Corporal Kirby Jensen's firstborn children, and Simon Goss, a fucking psycho terrorist, holding a gun to the heads of five good men in the middle of hell."

Flynn snickered at the recollection, running a hand through his mane of hair. It was a needed reminder, the tight buzz cut long gone. "Believe me, I took small comfort in knowing that Jensen wasn't one of the captured men. His wife, she rambled on, thanking me for taking such good care of Kirby—telling me how much he looked up to me, and that she couldn't wait to meet me. And here I am, jotting down weights and measurements, that they were blond like Kirby and that she'd already named the boy after him. Then in some military-issue voice, calm and steady, I offered Mrs. Jensen my congratulations. I told her not to worry about a thing, that Kirby would call as soon as he got back from patrol—I even went as far as to promise her that he'd be home to her and those babies soon."

A sympathetic smile curved around Mia's mouth. "Well, what else could you have said in the moment?"

"Nothing, I guess. In hindsight? I should have told Jensen to go AWOL, hop a fucking freighter home to his wife and babies, smuggle himself out of the country, and never look back, because if he had, it might have changed everything."

"I don't understand. How would that change anything?"

Flynn cleared his throat. He shifted in his seat, arms folding tight. "After hearing about my men, my first thought was that Alena had lied to me again—that her loyalty was still with Goss. I was furious with her. Maybe more with myself. It was right then that Ruiz and Jensen returned from their security detail. I . . . I didn't tell Jensen about the phone call, not then. I needed him to focus. There were too many other things going down. I told Ruiz and Jensen about our guys being taken hostage—too fast, not fast enough. I still can't decide. They knew Alena was an informant, but being subordinates they had no idea about my personal relationship with her. I told them what I suspected: She'd double-crossed me. Goss was holding our guys hostage—that he would most likely kill them before daybreak. Most important, I told them that Alena was the only person who knew where they were being held. We had hours, if that, to get them out. I left orders for them to hold the post while I went to town looking for her. I was praying that I could track Alena down through mutual contacts."

"Did you find her?" Mia asked. "Tell me you found her before Goss . . ."

Flynn felt his gut twist inside out. The sweat that the nightmare brought broke over him. He stared at the iron bars of the balcony, scrubbing a hand over his face. "Not before Jensen and Ruiz did."

"They found Alena?"

"It turned out that she had come looking for me at our base. That's . . . that's when things spiraled mercilessly out of control. Mia," he said, his voice hitting a dull, deadpan stride, knowing it was the only way he could get it out. "It gets . . . I want you to be prepared. It gets pretty gruesome from this point forward."

He watched her draw a deep breath, squaring up her shoulders as if bracing for the blow. "I'm still here, Flynn. I'm listening."

"Ruiz and Jensen met me outside my barrack. They were a mess, sweaty, out of breath. Jensen, he had scratch marks all over his face, his neck. I thought it was his own blood, and then . . . then I realized there was too much of it. Ruiz, he didn't look much better. I asked them what the hell was going on? Knowing we were down five men, I thought maybe some of Goss's thugs had counterattacked."

"But that isn't what happened, is it?" Mia asked, inching back in her chair.

"I'd give anything to tell you it was." He'd been staring into the night, focused on a single distant star. Flynn turned toward Mia. Her eyes were wide and unsure, like the moment they'd met, when he'd accidentally scared the hell out of her. This time it would be quite intentional. "Like I said, Alena had come back to base looking for me. Based on what I'd told them, Ruiz and Jensen, they took it upon themselves to interrogate Alena."

"They questioned her?" Mia asked

"It may have started out that way. It always starts out that way."

"What . . . what did they do?"

"They did what they were taught to do . . . what I trained them to do," he said, still unwilling to take anything less than complete responsibility.

"What does that mean?" she asked, her voice hardening at the prospect.

"Look, Mia, Elite Forces . . . it's not for the faint of heart. Part of our job was to deal with situations that the regular military wouldn't touch. And sometimes that required tactics— methods for extracting information that most human beings would not condone."

"I see."

"Do you, Mia? Do you have any idea what I'm capable of?"

She didn't answer, focusing instead on his story. "Ruiz and Jensen, they used those tactics on her . . . on Alena?"

"Ruiz and Jensen had an objective. The objective was to find out where the members of their unit were being held. There had been past situations where the information was vital to national security matters, or to avoid a loss of life—innocent lives. Because of the circumstance, because this was personal, Ruiz and Jensen saw it as an even graver situation."

"Goss was going to kill their colleagues . . . their friends . . . their brothers."

Flynn nodded, knowing that he was perched on the edge of a story he wasn't sure he could tell. *Finish it, you coward . . . Make her understand.* "The second I realized that their injuries were . . . *defensive*, I raced into my barrack. I'd been in firefights, hand-to-hand combat; I'd knocked the teeth out of some of those desert pirates myself. But I'd never seen anything like this." Flynn stopped, swallowing down the vomit that rose to the edge of his throat. "It was unbelievable. My barrack looked as if a round of mortar and a tank had rolled through it. The furniture was kindling, broken glass everywhere. Then I saw her. Alena was at the edge of my bed, on the floor—broken into more pieces than anything else in the room—blood everywhere. Ruiz and Jensen, they were standing behind me, giving me a report as if all they needed to do was to put a copy on my desk."

"Oh my God, they killed her?"

"Mia, you have to stop thinking of death as the objective. When you put a human being in that situation, it's what they end up begging for." Even in the dim light, Flynn could see her face go white. A hollow gaze cast over it, saying that she no longer had any idea who she was looking at. "It's worse than anything you could have dreamt up, isn't it? You can't believe what you're hearing, can you?" Mia didn't reply, retreating to the corner of the balcony. Still, Flynn wasn't sure he'd made his point. "That small ass-whipping you witnessed earlier—what I did to those boys—it doesn't cover the warm-up for what Ruiz and Jensen did to Alena. Every method they used was one they'd seen me condone—though," he admitted, "never all at once. Aside from the cops, it's most of why I got so rattled last night. Exerting force like that—well, it's something I saw very differently after Alena. I suppose Ruiz and Jensen figured if they applied the whole smash, she'd talk. I'd get back to base, glad to hear the news."

"And did she tell them?" Mia demanded, whirling around from the corner where she'd staked out safety. "Please tell me she gave them the damn information."

"Actually, you can take it as proof positive that *enhanced* interrogation doesn't work. She didn't. Alena didn't know Ruiz or Jensen, but she did know how situations like that worked. The way she lived her life wasn't without risk." He leaned forward and back in the chair, still trying to keep from climbing out of his own skin. "It was the thing I was most looking forward to, taking her away to somewhere safe. Alena was tough. I'm sure the worse it got, the more unyielding she became. Knowing Goss's location, Alena assumed it was the only thing keeping her alive."

"She was trying to hold out until you got back. She trusted you."

"Her mistake," he whispered, "my cross to bear. You see my ongoing issues with that . . . with trust." Mia wrapped her arms around herself, offering the comfort he couldn't give. "I told Ruiz to call Central Command for a med-flight team. They looked at me like I was crazy—then they followed the order. Alena was breathing, semiconscious, enough to know I was there. I told her not to talk, that help was on the way. She actually smiled at me, tried to speak, but she was just too battered. I could see it in her eyes; she knew she wasn't going to make it. I stayed there with her, on the floor, holding her—trying to keep the life from running out of her. Somehow, in the end, she managed enough strength to tell me two things."

"What were they?" Mia asked, swiping at tears.

"Zubara. It was a village about thirty minutes south of our location. I didn't even know what she meant for a second; I had forgotten why we were there. It's where Goss was holding my men. I nodded—I couldn't even think what I was supposed to do with the information, not in that moment. Then, with a last breath, Alena told me that she loved me, that she always loved me. And then," he said, drawing a shaky breath of his own, "she died." Flynn folded his hands, as if in a prayer, pressing the laced fingers to his mouth. "The hours after that are a blur, a smoky firefight—I can only remember bits and pieces."

"Tell me you got them out, Flynn. Please tell me that Alena didn't die for nothing."

He furrowed his brow and his gaze dropped to the floor. "Three out of five," he said quietly, still unable to accept anything that had happened that night. "Goss and his men put up a damn good fight. Bradshaw and Gilly—they didn't make it. Bradshaw had succumbed to torture tactics, not unlike Alena, not long before we arrived. Gilly was killed in the firefight. Jackson, Kroeger, and Lopez, we managed to get them out."

"And Simon Goss, did you capture him?"

"I killed him," Flynn said, emotion vacant from his voice. "Our exit came by way of a wicked firefight. They were pummeling the chopper with everything they had. Turned out Goss was a good shot, aiming at Lopez from about ninety meters out with a handgun. He missed his head by no more than an inch," Flynn said, absently brushing a hand over the scar on his shoulder.

"Bar brawl or jilted lover," Mia murmured. "Neither," she said, eyes closed, shaking her head.

"What?"

"It was neither. Your scar; it's from the bullet you took. It saved Lopez, didn't it?"

He didn't reply, continuing, "I managed to get the last shot—right through Goss's head. I watched him drop to the ground, and I realized that I felt nothing—not revenge or victory or satisfaction. There wasn't enough of me left to feel anything." Mia inched forward, a hand moving toward Flynn's scarred shoulder. He jerked away. He hadn't wanted comfort then, and he sure as hell didn't want any now. "On the chopper ride back to base, Jensen, he finally made eye contact with me. I could see it. The realization of what he and Ruiz had done. I swear to God he was going to jump. I grabbed his arm; I told him we'd figure it out. I told him he had too much to live for."

"You had empathy for them after what they did to Alena?"

"Empathy?" he asked, looking queerly at her. "No, I had a responsibility. I was their commanding officer, Mia. Those guys didn't take a piss without my say-so. Remember what I told you. I was their leader, their sole judge of what was right and wrong. As far as I was concerned, I might as well have been standing in the room, smoking a cigarette while they killed her."

"Come on, Flynn. They had to take some responsibility, they weren't robots. You would have never condoned what they did."

"Don't be so sure," he snapped. "I wanted those men back as much as they did." There was a visual standoff, with Mia's mouth dropping open. "There are days," he confessed, "when my sanity hinges on the belief that I wouldn't have. But remove that from the equation, remove what I felt for Alena . . . and really, I was worse, because I led them down the path."

"Okay, but that still doesn't explain how you ended up the fugitive, how you ended up in jail for mur—" Mia sat down hard on the chair, her fingertips grazing over her mouth. "Oh, Flynn, you didn't? No one has that kind of responsibility to another human being. I don't care what kind of code you lived by. Ruiz and Jensen were responsible for Alena's death, not you."

"It's not like I didn't consider that very point, Mia. But look at the situation. The place was crawling with MPs when we got back. As the commanding officer, I was debriefed first. It turned out that Alena had more than a few secrets. She wasn't just an informant to me; she was a top informant to the United States government. And it became clear fast that someone was going to pay for her death. I stood there, trying to figure out what to say, how to explain it, when I saw that piece of paper on the desk. The one with the information about Jensen's wife and his two babies. The ones he didn't even know about yet. I had told Ellie Jensen that her husband would be home soon. Ruiz, his situation wasn't much different: three kids, a wife, a widowed mother who lived with them. What did I have? Nothing—an old man who hated the fucking sight of me, a mother who I'd barely heard from since basic training. Two of my men were dead because of the mistakes I made. The woman I loved, she was dead because of the methods I condoned. And honestly, Mia, I was standing there with her blood all over my hands— Central Command never questioned my confession. And before you even ask, regretting my decision . . . well, that's not something I've thought about." *At least not until now.* He stood and walked to the opposite corner of the balcony, considering for a moment the twelve-story drop and the cement below.

Chapter 19

It was too much truth. Mia's head pounded with it. If Flynn said one more word, she was positive her head was going to explode. No wonder he didn't know how to tell her; she had no idea how to process it. He should have kept his damn secrets to himself. A jumble of thoughts stuck to her brain, like little yellow Post-its. *Flynn's everything I want. Not to mention, a convicted murderer. I want a life with him. Note to self: He's a fugitive; they'll never give him a mortgage. He understands everything about me. Friendly reminder: The simplicity of your life probably amuses him—like a board game.* Flynn had tried to warn her, over and over. She shouldn't have had the drink, gone for the ride, gotten in bed . . . fallen in love with him.

"Mia, please, say something, anything."

His voice was full of concern. Mia rose from the chair and walked back inside the room, snapping on the light. Somewhere in her mind she thought a change of scenery might alter the situation. It didn't. She clutched her stomach, pulling tighter on the tie of her robe. The whole sordid story made her insides ache.

While she knew there were secrets, she never expected anything quite so tainted. She turned, realizing that he'd followed her inside. Mia opened her mouth to speak, but nothing would come out. Her arm gestured in the air, delivering a stinging slap to her bare thigh. The story he told moved forward and back in her head as she tried to make sense of it. "There's no way out now, is there? No one would believe you—you're stuck with this crime as if you committed it," she sputtered between hiccupping breaths.

"Mia, I'm not going to argue responsibility with you. That's not why I told you. And, yes, it's who I am—Sergeant Peyton Flynn McDermott, dishonorably discharged for behavior unbecoming to a United States Marine. Convicted of second-degree murder, and sentenced to twenty years in a military disciplinary barrack. I've lived with it for a long time."

"And Jensen, Ruiz, they let you do this? They let you take the blame?"

"Not at first, not easily. But they were scared, more scared than I was. I'm sure it's cost them. Doesn't matter anymore. Ruiz died a few years ago—some god-awful disease. Last I heard, Jensen moved to Canada with his wife and kids. Back then, to be honest, they couldn't cart me away fast enough. I just wanted out of there; I wanted it to be over. Of course I had no idea that the worst was yet to come. Even when you think you've paid for your sins, the subconscious has a way of upping the ante."

"The nightmares," Mia said, realizing that like death, murder and jail weren't the worst things he might endure. "What are . . . will you tell me what they're about?" she asked, suddenly curious for the details.

"I can, but I'll tell you right now, any faith, any belief you have left in me is about to hit ground zero."

"Try me." She snickered. "How much worse could it possibly get?"

He shrugged, the eerily calm gesture sending a shiver up Mia's spine. "It's one nightmare, always the same. It starts . . . it starts in reality, exactly the way things went down—like a late-night rerun, the kind of thing where you know every line. Except . . . except when I rush into my barrack things begin to change, colors, smells—actions."

"How so?" she asked, watching his face turn wary and pale.

"I'm . . . I'm the son of a bitch killing her."

"You?" Mia questioned, wondering how fine the line was between his dream and reality.

Flynn's eyes closed, and he turned his head away. "It isn't Ruiz and Jensen who kill Alena. It's me—crystal clear," he said, opening his eyes. "Just like the way you're standing here in front of me. I've been trapped in that night terror so many times I can tell you how many flies are in the room, when they start to land in the splattered blood. After a few moments, Ruiz and Jensen, they're not even in the barrack—or the dream. I can hear Alena's thick accent, just as you hear your own voice. She always called me Peyton. I hear her asking me why—that she thought I loved her. But I can't stop, I don't. Then the panic starts—a dream or reality, I can't tell which is which anymore. The details, they're so vivid. I can hear her bones break; I know the pain she's in—because of me. It's my fault that this is happening to her. I want to get away from it and I just can't. I'm destined to stay there and watch her die all over again." It came out of his mouth in a blind ramble, and he didn't look at Mia until he stopped speaking. "I'm . . . I'm sorry. That was more than I meant to say. Are you . . . You look like you're going to be sick."

Mia's hands were clamped over her mouth, struggling to control the impending gag. She gathered just enough composure to ask, "The night you ended up in the field, you had this dream? You were afraid you'd mistake me for her." He nodded, a hard gulp passing by his throat. "My God, Flynn, you could have killed me!"

"Don't you think I know that! Why the fuck do you think you found me naked in a field? Since that night, every time we've been together, I've watched the sun rise over you. I'd never let that happen." He looked as if he wanted to gather her in his arms, wisely choosing not to. "I swear, Mia—you have to believe me. It's the truth."

Her gaze moved in circles around him, and she finally turned her body away. How much trust could you have in one man? One with half a name who'd just explained his sketchy past by way of murder—or some degree thereof, depending on which parts you chose to believe. Mia's hands wrenched through her hair, clasping tight to her head, squeezing. She wasn't good at making judgment calls, deciding between right and wrong. That was her father's job, not hers. And this wasn't a problem, it was an incomprehensible disaster. It was her whole life and it had just tumbled into some unforeseen black hole.

Mia turned, startled to find him so close. She backed away, seeing for the first time a different man. She needed to think— and damn, she couldn't think with him standing there looking so lost. With little else to go on, Mia relied on the same instinct she'd used that night in the field. "I want you to go." Flynn didn't argue. He'd meant what he said earlier, before he set fire to the fabric of what bound them. He'd applaud her for making a smart decision. As he gathered his belongings, Mia asked, "How will you get back?"

"Get back? I don't under—"

"I drove. How are you going to get back to Athens? It's two hours from here."

His eyes squeezed shut tight as he shook his head. The simplicity of the question seemed to confuse him. "I'm a wanted fugitive, Mia. Transportation issues aren't really a survival skill I worry about. And neither should you. I'll manage."

He would manage and she knew it. She also knew if he left like this she'd never see him again. He probably wouldn't even go back to Athens. There would be no way to find him. The power he had to do just that made her angry. *But maybe that's the right decision; maybe I should just let him go.* "Do one thing for me." The thought hurried out before caution and reason interfered.

"Anything."

"Keep your promise. Don't just vanish, not until I see you again. I need time to sort this out."

"After what I just told you? You would expect me to keep my word?"

"I'm going on the notion that you've never lied to me. Work with me."

"Why? What possible difference could it make? You think you can come to terms with this? Trust me, you're only going to get angrier. After everything, if you hate me . . . I can take a lot, Mia, but I don't think I could face that." He turned away, heading for the door, hesitating. "All right, if that's what you want. I'll stay until I hear from you."

"Flynn?"

"What?" His back was to her, the door already open.

She swore she heard his voice tremble. "Do you have any idea how much I love you?"

His head bobbed forward, shoulders slumping as if she'd hit him in the back of the head with a brick. "Yeah, it will make it that much harder, won't it?" The door closed and he was gone.

"Harder for who?" she whispered. They weren't the words she was looking for. She should have known better. He didn't want to give her anything to hope for, anything to sway the argument in his favor. The room went ridiculously silent. Mia never felt so alone or abandoned. A blind sense of survival dumped her on the edge of the bed before she fell to the floor. As if it belonged to someone else, Mia watched her own hand dip into the overnight bag. In the bottom was his T-shirt. She didn't even know why she'd packed it, like he wasn't going to be wearing one just like it? She held it up to her face, blotting tears, filling her lungs with its musky scent. It was strange comfort, a placebo for the real drug that had suddenly vanished. Everything he'd told her, it was like little knives jabbing at her heart. Was he at all responsible for Alena's death? Was he lying about his involvement? Maybe Flynn only convinced himself that he wasn't in the barrack when Jensen and Ruiz . . . *killed* her. Perhaps the subconscious made those kinds of accommodations too. Was there justification for any of it? It was a world and a code about which Mia had no understanding. Had they exchanged the lives of three good men for a woman who had betrayed Flynn? Who decides stuff like that? Mia wondered. Flynn was a fugitive, a wanted murderer in the eyes of the law, and the only thing that kept rebounding in Mia's brain was how much she wanted him back.

"What am I doing?" she snapped, throwing the shirt aside. "I have to be rational, reasonable. I need to understand this, see it for what it is. I need to think like Roxanne." This time there was no edge to catch her as she fell.

A crazy, outside-the-lines accusation barreled onto center stage. Possibility replaced absurdity. The words dropped from her mouth. "Oh, God, he couldn't have. Couldn't have killed those girls, the murdered coeds. It's insane." But only a few hours ago she never would have guessed the madness he confessed. Was it that much of a stretch? Mia had witnessed one nightmare. It was real, the violence palpable. She saw what he'd done to those college boys without breaking a sweat. How much of a chance would one woman have against him? He could have met up with each of those girls, had sex with them, fallen asleep, and . . . Look how close it had come to happening to her. He admitted it.

Peyton Flynn McDermott, not just tangled in the death of one woman, but—as Roxanne pointed out—possibly responsible for the murder of six others. Mia buried her face in the pillow, screaming. Tears were no longer a fitting emotional avenue for the man she loved and the serial killer he might very well be.

* *

The summer semester ended. For a few weeks Athens would be a ghost town. Usually a place naturally jammed with life, it was always unsettling this time of year. The sweltering August heat churned around the city like a pig on a spit. It was relentless and disconcerting. Even Roxanne packed up and went home for a few weeks. She'd been asked to crown this year's Watermelon Festival queen, and had invited Mia to tag along. They'd spend most of their time in Juliette, where Roxanne's family lived, take a day trip to Atlanta and visit Rory. Mia politely declined. That kind of trip would only remind her just how right Roxanne was about how wrong life could go. She stayed in Athens—alone. Flynn didn't call or try to see her. Mia didn't expect that he would. Instead she waited, thinking that at any moment an epiphany would strike, supplying her with the answers she needed.

Ten days had passed and Mia finally gathered the courage to call Flynn, indirectly. She dialed the bike shop, never worrying that he wouldn't be there—that he wouldn't keep his promise to stay. She left a message with the owner, asking Flynn to meet her downtown. He didn't call to say he'd be there. Yet a solid half hour before she'd asked him to come she sat at a corner table in an overly cheerful café. The bright blue place mats and sunny yellow walls made her want to retch. How could anything be so happy when the future was so dismal? But she'd chosen the public setting for a reason. *Isn't that what they say you should do when meeting someone who has questionable motives?* At the time she thought she was being savvy. Now it just felt absurd. She still wasn't afraid of him. Her appearance certainly wasn't any indication of a woman gripped with anxiety over meeting an unscrupulous killer. Shopping had been the only vice that offered a mild distraction. She bought new jeans (a skirt was totally out of the question) matched with a delicate linen blouse in pale pink. When Mia slipped it on she realized it was a color Flynn had complimented her on more than once. She'd cut several inches off her hair; it would be nearly the same length as his. The thought had caused her to smile idiotically into the salon mirror. Now, she tried to readjust her datelike attitude. There should be no anticipation, no fluttery nerves. She had questions and he was damn well going to answer them. And then, well, she'd see.

She sipped an iced tea, running her fingers over the pearls of water that dripped along the outside of the glass. Even air-conditioning couldn't completely fight off the heat. A group of four uncomfortable-looking suited men came in and were seated at the table next to her. One was wearing a hat, tipping it as he politely acknowledged her. "Miss." She smiled back. There was an aura of safety to their presence, something from her past that she recognized. They all ordered ice water and chatted on about the heat, just like everyone else. Mia glanced past them, out the window. He should be there any minute. If he was coming. The conversation next to her drifted on, from what they might have for lunch to their business at hand. She couldn't help but overhear.

"So what else did your buddy in Birmingham have to say?"

"Not much. They've eliminated all the local suspects. The guy's got to be a drifter. Stands to reason it's connected to the other five. Psych profile says he may be mirroring some kind of personal trauma. He's slick—in and out like a ghost. But he finally slipped up. They did get some blood evidence off the 'Bama girl. She put up a good fight."

"Well, I don't know about places like Birmingham or Austin, but if that ghost decides to rattle his chain here, he's gonna have a real Southern welcome from the Georgia contingency." The burliest member of the group pushed back his jacket, patting a holster.

Mia's eyes went saucer wide. The detective saw the shock on her face. Caught in his macho display, he quickly tucked his jacket into place and changed the subject. At that exact moment Flynn came through the door and she forced silent a gasp. Mia looked at the posse of detectives and back at Flynn.

One of them mumbled, "Damn, I left my wallet in the car. I'll be right back."

Mia bolted out of her seat before he was upright, racing toward Flynn who she shoved into the café's outer vestibule. "Kiss me!" she demanded in a panicked whisper.

* *

Flynn blinked at her in amazement, having tried out a thousand different scenarios as to what her first words might be. This had not occurred to him. "What?"

"Just do it."

He shrugged, following the order. His lips fell into hers with all the gusto ten days of pent-up passion could unleash in one kiss. Mia grabbed his shoulders, shoving him against the wall, covering him with as much of her body as possible.

Footsteps shuffled by and he heard a faint "Excuse me."

Opening an eye, Flynn sneaked a peek at the man who passed by. He thought about pulling away, apologizing. But hell, she was kissing him and damn hard. Mia had him pinned so tightly in the corner there was nothing to do but give in. His hands, which had been glued to his sides, came up around her, a needy groan vibrating from his throat. He pulled her body into him, wondering if they were making up or just making out. Flynn's hands began wandering to places unsuitable for public display. She didn't seem to mind, lost in the kiss. He wrenched his head back into the few inches of space behind him. His eyes were still closed tight. For once he didn't want to wake up. "Damn. This is a dream, right?"

Mia finally let go, her eyes flicking toward the door. "No, but it could be a brand-new nightmare for you. Let's get out of here." She grabbed him by the hand, pulling him through the exit. "I walked. Where's your bike?"

"Why, where am I going? What's going on?"

"Not now. Where is it? Don't talk, don't look at anybody!" With one giant step he was in front of her, lightly grasping her by the shoulders. Sweltering rays of sun left drops of perspiration on her brow. She pushed right past him, dragging him along. "I have to get you out of here!" Moments later they were on his bike, riding toward her apartment. "Don't go too fast," she warned at the traffic light.

"I'm not even doing the speed limit. What is with you?" She didn't answer, her arms grabbing tighter around his waist, her face buried in his back. Her heart was pounding against him in a panic that he could feel through to his chest. In the parking lot of the apartment complex, Mia jerked him away from the bike. He couldn't move fast enough for her. She wrenched off his helmet while he calmly removed his sunglasses. There was an exasperated gasp as the ground seemed to shift from under her feet. One hand went to her forehead; the other grabbed his arm to steady herself.

"That's enough!" he shouted, scooping her into his arms as the sweat ran down her flushed face. "Are you going to pass out from the heat or just the panic attack? What the hell is going on? I want an answer."

"Not here. Inside. We have to go inside." She kicked her legs furiously, her eyes pleading with him to move. "There were some men in the restaurant . . ."

His head went back and he rolled his eyes. "Don't tell me they were hitting on you."

"What?" She shook her head sharply. "No, I'm wearing jeans." He had to laugh a little. "Flynn, they were detectives."

"So?" he replied, shrugging his shoulders. Cops were a perpetual hazard of life on the run. They didn't even make him flinch anymore.

"So . . ." She wiggled more, attempting to get down, but he wasn't letting go. "Look, I can't just blurt this out in the middle of a parking lot, particularly when you're holding me like this. It is a little undignified. Can we just go inside?"

"Hmm, I was kind of enjoying it." He caught her somber if not woozy expression. "Yeah, I guess we better. Can you make it if I put you down?"

"Of course. I can walk."

"Never mind," he said. "It might be my only chance to do this."

Chapter 20

Safely inside the apartment Flynn gently deposited her on the sofa, telling her not to move, getting her a glass of water from the kitchen. "Okay, so they were detectives. And I'm guessing that the panic attack I just witnessed was because you were afraid they'd been flipping through their most-wanted snapshots this morning. If they saw me I'd be back in a cell in time for dinner?"

"Mmm, something like that," she murmured, sipping the icy water.

"And you don't think that's where I belong?" Every thought, every breath he'd taken in the last ten days hinged on that question.

Mia tipped her head back, glancing up at the ceiling. "Do epiphanies make any sound when they fall?" She frowned a little, her hand reaching to the soft beard and the blue eyes, apprehensive but focused. Mia ran her fingers over his lips and the sharp line of his cheekbones. "You suddenly look nervous. How come?"

"I don't know. Kinda feels like the day they sentenced me, only worse."

"It's not about getting caught or going back to prison, is it? You're afraid of what I'm going to say, aren't you?" The momentary pause was more than he could stand. "To admit that you don't belong in prison means I believe everything you told me. It's a lot to ask, Flynn."

"You won't get an argument from me."

"I've thought about nothing else for the last ten days. I've even considered the *evidence*, if someone like my father would believe your story." She paused, her gaze shifting away. "I don't know that he would."

"Smart man," Flynn murmured.

"Still, I can't come up with a reason why you'd tell me any of it, unless you were telling me the truth. Why risk it? Why not just disappear the way you showed up? Since I left that hotel room, I could have called the police a hundred times. And, really, there's nothing keeping you here."

"Except you." The words were a reflex, tumbling out of his mouth before he could stop them. In a way, she was right. Leaving would be the humane thing to do.

"Bottom line, I have nothing but your word." He scrubbed a hand over his face, sighing. Leaning back into the sofa, Flynn waited once again for judgment to pass.

"I'm grateful, Mia. Grateful that you haven't alerted the authorities, that you're willing to sit alone in a room with me. It's more than I deserve. I'll be gone by morn—"

"Flynn," she said, lurching forward, her hand grabbing his. "I believe you."

He jerked his gaze to hers, unsure if he heard her correctly. "You do?"

She nodded, pulling closer to him. "You'd never hurt Alena. It isn't in you. I'm sure of that much." She smiled at him, displaying the confidence he'd seen emerge in recent months. "I'm Lincoln Montgomery's daughter, and my instincts are that sure. As for everything else, how you took the fall for what happened . . . I don't claim to completely understand it. But what's done is done. My question is what are we going to do about it now?"

He looked into her expectant face. He hadn't considered a conversation beyond "I'll give you a ten-minute head start before I call the police." *What am I going to do about a future that doesn't belong to me?*

Mia continued on, reading his mind. "Well, it's not like we're in a position to seek a new trial now." His heart caught on the *we* and he pulled her close. But her body didn't relax into his. She pushed away, shifting on the sofa. "There's, um, something else I need to ask you about. It's something that Roxanne said." She wasn't looking at him anymore, her fingers nervously rubbing the nap of the fabric. "Flynn, you're not . . . Roxanne, she, um, she suggested something to me. I told her it was crazy." She stopped there, hanging onto the last word as her gaze trailed back over him. "I don't believe . . . I don't want to believe it, but Roxanne . . ."

"Roxanne what? You didn't tell her—you know, about me and prison."

"Of course not! I'd never tell anyone. Don't you know that you can trust me with anything?"

"I do trust you," he said, tipping his forehead against hers. She pulled away again. "I'm sorry. It's just that, well, I've only given you about a million reasons not to trust me, not to ever want to see me again. I know how Roxanne feels about me, and what she might say to keep us apart."

Mia's gaze dashed to his. "She would, wouldn't she?" Roxanne would say almost anything. "That's possible, isn't it?" He offered a vague nod, although she appeared to be waiting for something more. Mia laced and unlaced her fingers with his, almost examining them. "Flynn, tell me something. When you escaped, where did you go? Did you go to your brother's like you told Roxanne?"

He started to answer, but stopped, wondering exactly how much more confession she could take. "No, not quite."

"You mean you didn't head southwest? Your brother doesn't live in that part of the country?"

"Yes and no. I did go to Arizona. But Alec, he lives in California."

"Arizona, I see." He watched her expression rise and fall with the answer. "Well, if you didn't go there to see your brother, why were you there? What's in Arizona?"

"Look, what I told Roxanne were half-truths."

"Half-truths? What does that mean?"

"Well, she started asking all those questions. I had to say something and I wasn't really prepared for an inquisition. I just escaped from a federal penitentiary. Do you really think I'd run to a relative? Don't you think that's the first place they'd look? What I told her, it just popped into my head. I couldn't say what I was really doing there."

"Why not?" she asked sharply. "What were you doing that was so awful you couldn't tell her?"

"Because telling Roxanne that I went there to buy an untraceable vehicle from an ex-con who operates his fugitive-assistance program out of a doublewide in Bisbee might have thrown her already suspicious mind into a convulsion, don't you think?"

"Oh," she said softly. "I guess it would. How did you know to go there? For that matter, how did you escape?"

"Would you believe a clerical error and one fresh-on-the-job, overzealous guard?" He watched her face, the bend of her delicate brow. It was going to require details. "Okay, it goes like this. It was late afternoon, right around shift change. I was in the infirmary—"

"Infirmary? Were you sick?" she asked worriedly, her hand reaching to his face as though he still might have a fever.

"Ah, no," he said smiling, clasping his fingers around hers, drawing them away. "I kind of met with the business end of a shank."

"A what?"

"Homemade knife. The Marines had their how-to book, so did prison."

"A knife—somebody stabbed you?" she said, her eyes pulsing wide. "How bad?"

"Just a few stitches. Look, Mia, you have to remember where I was. Attempts on someone's life, it's not unusual. Anyway, this time the wound had gotten infected—"

"This time? How many times did they try to kill you?"

"Let's just say it happened enough to keep me on my toes," he said tentatively. "Being ex–special ops made me a rare commodity and a target, if not a trophy. Prison is all about pecking order; taking out former special ops would have gone a long way in assuring a place at the head of the mob. It stood to reason there would always be a next time."

"So you didn't just escape because of the nightmares. You escaped to save your life. They would have gotten to you eventually—killed you, wouldn't they?"

"Maybe . . . probably," he admitted with a dry swallow. "It was clear that I was going to die or just rot in that prison. At some point you either give into it—or you find another way. Anyway, the situation presented itself and I grabbed it. It came down to the untimely passing of one poor bastard and one wild insane mix-up. There had been an incident earlier that day. An inmate, Lyle Cochran, was killed. Particularly unfortunate for him because he was due to be released that afternoon. Seems he owed a debt that he wasn't going to make good on before his departure. Because the infirmary is the release point for inmates, all his paperwork had come upstairs, signed off, stamped, and ready to go. It sat on the table right next to me. The only thing left was for Cochran to be handed a change of clothes and to be escorted out. A call came in that a guard had been injured. It must have been serious, because all the medical personnel went tearing out of there. A minute later another guard, one who'd only worked there a month or so, buzzed in to collect his discharge. He already had a nasty-ass reputation, and I wasn't looking to rattle his stick. He demanded the paperwork and I handed it to him. I started to explain, and he told me to shut the hell up. Said part of his job might be putting scum back on the street, but he sure as hell didn't have to converse with it."

"And he didn't catch it? He thought he was releasing Lyle Cochran?"

"Funny thing about military mug shots, all perps tend to have a uniform look. With a shift change underway, that guard was my handler all the way out the front door, expedited me right through the system. He was cocky; more concerned about demonstrating who was in charge, telling me how I'd better watch my ass on the outside rather than doing his job. He never looked twice. I'm sure they realized what had happened fairly quickly, but it was long enough for me to land in a different zip code."

"And after that? What made you go to Bisbee?"

"A while back I'd been talking to a couple of inmates. Supposedly, this guy in Bisbee offered a pre-parole plan to fugitives. I didn't know if it was just folklore, but they even talked about the freight train you hopped in Oklahoma City to get there. I tucked the information away just in case. I made it to the train yard the next night. Short of drawing me a map it worked out like they said. I bought the bike from him."

"Okay, but how'd you pay for the bike? I assume he wasn't giving them away. Where'd you get the money, Flynn? Did . . . did you steal it?"

He leaned back into the couch, wondering how many crimes she thought him capable of? Guilty or innocent, time served had that effect. "Mmm, I see. What's a little thievery after doing a stint for murder?"

"You didn't murder anyone," she insisted. Then in a smaller voice, "You didn't murder Alena. I told you, I believe that." There was an awkward hesitation between them as Mia looked hard at him. It was as if she was trying to look right through him. "People steal for a lot of reasons. I could understand if you were scared or desperate. It might make you do, I don't know, crazy things."

"Crazy things? Exactly what kind of crazy things are we talking about? What's Roxanne filling your head with? No, I didn't steal it. Though I guess it's an obvious conclusion—for both of you. I earned the money. In prison. Unconventional methods maybe, but I did earn it."

"Earned it?"

"Yeah, prison details," he said, shifting again, unable to get comfortable with her and the topic. "You're not going to like it."

"I'm a big girl, Flynn. Unless you're going to start telling me stories that involve a shower and a bar of soap."

He held up a hand to stop her. "I assure you it never got that ugly, at least not for me. Long story short, prison is a dangerous place and protecting yourself is like the sun coming up. It's just going to happen every day. For some people, protection is a service well worth paying for."

"You mean you took money from people who would have otherwise gotten hurt? Flynn, that's—"

"That's prison, Mia. It wasn't the fucking Boy Scouts. It wasn't a vacation. It wasn't even the Marines. It was hell, and you do what you have to do. I was in for the long haul, and it was part of surviving." He got up from the couch, distancing himself from her and his latest confession. "I could have been the one doing the hurting. Maybe that would be easier for you to believe."

"You wouldn't do that," she said, rushing to his defense. "Would you?"

"I'm no angel, sweetheart," he said, looking hard at her. "I'm not going to stand here and defend my past; it's not worth defending. I'd like to think that that kind of violence isn't in me anymore. But like those guys at the concert, or a nightmare I can't find a way out of, you never know what will challenge it. You'll have to decide for yourself what you can accept and what's just too much."

"That's what I'm trying to do." Mia rose from the sofa and wandered toward the window, staring. "These past weeks, I've thought a lot about the things you did. Trouble is I only ended up thinking about where you were. I hate it, you in that place. And now, with what you just told me—you can't ever go back there."

"Mia, I don't want your sympathy," he said roughly. "It's not your cross to bear. What I want to know right now is what Roxanne told you. What's she got me doing, armed robbery? Maybe some drug trafficking through the Midwest?"

Mia moved silently across the room, standing opposite him. She picked up his sunglasses from the bar top, toying with the frames. "No, not drugs. Girls, it has to do with girls."

"Girls, what girls?"

"Along the way to here, were there a lot of girls?"

"You mean that I, um, picked up, had sex with? Is that what we're talking about?"

"Yeah, were they all college girls like me?"

"Like you? No, sweetheart, none like you." He laughed, but she barely smiled.

"That's nice, Flynn, but I wasn't fishing for a compliment. Could you just tell me, were they all college girls."

"I don't know, I suppose some were. I did tend to gravitate toward college towns, the bigger the better. It's the easiest place in the world to get lost. But I didn't ask them to fill out a survey before. Or after, for that matter," he said shrugging. "Conversation was, um, limited. Do you really want to talk about this? I think I'd rather tell you prison stories."

"Yes, I . . . I need to know, about the girls." She took a deep breath as if bracing for the answer. "So you went to lots of different college towns? There were lots of women? Like how many?"

He shifted his stance, imagining the sleazy stories Roxanne had dreamt up. "I don't know, a bunch, a few. I didn't keep a fucking diary—they weren't that memorable," he snapped, hearing Roxanne's voice more than Mia's. Flynn rolled his eyes. "What? You want me to do the math?" Mia offered the smallest hint of a shrug. "Okay, fine," he said tightly. "I've been on the run about two years. Let's see, that's three or four girls a month, maybe five on occasion—let's face it, I did spend a lot of years locked up." Flynn crossed his arms, squinting toward the ceiling as if in deep concentration. "Where does that leave us? Ninety-six, ninety-seven—ah, hell, let's just go with a round number and call it an even hundred." He watched her grip tighten around the sunglasses, realizing that perhaps he'd gone too far. His voice softened. "Mia, I'm kidding." She wouldn't look at him, her stare concentrated on the glasses. "Really, it was probably more like eight, ten at the most." Flynn moved forward, clasping his hand over hers. "Exactly what kind of details are you looking for, sweetheart?"

"Did you spend the night with them?"

Her willingness to pursue the topic surprised him—the prosecutor's daughter. He backed away. "The night?" he asked, beginning to wonder if gratuitous sex was really at the crux of Roxanne's accusation. "If I stayed more than a couple of hours it was a lot. We never got into a discussion of breakfast menus. But what I want to know is, why do you want to know?"

"It's just that Roxanne said . . ."

"Okay, hold it right there," he said, taking a step toward her. "I'm having a definite problem with sentences that start with 'Roxanne said.' I . . . I thought you were past this, buying into what Roxanne thinks. Exactly what is she accusing me of?"

"I'll be right back." Mia dropped the sunglasses onto the bar top and turned the corner into Roxanne's bedroom.

Chapter 21

Mia stared at the news stories tucked between two books on the shelf. She thought about just handing them over, demanding that he explain. Then she considered the hurt look on his face a few moments before, when she'd only accused him of stealing. Confront him, ambush him with this and he probably wouldn't even bother saying good-bye. Trust and blind faith were drawing a fine line between one another. She squeezed her eyes shut tight and reached for the papers.

A rush of guilt nearly threw her off balance as Flynn interrupted. "Mia? What are you doing?"

His soft voice held her steady. She spun around, looking at him, waiting to be accused, tried, convicted—all within the context of Roxanne's theory, some circumstantial evidence, and a road map. Mia guessed that his court-martial was as swift and calculated as Roxanne's rush to judgment. She'd made a good case for guilt, but what made him innocent? There had to be something. Mia took a breath, treading carefully with one fact at a time. "You know Roxanne, how suspicious she can be. Well, she thinks . . . She's got this crazy idea that you killed a girl," she said softly. "That girl from Birmingham, Alabama. You remember—on the news?" There was silence from the doorway and she thought he hadn't heard her. "Flynn?"

"Roxanne told you what? She said what?"

"The girl from the University of Alabama. She was murdered right before we met in June. Actually, it was the day before we met. You said that you came here from there. You told me that at the Odyssey. Do you remember?"

"Wait, this is just Roxanne's twisted sense of humor, right? Jesus, Mia, the girl needs to get a hobby or a boyfriend or maybe just a good . . ." He stopped. "Holy shit, she's serious."

"Answer the question, Flynn." Mia sensed the shift, felt the trust between them strain.

"No, I really don't remember. But does it matter what I say?" His voice was incredulous and cold. "Looks like you've already got your mind made up. Though even I have to admit, it's a very dramatic ending. Roxanne ought to rethink her major. Hollywood could use her."

"Ending for what?" He didn't answer, heading for the apartment door. Mia raced around the corner, his hand already on the knob. "Flynn, wait! Just listen to me. You told me the night we met that you'd never hurt another human being 'like that'— with your hands. Even then I could see it in your eyes, something so awful it made your stomach sick to look in a mirror. I understand. I understand how what happened to Alena makes you feel. You can't live with it when you're awake, and I've seen how it haunts you in the dark. Somebody who feels that much wouldn't do that to another person, not intentionally. But I do believe the guilt you feel over her death is—consuming." She grabbed the sunglasses, thrusting them at him. "Your hair, the beard, it's not a disguise to keep some cop from making a connection, from recognizing you. It's so you see someone else when you look in the mirror." He looked away, gripping his arms tightly around himself as if to hold in everything she exposed. "I believed what you said that night. I still want to believe it, but I want . . . I want . . ."

"You want proof, Mia, and I can't give it to you. I can't prove I wasn't in Birmingham any more than I could prove I was on the moon. Hell, I don't exist except for right here in this room with you. You are the only thing that has given me a moment's peace since . . . since that day. And God help me, I let you. But if this is where we're going, where we are—well, what the hell's the point?"

"The point is that I'm trying to understand everything you've been through, to put it into some kind of context."

"Yeah, well, good luck with that. If you can make sense of my life, sweetheart, you're a fucking giant step ahead of me," he said, his face stony, his expression bleak. "But I can tell you this; I won't defend myself to anything Roxanne has to say. Her dislike for me goes back to a cold stare from across a bar. And her need to judge is only outdone by her need to control. Influence, Mia—you shouldn't let either one of us have any over you. We both tend to lead you places you probably shouldn't go."

"That's not true!" she said, finding herself on the defensive. "She doesn't think for me and you haven't made me do anything I didn't want to. And don't do that. Don't make me feel the way I do about you and then tell me it's wrong, that I shouldn't be right here. I meant what I said in the hotel. I love you."

"I'm sure that's true. There just isn't much reason to trust me. You see the problem? That's a tough position to be in, isn't it?" He leaned against the door, still tense, still looking ready to bolt. But staring at her, his expression softened. "What you said,

I can't begin to tell you what that means to me. But it also scares me to death."

"And that's bad. Does it make you want to run all the more?"

"No, more like the opposite," he said, his eyes moving over her body. "But I strongly suspect it should make you run like hell. I don't deserve any part of you." There was an awkward smile, a small sign that neither one of them was going anywhere. "I'm sorry. What you do deserve is answers. Birmingham, huh?" he said, stepping away from the door. "Well, I'll tell you every detail I remember, about Alabama, about whatever you want to know. You'll have to decide if it's enough."

She backed up, sitting on a barstool, afraid that if she took her eyes off him he'd just vaporize. "I'm listening. Tell me how you got here, what happened in the days before."

"Did I come here from Alabama? Yes. From the university, no. I came here from Mobile where I was working a hotel construction site. But there aren't any pay stubs. No motel receipts, not even a postcard of the Gulf Coast. Nothing but my word." She nodded and he kept talking. "The job ended and I took off east, Interstate 10 all the way to Jacksonville. I admit, I did think about going to Birmingham. It was a logical choice. I can fade into the scenery in a place like that. Nobody asks questions, nobody looks twice. But I'd had my fill of Alabama by then."

"So you never went to Birmingham? You've never, ever set foot onto the University of Alabama campus?"

"No, Mia. I've never been to Birmingham," he said firmly. "We met on a Friday. Friday the thirteenth, if I recall. I spent the night of the twelfth in Milledgeville, Georgia. I remember because by the time I got to Jacksonville I was out of pot. I was getting anxious, looking for a place to score. I ran into a guy who told me about a big mental hospital there. Places like that, drugs flow like Kool-Aid. I went there, hung out for a couple of days waiting for a connection. That's what I was doing, committing a misdemeanor—not a felony."

"I don't suppose you got a receipt with that marijuana?"

He gave her a sideways glance. "No, but I do remember the afternoon I arrived here. There was a bad accident on 441 North. A guy was killed on a motorcycle. It was a Harley, like mine. I tallied up the parts while they scraped up the body. I wove through traffic for miles; thought I'd melt right to the pavement it was so goddamn hot. If I had been coming from Alabama I wouldn't have come from that direction, been on that stretch of highway. Look up the record of the accident if it helps. It's not much, but it's all I can offer you." She bit a fingernail, saying nothing. "Mia, I'd like to know, is this just crap from the warp cycle in Roxanne's brain or is there more?" She opened her mouth to speak, but nothing came out. "Mia? Answer me. Is there something else I should know?"

Believe him or don't. If he wasn't in Birmingham, he wasn't in any of those places. End it right here, because there are no alibis, there is no proof. He's paid enough for things he didn't do. While Mia let faith lead, she also felt resolute in the decision. "No, there's nothing else," she lied in a voice so calm and steady she hardly recognized it. "It was just a crazy theory Roxanne dreamed up. Can't you just hear her?" Mia said, forcing a laugh. 'If Flynn came here from Alabama, surely the two things must be related, him and that girl. Lord have mercy, Mia, no doubt he slept with half the state. What more proof do you need?' I told her that she's been watching way too much TV. I probably wouldn't have given it a second thought, except for, well, you know . . . the nightmares . . . Alena."

"Yeah, I can see how that would rattle you. Talk about bad timing." She edged toward him and he reached out, pulling her the rest of the way.

With his arms tight around her there was no room for doubt. As long as he was there, everything was all right. She couldn't imagine it any other way. "Just tell me everything's okay. Promise me nothing bad will happen, that things will just be normal . . ."

"I don't exactly lead your average life. It wouldn't be a promise I'd have a lot of control over, considering my situation. I'm not the guy you'd meet in a study group or even some asshole from your business law class—you'd have a better chance at normal with either one. Whether it's some detective in a café or Roxanne deciding to swipe my coffee mug and dust for fingerprints, this is only real until the past catches up with me. It's why fugitives run."

Roxanne lifting his prints, sending them to the FBI—it was a lucid vision. Startled by the prospect, Mia stepped back and looked at him, hearing a solution in his words. "That's why we should leave here, just the two of us! Think about it, Flynn, we could just get on the bike and go . . ."

"Yeah, that's a nice fantasy." He laughed, pulling her back into his arms.

"Why does it have to be a fantasy? Why can't we do it? What's stopping us? It's not like I have big career plans . . . well, not like Roxanne. I mean it, I'd go anywhere with you. The two of us could—"

"Mia, stop." Flynn pushed away, grasping her firmly by the shoulders. "Understand something—that will never happen. I was afraid of this, what you might be dreaming up in your head, where this is going to end up. Do you really think I'd let you throw away your future for some shabby hand-to-mouth existence? Maybe you don't have a grand plan at the moment, but you will do something incredible. Jesus, it's half of what gets me out of bed every morning." She tried to interrupt, but he gently put a finger to her lips. "Besides, it's not the romantic notion you're banking on, sweetheart. It's dirty, uncomfortable, and, hell yes, it's scary. You think I want that for you? Spend a few days and nights on a motorcycle, Mia. In the rain, the cold. There have been times when that seven-by-ten cell didn't look so bad, nightmares and stabbings included." He looked past her, trying to untangle himself from her pleading gaze. "I have a little bit of pride left, sweetheart. Don't take that away from me."

Mia dug in, clinging to fistfuls of T-shirt. To hell with pride, she'd dig her hands right through to his flesh if it kept them together. "I'd do anything to keep you safe. If they take you back to jail, they'll kill you. If running is what keeps you safe then I'm willing."

"Hey, it's not an option. So put an end to those ideas right now." He snatched her wrists, yanking her hands back. "Your future is not negotiable, not for my sorry-ass existence. You can't change who I am."

"But it's not who you are," she insisted, pulling away from his grasp, her fingers weaving through the mane of hair. "And you've no idea how much faith I have in you."

"Mia, you have to recognize the limitations, what I can promise and what I can't. I won't just up and leave, steal away in the middle of the night. But what we have is day-to-day; not because of what I feel or don't feel for you. That's not the issue . . ." He stopped, dangling perilously close to the words she wanted to hear. "But anything else is just that, a fantasy." Her gaze dropped to the floor and she backed away. He came right after her, dragging her chin up, forcing her to look. "And I know out of all the things you've heard me say in the past few hours, it's the past few weeks that hurt the most. But I will not promise anything I can't follow through on." She blinked hard, but a single tear got away and he caught it with his fingertips. "Damn it, if this is what I'm doing to you maybe it would be better if I just left."

Life-on-the-run fantasies and forever commitments, it wasn't what he needed to hear. He was right; his future wouldn't include landing a high-tech job or moving into an apartment with a view. It was about surviving to the next moment, with or without her. "I just want us to have a chance, Flynn. A chance to be together without you looking over your shoulder or someone making crazy accusations."

"I'd like that too. I'm just not sure how to get it."

"Well, I can't promise the future any more than you can." *But I can certainly hope for it.* "I'll be right here, from now until next June. I'm comfortable with things exactly how they are and I'm not asking for anything else. Stay with me, for now."

His staid blue eyes traveled her anxious face, his hand tucking a stray lock of hair behind her ear. A contemplative gulp echoed through the quiet apartment. "And what happens when June finally comes? And it will, Mia. Don't kid yourself. You're only borrowing a future."

She smiled at the glimmer of optimism. He was considering it. "Maybe by then we'll be able to figure something else out. Maybe by then you'll be so in love with me, you won't want to leave." It was a gauntlet of a statement, tossed straight from her heart in front of him.

"I haven't wanted to leave since the moment I first saw you."

There's a goal. Maybe I can get you to say it, tell me you love me before June. Mia reached up and pulled him into a long kiss that he didn't fight, sealing the precarious deal they'd just made. She felt him give in, felt the argument drain from his body as his hands traced the curve of her back, pulling her close. Mia melted into his embrace, needing him like air, in a way that far surpassed sex, although it appeared a perfectly logical place to start. Leaning hard into his body she roamed every tight muscle that tempted her. As he kissed her again, his hands flirted with the dance that came next, but he kept stopping, as if suddenly unsure of the steps. Then Mia remembered the hotel. "Please don't stop."

"It's just that . . . I figured I blew it, for good. I can't believe you still want . . ."

"Flynn . . ."

"Yeah," he murmured between the hard kisses that were plainly picking up the slack for the rest of his desire.

"Let me spell it out for you. We seem to have a body language issue. The real reason I want you to stay, what I'm really after . . ."

"Yeah?" He kissed her again, his hands easing from the self-imposed time-out, slipping beneath her shirt.

"It's my plan to use you for sex."

He stopped, staring willfully into her face and smiling. "Damn, why didn't you just say so?" He scooped her into his arms, exactly as he'd done outside. "Hmm, and I really thought that was my one and only chance."

Chapter 22

"Your hair. You cut it," Flynn said, gazing over her as it feathered around the mountain of pillows.

"Girl thing, part of life and death reflection. It usually involves retail therapy and a makeover. Too short?"

Tossing the pillows onto the floor, one by one, he answered, "It's fine, but I like it long."

"Hang around, it'll grow."

His mouth curved into hers, his body wanting to erase the doubts, to reclaim every inch of her that he'd hurt, inside and out. "Even with everything that's happened, the worst part was thinking about the last time we were together, at the hotel. About what I almost did. That would have been your last memory of us."

She put her fingers to his lips. "But it didn't happen. And I've already forgotten about it."

He smiled back, having finished with the pillows, busily removing each piece of clothing they both wore. "Part of retail therapy?" Flynn popped open the buttons on the pink blouse, his mouth following the lacy edges of the paler pink bra.

"You noticed. I'm impressed."

He liked the bra, the way it barely covered her, yet pushed her breasts together creating an inviting valley of flesh to travel. Sitting up over her, he left it on for now, caressing a body that could not have been clearer in his mind. "This isn't going to be anything like that. You understand, don't you? Never again, Mia. How you don't have a million little doubts, I can't figure."

"I have more than a little faith in you. This is what faith is, Flynn. Trust without proof. Is it so hard to be the recipient? But I will tell you one thing," she said, her eyes going wide, her fingers gripping his shoulders. "If you don't kiss me, like, right now, you will make me cry."

"Well, we can't have that, can we?" It washed over him. That implausible sense of peace Mia brought. Flynn couldn't get enough. She couldn't right the past, but for the first time in a hellish eternity, the future didn't seem doomed. Mia was as permanent and burned into him as any wrong he had ever done. Inside his head was a bright hypnotic vision, every part of her captured and bound to his soul. Not only the brilliant doll's eyes, but the tiny freckle-covered nose, the body he couldn't stop reaching for, and the scent of her, powdery soft, intoxicating. The way her skin felt next to his, clean and untainted. His mind could render each slim curve, knowing how she moved when his hands were on her. She soothed his ravaged mind, making him hunger for the life he had disavowed. Mia was salvation after a lonely, hard road, harder women, and a guilt that he suspected would only die with him. She was worth anything. He was beginning to think—no, he was sure he could live off it for years. Flynn sank back into her lips, soaking in the uninhibited growl of rapture from her throat. Mia's arms were around him, holding on tighter than usual. It was fine; she could hold on tighter if she needed. He wanted to lose himself in her faith. Flynn rolled over, pulling her on top of him, but thoughts of an uncertain future seeped between the cracks of what they shared. *What the hell am I doing? Staying is only going to make it worse. I should leave, go now. She's so in love, she doesn't know what she's doing. Who's in love with who? Idiot.*

Mia loomed over him, her hair tumbling every which way, running her hands hard over his chest, kissing skin that had earned nothing but sweat and grime for years. Eyes narrowed, she looked at him as though she were a sleek, graceful cat, ready to pounce. Her voice was a smoky tether of enticement. "Whatever you're thinking, stop. This is the only place you need to be. I'm very selfish that way. I want all of you. Your complete attention."

"Believe me, Mia, you're all I'm thinking about."

"Hmm, faith only goes so far. Prove it," she challenged, arching an eyebrow.

That much I can prove to you. In one deft movement she was under him again. He wanted it like this, to show her that the man she so blindly trusted could be what she wanted—at least here. Flynn took his time, making sure there was an equal sharing of skin, not really thinking about the act itself. *That* was the mark he wanted to leave. But each time he strayed from her line of vision, Mia pulled him back. It was as if seeing his face, looking into his eyes, was more important than any amount of foreplay. As he tried to move once again toward things that he knew would make her gasp with pleasure, she jerked away. Flynn saw the boldness fade from her eyes as she retreated to the top of the bed, pulling her knees close to her body. He finally got the message.

"I will not disappear. I promised you that much from the beginning." She nodded, but it was with uncertainty and distrust. Incredible, that she could accept his dark past, his actions that lacked a soul, yet was unwilling to believe a simple promise that he wouldn't walk out on her. She said nothing, having gathered the sheet up tight around her in an almost defensive gesture. Flynn gently pried her fingers open, releasing a fistful of flowered jersey knit. He threw it and the matching comforter to the floor, his own sweeping defensive gesture. There was nothing to cover her but him, his body a heated blanket of reassurance. "I will not vanish. That will never happen. You'll know what I'm thinking, no matter what." He left it at that, though he wanted to finish the sentence, to remind her that a promise not to vanish was not the same thing as staying forever. He couldn't do it.

The sun had gone down and Mia snapped on the light. "I need . . . I need to see your face." Her hands went to the beard, reaching for the skin beneath. Hearing the frustration in her voice, Flynn's mouth moved over hers, kissing her hard. The words were almost a whimper, her fingers digging into his back. The hours before weren't meant to be a tease; he just needed it to be the forever he couldn't give her. Flynn finally gave in to his desire. Mia looked up into his face, whispering, "Please . . ." He reached to the nightstand drawer, knowing where he'd stashed a few condoms.

Mia grabbed his hand. "No, I don't want it. I don't want anything between us."

"That's not smart, and you know it. Why?"

"Just this once. I need it, like I need to feel you breathe."

He guessed the why. He'd made such a point of being willing to go without at the hotel. If it was okay when he was such a bastard, why not when it meant so much more? Flynn didn't answer, but his hand dropped away from the drawer. Mia's eyes were focused, locked onto his. She traced her fingers delicately over his mouth as he kissed them one by one. Her hands gripped his body as he drove himself inside her, harder than he knew he should. Flynn felt her entire body tense, the rush break over her, surprising him when she came right away, crying out so loudly he barely managed to stay in control. But he needed it to last. He whispered huskily in her ear, "If I'd known that would be the effect, Mia, we would have done this a long time ago."

He caught a glimpse of a smile as she shyly buried her head in the crook of his neck. It was supposed to be slow and tender all the way. That was his intention. But after that she wanted no part of storybook lovemaking. Mia wanted everything he had. Slightly insatiable, she could literally wear him out. She amazed him. From the moment she crossed that downtown street, Flynn's image of Mia was someone small and delicate, easily handled. She had proved him wrong over and over—in and out of bed. Sex was just the first place she chose to show that steely underlying will. He wished to God that he could be there when she unleashed it on the world.

Not long after, the throaty words of encouragement were hers, whispering to him as he finally gave in, unable to control a writhing tremor that invaded his tarnished soul. That power she didn't even know she had, it was exotic and dangerous.

Mia combed her fingers through the mane of hair that had fallen free as she purred in his ear, still pressing tiny kisses to his face. He wanted to say something, forcing back the obvious, but his mind had drifted away from the erotic moment to something outrageous and sublime. For a split second, he saw tiny fingers and toes, Mia beaming over something no one could take away from her. Then like any real apparition it vanished as quickly as it appeared, gone. Flynn rolled away from her and sat up on the edge of the bed, reeling from the uninvited reverie.

"What's the matter? Are you mad that we did that?" Mia asked, leaning over, kissing his shoulder.

"No, I'm not mad. But it can't happen again, you understand that, Mia. You understand why?" He felt her head nod against his shoulder. Flynn reached to the floor and passed the sheet back to her. "I'll, um, I'll be right back." *I'll be right back, Mia, as soon as I figure out what the hell I'm supposed to do with that mental picture.* And in the wake of a fleeting image came his fate. The real price Flynn would pay for Alena's death and the life he would never have.

An hour later things had settled into a sweet lull, Flynn stealing comfort from the here and now. Mia was talking a blue streak, as he lazily revisited various parts of her sheet-covered body. The radio had turned on at some point. She was humming softly, having snatched his watch off the nightstand, twirling the metal band around her fingers. "Flynn, stop! That tickles," she playfully commanded, pulling the sheet off his head. "Come up here and talk to me."

"We've been talking nonstop for almost an hour," he said, sliding up next to her, pulling her into his arms.

"No, I've been talking. Your mouth has been preoccupied."

"Well, I figured if you're using me for sex, I'd better earn my keep."

"Oh, you will, I have no doubt. Do you know this song?"

He listened for a moment. The only sound he'd been hearing was passionate giggles mixed with Mia-driven chatter. "Oh, it's Gregg Allman. 'I'm No Angel,' I think. That's kinda funny. Remember I told you, his band, that's what I used to listen to under the covers when I was a kid."

"Well, isn't that a sign? You're still listening under the covers. The song is completely, totally you."

It made him laugh. "Hmm, really? I thought my theme song would have been more along the lines of 'Jailhouse Rock' or 'Back on the Chain Gang.'"

* *

From that moment forward, Mia set out on her own high-stakes mission. She was determined to keep Flynn focused on the here and now, as he clearly had issues with the past and future. She threw out the calendar, cancelled newspaper subscriptions and never spoke of plans beyond the current week. As his focus shifted, the nightmares eased, only making one more memorable visit. She thought maybe a passing thunderstorm had triggered it. Mia woke with a start, relieved to find him a few minutes later. He was fighting hard to keep a bad dream from turning into a raging night terror. The parking lot was under siege. Flynn stormed back and forth like the soldier he simply wasn't anymore. At three in the morning she stood in the doorway with a blanket wrapped around her, watching him. Forty degrees in a cold rain, barefoot, bare-chested, and still he couldn't stop sweating. Mia lit a joint and coaxed him back inside with it. As she towel-dried his mane of hair, he sucked in drag after drag, shivering so violently it made her heart ache for him. She'd witnessed two nightmares now. They were disturbing and frightening, but each time, he moved farther away, not toward her. She understood that it wasn't an alibi; it wasn't proof of anything except the awesome guilt with which he lived.

It was the normal things, the repetitive things, that Mia cherished the most. They were everyday things that in other relationships spelled boredom or monotony. Mia couldn't get enough, committing them to memory, just in case. Small moments were bound to her heart as if pressed between the pages of a thick book of memories. Silly things, like he always made the coffee too strong. She never could tell him, instead dumping in five scoops of sugar to counteract it. Crossword puzzles were a snapshot of his mind; Flynn filled in the blanks faster than Mia could absorb the clues. She was fascinated to find that he was a voracious reader, devouring novels, how-to books, cereal boxes. And it didn't stop there, as he admitted to a much different reason for frequenting those college campuses. "Pick a big lecture hall where the professor doesn't know one student from another," he revealed. "You can learn anything." Highly resourceful, he'd managed to tailor a life on the run to include a college education.

He unknowingly flattered her by remembering the most insignificant details—the oil in her car needed changing, she hated not only the taste but the smell and color of olives, and that Thanksgiving was her favorite holiday. And while he loved to watch her draw or paint, he was a one-man cheering section for those out-of-step designs. He'd compliment Mia's everyday efforts, but fervidly encourage ideas that hadn't yet found a rhythm. It made an indelible impression, making her believe that perseverance and passion would one day be in perfect tune.

Conversations, even silent ones, ignited possibilities. With Flynn's input, what-if thoughts found structure and shape. Inspiration came at the oddest times, from the unlikeliest of places. Places Mia would have never ventured to without him. A weekend road trip to the North Georgia mountains was among the most poignant. A defunct gem mine was a curious backdrop, set into the red and gold of October trees. They followed a trail and found an old rock bed, still lined with a rainbow of embedded stone. The colors were magnificent against the fall sky. Mia commented on their brilliance, saying something about marrying the natural elements with the simplicity of her designs. It was too bad, she quickly concluded, that mining semiprecious stone was counterproductive, not to mention costly. He didn't reply. But she did have to tug him by the hand as he stood, mesmerized by the sight.

They ended up spending the night there, the jewel tone setting also inspiring a keen sexual energy. Under a blanket of stars they made love until the campfire was nothing but a glowing ember. While Mia was surprised to find Flynn up and moving the next morning, she was less taken aback by her own achy body. The earthy surroundings were decidedly more comfortable when enhanced by moonlight and his heated body. But her sore muscles were forgotten as she glanced toward the fire's spent ashes. Next to her was a riverbed of color, a collection of what appeared to be motley stone. While mining it himself, after a night of exhaustive sex, didn't seem beyond him, she did realize that it was crushed glass. "Will that work like the stone?" he asked. "Plus it's recyclable, right?" Through the morning light, Mia blinked up at him, utterly amazed. There wasn't much he could have done to pass the hours before; but like only Flynn could, he managed.

Over time he even found a way to converse with Roxanne, albeit on a rudimentary level. There was a passive grunt when coming or going, a communicative glare as they crossed paths in the kitchen. Mia did have one fond recollection, fleeting and fast though it was, when the two arch rivals did connect. On a dreary Saturday afternoon, sitting at the dining table layered with textbooks, notebooks, and two calculators, Roxanne appeared oddly stumped. Meanwhile, Mia sat on the floor in the middle of the room reworking the design her professor had obliterated months before. Flynn's lanky body was sprawled across the sofa, his nose in a copy of *Car and Driver*, always opting for easy reading when Roxanne was around. After several exasperated gasps, a flying pencil and the final straw—a textbook, sailing past his head—he closed the magazine and sat up.

"What's the problem, Roxanne?"

"Oh, like you could help. Go back to deciding if motor oil should be a compound word."

Mia glanced up, suffering her own frustrations over the lack of aesthetics inherent to reclaimed concrete. She didn't say anything. By then she had learned to let them work it out on their own, unless bloodshed seemed imminent. He approached, his hands stuffed in his pockets, and peered over her shoulder. "Really, I'll take a look if you want."

Roxanne tossed him a wild-eyed glare, as if he'd suggested they take the problem into her bedroom. Mia snickered at the prospect, burrowing further into her work. "Ha! It's complicated, Flynn, a little beyond greater than or less than. My study partner and I have been trying to solve it. What makes you think you can do it?" He shrugged, not about to defend the offer. "Fine, have a look. I'm guessing your working knowledge of differential equations is, um, limited." She thrust her notebook forward, tapping her fingers on the tabletop.

Mia watched in silent curiosity, her eyes darting between her design board and the two of them. It was more dramatic than two warring nations agreeing to peace talks. Flynn studied the problem and picked up the pencil, calculating something. His brow furrowed as he refigured the problem, snapping the point against the answer. "Here."

"Here, what?" she said, giving a skeptical glance over his hand.

"In this problem the boundaries are between one and four. You were integrating the numbers wrong, zero through four—once you start down that road, you'll never get it. It's one through four, see?"

Roxanne snatched the notebook away, furiously punching numbers into the calculator. She pounded at the clear button, repeating the equation. "It's right. How did you do that?"

"Lucky guess," he said, returning to his position on the sofa. "Right."

"Roxanne, don't you have something to say?" Mia asked, concentrating on her project.

"Oh, yeah. I guess, um, thanks," she said, her eyes still curiously trained on Flynn.

"Don't mention it." He flipped the magazine open and things faded back to normal.

After Flynn had left that night, Roxanne poked her head inside Mia's bedroom. "Michael Wells and I worked that problem for days—neither of us could get it. First those chemical compounds, now the math. He's very smart. Why doesn't he use it to do something with his life—why doesn't he want anyone to know?"

With closed eyes, from the brink of the dream she wanted, Mia murmured, "Not everybody has to scream to the world what they're all about. He's got other things on his mind."

The Widow Montgomery, as Mia fondly referred to her mother, was an intermittent disruption, generally relegated to weekend phone calls. Most conversations gravitated back to her social calendar and what she perceived to be her daughter's nonconformist pursuits, namely what defined good interior design. She just didn't get it. After a time, Mia cut the calls short or avoided them completely. Clarice Montgomery would never appreciate an interior that didn't involve a high-gloss cherry finish or pinch pleated drapes. She hadn't seen her mother since spring break, since before Flynn. Thankfully she'd been preoccupied dating a defense attorney against whom her father had often faced off. Mia could imagine how that bit of news would sit with Lincoln Montgomery's sense of symmetry. No doubt her father would see it as sleeping with the enemy. Then she realized how it might apply to her as well. Her mother was adamant, insisting Mia fly home for Christmas, wanting to know what possible excuse she could have not to. In all those months, she never said a word about Flynn. As nonconformist pursuits went—well, even Mia had to admit that Flynn made innovative interior design seem tame.

There was no way out of it, and worse, Mia knew she would have to go alone. She couldn't consider asking him; airplanes meant security checks and proof of identification. It was nearly equal to the risk of turning her mother loose on him. She wouldn't allow it. Mia left Flynn for five dismal days in December, making polite conversation with the man who was obviously being groomed to be her mother's replacement husband. Listening to him say he was thinking of switching sides, taking a run at the DA's office, Mia was doubly glad Flynn wasn't there. But it did make her think. What would her father have said about Flynn? Would he have only seen the fugitive, or would he have considered the whole story? The probable answer seemed grim enough. It didn't matter; Mia had made this choice on her own and with no regrets. Lying awake alone on Christmas Eve and Christmas Day night, she promised herself that next Christmas would be different.

The days apart agitated nagging worries, rubbing raw like a blister. A million horrid things could happen in five days, and she couldn't do a damn thing about a single one. Things like Flynn getting busted for that medicinal dime bag he carried. Not so bad until they fingerprinted him. No doubt the state of Georgia had its own zealous lot of DAs; they'd take him away before she ever made it back. Smothering that scenario, a different fear cropped up as her flight landed. Airplanes, lunch dates, meet me at the mall at two—would he be there? Or would he decide to call in the marker early on that borrowed future? The time away was too costly. Winter didn't last long in Georgia. Spring was a heartbeat away, then would come June.

It was all momentarily forgotten as she stepped from the gate. He was waiting. That day it was all fine. Flynn was very much there, greeting her with a tremendous kiss, grabbing her up in a hug so warm and full that the worry melted away. Before letting go, he whispered in her ear that it felt longer than all the days he'd spent in prison. As she held tight to his arm they made their way through the bustling airport to the parking lot. A small package wrapped in the prettiest Christmas paper she'd ever seen lay on the front seat of her car. "For me?" She gently unwrapped it with every intention of keeping the paper. Inside the velvet box was an antique silver cross with filigreed edges. Her mouth dropped open. "I . . . You're not going to believe . . . "

"You don't like it."

"Oh, no, no, I love it. It's just that . . . Well, here." She reached into her purse and handed him a similarly shaped gift. He tore off the paper, opening a slightly larger, black velvet box. The smile was instant. Flynn pulled it out and held it up for her to fasten around his neck. She did so, smoothing the handsome cross down around his chest. "A sign of faith," she murmured, falling into his arms.

Chapter 23

After he vanished it was moments like that to which Mia held tightest, eventually taking a reflective inventory of what Flynn did leave behind. When the initial shock didn't kill her, which took some realization, Mia compiled a tidy checklist. She thought it might be a route to comfort, a Band-Aid over a deep gash. She should have known better. Even the memory of such a complex man required a learning curve. And Mia soon discovered that everyday life best demonstrated his impact. Hers for the taking, time revealed an amazing cache of resolve. Mia latched on to that steely will, finding a starting point—or at least a way out of bed. She thought it was a monumental accomplishment, but it hardly stopped there. Flynn hadn't just influenced Mia; he'd changed her in every imaginable way. And while the hurt and disappointment were excruciating, Mia found that she much preferred the *woman* who now looked back in the mirror. So it was something like that, along with a shiny coat of armor and lipstick, which she hesitantly donned upon venturing into a world that no longer included his physical presence.

It was a rite of passage. The graduates who'd earned a degree in Textile Applications were invited to display their senior thesis at an on-campus gallery. If you managed to make it through the program, which was significantly more difficult than someone like Roxanne might believe, there was the prospect of a big-name furniture manufacturer or mid-level design house scooping you up. It was unnerving, the heated competition for fresh-out-of-college grunt work. Along with everyone else, Mia was considering it. There was the Atlanta internship—hers if she wanted it, but it would barely pay the electric bill. The idea had more appeal when it included Flynn. Now she'd have to go it alone, supplementing a meager paycheck with what was left of her trust fund. It didn't seem like a wise choice. The balance of the trust fund was a nest egg. For what, she wasn't exactly sure. Perhaps a life that didn't include a significant other; she felt prepared for as much. Then again, the money could back a design studio of her own. But that was an unlikely scenario. Mia's ideas about what she wanted to design didn't seem to mesh too well with the industry's stamp of success.

As she hurried into the gallery on a steamy June morning, she was having trouble negotiating the high heels she'd swiped from Roxanne's closet. She figured if her design didn't impress anyone, perhaps she'd better. Mia stuttered along feeling oddly dressed and out of place. She glanced left and right, seeing elaborate three-dimensional mock-ups, postmodern fare, and themed rooms. They ranged from the glitz of the Taj Mahal, complete with working fountains, to chic urban lofts involving more metal rails than a train track. Her design was not among them. A flutter of nerves eased when she saw familiar faces, other students who'd made it through the program and some she'd socialized with in the years before. While her work didn't reflect theirs, she'd always found them to be a fun crowd.

A few moments later Mia was absorbed by the small talk. She was distracted for a time, dabbling in topics that didn't remind her of Flynn. Memories, freshman through junior year, that didn't include him. Reacquainting herself with the crowd while drinking watery punch, she was amused by the mindless chatter. During the past year, socializing with a group had fallen to the wayside. There had been no need to put Flynn in a situation where someone might look twice or ask an unnecessary question. Roxanne instigated enough issues on that front. Mia never thought of it as sacrifice and had no regrets. Even so, her close friends were something that always mattered to Flynn. He'd gone out of his way to keep them in her life, and now she understood why. Every so often he'd insist that Mia spend an evening with her usual crowd—Roxanne, Lanie, Sara, a few others. She'd begrudgingly agree, unable to get back to him and the cottage fast enough. The lost time dug at her now. Mia glanced around a room filled with perfectly nice people, none of whom she'd ever see again. She'd swap them all in a heartbeat for one more day with Flynn. The improbable fantasy faded as Mia took a cleansing breath. She crumpled a napkin and tossed it into an overflowing trashcan. She was stuck in reality. There was no cottage, no one to rush back to.

"Mia . . . hello? Earth to Mia . . ."

She looked up, startled to find Charlie Jewel staring at her. He waved a white plastic cup like a peace offering. "Charlie," she said, trying to focus. "I didn't know you were here."

"Well, you're definitely not," he said, grinning. "I've asked twice what your plans are. You're still not trying to avoid me, are you?" She smiled, raising a brow. Now there was a memory she'd rather forget. Charlie Jewel was the boy from Alpharetta. The boy she'd lost her virginity to freshman year, the one whose name she couldn't recall the next morning. "If I wasn't looking at that pretty face, I'd swear you weren't in the same room."

"Not the same room, not the same girl . . . not even the same universe," she mumbled, forcing down the lump in her throat.

"Mia, are you okay?"

"Yeah, sure. It's a little warm in here, that's all."

He plucked at his damp polo, agreeing. "I hate to say it, but I think they've cut the air off—maybe with us graduating the university's fallen on tough times."

"Maybe so," Mia said, sipping the rest of her punch. A good sense of humor and a lightning grin; she could see how that silly girl had fallen for it.

"Take a walk with me. I saw your project. It's over there," he said, pointing to an obscure corner of the room.

She was amazed that Charlie Jewel knew her major, never mind where her project was located. Not having seen her final grade, Mia wasn't sure she wanted company on the reveal. "You know, Charlie, I'm not feeling particularly social." Since their infamous one-night-stand they'd barely had a conversation—including the morning she'd woken up in his dorm room. Since Flynn, Charlie Jewel hadn't done more than smile politely passing by on campus.

"Come on, take a quick walk with me. I won't bite," he said, flashing that grin. "Promise."

She followed tentatively, unable to imagine what he was up to. It became clear a few steps later. Charlie Jewel didn't intend to gush over her outstanding achievement. Having revamped her Interiors Concepts project, which had gone from a flat design board to a 3-D model, Mia had higher hopes for a good grade. Tossing back her head, she grimaced at Professor Grinley's burning-red B-. Even Flynn agreed that the changes were substantial when he loaded it into her car the day he vanished. She'd revamped the entire project, focusing on the whole design rather than individual parts. Everything centered on energy, orientation of flow, and a thoughtful selection of materials. While the surrounding designs were wow-factor inspired, fringe-covered dog and pony shows, Mia's model relied on a minimization of impact to the footprint. It was, in fact, the physical opposite of everything else in the gallery. "And your point is . . ." she said, wondering if he was going to make a grading comparison to their drunken tryst.

"My aunt, well, actually she's my great aunt from Virginia; she wanted to come to the gallery. She's the one who noticed your design." He stopped, his gaze trailing over Mia's simplistic model. From the vague look on his face, it was clear that he didn't get it either. "Anyway, I told her that I, um, *knew you*."

"I'm flattered," she replied flatly. She supposed it was nice to have someone notice, even if it was only Charlie Jewel's great aunt from Virginia. "I'm glad she liked it."

"She said she'd love to meet the girl who was ballsy enough to pull it off." Mia's eyes widened along with his grin. "You have to know my aunt. She's, um, colorful, not exactly your regular relative."

"Like I said, I'm flattered." Mia looked back toward the thinning crowd. Chatty conversation with Charlie Jewel had its limits. "Thanks for telling me. It's encouraging," she said, though it really wasn't.

"That's not all," he said, grasping her arm as she tried to walk away. She pulled it back. It only required a firm, confident look—the one she'd grown into—informing him that contact of any kind was out of bounds. He got that message, stuffing his hands into his pockets, stepping back. "Listen, Mia, there's something else I've been wanting to say. What happened between us—"

"Nothing happened between us," she said calmly, because really, nothing had. Nothing that couldn't be condensed into a sex education pamphlet. "It was a long time ago, and it could have turned out worse."

"I suppose," he said. "But it might have turned out better if I'd been more, um, considerate." He had a point, and she allowed him the moment of remorse. It really wasn't his fault that she'd been immature, drunk, and plain stupid. "Look, it's an awkward thing to talk about. But I didn't want you to leave school feeling as if—"

"Don't beat yourself up over it. It was bad judgment, one too many Jell-O shots. It's an anecdote I'll use to forewarn my own kids someday." Mia closed her eyes, snickering. *Kids, what kids? There won't be any children, not without Flynn.*

A colorful voice moved hastily toward them, rescuing Mia from both the conversation and her thoughts. "Charlie Jewel, there you are! I thought you'd gotten thoroughly bored and gone off to the pub without me."

"Would I do that, Aunt Gi?" Mia shot him a sideways glance, recalling that Charlie Jewel would do most anything for a beer, including ditching his great aunt. "Here she is. This is Mia, the girl you wanted to meet."

Turning toward layers of bright hues, it was difficult to focus on her face at first, the word *gypsy* jumping to mind. Her hair was the color of flames. It was only trumped by her attire, which was complemented by a layer of jewelry. It took Mia a moment to put it all together. First to grasp that it wasn't gaudy, but rather an artsy and original ensemble, and second for her to realize that she recognized the woman. "You're . . . you're Gisele DeVrie," she said, the words stumbling from her mouth as if she were reading from a first grade primer.

She smiled at Mia, leaning in, the smell of perfume sharing an equal presence. "In some circles, yes. In this room I'd rather be Aunt Gigi. Thought I'd sneak in and out, have a peek at what's about to be unleashed onto the design world, but damn if I didn't get caught. I just spent the last ten minutes ensuring two of your overeager classmates that they'd make something of themselves. Redecorating Barbie's dream house—maybe," she whispered with a smile.

Mia nodded, wide-eyed and speechless. Gisele DeVrie. It was like having the Queen of England come to your backyard tea party. She was a legend: eccentric, definitive, inspiring—the Paris runway of interior design, spotting trends a mile before industry insiders. And the only thing Mia could do in the presence of greatness was toss a look of disbelief at Charlie Jewel, mumbling, "You didn't tell me your great aunt from Virginia was Gisele DeVrie."

He shrugged. "Well, she's not. To me she's just Aunt Gigi." Not surprising. Along with Charlie's blinding grin and sense of humor was a layer of denseness. Clearly she was his aunt by marriage.

"So you're Mia Montgomery. This is your project?" she said, waving her hand over the display like a wand. Looking at the B- and the professor's mediocre review, Mia guessed the expert designer wanted to make it disappear.

"Well . . ." she began. Mia tried to take advantage of the high heels, forced her posture tall and prepared to stick up for her effort. "It, um, it is . . . mine, all mine," she squeaked out. Then she just waited. Maybe Gisele DeVrie just needed a good belly laugh. Perhaps she wanted to suggest an alternative occupation, one that didn't involve any thought. But she appeared to be waiting for more, so Mia began again. "The basis of the design is the environment and the user, to integrate sustainable resources, artistic components, natural light, and reclaimed lumber to—"

"I know what it is, dear," she said, smiling. "Your material source for that artwork?" she asked, pointing to the intricate mosaic displayed next to the model.

"Soda and beer bottles mostly." She glanced at Charlie, who was examining the accompanying artwork with renewed interest. Flynn had convinced her to include the mosaic. Mia worried that it would be viewed as frivolous art, but he insisted that it brought a whole other dimension to the project. "All recycled goods. There's a separate bin at the landfill for colored glass. They, um, they let me pick through it," Mia said, nervously glancing at her fingernails, inspecting for dirt. "The environment and art, I wanted to show how the two things could work in unison, natural resources in step with reclaimed resources, like the glass. I just think . . . I think it should all connect: the user, the resources, the benefit."

"And you did the design and the artwork yourself?"

"The mosaic, yes, absolutely, except the adhesive. I wanted to find something nontoxic, but I haven't come up with anything yet. It's one of the components I'm still working on—not just zero impact, but a positive gain. I believe you can achieve both. It's kind of an untouched area in interior design," she said, wishing she'd prepared cue cards.

Gisele was nodding now, pulling her bifocal spectacles down to the point of her nose. "Very intriguing," she murmured, examining the project closely. Her steady gaze panned to Mia. "The originality is brilliant and the art brings it to a new level. It deviates from anything we're seeing right now, the way you've simplified the composition to make energy use paramount, not secondary. This uncommon blend of artistry and environmental impact—surely someone's pointed that out to you?"

Assuming she didn't mean Flynn, Mia shook her head. "Not really. Professor Grinley hasn't thought much of my work—as you can gather from the grade."

Gisele DeVrie looked squarely at Mia. "Oh, don't listen to him, dear. Haskell Grinley's an old-school pompous ass." Mia's eyes widened, amazed. Partly because of the huge compliment, and partly because it was what Flynn had said—more or less. "Hmm, perhaps I shouldn't be so forthright in my opinion. And to be perfectly honest, that design is so Tomorrowland . . . Well, it seems to me that you're marrying ideas—art, the environment, and impact—that won't come to fruition for some time, maybe another decade. But eventually . . ." Removing her glasses, she tapped the frame against her teeth, giving Mia a more inquisitive look than she'd given the design. "Can you do standard interior design with this kind of passion, enough to earn your keep?"

Biting her lip, Mia thought there was a definite right and wrong answer to that question. She answered truthfully, suspecting there was no hedging with Gisele DeVrie. "Everyday interior design isn't my passion—but yes, of course I'm capable." There was a burst of confidence; she even felt comfortable in those high heels. She *was* more than capable of producing work that would appeal to the masses. Up until then, she simply hadn't seen the need.

Snapping the glasses back onto her face, Gisele DeVrie continued to look Mia over. "And sixty-hour work weeks, how do you feel about those? Saturday night out . . . girlfriend, boyfriend, whatever your cup of tea, you won't have time for it."

You left out fugitive on the run. "I'm fine with that. In fact, I'd like nothing more than to focus on my career."

"We'll get to the career. For now just be a sponge. There are a thousand steps, dear." Mia's brow crinkled at the familiar words—Flynn's words. "You'll spend half your time at my design studio, half in the field—traveling, trade shows, dirty warehouses, impossible clients—learning every inch of interior design that has nothing to do with passion or creativity. That will be difficult for someone like you. Generally it's the other way around, people trained in textbook design fighting for their next inspiration. Are you game, Mia?"

"Yes! Absolutely. I'll be there Monday, tomorrow, yesterday," Mia said, feeling the spark of her out-of-step designs catch. It was an ember that would not have existed without Flynn, and it was empowering. Mia was suddenly willing to design a Vegas lounge—strobe light included—if it meant a chance to work with Gisele DeVrie.

"No need to rush. I won't be back in the office for another week. Just give my assistant a call; he tends to the everyday matters." Mia nodded, her heart pounding. "Take a moment to pack a bag and take a good look around. Life is about to change." Tucking a business card into Mia's hand, she motioned to her nephew, instructing him to follow.

Mia was on a roller coaster moving backward. There was a sudden thrill, a steep climb she couldn't see, not even a guess. She wanted to scream with excitement. The expectation was exhilarating, her stomach rolling on the hairpin turn she'd just taken. It was beyond huge. And, perhaps, the awkward answer to a difficult prayer. Mia left the gallery, gaining momentum with every step, creeping toward a beginning. There was that. And the melancholy prospect of riding a roller coaster alone.

* *

Like snow in June, unexpected events continued to blanket those last days in Athens. Roxanne's reaction to Flynn's disappearance had been oddly subdued. She didn't damn him to hell with her convoluted theories or even offer an "I told you so." But Mia was wary, knowing her silence was temporary at best.

They were on their way to an engagement party of all things.

It seemed the Odyssey had been full of cupid's arrows the night Mia and Flynn met. Lanie and the frat boy she danced with had decided on a diamond instead of desertion to typify their union. It only caused a moderate gush of pea-green envy. Though she had little desire to attend, Mia thought it selfish to let her loss overshadow a friend's happiness. Besides, Roxanne, who had no use for romantic ritual, insisted they go. It would be a chance to say good-bye, to wish everyone well. Mia had to agree, although it seemed that her relationship with Roxanne would be safe. It turned out that Georgetown School of Medicine and Gisele DeVrie's design studio were less than twenty miles apart. "Imagine that," Mia had murmured as Roxanne smiled with delight.

Mia drove to the engagement party, a back road weaving past the seedy motel where Flynn spent his first night in Athens. She made a tiny reference and a simple conversation flipped fast, like a high-speed collision. The remark led to Roxanne's tainted recollection of that same night. It spiraled from there, with Mia vehemently defending him and Roxanne countering. It escalated until she struck a final nerve, equating Flynn to something just below flesh-eating bacteria. "Because with that," Roxanne insisted, "those dead girls might have stood a chance. Had that been their fate, instead of someone like him, there might have been an antidote."

Like a missile, the car rocketed from a winding curve onto a soft embankment, with Roxanne clinging tight to the dashboard. "Have you lost your mind? What are you doing?"

"Get out!" Mia demanded.

"What?" Even in the fading summer light, Mia could see the confusion on Roxanne's face. "We're in the middle of nowhere."

"I don't care!" She reached down and unbuckled Roxanne's seatbelt. "Get out of my car. Get out of my life."

"Come on, Mia, you don't mean that."

"Don't I?" she challenged, firm and fixated.

"Be serious. I'm not getting out here. Forget the party, it was a bad idea. Let's go home. I think I have a Valium in the medicine cabinet." She looked straight ahead, waiting for Mia to comply. Instead, she thrust the car into park, stretched past Roxanne, and popped open her door. Roxanne turned back, appalled. It didn't matter. She no longer needed a surrogate parent, or led a life that required Roxanne's judgmental eye. "Lord have mercy," she squawked, "I'm wearing three-inch heels! It's a cow pasture out there. Do you know what's in a cow pasture?" Mia cocked a brow, picturing Roxanne sinking fast into a pile of cow shit. "This is what I mean. See what he's done to you! The Mia I know would never behave this way," she said, finally getting off her chest what had been burning in her head. "Consider yourself lucky, Mia. Be grateful that his leaving you turned out to be the worst of it."

The argument was poised to end a friendship; Mia felt ample fire. And it would have ended had she gone with her gut. But easing back to her side of the car, shoulders pinned to the window, Mia realized how, in Roxanne's mind, abandonment was a token price to pay. She stopped, considering the *whole* story, and everything that made Roxanne who she was. Flynn's departure, while devastating, couldn't compete with Rory Burke's fate. "If only Rob had left Rory, right?" she said, her voice softer.

Roxanne turned in her seat, staring hard at Mia. "If only," she said in a whisper that lacked drawl or attitude. "I'm sorry, Mia, sorry I can't ignore the blatant similarities."

"What similarities?" she asked. "Flynn wasn't some rich boy-toy, Stanford student by day, drug dealer by night. He didn't steal me away from my family and friends. He didn't turn me on to a life that barreled down a dark tunnel."

"No, thank God he slithered out of town before anything

like that happened. And it's the part you refuse to see—drugs, dead college girls, pimping a prostitution ring—his personal flaw is irrelevant," she insisted. "It has everything to do with giving yourself to a man who roams through his life disregarding yours. That kind of recklessness, it was Rob . . . it was Flynn."

"Roxanne, you couldn't be more wrong. Rory and I—the two situations have nothing to do with one another. Yes, what Flynn did hurts—it will forever," she said, unable to find fitting words. "That's no secret. But he wasn't some random hit of LSD; I wasn't his acid casualty." It was hard to say aloud, and brutally hard for Roxanne to hear. And for the past year it had been an unspoken truth they'd teetered around. "Let me ask you something. When you visit Rory, what do you think about?"

"What do I—?" Roxanne continued to stare, looking wildly uncomfortable with the question. With her prim mouth agape, her eyes welled with tears. She looked forward into an endless pasture of simple scenery. "Well, at first I think about how things used to be. Rory's three years older; she was my motivation for everything. If Rory was smart about something, I was going to be ten times smarter—and that was hard to do," she said, an aimless smile and peaked cheekbones diverting a tear. "The truth is she *was* smarter. Of course Rory never let me know that."

Mia nodded, trying to fathom that kind of brilliance, still trying to grasp how one hit of LSD could snuff it out. "I find myself thinking about what she would have been—first a renowned surgeon, maybe later a mentor—a wife . . . somebody's mother," Roxanne said, her gaze dropping to her clenched hands. She turned toward Mia. "When I visit Rory, I let that stuff run through my head for a minute or two, then I let it go, or I'd go nuts." She shrugged. "It's pointless to focus on things that won't happen . . . her graduation from Stanford, and the

life she'll never have. Besides," she said, dense sarcasm doing its
job, soaking up the hurt, "Rory demands my complete attention. We're far too busy hot gluing macaroni to cardboard."

Mia sucked in a deep breath, her fury fading. She reached
past Roxanne and closed the car door. Rory was the reason
behind Roxanne's every thought, her drive, her need to be the
guard dog in someone else's life—and you had to factor it in.
She'd gone there once, to visit Rory, feeling privileged that Roxanne was willing to let her in so far. No one had that kind of
access to Roxanne. Having seen the academic accolades that
shrouded the Burke home, Mia was nervous as they entered
Rory's group home outside Atlanta. A woman wearing purple
pajama pants and a shirt that was inside out bounded toward
Roxanne, thrilled to see her.

Rory was beautiful, every bit as stunning as her younger
sister, but sadly possessing the mental capacity of a five-year-
old. "One day she was taking a biochemistry midterm," Roxanne had explained, "the next Rob dropped her off at the
emergency room entrance—pretty much like this." They went
into the craft room, Rory's favorite place. There Mia sat in a
chair, dumbfounded, mostly watching, sporadically—at Rory's
insistence—hot gluing the round macaroni to construction paper. "A random experiment with LSD, courtesy of Rob—who
probably hadn't peddled all his wares that week," Roxanne had
said. "It's a popular drug with some in the med-school community. But with LSD you never know what kind of bad trip
you're going to take. If it so happens that your brain's wired a
certain way, it's your last trip. And it's what happened to Rory,
thanks to him."

Mia and Roxanne skipped the engagement party that night,
neither of them able to feign happiness. They went back to the
apartment, the evening ending on a somber note. But the con-

versation continued a day or so later, the two of them agreeing
that they'd never agree on Flynn. Acquiescing as best she could,
Roxanne made Mia a promise. Since Flynn was gone, since there
was nothing to be done about it, out of respect for Mia's loss,
Roxanne would never bring him up again—not her theory, or a
man whom she was sure meant certain harm.

Chapter 24

MARYLAND

"Sitting here like this, making yourself sick, isn't going to help anyone—not even him. I swear, I thought he was the most stubborn person I'd ever met." Roxanne stood on the opposite side of the bed with Flynn between them. Her voice pulsated through Mia's cobwebby head as if it were on a loudspeaker; there was no getting away from it. Reaching across his silent body, she thrust another box of Kleenex at Mia. "You passed unreasonable two days ago. You have to go home at some point, don't you? And how are you planning to explain yourself? I know Michael's been away on business, but he's back tonight, right? From the stress level on your face, he's going to think Aaron Hough dumped you and decided to go with the design team from Walmart. You look worse than he does." As if on cue, both women's eyes trailed over Flynn, who was back on the ventilator, life being pumped into him.

The vigil had turned ugly. For three days Mia sat at Flynn's side in tense negotiations with God, bargaining with the devil in the off hours. It was too bad she was already burning in hell, she

thought; it left her little to work with in the way of sacrificial of-
ferings. She did look worse than he did, with dark circles under
bloodshot eyes and a red runny nose. She was in desperate need
of a shower. Mia had left Flynn's side only to use the bathroom.
Food was barely a consideration; she forced down a morsel or
two to keep Roxanne quiet. At some point, she'd decided to join
the vigil. Mia figured that somewhere there was a stalemate in
the offertory of souls; Flynn's hanging in the balance. Real sleep
had been an absurd notion, dozing here and there in the chair
and never letting go of Flynn's hand.

"Enough, Roxanne," Mia said in a hoarse voice that didn't
sound like her own. "You can't stop me from being here. Aren't
you getting the least bit tired of this argument? Are you sure no
one has come in asking about him? The police, maybe someone
from the DA's office? They know to tell me, right?"

Roxanne heaved a frustrated sigh as she leaned against the
wall, pounding the heel of her hand on her forehead. It was the
way the conversation had gone since she, of all people, managed
to shock Flynn back from the dead. "No, Mia, no one has come
in. I told you, the DNA test will take weeks. And yes, the desk
has strict instructions to inform you, not *if* but *when* the cops
show up looking for him. Maybe that will finally knock some
sense into you."

"I told you, I'm not worried about the DNA and those girls."
*What I'm concerned about, Roxanne, is the prison they're going to
ship him off to when he wakes up, the look of satisfaction on your
face when you find out he's a fugitive, that he confessed to killing
a woman. The microscopic chance that you—or anyone else—will
believe what really happened.* Mia sighed, scrubbing a hand over
her tired face. "I've been meaning to ask you," she said, straightening the blanket that had been straightened at least twenty
times in the last hour. "All these weeks and you still haven't told

me what you meant the night you called. You said you owed me that much. It's not something you say, Roxanne; it's not something you do. What do you owe me?"

Roxanne pushed herself off the wall, now straightening the blanket on her side of the bed. "Nothing. It's not important anymore." There was a sympathetic smile as her tone softened. "How about something to eat? Will you at least let me get you a sandwich? Cheese fries? Something?"

Mia ignored her as if she hadn't said a word. "I keep thinking, if only he would wake up—just long enough for me to say good-bye. Like you said, if I got the chance to say it this time, maybe I could let him go." Mia tipped her head to one side, her mouth turned down as she stroked Flynn's arm. She looked over the monitors that she really couldn't read, but understood enough by now to know good numbers from bad. "Yes, there is something you can get for me. Michael."

Roxanne's blue eyes bugged out of her head. "You want me to call Michael. And tell him what?"

"Tell him to come to the hospital. I'd do it myself, but I can't use my cell phone in here."

"Mia, I—exactly where would you like me to start?" she said, her arms widening at the awesome prospect. " 'Gee, Michael, I hope you won big in Vegas because your luck's just about run out here. In fact, you won't believe what your wife has waiting for you.' Better yet, why don't I just shoot him in the head when he comes through the door, save the poor guy some misery?"

"Are you finished?" Mia asked, her eyes narrowing, her hoarse voice rigid.

"Quite."

"Tell him whatever you have to, as long as he comes."

* *

Michael was on his way to the ICU; that was the text message Mia received from Roxanne before she had been paged to the ER. A five-car pileup was going to keep her occupied for some time. Maybe that alone was a token reply from God—or someone else. Mia took a few moments in the restroom and splashed cold water on her face as she made final peace with her decision. It was a grim reflection. Whatever happened to that unaffected college girl with no problems, no worries? She had been so carefree, such a silly flirt. Mia offered herself half a smile, mumbling into the mirror, "She went for a ride on a motorcycle and everything changed." A quivering breath blew from her lungs, her bangs flying up from her face. It wasn't her best moment.

She thought about putting on a little makeup. The wild-eyed, unkempt look wasn't going to help matters. Michael always did favor a neat appearance. In a halfhearted effort to look like Michael Wells's wife, Mia snatched her purse off the narrow ledge, the contents tumbling into the sink. Her hand bypassed the tube of lipstick, reaching for the leather change purse she'd carried for the past twelve years. Inside there wasn't a penny's worth of change, only a worn piece of Christmas paper. She ran her finger over the smooth edges. It was neatly preserved, folded into a small square—somewhat like the past. Well, before Flynn had turned up again.

Mia tilted her forehead against the cool glass. She was so tired, her mind drenched in exhaustion, not quite sure how she was going to get through the next few hours. Still, it had to be done right now. She was sure about everything, but worn through, dismissing visions of her own bed, thick downy comforter, and fluffy pillows. A near-perfect husband and a comfortable existence; it was a worthy temptation. She shook her head. *I can't do this anymore. It's not fair to Michael or to Flynn.*

On the way back to Flynn's room, Mia shot a pensive glance

toward the elevators. Michael wasn't there yet. She had every intention of meeting him in the privacy of the conference room and starting from there. *What's the point?* She sighed, stopping at the nurse's station. *When somebody blows your life apart, does the location really matter?*

"Excuse me, Margaret."

"Yes, Mia, what can I do for you?"

A most compassionate nurse, Mia was always pleased to find Flynn assigned to her shift. "I'm expecting my husband in a few minutes. Would you please tell him I'm in with . . . you know."

"Your husband? But I thought . . . Never mind. Of course, I'll send him right in."

The future was being coolly disregarded as the past and present prepared to get reacquainted. Mia sat; she stood; she adjusted the pillow under Flynn's head. She looked around the room at the many sketches she'd pinned to his walls, appreciating the support he'd provided, even from his prone state. Her fingers were caught around the new chain on his cross, smoothing it over Flynn's chest when Michael showed up at the door.

Still dressed in a suit, the red tie that hung open around Michael's neck was the only casual thing about him. He was his own breathless state of nerves as he rushed through the door. "Mia! What's going on? Are you all right? I've gotten nothing but vague messages from you for days. And then on my way from the airport I get this crazy text from Roxanne to meet you in the ICU." Michael's dark eyes jerked from his wife's face to her hands splayed across the body that lay between them. "Who the hell is that?"

"Shh, come to the lounge with me. We have to talk."

Michael followed Mia down the corridor, past the nurse's station where Nurse Margaret hid a slack-jawed gaze. Mia looked straight ahead, keeping a step in front of her husband. Her heart thumped hard as she carefully held his in her hands. They sat together on the sofa in the vacant lounge. Even his bewildered expression was more than she anticipated.

Michael Wells was the kind of guy who always had the answer without being condescending, a natural-born success. He had been on a winning streak his whole life—business deals, calc equations, the first grade—and got a little more than he bargained for when he captured the hand of the girl who just wouldn't say yes.

For a split second Mia wanted to keep the streak alive, just tell him everything was fine, go home and fall into that downy bed. She didn't want to do this to him. But it would be the biggest lie of all. There didn't seem to be a starting point that offered the rational explanation he would need. She hesitated too long and he leapt to his own conclusions.

"What happened, Mia? Did you have an accident? Wreck the Mercedes? Did you hit that guy? Jesus, you look awful. How long have you been here?" She put her hand up to stop him, but his fingers automatically locked with hers, his face looking just as it should. A husband gone mad with concern over the wife he loved. "You're scaring me, baby. What's going on?"

Mia focused on her hands, which were clasped loosely in his. Michael pulled her forward into a tight hug that was so familiar she couldn't help but fall into it.

"It's okay, Mia, I'm here now. Whatever it is, I'll fix it."

Exhaustion crushed down on her. Mia's tears fell onto his broad, welcoming shoulder. There hadn't been a shoulder, nothing in recent weeks on which to rest her grief. God, she had never, ever meant to use him like this. Mia pulled back, the gross unfairness of it all making her stomach sick. She struggled to gather her resolve. Like she'd told Roxanne, she owned this.

"It can't be that bad." He was smiling now, assuming the

worst had passed. "You're here, you're in one piece. How awful could it be? Please talk to me." Capturing a wild strand of hair, he tucked it into submission.

She shook her head, loosening it. "I thought I knew where to start . . ." she said, her nose running again. "How to make you understand, but . . ."

Preparedness always a given, Michael pulled a handkerchief from his pocket and dabbed at her nose, at the dripping tears, and planted a soothing kiss on her forehead. "Listen, let's go home. You can tell me all about it—"

This time she pulled away. "No! I can't leave here. I can't go with you, Michael."

"What do you mean, you can't go with me? Why in the world not?"

"I have to stay with him."

"Him, who? The Jesus look-alike on the vent?" He stopped dabbing, the frustration beginning to mount. "Mia, start making sense. Roxanne said you were upset, but I think hysterical would have been a better description—this isn't like you. Maybe we should call her."

It was the last thing she needed, Roxanne and Michael tag-teaming her. "No, don't call Roxanne. I'm sure you'll hear plenty from her later." Stifling down the last sob, Mia wiped her nose with the back of her hand, twisting the narrow end of his tie tight around two fingers—like a tourniquet trying to stop a hemorrhage. "Michael, let me start by saying that I understand that you're going to walk away from this hospital hating me. And so you hear me now, while you're willing to listen, I want you to know that I'm so incredibly sorry—sorry for what I'm about to do."

"Okay, Mia, I'm already bordering on irritated. Who is that man and what does he have to do with you?"

"Everything," she said, the word sounding like a gushing dam. The tie unraveled from her fingers, and she pressed her sweaty palms into her skirt. It was the first word that made sense. Mia's gaze jutted up from her lap, meeting his. "You . . . you don't remember him?" she asked, searching for a starting point.

For a moment there was a blank look on Michael's face that said he had no clue about the stranger in the room down the hall. Slowly his breath drew in; maybe calling forward something that lingered in the back of his mind. "He's, um, he's not a stranger." Mia shook her head. "He's not some random, meaningless man that you've never seen before."

"No," Mia said, her voice a featherbed under a furious fall. "He's not."

"Flynn," he offered, the sharpness in his voice startling her.

"I . . . I wasn't sure how much . . . if you remembered that much," she said, sucking in her own deep breath.

"Sometimes the less someone is willing to share, the more there is to know. And you were never willing to share—were you? Let's just say I'm aware."

"How aware?"

"That's a hell of a scary question, Mia." But the panic in his voice was gone, replaced by something so serious it made her skin prickle. "He's an old boyfriend," Michael said, labeling Flynn as little more than the guy from a high school reunion. She stared, expressionless. "Okay, someone who fascinated you back then—dark, mysterious . . . I can see it." A hard swallow rolled through Michael's throat as Mia's eyes filled with tears. "All right, if you want to make me say it, your ex-lover. That still doesn't explain what you're doing here, looking as if your entire life is hanging in the balance."

"Michael, I have to tell you something you're not going to

want to believe. You're going to have a lot of questions, and I'll try to answer them all. Flynn wasn't just an old boyfriend, or even my ex-lover. If it was that simple, I would have told you weeks ago that he was here, in a coma." Inching back, Michael's brow knitted the way it did when tough negotiations weren't going his way. "We wouldn't be having this conversation if that's all there was to it."

"I don't understand, Mia. What more could it possibly be? You haven't seen the guy in years." He stopped, his brow knitting tighter than she thought possible. "You haven't—have you?"

"No," she said quickly, claiming the honesty she could bring to the conversation. "I haven't seen Flynn since the day he vanished, right before I graduated. I haven't heard from him, or known where he was, or even if he was alive." She stopped, weighing her next thought. Owning up to things was just a tad more difficult than silently living with them. "But I do know that if given a choice all those years ago, I'd still be with him." It was cold and hard and unfeeling, and he didn't deserve a word of it. But it was the only way Mia could think of to make it big enough, to keep Michael from dismissing it as an old flame she'd gone a little mental over.

The always composed Michael Wells caught his stunned reaction. She watched him force a poker face of calm. He closed his eyes, shaking his head in a tight, agitated stroke. "You're going to have to say that again."

Mia touched his arm. He opened his eyes wide, looking more bewildered than before, perhaps slightly less concerned for her well-being. "I've never talked about Flynn—about us—because . . ." She hesitated, trying to corral six years of reasoning into a sentence. "Because I didn't want you to touch it. There were a lot of, um, issues . . . things that kept coming between us—Flynn and me. Michael, I can't begin to tell you how much

I loved him." She paused, waiting for him to digest, or just choke on the information. An exaggerated breath blew in and out of his mouth as he scrubbed a hand over a five-o'clock shadow. His body stiffened and his fingers fell away from hers. "Parts of it are extremely complicated. I'm not sure now is the right time for the details. Like I said, in the end Flynn left, he just vanished one night." It had taken Mia years to hear it in her head. Sharing it out loud with Michael was surreal. "I haven't known where he was until Roxanne called, not until he turned up here."

Michael made several attempts to form words before something actually came out of his mouth. "What . . . what's wrong with . . . Why is he in a coma?"

"An accident. He was on a motorcycle when he was hit by an SUV, about a mile from Roxanne's house, downtown. This is where I've been for the last month, working on Hough's project from the inside of Flynn's room. It, um, it all started the night I had that dinner meeting with Hough—the one you didn't come to." Mia forced a dry gulp, trying to read his face. She'd never seen anything quite like it. This was going to be a Michael Wells she had never experienced.

Oddly, a crooked smile formed over his lips, his face brightening. "This is a joke, right? Did Hough put you up to this?" Mia shook her head; she felt a wave of empathy for his confusion. Michael didn't even know Aaron Hough.

"Oh, wait, I get it," he said, the grin widening. "You and Roxanne cooked this up because I've been away so much. You wanted to teach me a good lesson. You win; I'm working out of the house starting tomorrow. Where is she?" he asked, peering over her shoulder. "This is Roxanne's brand of humor, cruel and twisted, but ridiculously funny. I give you two credit; you had me going there for a minute. Who's the guy, really? What, did she give some bottom-rung orderly twenty bucks to lie in bed and suck on that ventilator?" He hesitated and looked hard into his wife's eyes, waiting for her to join in the macabre humor. Her blank response struck the nerve that harbored the truth. He jumped from his seat, frantically pacing around her. "Come on, Mia, give it up. This is a bad joke, right?"

Mia's thumb ran over a frayed edge of the cushion, concentrating hard on the tattered fabric. She couldn't bear to watch him come unglued; it was so unlike him. "There's a part of me that wants to tell you just that, to save you from any of this. But I've made a decision. And it's not fair to you—"

Firm hands reached around and plucked her from the sofa. His eyes met Mia's in a tumultuous explosion of betrayal. "This is not happening! You can't be serious. This is insane!" he shouted. The last time she heard that tone he'd lost twenty thousand dollars in the stock market. "What exactly are you telling me? That you want to stay with him until he recovers, put him up in our guest room? Maybe donate a kidney?" He narrowed his eyes, his hands drawn to his hips. "You and your hopeless causes," he sneered. "Jesus, if this isn't coming from the part of your brain that believes good vibrational energy holds the cure for cancer."

"I know it's a lot, Michael. But this really isn't about Flynn. It's something I should have done a long time ago." She stopped; it was coming out all wrong. "No, it's about things I should have never done in the first place."

He threw his head back, a frustrated growl seeping from his gut. "Well, what does it have to do with? If you didn't summon me here to shove an ex-lover in my face—excuse me, an ex-lover who apparently means more than the guy you're currently married to—then what the hell am I doing here?"

"Stop twisting my words. I'm trying to explain." She looked toward Flynn's room, craning her neck a bit as she caught a glimpse of a nurse going in.

"Hey! I'm over here," he said, grabbing an arm. "Don't you think trashing six years of my life, our marriage, is worth your undivided attention? I mean, he is in a coma. Won't he keep?"

"That's why I had to do this now, while Flynn still is in a coma." Her eyes jutted back. "What happens to him doesn't change this decision."

"What decision?"

"I can't be married to you anymore, Michael." She rushed through the sentence as if it might soften the blow. His mouth opened and Mia clamped her hand fast over it, the confession spewing forward before he had a chance to stop her. "I have absolutely no idea what's going to happen when he wakes up, *if* he wakes up. There's a lot to this story you don't know. I'm not leaving you for him. I'm leaving you because of him."

He roughly pushed her hand away. "What the hell is that, semantics?" Michael sat back down. His face fell into his hands as he mumbled something she couldn't understand.

"I've been ignoring the signs for the last year. I can't, not anymore. Michael, you're the most generous, patient man I've ever met, and you deserve a lot more than me. I can't do this to you anymore. The first week Flynn was here I thought about how to tell you, what I would tell you. I reasoned that if he died, maybe I would save it until we were old and it didn't matter so much anymore. It's undoubtedly the most selfish thought I've ever had." She eased into the seat next to him and reached over, dragging his chin up, forcing him to look, owning it. "Do you hear what I'm saying? I was willing to go on with our marriage because it was safe and warm and convenient. I was willing to keep right on hiding everything from you. Don't you see how wrong that is? How unfair?" His pain was excruciating to witness, an amputation with a dull knife and no anesthesia.

"How . . . how could I not know any of this? I know you,

Mia. Sometimes you do impulsive things, follow a train of thought I can't appreciate. But this . . . this makes no sense whatsoever."

"This is the least impulsive, most careful decision I've ever made. I know it doesn't make sense to you right now."

"We have a good marriage. We've been talking about starting a family—it was a two-way conversation, wasn't it? I'll admit you've been a little distant lately, but I thought you were just wrapped up in this Hough thing." Michael sprang to his feet. He paced a few feet and turned back toward her. "The woman I know wouldn't do this; it isn't in her. I'm sorry, I can't wrap my mind around this. I feel like I got off a fucking plane from Vegas and stepped into the Twilight Zone."

"It's a lot to take in. Roxanne wanted me to tell you weeks ago, but I kept . . . I kept looking for the right words," she mumbled, feeling every bit of the shame she deserved.

"And what is Roxanne's take on all this? You can't tell me she has no opinion; that's an impossibility. From what I recall, she never was a big fan."

"To say the least," Mia said, fingers rubbing her forehead. "In fact, I'm surprised she's never filled you in. I suppose her vow of silence extended beyond conversations with me. Roxanne doesn't dislike Flynn. She hates him; she always has."

"Why? Why does she hate him?"

"God, it's Roxanne. I'm sure a copy of her reasons, real and fictitious, will soon be available to you." The flash of sarcasm was unappreciated, his handsome face confused and despondent. "Mostly she hates him because he hurt me, just like she said he would."

Michael paused, searching her face for the bottom line. "And this is what you want? To leave me—a man who has vowed to love you forever and has done a damn good job of it—for that? I didn't get a very good look at him, but to me he still has all the markings of an escaped convict!"

She sucked in a deep breath. It was enough conversation for one night. He would learn it all soon enough. "I'm not sure what the next step is. I didn't get that far . . ."

"Not thinking things through! How typical," he yelled, pounding his fingers to his temple so furiously she thought he'd knock himself over. "Like the time you told my boss, the guy who signs my paycheck, that if his banks were greener the money that passed through wouldn't be so dirty." A surly tone rose over the tension, cutting apart vows and promises. "In practical terms, babe, what is it you want? Shall I bring you a change of clothes, have your mail forwarded? Or do we just talk through our attorneys from here on out? I'd really like to know." Michael reached into his jacket pocket then thrust an envelope into her hands with such force it caused her to stumble back. "Seems one of your crazy, eco-centric projects is about to hit it big. After the deal goes through, I was going to surprise you—take you on a celebratory cruise. So let me know," he said, the surliness shifting to a pitchy tremor. "Maybe I can get one of the tickets swapped out for your . . . your soul mate. Maybe the sea air will snap him out of it." He stormed to the elevators, ramming his fist into the call button.

Mia couldn't stand it, succumbing to his pain. "Michael, wait!" She raced to the opening doors and hit the button for them to close, grabbing at his arm. For six years he'd been the buffer between layers of hurt that wouldn't heal. Now he was the enemy. Or she was. "Don't leave like this. Please."

"You've got to be kidding me. You can't have it both ways, Mia. Drop a bombshell like this and you want comfort? If I do that, you're coming home with me and I'll make damn sure you never come back here." As Michael spoke he raked his fingers through the tangles framing his wife's dubious expression. "This is what he does to you, and I'm supposed to do what? Just excuse myself from your life and let this happen? Look at you, you're a complete wreck. I don't know why you insist on wearing your hair so long. It's always in your face." The senseless observations fell off, his voice pinched. Michael moved out of reflex, jerking her hard into his arms. "Don't do this to us, Mia. God, you must know how much I love you. Just come home with me, for now, for tonight. You can't make me believe that you don't love me."

Mia took a small step back as her hands clutched his shoulders. Hurting him like this was unforgivable. Burning in hell was child's play. There had to be something worse awaiting her. "Michael, I never said that I didn't love you . . ."

Squeaky sneakers, loud on the linoleum floor, interrupted as they came up fast behind the two of them. "Mia! There you are. We couldn't find you!"

Her thrashing heart stopped cold. Reflex again, her body braced against Michael's. Mia half-turned in his arms to see Nurse Margaret approach, rushing down the corridor as if the world were on fire.

Oh, God, here it comes! He's dead.

"He's awake, Mia! Flynn's awake!"

Chapter 25

Jesus, it's bright in here. What the hell? I can't breathe. What is that thing? Am I alive? Okay, I must be alive; people are talking. In hell they'd be screaming.

"Mr. McDermott, can you hear me? I'm Dr. Logan. Can you understand what I'm saying? You're on a respirator. Just blink if you understand what I'm saying." One solitary, firm blink was the response. "Good, excellent. You've been in a coma, Mr. McDermott. I'm glad to see you've decided to join us again. You were in an accident. I'm going to examine you. Just try to stay relaxed and then we'll see about getting that vent disconnected, all right?"

Flynn blinked again. He was paralyzed with fear, or maybe he couldn't move at all. *What happened? I was on the bike. I had to be . . . I was going somewhere. I was so angry, furious about something. Mia's voice . . . I didn't want to wake up. I kept hearing her voice. It was like she was right next to me. God, let me go back to sleep. At least she was there.*

"Mr. McDermott, stay with us. Try to stay awake." The voice

was coaxing and loud. "You're doing fine. Can you give my hand a squeeze?" In an agitated reflex, he gripped the doctor's hand. "Excellent, that's pretty impressive strength for someone who's been out of commission for a while. How about your legs, can you bend them for me?" Flynn complied again. "That's great. Nice and slow, good range of motion. You had a substantial fracture to your pelvis. We'll get a new film as soon as possible, see if we can get you up and moving."

Moving? I need to get the hell out of here... Mia doesn't know... something... His right arm swung over to his left side. He groped around; the arm was taped to an IV board and strapped to the bed. Forcing his lethargic body to move, Flynn anxiously clawed at it. He had been chained up long enough. He couldn't stand it, wouldn't allow it.

"Whoa! Mr. McDermott, don't do that!" the doctor yelled. The fuzzy image of a nurse, as wide as she was tall loomed over him, pulling hard at his arm. Even in his weakened condition she was no match. He swung and she ducked just in time. The doctor's voice was harsher. "Mr. McDermott, we're trying to help you. If you don't settle down that arm will be in a restraint too. Do we understand each other?" He blinked again, but furiously this time, feeling the veins in his neck tight and extended. Helpless to do otherwise, he tried to relax. From the corner of his eye he could see drawings. Pages of paper surrounded him like an embrace—so different from everything else. His gaze focused up onto the stained ceiling tiles and fluorescent lights. He thought it smelled like antiseptic. When he was asleep he had been breathing in something powdery soft . . . Now it was gone.

I can't remember. I was going . . . somewhere. Why the hell can't I remember? It wasn't to see Mia. I can't find Mia. It was to see . . . Roxanne? Jesus Christ, maybe this is hell. His gaze dropped back, darting between the unfamiliar faces of the doctor and nurse.

They rapidly passed medical jargon to each other, talking about oxygen and reading monitors that beeped in his ear like a homing signal. *I am alive. I have to find her. She doesn't know. Doesn't know what?*

"All right, Mr. McDermott, if you think you can control yourself, we'll work on getting you off this vent. Now when I say, I want you to cough hard."

* *

Like Christmas in August or the dead showing up bearing armfuls of beautifully wrapped gifts, Mia could not have anticipated a more bizarre scene. As she waited outside Flynn's room, Michael stood at her side, both of them suffocating in silence. When Nurse Margaret announced that Flynn was awake, Mia thought that would be it. Michael would get on the elevator and leave, hating her, just as he should. Hindsight suggested she hadn't thought that part through too well either. Michael never gave up easily on anything. She watched him reach hard for the self-control he used in high-stakes business deals and when firing his stockbroker.

"What are you waiting for?" he'd asked. "Obviously your prayer has been answered. But if you don't mind, I'll go with you. Just in case there's some confusion about which one of us you're married to."

In six years they had talked about almost everything that mattered. One conversation later and it counted for nothing. They might as well have discussed the weather for the last half dozen years, leaving her to feel as if she was standing in the hall with a total stranger. She guessed he felt exactly the same.

A curtain was drawn and the door closed. Dribs and drabs of information seeped out as the staff occasionally passed by. Her stomach jumped when she heard the respiratory therapist say he was responsive, that he understood where he was. After an hour that seemed like the last twelve years plus thirty-four days, Dr. Logan emerged.

"It's good news, Mia."

She couldn't help herself, even with Michael standing there. A trembling hand covered a thankful smile as tears rushed out and she hugged Dr. Logan.

Understanding her intense vigil, the kindly doctor patted her shoulder and gave Michael a curious glance. "I'm sorry. I don't know that I can discuss his condition in front of . . ."

Michael stepped right up, offering a hand. "I'm Michael Wells, Mia's husband. You can say anything in front of me. Seems we're all related." Mia nodded, quietly hoping she wouldn't have to explain any further.

"I see. Well, he's tough. He's awake and he's off the vent. He's responded well to a short series of cognitive reasoning questions. He's got a harder head than most people. I don't know what made him fight like he did," the doctor observed, "but whatever it was, apparently it kept him alive. We'll have to run some more tests. Of course there is the cardiac arrest he suffered, but I'm fairly comfortable projecting a complete recovery."

"Thank you. Thank you, Dr. Logan. Um, does he know that I'm out here?"

"No, after the time you've put in, I thought you'd like to tell him yourself. I suspect it's going to be better medicine than anything we've dripped into him so far." Aiming for a compliment, he was unaware of the tension. "Your wife is quite exceptional, Mr. Wells, the way she worked those fabulous designs *and* kept track of his every breath."

An uneasy sigh hissed from Michael. "Yeah, my wife's a real multitasker—responsible to a fault."

"I'll be back to check on him in an hour or so. Go on in. But,

Mia, one word of caution," he said, looking between her and Michael. "He was easily agitated when we examined him. Let's keep him quiet until we get him on his feet, give him a chance to gain his bearings. Keep it short. Ten minutes max." He smiled at both of them and headed off down the corridor.

Mia exhaled the breath she'd been holding since she first saw Flynn. The future couldn't be more uncertain, but all she felt was relief. He was going to be all right. For a solitary instant she'd forgotten that Michael was there, but his stern look was a poignant reminder. It came right back into focus as she wiped away the tears. "I, um, don't think it's a good idea if . . ."

"If what? If I come in with you?" Michael shook his head, a sarcastic snicker rumbling out. "No, thanks. I'm not that much of a masochist. But I will be right here to take you home when you're done, and that's exactly where *we're* going. Like it or not, and as the good doctor noted, you're *my* wife. I'm going to have a say in what happens here, Mia. This is far from over. Ten minutes, or I will be through that door to get you." She nodded, taking a deep breath as she pushed it open.

* *

Mia hesitated between the closed door and the edge of the curtain. It was all that separated them. She stole a glance over her shoulder at Michael, whose head was down as he contemplated the wrong turn his life had taken. Loss of any kind was unfamiliar territory. She faced the curtain, suddenly wondering how it all could possibly live up to her expectations. *Be patient. He may not remember the past.* She took a small step and stopped short. *What if he doesn't remember me?* It hadn't occurred to her. *Keep it simple. Don't upset him.*

Flynn's eyes were closed, like before, but he was free of the ventilator. The feeding tube was gone and his head was propped higher. Somehow he looked more alive. Not making a sound, she edged her way over. A hand went out to him. She snapped it back. For weeks she'd touched him, brushed back his hair, run her fingers over those lean muscles in his arms. But now he was going to react. Flynn could tell her to stop, admit that he didn't quite recall her. She was too many women ago. He could tell her to get out, laugh at the fact that she'd stayed by his side. Or worse, ask her to call his wife—the one that he'd been married to for five or ten years. Mia shuddered, closed her eyes, and prayed for the right words. Her trembling hands balled into two tight fists trying to rein in the fear. There were too many unknowns. Michael was right; she dreamt too big. She nearly retreated. But then there was a gift, unlike any she had ever received. It floated into her ears on a path straight to her heart. The sound was raspy and weak, but familiar as her own skin, a deep voice breaking over that silent prayer.

"I was wrong. I thought this was hell, but I guess—this would be heaven."

The fists relaxed. Mia's hands flew up over her chest, trying to hold in that bursting heart, her eyes flashing open wide. *Breathe, breathe, breathe. Say something!* "Hi . . . I've missed you." They were the perfect words.

"Hi, yourself," Flynn said, as if not a day had passed. The ease in his voice was enough. He remembered everything. "How long have you . . . have I . . . have we been here?"

We, he said we! "You've been here, in a coma, for about a month."

"A month? What month is it?"

"September. It's September, Flynn. Did the doctor tell you about your injuries?"

"Yeah, some I guess. Your birthday is . . . September . . . Soon? Everything's . . . foggy."

My birthday . . . He remembers my birthday!

His eyes rolled up in his head. Dr. Logan was right. He was shakier than he'd ever admit. Mia smiled, wanting to touch him, wanting to throw herself right on top of him, but wrapping her fingers around the cool metal guardrail instead. "No, today's the second. It's not for a few weeks. Does anything hurt? How do you feel right now?"

"Like I got hit by a truck." His Adam's apple bobbed with a deep swallow. "Thirsty."

"Oh, here," she said, grabbing a cup of ice water that she'd seen the nurse bring in. "It was an SUV, actually," she explained as he sipped gingerly through the straw. It was amazing. God had come through. This had seemed impossible a few hours before. Now he was breathing, talking, sipping water through a straw—it was a beautiful thing. "Enough?" He gave a small nod. She couldn't stop staring. There were deep, etched lines around his eyes. They weren't there when he'd left. She couldn't see them when he was in the coma. She loved them, a heavenly afterthought for those angelic eyes. "Do you know what happened? Do you remember anything? About the accident, I mean." *Well, I really don't mean about the accident. What I want to ask is do you remember leaving me, not a word, not a note, nothing. Could you explain that to me? I've only been waiting for twelve years, two months, and sixteen days.*

"About the accident, no. I remember being mad about something . . . I was on my way . . . Ah, I must be dreaming."

"What? What were you on your way to?"

"I think . . . I think I was on my way to see Roxanne. That's crazy. Why the hell would I do that? How would I know where to find her?"

"Flynn, Roxanne is a doctor at this hospital. The accident happened in between her house and here. I don't understand."

His eyes searched hers for a moment. He tried to lift his head from the pillow, but it flopped back down. "Shh, don't move." Mia gently touched his shoulders. It was nothing more than a small gesture to calm him, but the urge to hang on was overwhelming. She forced herself to let go. "You need to rest. They don't want you excited."

"Mia?"

My name, he said my name!

"I don't understand either. Wait, what state are we in?"

"Maryland, just north of D.C., south of Baltimore. I live about half an hour from here. Where did you think we were?"

"I don't know . . . Did I find you?"

"Find me? No, I found you. Roxanne called me the night they brought you in. I've been kind of, um, waiting around. Waiting for you to wake up."

"Then I didn't imagine it? These . . ." he said, pointing weakly toward the drawings. "These are yours?"

"Yes, they're my sketches."

He smiled, his eyes closing for a moment. There was a slight nod as he swallowed deeply. "And your voice. You've been here all this time? But I don't get . . . Why . . . Why would you wait like that?"

Why? It wasn't exactly the thunder of heartfelt appreciation she was hoping for. *Flynn didn't want me then, he doesn't want me now. For twelve years he could have found me, and nothing.* Mia struggled for an "I don't love you either" explanation. "Well, there wasn't anyone else that I knew of. They couldn't find your mother . . ."

"She's dead. Five years ago."

"Oh, I'm sorry. Anyway, I just thought someone should be responsible," she said, stealing Michael's word. "Is there . . . is there someone you want me to call? Your sister, a friend"—*say it, say it, say it*—"a wife maybe?" The word stuck in her throat like hot tar. There was that horrible picture Roxanne painted. The trailer, a bunch of runny-nosed kids, none of whom resembled him. They all looked like his fat, dowdy common-law wife, maybe the postman. There was even a mangy dog.

* *

Wife? Whose wife? He stared into her face. Mia's face. What was she doing there? Questions pelted his mind, vast as raindrops on the ocean, but he couldn't put them in order, couldn't get them out of his mouth. She was so beautiful, and she was standing right there. Something wasn't right. The pain in her face was incredible and just as real as her. Goddamn, there was that anger, burning at him. Surely it wasn't meant for her . . . He was riding fast, going somewhere. He wasn't paying attention. So furious he couldn't see the road. Murky scraps of information tumbled in and out, a whirling vortex. He couldn't stop it long enough to connect it. *Wife?* Then, like a rush-hour train, it slammed back into his head. *Mia's married. I know she's married! Why shouldn't she be? She didn't come. She didn't want to wait. Mia loves someone else.* He gasped in a trembling breath, turning his head away, as far as his neck would allow. Flynn couldn't recall the accident, but he remembered that horrific pain, right before, minutes before. Mia belonged to someone else. "No, there's no one to call." There was a tremendous sigh from Mia, so deep he couldn't miss it. *Terrific, now she thinks there's no way out, she's stuck here.*

"Are you all right? Should I get the nurse? Does something hurt?"

"Hurt?" he mumbled, trying to clear his throat. "No, I'm just having trouble remembering things, that's all."

"Dr. Logan said that's normal. The medication they're giving you for the pain is making you groggy. Maybe I should go for now. It's late." Mia glanced toward the door. "I'll come back tomorrow, okay?"

"Is that . . . is that okay with your husband?" He turned his head back; he had to see her reaction. "Does he mind you visiting your ex . . . ex what? How'd you explain me, Mia?"

"Not very well," came her shame-filled whisper. Their gazes drifted together then down to Mia's fingers wrapped tight around the bar. The fat wall of diamonds on her left hand sparkled and danced under the fluorescent lights. She clumsily yanked it away, the diamonds bumping along the rail, a clinking calling card of betrothal to someone else. "Don't worry about that. Michael's not your problem."

Michael. Jesus Christ, he has a fucking name. And why is it familiar? "Whatever, Mia."

"Does that mean you want me to come back?" She reached over the bar and picked up his hand. "I spent a lot of time here. I'd like to at least see it through, until you're better. If you'll let me."

Her touch was every memory he harbored come to life. He wanted to, but he couldn't close his fingers around hers. *Great, fucking pity. What's next? Maybe her husband—that's right her husband, the guy she's been fucking sleeping with for who knows how long, five minutes after I was gone—maybe he'll come by to shoot the breeze, bring a nice house plant.* Her eyes, he couldn't avoid them. There were those sparkling doll's eyes, so clear and beautiful—and sad? Everything about her was more perfect than he remembered. Almost everything. She let go and his stare moved to her hand again, to that cluster of diamonds. If he hadn't known better, he would have said she was trying to hide them, tucking one hand behind the other. "Yeah, Mia. Come back if you want to," he said, swallowing down that last bit of pride.

Chapter 26

Mia rolled over, burying her head in a thick goose-down comforter. She lay there, half awake, fighting to stay inside a beautiful dream where everything was all right. Like the fat, dowdy common-law wife, none of her fears were real. Flynn told her that he loved her. Finally he said the words, confessing that he'd made a terrible mistake, spending years searching for her. It was just the coma. He was confused when he didn't say it last night. But she couldn't keep it going; the dream was over.

A stream of sunlight broke through the plantation shutters, drilling a narrow passage into the folds of the fluffy cover. She opened her eyes and bolted upright in bed. *Eleven thirty!* She snatched the clock off the night table, making sure she'd read it right. Darting from the bed, Mia grabbed her robe and raced into the hallway. The aroma of brewing coffee halted her steady charge. Michael was home. He didn't do anything without two cups of coffee—God, by now he'd probably had twenty. She inched toward the top of the staircase, like a prowler in her own home. The low mumble of the television confirmed her suspi-

cion. Mia didn't know why she was so surprised that this morning was going to require further explanation about last night.

It was after midnight when they'd pulled in the driveway,
Michael's car behind hers the entire way. Mia headed straight for
the shower, thinking he might be asleep by the time she came
out. Then she could go quietly to the guest room. She had mis-
judged him again. Michael was right where she'd left him, in the
middle of the bedroom. The only move he made was to take off
his suit jacket and tie. The moment was so awkward she would
have felt more comfortable climbing into bed with her last client, a gay man who smelled of lemony aftershave and had a
fetish for fringe. She looked around as if searching for the escape
hatch, tugging at her terry cloth bathrobe. There wasn't even a
way to say it. It was salt poured straight into the wound, but she
couldn't do it, couldn't sleep in the same bed with Michael. It
would have been a sign of hope.

"It took a whole year to get you to sleep with me, two completely redecorated rooms—not cheap either, mind you—and
then, the first time, an entire bottle of champagne. It had nothing to do with commitment jitters, did it?"

She hadn't answered, amazed by his ability to read her mind.
Neither one knew what to do next. She avoided his stare, offering to go down the hall. Michael refused, saying he had no
desire to sleep in their bed without her, then stalking off to the
guest room.

Now at the top of the stairs, she listened for any sound to
gauge his state of mind. There was only the TV. Peering over the
top of the rail, Mia could see the entire foyer, blank contractor-
white walls. The rest of the interior looked the same. They'd
lived there for a year and she'd never bothered to decorate a
single room. Michael attributed her lack of interest to not wanting to bring her work home with her. Mia knew better.

She tiptoed back to the bedroom and closed the door. Having memorized every prompt to get her straight through to the ICU, Mia picked up the phone and hurriedly dialed. In a breathless fluster she asked how Flynn was. Had it all been a crazy dream? Her smile widened with each minor detail the nurse offered. Flynn had slept on and off last night, ate real hospital food for breakfast, and was waiting to go down to radiology. If things looked good, they would get him on his feet that afternoon. Mia asked the nurse to give Flynn a message. "Tell him I'll be there shortly."

Meeting Michael's complex stare a few minutes later, she mentally recanted. "Shortly" was wishful thinking. He didn't look as if he'd slept five minutes; his hair was oddly rumpled. He was poised at the center island in their kitchen wearing a wrinkled polo shirt and sweatpants, his arms leaning so hard on the countertop they looked like an extension of the granite. She was a bit taken aback not to find him in a power suit, prepared to handle his business. There was a confrontational exchange of posturing glances as she passed by, getting out a favorite coffee mug, filling it. When Mia approached, Michael instinctively shoved a sugar bowl at her from the other side of the island. She said nothing, catching it before it sailed past, dumping in the obligatory five cubes of sugar. Mia pivoted toward the refrigerator. He blocked her path by opening the door himself, handing over a small carton of skim milk. The only sound that resonated was the tinkling of her spoon in the mug.

Wielding a chainsaw of observation, Michael cut through the tension. "I know exactly how much sugar goes into that cup and that you're not even going to drink it if there isn't any skim milk. I also know that you don't get what an asinine contradiction that is. Last night you informed me that you're in love with someone else, that you've *always* been in love with someone else. I'd like to know how I missed that one."

Nothing like getting right to the point. If he stared any harder, he'd burn a hole right through her—problem solved. "It's a better question than I have an answer for." Mia wiped the spoon on a napkin, looking for something to prolong the moment, giving her time to come up with the structured list of reasons that had landed them both in this place. "Since the day I agreed to marry you, I thought that this—what we have—was what I was supposed to have. I mean, who wouldn't want this life?" she said, pointing out the gourmet kitchen as her example. "More important, Michael: Who wouldn't want you?"

"Am I supposed to be flattered?" He leaned against the refrigerator, locking the tight muscles in his arms into an unimpressed fold.

"No, it's just the truth. I understand that it's a natural reaction to make this all about Flynn." She afforded him a courteous pause while he rolled his eyes. "But it's not. It's about fixing a mistake I, and I alone, made when I gave up on what my heart said. By the time we met—again, it had been years since Flynn vanished," Mia said. "Common sense, logic, loneliness—they all said to get a life. And I thought I was ready. A first date, sleeping with you, marrying you . . . I wasn't resisting because of Flynn—at least not consciously. I was trying to find my way. And I did try. I swear, Michael, I tried so hard . . . at first," she finished, averting her gaze.

"Oh, so I was an experiment in life skills, to see if you'd healed enough to move on."

"Come on, Michael; it wasn't deliberate. You weren't a theory I was testing," she said, her voice pinching. "I was just trying to live my life." Her stomach began to churn, and Mia walked to the sink, deciding she didn't want the coffee after all. She felt drenched in black, a soot-covered villain for whom mercy would be a moot point. But glancing down, the blackness eased as evidence of what her husband had been up to all morning, a third coffee mug, sat in the sink. *Roxanne never could manage to find the inside of a dishwasher.* He'd been doing his own calculating. No doubt Roxanne had been to the house before dawn, the two of them comparing notes all the way back to Athens. With her back to him, Mia hesitated, trying hard to think like Michael Wells.

His approach shifted, the tone gentler. "I guess you slept well. That's good. No doubt you'll benefit from a clearer head. We need a new mattress in the guest room. That one's like cement. I came back in for another pillow and you were sound asleep." He moved closer and his expensive aromatic aftershave wafted around her, like a lasso. "I wanted to get into the bed with you, Mia. And I had to stand there and ask myself, what the hell is so wrong with that?" His hands were on her shoulders, and she felt his mouth press into her head as his fingers dropped, riding along the small of her back. "I think you're very confused, honey. You haven't slept in weeks, you're exhausted. I've been thinking about it all morning. To be honest, I knew something wasn't right—something bigger than a design project." Michael slid his arms around her, the embrace tightening. "Can we slow this down a little? This man, Flynn—he isn't what you think. Maybe if we talk it through, you'll see things more clearly."

Mia twisted around, finding herself pinned between him and the apron of the sink. "Tell me something, Michael. Exactly how long did you and Roxanne end up brainstorming? That's two brilliant minds; I just want to know what kind of firepower I'm up against."

"I don't know what you're talking about."

Mia reached around and picked the mug out of the sink. "Coral lip gloss goes terrific with blond hair. What did Roxanne tell you?"

Anger flashed through his dark eyes and he backed away from the possible bargaining power of seduction. "Everything you didn't. You know, it was bad enough when I thought my wife wanted to leave me for her old college flame. But you left out a few pieces of information, hon. This man—"

"Stop calling him that. You know his name."

"Yeah, and I understand he wasn't too forthcoming with that either."

She nodded, biting her fingernail. "Okay, so now you know it all." *Well, not really all, but all you're going to know for now.* Mia paced the cold tile floor, launching into a recitation of facts. "Let me know if I miss anything. According to Roxanne, Flynn was a drifter who rolled into Athens and right into my bed. As you might have guessed, and she confirmed, I had a torrid affair with him. He had some lowly job, a sketchy background, and didn't mesh so well with the status quo. Oh, and a criminal record, which I never got around to mentioning to Roxanne. She told you that she distrusted him from the second she saw him, that he was only using me for sex, or worse. She was sure he was going to break my heart, if not my neck! Come the following June, Roxanne wallowed in a moment of 'I told you so' when he did just that, simultaneously confirming all her suspicions. But because she prevailed, because Flynn was gone for good, she was compelled to offer a gracious consolation, agreeing to never mention him again." Dizzying herself with the lack of breath, Mia ignored it and forged ahead. "Did she happen to use the Antichrist comparison? It makes for such a nice visual. Oh, and of course there's the pesky detail about Flynn being a serial killer. I'm sure she managed to squeeze that in."

"Do you hear what you're saying? Any of it? It doesn't exactly cast him in a positive light."

"And every word of it is her version of what happened. I have a slightly different perspective, but I'm sure it doesn't interest you."

"No, it doesn't, and let me tell you why. I wouldn't give a flying fuck if he had been the captain of the goddamn football team and carried a 4.0 GPA. You're married to me. He left you! Where the fuck is the question?" Michael slammed his coffee mug into the sink, fat chunks of ceramic flying everywhere. "You and I have six years invested in one another. You had one lousy year with him!"

"Well, maybe that alone tells you something about what we had." Mia stopped short. She didn't want to do this, to taunt him or make comparisons. It wasn't about that. "Like I told you, there's a lot to this story that you don't know, and neither does Roxanne." Mia turned and headed out of the kitchen. Halfway up the stairs, Michael was right behind her.

"And where exactly do you think you're going?"

"To the hospital," she said firmly, continuing to climb the stairs. Michael grabbed an arm, spinning her around on the landing. It was startling; he never passed by without less than an "excuse me."

"I don't think so. We're not finished. I told you last night I'm going to have a say in this, and I meant it. Walking away from this marriage isn't going to be as simple as you think, Mia."

"What are you going to do, lock me in the bedroom? You can't stop me from seeing him."

"Maybe. But I sure as hell can delay it."

"What's that supposed to mean?" She gave a hard yank, surprised when her arm didn't break free.

Michael stepped up to the landing, rising above the level eye contact they were making. "All right, I'll put my cards on the table. Roxanne and I had a very long talk this morning. She's concerned, extremely concerned, about your mental state."

"My what?"

"She saw what he did to you all those years ago, what he's doing to you now. Roxanne said he's got some kind of insane hold over you. From the time or two I saw you with him, I sure as hell didn't get it. What you saw, or why you'd want to— Anyway," Michael said, averting his gaze, "she says that you're not yourself around him. From what I've witnessed, that's a fair observation. According to Roxanne, you show all the signs of someone completely obsessed, irrational. Obviously you're not thinking straight."

"Remind me, when did Roxanne get that degree in psychiatry? Cut to the chase, Michael. What are you getting at?"

"I want you to not see him for a few days."

"You want me to what?" He might as well have asked her to cut off an arm. "No way. I'm not playing games, jerking him around. He just came out of a coma. I told him I'd be there, and by God, I will be!"

"No, Mia, you're not." He finally let go, though his voice was eerily cool. His height, his frame, his willingness to navigate their everyday lives, it had been a protective trench. Now she wasn't sure how to get around it. "You're going to listen to me, answer a few more questions. Look at me and tell me you feel nothing, that our marriage is based on no more than me being second choice."

No, Michael, you were the only choice—but it doesn't change anything. "You and Flynn, you're never present in the same thought," she insisted. "I was trying to move forward with what we had. Even so . . ."

"Even so what?"

"It's not working, Michael. I can't give you what you need regardless of Flynn." Mia sighed, swallowing down the lump in her throat, saying out loud things she'd been thinking for the last year. "Is this what you want?" she asked, looking over his strong frame, his handsome face, the presence that said he was somebody. "For God's sake, you're Michael Wells—is this what you deserve from your wife? From your marriage?"

"No, it's not," he said, the two of them agreeing. Silence followed his admission, and Mia turned, continuing up the stairs. "But I'm also willing to fight for what's mine. You can't erase the last six years, Mia. We have too much going for us." She stopped, moved by the desperation . . . the determination in his voice. "I want . . . I want you to come away with me for the weekend."

She turned back, his anxious face waiting for something to go his way. A part of Mia wanted to say yes, to give him time to adjust to a truth that had shadowed the past twelve years. But he wouldn't see it that way. Like sleeping in the same bed, it would be a sign of hope. "I can't do that, Michael. I'm sorry."

"Okay," he said, nodding. "Here's an alternative plan. How about spending a couple of days chatting with the nice folks on the ninth floor at Good Samar—"

"The pysch ward?" Her eyes bugged out of her head, appalled at what had just come out of his mouth. She'd sorely underestimated the lengths to which he was prepared to go. "You've got to be kidding."

"Anything is possible, Mia—" He stopped short, collecting his demeanor. "Of course not. But I do think two days on an analyst's couch and a mild sedative might do you a world of good."

"And what's behind door number two, Michael? Thinking about having my memory erased?" She sourly spit the words out, but backed up one more step.

His hands shot up in an apologetic gesture. "I don't want the conversation to go like this. Maybe you can understand that I'm a little upset. One minute I'm booking a cruise and the next I'm mentally dividing community property. Can we at least sit down and talk?"

She agreed, walking to the bedroom. Mia sat in her favorite chair near the window; Michael pulled over her vanity bench and sat close beside her. She watched the cleverness in his eyes as he mentally arranged his game plan.

"Mia, he had his chance twelve years ago. He could have married you, asked you to drift away with him, or just kept using you like he did for that year." She rolled her eyes in frustration. "Now wait. Just hear me out. According to Roxanne, what he chose to do was leave. Without a word, nothing. That's what she told me. The fact that he could do that to you, it's reason enough to hate him, in my book."

"I don't hate him for it. Why should you?"

He laughed a little, revealing deep dimples that caused his stone-chiseled face to go soft and kind. Michael gathered her hands in his, twisting around the platinum set of diamonds she wore. "Mia, you're too forgiving. The way he lived, the way Flynn showed up in Athens. Can't you see how he took advantage of you? Do you think you're the only wom— Don't you think that was his pattern? The man used you in ways I can't begin to think about." Michael's concerned expression traveled her body. Mia clasped the front of her bathrobe together, the thought making them both uncomfortable. "All of this," he said, his voice catching, "it makes me sick and hurt and angry. But the more I hear, the only thing I want to do is protect you from him."

"Michael," she said softly, her fingers grazing his cheek. "I don't need anyone to protect me from anything, but especially not from Flynn."

"Okay, tell me one solid thing about him that should make me believe that." Her gaze avoided his, silently answering. "All right, help me to understand something else. When he left you, how long did it take to get over it, or at least go on with the part of your life that didn't include interior design or passing time with some wayward teenager?"

Mia looked down at her fingers, locked with his. "Six years," she quietly admitted. "I had three dates until you and I both showed up at that alumni function."

"Damn, all the stars must have been perfectly aligned." He shook his head, snickering. "At least it finally makes sense. I never could figure out why someone like you wasn't engaged or married. Fate and then some," he murmured.

"Fate and . . . ?" Daydreamy platitudes were not how Michael handled life.

"I'd asked Roxanne about you once or twice back in Athens. But I was in a different place, serious about getting my masters, taking the business world by storm. The timing wasn't right. When you showed up at that alumni dinner, I thought fate was so kind . . . incredible, actually, giving me the chance I should have pounced on all those years ago." Mia squirmed at the romantic notion. He cleared his throat, moving back to the business at hand. "Now I want you to tell me something else. When you saw him, saw Flynn last night, what did he say? Be honest with me—whatever it is."

Her lip quivered a little. She'd been fighting the lack of enthusiasm Flynn had shown in and out of her dreams. "He was in pain and he was groggy, Michael. It was hard for him to focus."

"Nevertheless, if he shared this great passion you seem to have for him, wouldn't he have said as much? I'm not saying this to hurt you. I'm saying it to keep you from getting hurt again."

She dabbed at a stray tear. "He, um, he wanted to know why I had waited there for him to wake up . . ."

"I see. Not exactly the words of a man desperate to see you." She wrinkled her forehead at him. It hurt more now than it had last night. "Now, let's add something else to this equation, just a possibility. I know you don't buy into Roxanne's theory about those girls, and I'm not saying I do either. I don't know enough about it. I'm willing to wait for the DNA."

"Roxanne is determined to chase that stupid theory of hers to the end of the earth. That DNA won't prove he killed those girls." *On the other hand, it will remind the world he's a wanted fugitive.* "She's taken a bunch of sketchy facts and decided it's a slam dunk for motive and opportunity. You know how she is—"

"Maybe so, but you can't fault her for wanting to know if this man is a killer. Roxanne can be acerbic, opinionated, and blunter than a two-ton anvil—but she loves you. She's only ever wanted your happiness. We both do." The deep breath came from both of them; Mia knew how true it was. "So, based on everything we've just talked about, you tell me how I'm being unreasonable. I want to take my wife away, just for a couple of days, to clear her head and think things through." He held tight to her hands, waiting for an answer. "It's not an outrageous request, Mia. If you do love me at all, I should think it's an easy decision."

All her doubts, highlighted in such meticulous order, delivered with such confident composure. Mia didn't want to hear the sense he was making. "I don't believe for a second that Flynn killed those girls. I'm not worried about the DNA for that reason." She stopped. The urge to protect his secret was still strong. "You're right, Michael, it was six years of hell after Flynn left. I didn't care if I ever met anyone, ever loved anyone again, until I met you. That says something about us."

"I'll take it, for now." He hid a shaky sigh beneath a wall of confidence that was showing tiny fissures of stress.

"But I can't go away with you," Mia said, her voice cracking under the strain, knowing how much it was hurting him.

He nodded. There was a defeated look in his eyes that she couldn't bear. "Okay, an afternoon," he said, managing a smile. "Get in the car with me and just go for a drive. Maybe it will clear your head—or mine. Maybe the time will help me understand."

Mia opened her mouth, unsure what to say. But something else weighed in on the decision. "My final presentation. It's scheduled for late this afternoon at the mock office—then dinner to discuss the details," she said, having lost focus in the whirlwind of drama. "I haven't even moved the last drawings to computer graphics."

"You'll make your meeting. And if you need an extension, I'll see to it that Aaron Hough grants it."

She smiled into his sober face, shaking her head. "Michael, you don't even know Aaron Hough. While your negotiation skills are legendary, I doubt a multimillionaire mogul is going to cave to your demands."

"He'll do it," he assured her. "It's a few hours. Please, Mia, tell me I'm worth that much to you."

He was worth far more than she could offer, but Mia couldn't make him understand. It was absurd to think that she'd come up with words in an afternoon, delivering a realization that only time could provide. On the other hand, it seemed beyond cruel to refuse.

As Mia dressed, pulling a sweater from the closet, her gaze filtered over the dusty past on a shelf. A bag of broken glass and a filthy pillowcase. A worn cotton T-shirt and a pretty box filled with photographs. She'd bought the box from a boutique on her last trip out of Athens. Years later, when Michael and Mia bought their home, there was the obligatory discussion about warranties and insurance, the subject segueing to what you might save first in a fire. For this reason Michael insisted on a fireproof safe, keeping important possessions out of harm's way. That was good, she'd thought, that way there would be nothing to stop her from saving what was most valuable.

Chapter 27

"It's all right. I understand. I can barely hear you," Flynn said, sitting in a chair, poking at a bowl full of lime-green gelatin. "Mia, are you crying? Well, you sound like you're crying, sweet—" He didn't say it. "No, okay . . . Yeah, they've got me up and moving, must need the bed space. I'm already doing laps around the ICU . . . Yes, I'm kidding. A slow walk . . . Sure, we'll talk then . . ." Before he could say good-bye she hung up. The only part that seemed authentic was a brief exchange about the sketches surrounding him. There was a gust of happiness in her voice when he'd asked about them. Staring at the wobbly mass of Jell-O, he shoved the stand across the room, the wheeled cart almost taking flight. But a white lab coat breezed around the corner just in time to prevent anything from happening.

"Temper, temper. I see even a coma hasn't curbed your ugly outbursts, as I might have predicted."

His dismal expression turned positively black as the brewing blond storm approached. "And I see your bedside manner sucks—just as I would have predicted." He squinted up at her, wishing he could jump to his feet. Having Roxanne bearing down over him was an untenable position to be in.

With a predatory gleam in her eye, like a barn cat preparing to bat around its prey, she asked, "Mind if I sit?" He shrugged and looked out the window; at least it leveled the field. "Did you know I saved your life? Twice? First in the ER when they brought you in, and then up here when you coded. How's that for twisted irony? No need to thank me. You probably ought to just thank God for that Hippocratic oath. Otherwise, it might have gone another way."

His head did a slow turn from the window, giving her a long once-over. Time had frozen, having little effect on her. She was an ice sculpture, a cold sparkling beauty full of sharp edges. "Must have been a tough call. Great, now I owe you. Had I known, I would have just stayed in the coma. Is there a reason for this unholy reunion, or did you have a change of heart, decide to do me in after all."

"Mmm, murder. Not really my area of expertise." She cocked her head, meeting a look that he was trying hard to hold neutral. "I understand you don't remember much from before the accident. A blow like that usually knocks out all short-term memory, maybe more." She paused, waiting. Silence was the only response he was offering. "Frankly, I'm amazed you're able to recall your own name, never mind what you were doing here. Is, um, is any of it coming back? Do you remember anything?"

You're nervous, Roxanne. What are you so worried about? Why do you want to know what I remember? Okay, I'll play. I've got nothing to lose. But you, Roxanne, what's at stake for you? "No, it's all a big blank, fits in good with the rest of my past. I do remember that I was trying to find Mia before the accident."

"Why couldn't you have just stayed gone? Good Lord, she probably had herself convinced you were dead."

Why would she think I was dead? She knew where I was. Once more he tried to put it together in his head. He'd spent the past five months searching for Mia and found nothing. He'd gone back to Athens, to Atlanta where she was supposed to have taken an internship, to her hometown in Maryland, nothing. Her mother had moved away, a dead end. That's when he decided it might be easier to find Roxanne. And apparently, he had. His eyes flew open wide as the first piece of the puzzle clicked into place.

"Well? Surely you were up to something, and I can only imagine what. Your ego amazes me. Did you really think she'd be hanging around waiting for you? You ought to try pursuing someone closer to your own socioeconomic scale. Prostitutes come through the ER all the time. Maybe I can hook you up."

"Shut up, Roxanne." Lord, he'd forgotten how she could make his head pound. He raked a hand through his hair and turned back toward the window.

"Look, I just came by to give you fair warning. You're alive because of me, and don't think that hasn't kept me up nights. After saving your life twice, let's say I feel responsible. The secrets you keep, they're dark and ugly, of that I'm sure. No one lives like you unless they've got something to hide or they're plain crazy. You're many things, Flynn, but you're not crazy."

"Your point being?" Flynn only glanced at her, but was listening harder. She was scheming something.

"I've looked at your chart. You keep improving like this and before you know it the freebies will be over; they're going to cut you loose." She shrugged. "Feral animal species always tend to heal faster. I assume Mia didn't tell you—I've sent your DNA to the state crime lab for analysis."

"You did what?"

"Don't give me that incredulous look, like your fingerprints wouldn't flunk a background check and your photo's not part of the FBI's best-of collection. Besides, comatose patients are very generous with their saliva. I'm expecting those results within days. When my theory turns into hard evidence, more than one law-enforcement agency is going to want to chat with you about some dead college girls." He said nothing, his expression only a tad more concerned. "Here's your chance to save a nice girl further misery, plus save your own sorry behind. Before the DNA comes back, before the cops show up—leave. You did it before and she got over it. If you end up going to jail, this will only persist. It will force her to keep a twenty-to-life vigil for whatever you've done. For God's sake, if you get the death penalty she'll spend the rest of *your* life writing letters to the governor. Don't do that to her."

"What the hell are you babbling about?" *Mia didn't wait last time . . . because Mia didn't know . . . didn't know . . . didn't know I spent the last twelve years in prison!* Flynn's head whipped around, meeting his own shocked reflection in the glass, the bolt of truth hitting him hard. *I left her the letter, but she didn't answer it, not a word. She did exactly what I told her to do if she didn't want to wait.* Roxanne droned on in his ear, but Flynn wasn't listening anymore. Mia didn't know, but how? It was like wet glue; the pieces wouldn't stick. Pieces were missing. Roxanne kept a venomous buzz going, interrupting, infecting his train of thought with tidbits of Michael and Mia's happy, well-to-do life. He couldn't concentrate.

"Fine, that's the way you want to play it. We'll see what her husband has to say about that. Michael isn't easily intimidated. Mia loves him."

Flynn's entire being swung around in the chair, wanting to take a dive right at her. He winced as his bruised body followed through. "Mia loves me," he said through gritted teeth. He surprised even himself with the ferociousness of the words.

"Ha! You keep telling yourself that. Why isn't she here? She's a little obsessed, caught up in the past maybe. But does she love you? She's smarter than that. Do you really think that stupid spell is still holding?"

"She called, said there was something she had to take care of . . ."

"But she didn't say what, did she? Would you like to know what that something was?" The predatory gleam grew brighter. "She's gone off with her husband on a romantic getaway. Yes, she spent a fair amount of time holding your pathetic hand, but you're on the mend. In the end"—she shrugged—"things turned out just as they should. Michael was such an obvious choice. Really, you should have been at the wedding. Big wedding," she said explosively, emphasizing with her hands. "Mia was the most beautiful bride . . ."

Flynn's head snapped to the side as if someone had slapped him, and he squeezed his eyes shut tight. He could see the picture and feel that sickening punch to the gut. She was married. This was no vision; it was real. He was holding the picture. Mia was wearing her hair up; he didn't like it. She looked beautiful anyway . . . but she didn't look all that happy. Those doll's eyes—they didn't sparkle. Roxanne, she was in the damn picture too. Pieces were coming together, shooting in at random angles from the corners of a fractured memory. He had wanted to throw the picture across the room, holding it so tight he cracked the glass. He laid it down. On the desk was a newspaper clipping; Mia was pictured with a silver-haired man. He hesitated, reading the story, breathing in calm. There was a swell of pride that stretched all the way back to Athens. She'd followed her dream, found the path for those extraordinary ideas. He'd spent years wondering. He put it aside, kept searching. An address book in the desk drawer. "Wells," he blurted out. Flynn turned back toward Roxanne, who was yapping away about Mia and her husband.

"What did you say?"

"Mia's last name, it's Wells."

"How do you know? You must have heard it from one of the nurses."

Flynn turned away again. He could feel it; he was so close. With his eyes closed and Roxanne buzzing in his ear, Flynn tried to find that quiet place in his mind, the one that held the other pieces. The address book. He had been searching for Mia's address . . . at Roxanne's house, while she was at work. He had paged through, all the way to the W's until he found it: Mia and Michael Wells, Willow Creek Court, Silver Spring, Maryland. For an instant he almost gave up. Maybe it was time to let go. She had found someone else. Too many years had passed. How many ways did she need to say it? She didn't want him. Everything pointed to a beautiful life. Who the hell was he to drop in on it? He put the address book away. There was something else there, at the bottom of the drawer. The corner of a familiar lavender envelope. His fingertips grazed against it, nudging it from underneath some papers. He uttered a rash of swear words at the sight of his own handwriting, at seeing Mia's name on the front. Twelve years and finally it all made sense.

Mia had never come because she didn't know. He slumped back into the chair, the last piece snapping into place. *Roxanne managed to get to the letter first. She took it, kept it from her. Mia thinks I walked out, vanished, exactly like she always feared I would.* Control, it had been about control from the moment Flynn and Mia met and Roxanne finally had her say. He had been absolutely livid when he left her house, the letter in his pocket, on a mad tear to the hospital with every intention of confronting Roxanne.

"Are you listening to me?" she sniped, their blue eyes meeting in one fixated steely glare of hatred. "Do yourself and Mia a favor and take off while you still can."

She was a brilliant, beautiful, manipulative thief who took away any chance the two of them had. Vengeance or making this right, Flynn had to decide which one he wanted. He choked back a laugh. Was it really even a question? Suddenly, he was thinking and talking as fast as he could. "Jesus, Roxanne, but you are awfully anxious to get rid of me. But then again, you do have a point." He paused; it had to be everything she wanted to hear. He had no chance of convincing her of anything else, the truth in particular. "Hell, you're right. As much as I want Mia, I don't want to be hanging around here when those DNA results come back."

As if finding a winning lottery ticket, Roxanne gasped loudly. "Oh my God, you did do it! I knew you killed those girls! I was right!"

"Yeah, like I'd confess to you. Speculation, circumstantial evidence, I can deal with that. DNA," he said, raising an eyebrow, "now that might be an issue. But you know, Roxanne, I'm not the only one with a secret. You have something of mine and I want it back. Considering my situation, I'm comfortable adding breaking and entering to my resume. I was on my way here from your house when I had the accident. But you already know that, don't you?"

"I don't know any such thing."

"I think you do. The nurses told me the only thing they found on me was this cross," Flynn said, looping a finger around the chain. "But there was something else. Something tucked inside my pocket. You were my ER doc, calling the shots. When you saw me, I'm sure you told them to hand over everything they found." He leaned forward, hissing out the question. "Where's the letter, Roxanne?"

"I threw it out," she offered without a modicum of guilt. "What does it matter? It only confirmed every suspicion I ever had about you. Escaped convict to serial killer—I haven't been wrong about you from the first second I saw you. I passed you that morning, Flynn, as you were heading out of town. An unfortunate turn of events for you, I left all my organic chemistry notes at the apartment. I couldn't very well prepare for a final without them, and I couldn't spend half the day driving. I had a family obligation that afternoon—in Atlanta." He tried to interrupt, but could only manage an incredulous stare. "I was back in Athens before the sun came up that morning. When I saw the letter I figured it was fate, destiny, my prerogative—call it whatever you like. You're damn right I took it. Do you really think I was going to let her read it? Buy into the garbage you were peddling?" She looked him over as if he were still in need of an exorcism. "I wasn't about to let her throw her life away while you rehabilitated yourself. Tell me, Flynn, do you know of any prison romances with a happily-ever-after ending?"

"Goddamn you. Who the hell do you think you are? The letter was for Mia. It was up to Mia to decide."

"She would have never made a clear decision, the right decision. The way she feels—felt about you . . . I've seen what that can do to a person, and I wasn't going to let it happen to her. Let her think the open road called you back or you got bored, the cops were breathing down your neck or you found someone else. Pick one," she said, spitting the words at him. "The reason you left didn't matter, the truth included. You were gone and you weren't coming back. My way was better. I understand your frustration, though. What a wasted spark of nobility, turning yourself in like that." Her head cocked to the side, looking him over. "Did you think time served would be absolution, make you good enough for her?" He turned away and she sharply recalled his attention. "Look at me! It didn't turn out so bad. Think about it. She's married to a man who's never been strip-searched or considered orange a staple color in his wardrobe." Roxanne rose to her feet, her posture as rigid and narrow as her conclusions. "The better man won, Flynn. And now, with what you've practically just confessed, you tell me how what I did was so wrong."

He struggled to get out of the chair, helplessly falling back into it. Then Flynn thought better of it. Playing right into her hands might be worth the gamble. He needed that letter. It was the only proof he had that he didn't walk out on her—that he did it so they could have a future. He kept chipping away, steadily baiting her. "Another good point, Roxanne. She would have followed me anywhere, done anything I asked. You know Mia could never keep her hands off me," he said, shooting her a smug stare. "Sympathy, sex, and six hot meals a week. It was a package sabbatical for the criminally insane."

"Do you hear yourself, you twisted bastard? So finishing that first prison sentence was what, throwing yourself on your sword?"

"I like to think that if I had Mia, there was a chance I could turn myself around. And, well, I was concerned about how long I could hold out. Damn, there was an entire campus full of girls at my fingertips," he said, rubbing the back of his neck as if it were an itch he couldn't quite scratch. "Prison was the only way I could think of to keep my hands clean, so to speak. I mean, that's a tough thrill to replace." He froze, looking hard at her. "You know that feeling, Roxanne, the power. I'm sure you do." She blinked, taking a step back. His voice dropped into an eerie cadence, the one he saved for court-martials and murder confessions. "That moment when somebody's life hangs in the balance and you control it. You decide their fate—whether or not they go on. It's up to you if they ever see the people they love again.

You control it all, their next breath—or not," he said, shrugging. "Believe me, Roxanne, I know the high."

"You are out of your mind," she said, dismissing him as she fiddled with some papers. Then, looking boldly at him, "Letting you rot away in that prison was the best thing I ever did for Mia."

"I'm sure you think so."

"Did you really think I'd let her waste years waiting for every other Sunday, maybe an occasional conjugal visit? Knowing you were locked up, I have to say, I've slept fairly well ever since."

"And these days, how are you sleeping, Roxanne?" He nodded at the lack of reply. "That's what I thought. So, do you still want me gone? Would it help get you through the night, or will you be dropping a dime to local law enforcement, offering up your grand illusions?"

"Grand illusions that will be crystal clear when that DNA gets back. No, as much as I'd like to see you back in prison, Mia comes first. I've done my best to see to her happiness; I won't quit now. I want you gone. You'd be front-page news for years. I won't put her or Michael through that humiliation. I'll keep protecting her. She's suffered enough because of you."

And you. "Good," he said, nodding. "Tell you what. In appreciation of your, um, discretion, I'll go. She'll think I vanished, just like last time. But I want something first. I want my letter back."

She laughed, shaking her head. "Why? What do you want with it? Keeping a scrapbook?"

"Nah, let's just say I don't like the idea of you holding on to any evidence of me. If I'm going, that letter goes with me. Game over. Part of coming back here was just to see what kind of trouble I could stir up. Hell, maybe if she left him she'd get to take a little of that well-to-do lifestyle with her. I'm thinking I'd only have to rehabilitate myself as far as a La-Z-Boy and a six-pack.

Shit, knowing Mia, she'd be happy to put my 1-900 numbers on speed dial for me." He stopped as Roxanne's jaw grazed against the floor. Maybe it was one visual too many. "Listen, if I learned anything from that last little go-round in prison, saving my own ass comes first. Prison isn't worth any woman, not even Mia."

"I was so right. Men like you are all the same." She pursed her lips, looking past his head. "Naturally though, it was the sweet girl you went for. Easy prey, right, Flynn?" Roxanne folded her arms. "I told you, I threw the letter out. Besides, why would I give it back?"

"Because you'd do anything to keep Mia from finding out that you took it. She'd never forgive you. That makes me, and what I know, a pretty damning threat. And that letter still exists, I'm sure of it. You kept it all these years as a souvenir that you were right, that I was never good enough for her. Every time you looked at it, you patted yourself on the back. You thought, hell, she has that great guy, that life, thanks to you. Am I right?" With each accusation Roxanne's chin tipped higher, her haughtiness serving as ample cover for any wrong she'd done. Flynn turned his attention out the window, thinking aloud. "Besides, what would she have if she waited for me? A box of old letters, a guy with nothing but a criminal record, and free Sundays." His breath caught, the thought hanging over him like an eclipse. It wasn't part of a ploy to outwit Roxanne. It was the truth.

"And that's the best-case scenario," she said softly. "She has a real life, Flynn. She also has a man who wants nothing but her happiness—no dark past, no questions about the future. Michael was the only choice."

"Right," he said, a weathered sigh churning from his gut.

"So if I give you the letter, you'll go?" He wasn't looking at her anymore, taking in the empty view of the hospital window. "Flynn?"

"Yeah, sure, Roxanne. By week's end."

She walked to the door, contemplating the deal with every click of her heels. "Fine, we have an agreement. We can burn it together. And then we're done." He looked back as she pivoted sharply, flicking her arctic eyes over him. "Understand something: Had anything you felt for Mia been genuine, if that DNA didn't prove you were viler than I always knew . . . if college girls had kept on dying *after* you turned yourself in, while you were in prison, I might have given you the benefit of the doubt. And, well, this might even have been a different conversation."

"Why? Do you really think any of that would change what you see?" She didn't reply, leaving with what she'd come for: the satisfaction of being right. It left him alone in a room filled with nothing but opposing truths.

Chapter 28

They drove east. And without a hint or map, Mia knew where they were headed. She said nothing as they approached the Chesapeake Bay Bridge, connecting busy metropolitan life to the simple shores of Kent Island. It held the allure of his third marriage proposal, when Mia had agreed, unable to deny the promise of a fresh future. Driving through the village of Stevensville and onto the rural roads that hugged marshy wetland, it felt more like a Sunday outing than the backdrop for life-altering decisions. She assumed that was the idea. Michael had kept the flow of conversation neutral, Mia answering with "Yes, September is always the prettiest month here." And "No, the air-conditioning's not too cold." She pulled in a low breath as they arrived at Love Point. The Bay's Bed was a waterfront inn, a romantic place filled with charm and memories.

"It's not what you're thinking," he said, pulling off his sunglasses. "I mean, I didn't book a room or anything. I just thought we could have lunch, take in the view." She didn't object, nodding. "If nothing else, it's a different perspective from the last month—or the last twenty-four hours, depending on which one of us you are."

But Michael was craftier than that. Mia saw the rocky point from where he made what he insisted would be his last proposal. That if she didn't agree to marry Michael and make him the happiest man in the world, he'd chuck it all. In a grand, Michael-like gesture, he said he'd buy a sailboat and spend the rest of his life drifting from port to port. Hindsight considered, Mia guessed the coast of Spain didn't sound like a bad plan at this point. But he kept the moment in focus, negotiating with the waitress for the seaside table with the best view, even as she insisted that it was already reserved. Naturally, he prevailed, holding Mia's chair as she breathed in salt air and memories.

He took a slightly different route, forgoing the obvious. "Do you remember the time we decided at noon on a Friday that we needed a vacation?"

She sipped a glass of wine, unable to keep from smiling at the recollection. "Of course I remember; I booked us a last-minute flight to Miami."

"But we never checked the weather, did we?"

"Well, let's be honest. *I* never checked the weather," she admitted. "We spent the entire weekend in a hotel, bracing for hurricane-force winds and watching the Weather Channel," she said, taking in the silky sky and high clouds of this day. "We couldn't figure out why we were the only people going out of the airport."

He reached across the table, fingers linking with hers. "We did a lot more than watch TV, Mia." His hand tightened. "It was really a wonderful trip." She tensed, pulling back, breaking away from his grip. "You cried, Mia, the next month, when the little arrow didn't turn blue and you weren't pregnant. You wanted that baby."

I wanted to give in to fate. It would have been a reason to let go . . . and it didn't happen. It had occurred to Mia, not long after, that needing a new human being to cut the ribbon on your future probably indicated a flaw in your plan.

"You can't dismiss those memories, and we have a lot of them."

There was no point in hurting him with any more truth. "But you were right, Michael. You said it was too soon. We were barely married six months. It wasn't meant to be."

They sat in silence, Mia taking in the view, Michael surely taking an inventory of their life together. She could see him debating the next heart-rattling memory, swallowing down the scotch he'd ordered. A calm drive and pleasant scenery aside, it was proof of his state of mind. Michael barely drank beer with his buddies. Hard liquor was reserved for hard-nosed business dinners and tough negotiations. She braced for whatever he brought up next, aware that no memory would trigger the feelings for which he searched. There was one, however, guaranteed to make her squirm in her seat. *My thirtieth birthday, now there's a kicker. A surprise trip to Athens, a football game. Thought you'd thrill me with a fun-filled nostalgic weekend. It was all I could do to keep my head from exploding. Everywhere I looked, there was Flynn.*

Thankfully, he abandoned the past, opting for generic conversation. "I think the vacation crowd has cleared out," he said, his gaze scanning the sparse collection of boats on the bay.

Mia shrugged, finishing the glass of wine. "Or just haven't arrived for the Labor Day weekend."

"Maybe," he said, also downing his drink. Glad for the waitress's interruption, they ordered, the food arriving mercifully fast. It did look fabulous; Mia recalled the cuisine was exquisite. "It looks wonderful," she said, ordering another glass of wine.

"You, um, you never did say. Did you accomplish everything you needed to in Vegas?"

"Vegas," he said, poking at a plate of pasta. "Seems like a light-year ago instead of yesterday." They exchanged a wary glance, Mia keeping the rhythm of food moving toward her mouth. "No, not really. I may need to fly back later this week, take another meeting."

"That's fine, Michael, you do what you need to." She meant it as no more than a benign comment, the kind of thing she always said, never wanting to get in the way of his work.

He took it as a direct dismissal, his fork dropping onto the plate with a resounding crack. "I guess that would suit you fine. Maybe you'll get lucky, maybe the plane will wreck. Damn, it certainly would go a long way to solving your problems. You could come to my funeral, stand by me, continue to play the devoted wife. Then the two of you can quietly cash in the life insurance. Take that European vacation we've always talked about. When you get back he can just move right into the house—the neighbors might talk a little, but what the heck."

"Michael, I . . ." She could only stare, stunned by his train of thought. A plump shrimp stopped midway to her mouth, which was gaping wide at the accusation. "I'd never . . . That's . . . that's a horrible thing to say!" She lobbed the shrimp, fork and all, onto the table. The cooked crustacean broke free and he watched it bounce, jumping the rail and falling back into the sea. Mia reared back in her seat, doing everything she could to keep a civil tone. "Understand something, Michael. I didn't go looking for this. You can think I'm an unfeeling, self-centered bitch, think I've wanted him back since the day he left, but don't think I'd ever wish anything like that on you."

He pushed the plate away, shuffling back in his chair, distancing himself. "I know you wouldn't. I'm just really angry and frustrated. I don't even know who to be angrier with—you, him . . . or myself."

Scrubbing a hand over her face, Mia had to agree. Anger would be the least of her emotions had the scenario been reversed. Well, that wasn't entirely true. Last year, at a Christmas party, Mia watched as a beautiful young lawyer from Michael's office cornered him by the pastry table. He was friendly but unaffected by the woman's flirtatious advance, which was clear from across the room. Naturally, nothing came of it. But as they drove home, on the seat next to Mia sat a pesky guilt. Instead of politely approaching, introducing herself as Michael's wife, she stayed on the opposite side of the room, considering what a lovely couple they made.

There was even less conversation on the way back to Silver Spring, Michael having spent the majority of the ride on the phone with work, Mia looking out the window. She wasn't sure what the afternoon had accomplished, other than driving something sharp and unbendable farther into his wound. They pulled into the driveway as Michael discussed a business matter that did sound urgent. "I have to get some paperwork, go into the office for a while," he said, flipping closed his phone. "Are you—"

"I'm going to my meeting with Hough . . . and then, yes, I'm going to the hospital."

"It'll be late," he said, getting out of the car.

"Does it matter?"

"I suppose not." He stopped, a hand clasping around her arm. "Then what?"

"Then . . ." Mia took a tumultuous breath, wishing there was some way to fast-forward, allowing Michael to glide past his immediate future. At the moment, she had no answer that didn't convey his worst fear. "I guess we talk some more." She meant about an amicable end to their marriage; she guessed he was still thinking of ways to reconcile it.

They walked toward the house, the two of them stopping at Mia's car, which had a flat tire. He shook his head, hands stuffed into his pockets. "Damn, I suppose you'd like me to change that."

She stared at the deflated tire, realizing the depth of humiliation it would require for him to do so. "Of course not." She glanced at her watch, seeing that time was short. "I'll call for a cab."

Inside the house, Michael changed into business attire and disappeared into his study. He left moments later, without a word. Mia had no more time to wallow in outcomes or think of words to soften the blow. She had to switch gears fast and get to her meeting with Aaron Hough. Flipping through the phonebook, she called a cab company, gathering her things as she spoke, sketches and her portfolio. It was a magic-act change, grabbing a suit from the closet and negotiating the stairs while tugging on high heels. Looking into the foyer mirror, Mia pulled a brush through her hair and applied a hint of lipstick, a layer of guilt draping over her grim expression. It was almost comical after the hours spent envisioning the preparations for such a meeting. A FedEx driver was on his way up the walk as Mia opened the door. As he delivered a slim envelope, she considered asking him for a lift. But as she was tucking the envelope into her portfolio, the cab pulled into the driveway.

* *

Flynn exhaled a restless breath, tapping his head against the window in short, terse strokes. Late afternoon sunlight pulsed in, and he saw his pale eyes reflected in the glass as he stared into the distance. The sun inched toward the Potomac, its baking rays penetrating the window. He could tell it had been a hot day for September. Heat always caught up with him. An aimless smile crept across his face. He now leaned his body against the glass. Maybe he'd move to Alaska when this was over. The smile vanished, raw nerves riding him like an addict on his third day without a fix. If he had to wait one more minute for Mia, he was absolutely going to lose it.

A nurse had come by after lunch and told him he should be resting in bed. Flynn ignored her, firming up a shaky stance. He'd gladly continue to endure pain for his freedom. It belonged to him now, the ability to say what he wanted, be where he wanted. And he was ready to make good on everything he'd promised himself and Mia, even if she didn't know it.

Worse than any nightmare, he'd endured a sticky, heat-filled vision. Mia and her husband making up for lost time. Had Roxanne been lying about that? It could very well go that way. Mia might tell him, thanks, but she'd made other plans with her life. Who could blame her? Michael Wells surely didn't have the kind of past that hung on post-office walls. He'd seen Mia for ten lousy minutes. Twelve years and it was all he got, ten hazy minutes. Even so, the conversation was seared into his mind. He had replayed it endlessly. Everything about her said she was something more than an ex-lover who'd come by to hold his hand. When she learned the truth, maybe it would make a difference. Or maybe he was just setting himself up for one horrific fall. Who was to say it wasn't exactly what he deserved? Maybe punishment for the past went far beyond time served.

Flynn sipped cold coffee. The lunch went untouched; it had an unsavory kinship to prison food. Didn't matter, he wouldn't have eaten it had a four-star chef prepared it. He thought about the fried chicken Mia had cooked, that silly dinner with Roxanne. She hadn't come back yet, didn't bring the letter. She was probably waiting in the shadows, figuring the police would show up sooner rather than later. *Go ahead and wait, Roxanne. Bet it all on your damn DNA.*

Flynn left the coffee, returning to the window. He couldn't help it; there it was again. Mia and this man to whom she was married, he couldn't force it together in his mind. All those years, he knew it was possible. Hell, it was probable. It didn't make it easier though he'd prodded himself with countless reminders. Mia didn't know; she thought he'd walked out on her. And this man, did he pick up the pieces? Was he the comfort at night? Did he help her through it? Maybe Mia realized what a mistake he would have been before he hit the state line. Wasn't he the one telling her all along that he'd hold the door open, applaud her if she decided to leave? Maybe she had taken his advice. Maybe she would have rolled her eyes at the letter and said, "He's got to be kidding . . ."

The IV was gone, not so gently yanked out by the same nurse who came back at three. The stronger he felt, the more uncomfortable the hospital attire became. Flynn gingerly paced the room, moving awkwardly on unsteady legs. Then he stopped sharply, as if he'd hit a wall. *Kids, what if they had kids?* It could change everything, no matter how she felt about him. Surely Roxanne would have mentioned that, thrown it in his face. Maybe not. Even Roxanne would protect a child. She wouldn't want him to know. He was back at the window, knocking his knuckles against the glass. *God, let her come soon. Either way, let this be finished.* A take-charge voice broke into his thoughts and he turned from the window.

"Excuse me, you're Flynn, aren't you?" The man was all confidence, coming right at him, never hesitating as he extended a hand. Without thinking, Flynn automatically shook it. "I'm

Michael Wells, Mia's husband. I'd say nice to meet you, glad you're feeling better, but . . ."

"But that would be a load of bullshit," Flynn said, assessing the sudden, if not polite, ambush.

"Something like that."

He turned back to the window, not affording Michael the courtesy of eye contact. There was no point to this conversation. He'd learn everything he needed to from Mia. Yet there he was, standing in front of him in his thousand-dollar suit, clean shaven, dripping with success. Even his aftershave had the scent of a born winner. "Where's Mia?" he asked, speaking into the window. The reality of it disgusted him, needing this man to tell him where Mia was as if she belonged to him.

Flynn heard his contemplative sigh. "Ah, Roxanne said you could be . . . abrupt. I'd like to speak with you about Mia."

"Roxanne's a fucking lying bitch. How's that for abrupt? If you've been talking to her, I already know what you're thinking. I've got nothing to say to you about Mia." Cold, impassive, Flynn turned, demanding again, "Where is she?" It was reflex, that defense mechanism. The one that guarded against society, against the assumptions people made. Flynn returned his vacant stare back to the window.

Michael cleared his throat. Evidently blistering hostility didn't enter into his usual high-stakes negotiations. In the reflection, he could see Michael's stance shift, looking as if he was trying to figure Flynn out. Perhaps it was dawning on him that this man was not approachable from within the norms. "Look, this is a difficult situation. For everyone. But Mia is my wife . . ." Flynn's head whipped around as the words lashed into him. He understood that Michael was prepared for the challenge. "And if you want her, you're going to have to go through me, you son of a bitch."

"Not a problem." Flynn turned away again.

"I see. I suppose that answers my first question. Do I understand you correctly? You can just grunt once for yes. You want her back? You came here to find her, after all these years? My wife is not delusional?"

"Yeah, bad weather in Cleveland, took a little longer than I thought."

"Hey, why don't you lose the fucking attitude," Michael snapped. "This gets more absurd by the second. I can't believe this is what Mia wants."

"What Mia wants." He wouldn't be here if she didn't want me. This guy is about two seconds away from ripping my head off. Flynn drew strength from the hint Michael unknowingly offered. "Look, Mike, don't take it personally. I'm sure you're a great guy. Under any other circumstance, you and I might have . . ." He took in Michael's well-groomed but appalled expression. Flynn shrugged. "Might have passed each other on the street without incident?"

"Except for this one very unlikely thing we seem to have in common." Michael shoved his hands into his pockets and tipped back on his heels a little, examining the floor for a moment. It was as close to civil conversation as they were going to get. "Mia will be here this evening."

"Good, the waiting is really getting tedious." Flynn shot him a contemptuous glare, shifting his weight. He didn't dare sit down.

"And arrogant. Roxanne mentioned that too. Look, I don't have time to negotiate with you, so I'll just say my piece. A couple of days ago you were nothing more than a vague college memory, and now you're in a position to blow my life apart. I'm usually more prepared, so you'll have to understand, I'm at a significant disadvantage here." Flynn didn't buy a word of that, staring steadily out the window. "Generally I'm afforded more time to gauge an opponent," he said, equating Flynn to a challenging business maneuver, "evaluate his assets, exploit any weaknesses."

Flynn turned slightly. "Let me help you out. I don't have any fucking assets, and even fewer weaknesses—which, from your perspective, gives me an unknown value. My guess is that's not a position you're used to finding yourself in."

"Hardly," Michael said. "Either way, it's an unsettling circumstance, so you'll forgive me if I'm blunt here."

"Blunt? I was wondering if you're always this polite when somebody shows up to claim your wife. Must work for you though," he said, scanning his polished appearance. Flynn guessed he was the kind of man who couldn't fathom loss. "You don't look like you're wanting for much."

Michael ignored the remark as he folded his arms across his chest, moving closer. "Everything I have is nothing without Mia. It might be the last thing you want to hear, but I love my wife. All I'm asking for is the opportunity to be heard, before she gets here. Look, you don't owe me a damn thing. But regardless of what you believe, Mia has been happy these past few years. It's something you might want to consider before incinerating the life she has."

The guy was shrewd. No wonder he was wearing a thousand-dollar suit. Apparently he'd earned every thread. "I'm listening. But like I said, if you've been talking to Roxanne and you're about to accuse me of knocking off college coeds, we can all just take a time-out until the DNA gets back."

"First of all, it wouldn't solve my problem. Secondly, I doubt that DNA will show much of anything."

"What makes you say that?" Flynn said, surprised by his generous assumption.

"Mia, mostly. I can't believe she'd be that wrong about someone she feels . . . Well, I'm sure as hell not going there. Listen, even if Roxanne saw you in the library, standing over Professor Plum with the candlestick . . . well, in Mia's eyes it would only hang you higher on the cross. Besides, I've known Roxanne a long time. There are a lot of things that drive her . . . Not all of them are easy to understand."

Flynn glanced back. "Her sister . . . I know."

Michael nodded, crinkling his brow. "Roxanne confided that to you?"

He shook his head. "Mia did—eventually."

"Anyway, I want to show you something. Like I said, I don't have time for long negotiations. If you could just take a look, maybe you'll understand how solid, how safe Mia's life is."

Flynn watched as Michael pulled an envelope from his jacket pocket. *If they're fucking baby pictures, I'm throwing myself out the window.* It was close. Inside were a dozen or so pictures of Mia looking as happy as he'd promised. Flynn hid short, nervous breaths as he passed by each photo. At first he was just mesmerized. She was as beautiful as every memory he carried with him. When he left Athens, he took a few pictures with him, but once she didn't come, it was only on rare occasions that he looked at them. Michael moved closer, obviously feeling the need to narrate.

"They're just everyday pictures, from home, from the holidays. That's Mia with my family. She's very close to my sisters. Here she's in the kitchen, Thanksgiving. She loves to cook. It's her favorite holiday."

"I know," Flynn said dully.

"And this," he said, pointing to the next one. "Mia broke her ankle skiing. Six weeks on the couch. That was actually before we were married."

"How, um, how long have you been . . . married?"

"Two years this fall. It took me four years to convince her. I never could understand the hesitation. She claims it was cautiousness." He looked at Flynn, pulling in a difficult breath. "Now I suspect that's debatable."

Flynn nodded. The first six years. Mia spent that time believing he'd vanished without a trace, hurting, wondering why. There was an unnerving pang of gratefulness toward Michael Wells. He didn't want to think of Mia as lonely and miserable. It was small comfort, but Flynn had spent the last dozen years under the impression that a life without him was what she'd chosen. He looked at Michael, feeling a little ill. He didn't want to owe him anything either.

But the photos weren't as simple as Michael claimed. Flynn was wise to the story they told. They graduated; from innocent family candids to the broken ankle he'd nursed, straight on to the big-ticket items strategically placed last. Mia posing in front of a Sold sign, a handsome two-story brick house behind her. Then in another, pulling a giant red ribbon off a shiny Mercedes-Benz. Flynn stared at the last one longer than the others. They never had talked much about the future. Mia because she was hiding from it, Flynn because he knew he'd have to surrender it.

"Actually, there's something more important here than Mia smiling or the material stuff."

"Really? You mean you didn't bring your stock portfolio along too?"

"I wanted to give you a sense of the security she has. Mia doesn't worry about where she's going to live or how long it will be until I tire of her and decide to take off. Questions, doubts like that, they don't enter this marriage. And they never will as long as I'm her husband. I have no idea what you're prepared to offer her, but unless you can do at least as good as this, think it over. Because if Mia goes through with this, makes what I believe is a terrible choice, and you end up hurting her again . . . you will be dead to her, because I will fucking kill you myself." Flynn shoved the pictures back at him, turning away. "Are you listening to me?" The lack of response baited Michael's anger. "I've got to wonder about a guy who drifts into town and spends a year taking advantage of an innocent college girl. When he's had enough, he cuts and runs. I was there, you know." Flynn turned, furrowing his brow. "Not in any meaningful way . . . not to Mia. I was a grad student; Roxanne and I were study partners. But I noticed Mia. Hell, who wouldn't?" Flynn had to agree, offering a barely perceptible nod as he turned back to the window. "Even then I wondered what she saw in someone like you. If you ask me, she was spellbound, if not brainwashed."

"What the hell is that supposed to mean?" Flynn said. He turned fast, taking a foreboding step in Michael's direction. It set off too many visions from a past he couldn't forget.

"What were you doing to her? Her attachment to you is twisted at best. How could someone like you keep such a tight hold on a woman like Mia? Of course, she wasn't quite all grown up back then. She was a naïve college girl with a fat trust fund at her disposal."

"Mia and I never discussed that, not once. And you underestimate her. She was smarter than that."

"Regardless. Your influence was inexplicable . . . unsavory. You didn't belong in her life. Yet you managed to maintain the kind of control reserved for military interrogations and POWs." Flynn swallowed hard as Michael struck a frayed nerve. He closed the distance, taking a sharp poke at Flynn's shoulder. "So you tell me, Sergeant McDermott, what were the rules of engagement? A questionable past, no apparent future—what kept her attention? With your military background, you were wise to control tactics she's never heard of. You were in total control of that relationship, giving the orders. Who knows what else, maybe slapping her around a little if she got out of line—"

That was it; the trigger was pulled. Flynn's hands gripped the lapels of Michael's suit, prepared to redefine the concept of slapping someone around. Michael was having none of it, grabbing Flynn with equal bravado, quickly shoving him against the wall. His weakened state put Flynn at a momentary disadvantage. His mind took over, containing the screaming pain. He deftly turned the tables, flipping Michael around, his back now pinned to the wall.

"I don't have to explain a goddamn thing to you. You got to be with her for six fucking years, married to her for two of them. I can't begin to tell you how that makes me want to 'slap somebody around.' Mia belongs to me! Houses, cars, ski trips, stock in Disneyland—it won't change a thing."

"I don't have to change anything. I'm married to her!"

"A temporary problem, I assure you." Flynn's forearm jammed sharply into Michael's throat. But after a near-lethal second, he let go, backing away. He wasn't that man anymore.

Smoothing the front of his suit, Michael appeared undaunted if not disappointed. "Shame, had you done some real damage it would have gone a long way toward making my point. She'd never forgive you."

"Believe me; if I'd done some *real* damage, you'd need this hospital more than me."

"As for Mia belonging to you . . . well, I have a life, a marriage certificate, and a bed that says otherwise." Michael's confidence was too steady. Flynn took a harder look, guessing there was more. "I also know how far I'm willing to go to ensure Mia's happiness. So let me ask you the same thing: What are you willing to do for her?"

He wanted to answer, *twelve years in prison, minimum*, but he couldn't see the advantage. "Anything. I'd do anything for her."

"And if getting out of her life is what's best, would you do that?" Michael stepped back, allowing for distance and doubt.

"If that was what she wanted . . ."

"As I said, Mia's happy—or was, until you disrupted what was a very pleasant life. In fact, her happiness is about to expand tenfold. Mia's about to see a dream come true . . ." He hesitated, clearing his throat. "One that doesn't include you. I've spent months seeing to it. There's something to which she's totally devoted—more so than you or me. Actually, I'm willing to bet that its genesis was sparked by another man entirely. Eco-friendly, green commercial . . ."

"Holistic design. I'm aware; I was there at the beginning, long before she even understood what it meant, what she was designing."

"Good, because I've been around for the trial-and-error phase, watched the years go by as she's tried to get it off the ground, make it sell. And you know Mia. It has nothing to do with money; she's only interested in the impact, the benefits—whatever she believes them to be. Right now, she has an opportunity to see that happen. And, Flynn, take my word for it when I tell you it's a sure thing."

"What'd you do, convince Congress to pass a law mandating holistic, eco-friendly design?"

"Not quite, but know this: For what I've invested, Mia's happiness is the only return I'll be getting. And I will protect my investment. One thing I've learned about holistic design: Lots of people talk, but very few are willing to commit. At least not to the standard she's looking for. There's no steady demand, not like with her regular designs—which are fabulous, not to mention lucrative. That makes these designs a risk and nearly impossible to mass market. But thanks to some creative financing and project specific negotiations, an investor has stepped forward. Aaron Hough. Maybe you've heard of him?"

Flynn recalled the news article, Mia pictured with the developer. The one who said he was wildly enthusiastic about her work. "Yeah, it's familiar."

"It seems he was able to acquire commercial property on a national scale, at a more than fair interest rate and exceptional terms." Michael held up a hand, warding off any assumptions. "All quite legal, just incredibly stacked in his favor. Sometimes you have to go beyond what's customary to secure what's necessary—I'm sure you understand, not everything in the world can operate on altruism."

He snickered. "Yeah, you could say I have a clue about that."

"Part of those terms includes Hough's dedication to Mia's project. He's willing to go green all the way—mainstream every one of her ideas."

Flynn's chin tipped higher, piecing together Michael's plan. "Not because he believes it, but because of the financial deal you cut for him?"

"Like I said, not everything in life can be based on an altruistic cause."

"And she has no idea you finagled this? Mia believes she achieved this on her own?"

"Do you want to tell her otherwise?" It was a risk-filled question for both men, Flynn seeing the wager in Michael's eyes. "She gets there. That's all that matters to me. I'm going to see that Mia's dream comes to fruition—guaranteed."

"But now there's an addendum to that guarantee. You'll see to it as long as I'm not in the picture."

Michael shrugged, his stare intent. "Look at it any way you need to. But there's something else you might want to factor in. According to Mia, executed on a mass scale, holistic design could increase the average life expectancy, save a few people from an early grave." He paused, laying down his bottom line. "Don't you think her father would be incredibly proud? *If* he was alive to see it—he's the third guy in this curious triangle. The success of her designs won't bring him back, but it will give her peace of mind and some residual approval."

A huge sigh heaved in and out of Flynn. Roxanne's voice rumbled through his head: no dark past, no questions about the future, that's what Michael Wells offered. And while his methods were doubtful, they weren't without merit. Flynn couldn't take that away—and offer Mia what in return? He'd leave this hospital and do what? Go where? It wasn't the life he wanted to give her back in Athens; it was no better now. Sure, he was a free man, having paid a debt that wasn't his, but was that what mattered?

It was as if Michael was in his head, reading his thoughts. "Like I said, unless you can do at least as good, you might want to reconsider what you're doing here. Maybe this isn't about what you want." For two men who couldn't have more in common, their mutual stare was filled with distrust. "Do the right thing, Flynn. Bow out; if you truly care for Mia, ensure her happiness. You're equally in a position to do that."

Chapter 29

"I understand, Aaron. I know you're a busy man. I had a flat tire, but I'm on my way. I have the rest of the presentation with me." Mia pressed her hand over the cell phone. "Could we speed this up a bit? Whatever the fare is, I'll double it."

"You got it, lady," the cab driver said, darting from the right lane into the left.

"Yes, Aaron, of course I'm still here. Well, yes," she hedged. "I understand that I'm a half-hour late." Mia glanced at her watch for the tenth time, having hoped it was running fast. "There was a personal matter that came up and I— No, not another accident," Mia said, her credibility ticking away with the time. "I understand that you're waiting at the site right now." She tried countering his sarcasm. "No, I don't know what your time breaks down to at an hourly rate . . . Really? That much. If you could just—" But he hung up before she could come up with a reply to "You've got five minutes to get here."

They were still blocks away, rush-hour traffic slowing them down. Raking a hand through her hair, Mia guessed a tripled fare wouldn't convince the cabby to drive on the sidewalk. She took a deep breath, thinking about what she could control. Organization. She unzipped her portfolio, realizing that she had never transferred her final drawings to computer graphics. How incredibly professional, she thought, rolling her eyes. Perhaps she could dazzle Hough with some evidentiary data. People in his position always liked to talk numbers. Shuffling through the paperwork, the FedEx envelope slipped from between the pages. Her eyes glossed over it, ready to tuck it aside. But the return label caught her attention: HOUGH DEVELOPMENT—yet it was clearly addressed to Michael. "What in the world . . ." She tore it open, and pages fell onto her lap, something that looked like an invoice. "Nineteen thousand . . ." she said, looking at a page six total. *$19,999.63.* It was a curious number, the kind that stuck in your head. It was also the exact amount that Hough's foreman, Sam Kramer, was short. "This doesn't make any sense. Why would Michael pay for . . ." Scanning the other pages, Mia's brow furrowed tighter. It was an invoice, detailing every purchase she made for the mock office—the one that Aaron Hough was supposed to be financing. "What's Michael doing with . . ." Her hands gripped the pages tighter, snippets of conversation filling in a few more blanks. *"I already feel as if I know Michael . . ." "I'll see to it that Aaron Hough grants you an extension . . ."* And the cruise tickets. Michael bought them knowing it was a sure thing, that Hough would offer Mia a contract. She thought back to Aaron Hough's initial phone call. It was more than out of the blue, and it never did add up. Ecstatic over his interest, she'd excused his lack of knowledge as eccentric grassroots initiative. And she was happy to be the professional in charge.

As the cab pulled up to the vintage brick building, scraps of another conversation, something her brain overrode at the time, seeped back in. Sam Kramer had all but given them away.

He said that Hough and a man had been by the mock office. A suited, savvy businessman who fit Michael's description, someone who bragged on her work and those everyday designs. "But why?" she whispered, her gaze trailing out the window. "Why would Michael do that?" Mia sank back into the seat, forced to entertain a truth about a man who never gave up on the notion that big gestures would win her heart. This, however, went beyond ribbon-wrapped vehicles or cruises to the Caribbean. Not for a moment did Michael ever believe she'd succeed on her own. Staring through the taxi's window at a broken, unsalvageable layer of brick, Mia guessed it represented her entire professional existence.

"Hey, lady, you gettin' out or you want to change destinations?"

She glanced at the meter, which read seventeen dollars, and tossed two twenties onto the seat. "Here is fine. I'm guessing we're at the end of the road," she said, scrambling out of the cab.

* *

The hospital had provided Flynn with a small duffel bag and a change of clothes. His sister had wired him enough money for a bus ticket to Texas, while Michael Wells had severed any lingering hope. Circumstance had managed to totally fuck up the rest.

Never having been a big believer in fate—or just fighting it his whole life—Flynn decided that it was time to give in. After Michael left, the argument continued in his head, weighing the misery he'd caused and that he would continue to bring if he stayed. He wouldn't be responsible for taking away the one thing Mia had worked for since . . . well, since before him. It trumped his existence, and it was an uneven trade. But it wasn't everything. As much as he hated to validate anything that spewed from Roxanne's mouth, she was right about a lot of things. Mia would have wasted a dozen years of her life had she waited for him. She'd waste the next dozen while he tried to resuscitate his. Flynn thought time served, and then some, earned him the right to a future. Maybe it did. It just didn't earn him the right to hers.

"You're going?" A soft drawl came from across the room from where he stood, packing up his few belongings.

He glanced up. "Roxanne. I didn't think you'd be back—at least not without the National Guard and an attack canine."

In her right hand, pinched between two fingers, was a once-lavender envelope. It was dirt covered and streaked with dried blood. It was nearly unrecognizable. Neither was Roxanne, now that he took a closer look. He knew every line of that sculpted face. But something had changed. A marked shift in glacial form. "You bring the lighter?" he asked, ignoring it, sure she'd only come to seal her end of the bargain.

"No," she said quietly. "I, um . . . I had some unexpected news this afternoon." Tucked tight to her body, in her left hand, was a larger envelope. The set line of her pursed lips bent to a frown, as if trying to hold something back. "Raymond Allan Mallard," she finally choked out.

It was the way she said it, like she couldn't breathe. She looked absolutely ill. Flynn even thought she might pass out. Everything considered, he wondered if letting her hit the floor would be bad form. "Raymond Allan who?"

She held out the larger envelope. "The DNA, it came back. Seems I've assisted in solving a twelve-year-old string of homicides. My zealous demand for the FBI to examine your DNA re-energized the case, leading them to information that identified the real killer. Go figure," she said, dumbstruck. "There's a letter from the FBI; they're making a formal announcement today—giving me a citizen's citation."

"Congratulations," he said dully, going about his business.

Yet she continued. "Eleven years ago, Raymond Allan Mallard was arrested in Gainesville, Florida—just outside the university." She looked at Flynn, her porcelain brow gathering. "He killed a girl there, in Florida. Because he shot her, because she wasn't a student, they never linked it to the other murders. The gun didn't fit the pattern. All the other girls, they were beaten to death, and he used that fact to deflect suspicion. He told the police that he knew the girl he shot; that they'd been on a date gone bad. The authorities concluded that it was an isolated homicide. He was sentenced to twenty years. Based on my query, further investigation revealed that Raymond Mallard worked at a dozen different colleges—a drifter who moved from town to town. Two days ago, there was a match to the blood evidence taken off the girl in Alabama. His DNA—not yours."

Flynn nodded, not feeling particularly surprised. "Makes sense. His DNA wouldn't have been on file twelve years ago when I asked them to test mine."

"What? Why would you request that kind of test if you knew—"

"I didn't know, not for sure. It's why I left the letter, left Mia, left Athens in such a goddamn hurry." He stopped what he was doing and looked at her. "Fine, you want to hear it. It was the day I left; I was at your apartment—alone. Mia had gone to turn in her final design project. I was looking for something to read. I found a little more than I was bargaining for. I found the news clippings in your room. It was quite a jolt, your neatly compiled day-in-the-life-of-a-serial-killer. But it only served to speed up a plan I already had in place to turn myself in." She seemed confused; it was an odd look for Roxanne. "It's complicated— things from my past that are still none of your business. But I will tell you that back then I lived with some seriously scary demons. Scarier than you. There were blocks of time I couldn't account for: random, inexplicable—and, yes, violent. I don't know that I would have ever come up with your theory. But when I read the accounts of those murders, how each girl died, and saw the map—well, it scared the living hell out of me. The timeline was . . ."

"Remarkable?"

"And then some. Because of those missing hours—days, in some cases, I couldn't dismiss or deny the facts. I just couldn't be sure. If there was even the slightest chance . . . Well, I couldn't spend one more night anywhere near Mia. The rest played out like you figured. Except, of course, the part about the DNA not being a match. Afterward, when Mia didn't come, I assumed that was her choice. I'm sure you're clear on what I'd asked her to do in the letter if she wasn't coming."

"Yes," she said, "I am." And for the first time Flynn heard remorse, some admonition that Roxanne had stuck her nose in where it didn't belong. "Turning yourself in, it was . . ."

"It was the only way out. The only thing I could do if I wanted a future with Mia—someday. And it's still not something I have to justify to you." He turned away, reshuffling his things around the duffel bag. A heart-to-heart with Roxanne was too bizarre, not to mention pointless.

"Interesting, I've recently had that pointed out to me." With their business finished, Flynn figured she'd go. But the white lab coat didn't disappear from his peripheral vision, and he was compelled to look. It seemed she'd been waiting for eye contact. "I'm . . . I'm sorry, Flynn."

"You're sor—" He laughed. "A lot of good that does me now." He shook his head, shrugging. "Doesn't matter. A lot of things didn't turn out the way I would have liked. Not all of them are your fault." He stared for a second, wondering if absolution was within him. "I've recently had it pointed out to me that Mia's happiness was your only intent." The line of her mouth turned to a frown as she nodded. "Anyway, at first I'd hoped for a new trial; it didn't happen. When Mia didn't come, I figured, what difference did it make? Prison, roaming the earth . . . Without her, I really didn't give a damn about my address."

"So you came back because . . ."

They were words Flynn imagined he'd say to Mia. "Because if nothing else I wanted to tell her that I loved her—out loud. It was the one thing she wanted to hear and the only thing I couldn't say. If I had given her that back then . . . Well, we'd still be running. No matter what you think of me, it wasn't the life I wanted to give her. I would have never done that to her." *I still won't.* "But now, even if she found fucking happy-ever-after with somebody else, I earned the right to say it. She should know that what we had got me through the last twelve years." Sucking in a weathered sigh, Flynn zipped the bag shut. "I found a lot of peace there, knowing we were under the same sky."

"So you came back for a second chance."

He glanced at her. "If that's how you want to look at it, I guess I did."

"Mia's good at that, second chances. She always had a heart too big; an ability to overlook a person's flaws, no matter how unyielding. She even managed to understand mine, that I only wanted what was best for her—that I wanted her to be safe, happy . . . to have a whole life."

"But she'll never understand—or forgive this."

Roxanne smiled, a tear trickling down her face. "No, I don't expect she will." He watched as she tossed the dirty lavender envelope onto the bed. "I won't be getting a second chance. And you don't need one. You never did."

Flynn touched the edge of the envelope, but he didn't pick it up. "I'd love nothing more than to find out if that's true. It just isn't the right thing to do."

* *

The vintage brick rehab provided the canvas for Mia's groundbreaking effort. Aaron Hough was the puppet for opportunity while her husband pulled all the strings. Circumstance had managed to totally screw up the rest.

Expecting complacent and apologetic, Aaron was caught off guard when Mia came through the door of the mock office demanding an explanation. It gave her an unlikely upper hand after establishing what she'd discovered, wanting to know why her husband was paying for a project that the wealthy investor was supposed to be financing. After a few sentences of doubletalk, he confessed that Michael's bank was providing the financing for his latest business venture while her husband personally picked up the tab for the office. It seemed that Hough's portfolio had taken an economic hit in recent years, and Michael had offered some creative financial aid. The two of them had struck a deal, which involved a few extraneous clauses centering on Mia's holistic designs.

"Mia, I'm having a difficult time understanding why you're upset. If you think about it, the gesture was quite benevolent on Michael's part. He took a sizable professional risk to arrange everything, in addition to agreeing to pay for this," Aaron said with a wave of his hand, taking a seat in the mock office. "Perhaps his methods were unorthodox, but he only wanted you to have the chance to pursue a dream."

Mia shook her head. "Believe me, I understand Michael's motivation. It's yours that has me bewildered. In the long term, it doesn't make sense. No matter what the financing, even if

Michael got you zero interest and a forgiveness clause if you default, why would you agree to holistic design for all your commercial holdings? My guess is you're not any more sold on it than he is."

"That's not true; I think it's a commendable idea," he insisted, arms widening as he gestured toward the space. "What you've accomplished here, it's, um, bold, cutting edge . . . colorful," he said, toying with the phone wire desk accessories. "Why, I'm willing to bet the EPA would give you a gold star for your effort."

Mia snickered, scrunching her brow. "You don't have the first clue what I've done here, do you?"

"That's not really my job, is it, Mia? You're the decorator."

"Designer," she said, as if he didn't comprehend English. "I design holistic, eco-friendly commercial interiors; that's why you hired me." She stopped, arms leaning on the desktop, almost nose to nose with Aaron Hough. "You had no intention of going through with it, did you? Somehow, some way, after the mock office, you were going to pull the plug on the entire design effort."

His gaze never averted from hers, even smiling a bit. "All right, if we must. I've nothing to gain by perpetuating this— there are lots of talented, willing *designers* out there. Yes, the mock office was going to be a one-of-a-kind proposition. Your husband offered me a financial aid package that I couldn't refuse. While Michael was under the impression that other offices would follow, there was to be a small addendum in your contract. If at any time I rejected your eco-friendly designs, I reserved the right to revert to a design of my choosing. It was to be a fine-print, nominal risk I assumed you'd take. Especially if you thought I was sold on holistic design."

"That's . . . that's horrible," she said, backing up, at a loss for big business words that conveyed her disgust. "Not only did you disrespect my time and expertise, you totally misrepresented yourself to Michael. That makes you nothing more than a con artist!"

"That's savvy business, Mia. Grow up. It's not like you would have lost the contract or lost any money. On the contrary; your standard designs are exceptional. I know that. I would have leased or sold those office suites for a fortune, and you would have made a tidy profit. It hardly makes me a monster. It's, um, commendable, albeit odd, what you've done here," he said, glancing around. "But what's the point of five hundred or a thousand holistically designed offices if they're empty? I'm a businessman, not a magician. Your holistic designs might be everything you said and then some, but you can't force your ideals on people. Cherrywood conference rooms are sure sellers, and unfiltered air is free."

Mia closed her eyes, shaking her head. "So your plan was to dupe both Michael and me."

"Granted, he wouldn't have liked it when things didn't go your way. But other than an unpleasant phone call, he has no recourse. My dealings with Michael are ironclad, and over. Besides, I doubt he'd want to draw attention to higher-ups with the deal he made me. But I'll tell you what, just to appease all parties involved, I'm willing to compromise. You design my suites in traditional decorator methodology, and for every . . . let's say hundred you complete, I'll let you have one that caters to your cause. It does give me something munificent to chat up with the press." He stood, buttoning his jacket, smoothing his tie. "I assume this," he said, waving his hand dismissively, "falls under some government-sponsored, tax-deductible program?"

"You know, Aaron, I might be willing to take you up on that if it wasn't for one small problem."

"What's that?" he asked, looking as if the entire conversation was boring him.

"I don't think I could stand in the same room with you and not be physically ill."

He tipped his chin and walked to the exit, where he stopped. "I'll give you a week to get your, um, furnishings out of my building. Then I can tear up the floor, turn this into something practical." Mia nodded, taking a disheartened look around her masterpiece, about to be crated off to a warehouse. She watched him go, the door swinging shut behind him. It was mind-boggling. The time she'd invested, the hours Michael watched her slave over the tiniest of details, knowing it was nothing but false hope and manufactured success. It made her stomach sick to think about it. It was humiliating at best, a sobering insight to the respect Michael had for Mia and her designs. Her finger-tips trailed over a mosaic partition, the light catching the glass just right. It *was* beautiful, reminding Mia that it was only half a dream gone.

Chapter 30

The same cab driver thought he'd hit passenger pay dirt when Mia tossed another twenty onto the seat, racing for the hospital. Though she was familiar with the internal route to the ICU, it took her a few minutes to gain her bearings. The hallways leading to the hospital's general populace were a maze. Frustration mounted as Mia took a wrong turn on the fourth floor, which wasn't as direct or compact as intensive care. It reinforced a gut feeling that she was on a downward spiral. She disregarded it. Flynn was right there, only steps away. But the omen didn't ease, some yellow caution tape providing a last roadblock. A hazmat crew had sectioned off the corridor that supposedly led to his room. What might have been the ultimate environmental irony brought Mia to the verge of tears. She rounded another corner, running headlong into Dr. Logan.

"Mia, I'm so glad you're here—for a couple of reasons. I was going to call you."

"Is Flynn okay?" she demanded, her heart instantly thrashing. "You wouldn't have moved him out of the ICU if he wasn't better."

"Calm down. He's all right," he said, patting her shoulder. "But against every piece of advice that I could offer, he signed himself out of this hospital."

"He did what?" she said, her eyes pulsing wide. "He just . . . He can't, he wouldn't!" She searched the corridor, whipping her head in every direction. "Where, what room?"

"That way, 4412," he said, physically spinning her in the opposite direction. "But I think he's already . . ."

She ran. Plowing through the door, Mia stopped short, braking hard into a bed stripped of sheets and a body. The emptiness crashed down on her. That same raping, ripping sense of abandonment she felt all those years ago. The tears stung, her breath jerking in and out as she prayed for a last one. She could feel her mouth twitch. But there wasn't a word, not even a sound that could convey what she felt. It all screeched to a halt, pivoting sharply, like a well-trained soldier, a deep voice coming from the doorway.

"Thanks for the help—Suzie, was it? Have them send the bills to that address. It's where I'll be until everything heals."

"My pleasure, Mr. McDermott—Flynn," Suzie purred in a voice that was a bit too helpful. "If there's anything else I can do before you go, just buzz me."

Mia turned, several sights adding to her disbelief, not the least of which was a perky red-haired nurse with her hand clamped on his arm. It was an adolescent, off-the-radar assumption. Some backlog of instinct, a claim that affirmed she had never let go. The urge to assert herself—right in between them—was automatic. And she might have if Flynn had offered a glance of encouragement. But as the nurse left, he only stepped aside, ending one visual as others kicked in. He was standing upright, wearing clothes, not connected to tubes or wires, or anything else apparently.

Reaching for a small duffel bag, he tucked some papers inside. Finally, he looked in her direction. "You're back."

"You're going?" she eked out. Her head and heart pounded so violently, Mia guessed that the hospital services might prove useful.

"Yeah, I was just waiting for you to come by."

"Waiting for me to—" She inched closer, dumbfounded by his dismissive demeanor. Even his voice was different, that penetrating timbre gone. "Where . . . Why are you leaving?" Twelve years later and she was still asking the same question.

And still, he didn't answer.

"I called for a cab a while ago. I appreciate what you did, Mia, sticking around here while I—"

"Whoa! Just wait," she said, a hand tearing through her hair, trying to decipher whatever code he was speaking in. "Stop talking to me like I'm less important than that candy-coated nurse who just slinked out of here!"

"The what?" he asked, his eyes jerking fast to hers.

"If you think for one second that I'm letting you walk out of here without an explanation—" Mia's throat went numb, her voice catching on the past. She walked to the door and shut it, gathering her composure on the way. "If you think that, then you seriously underestimate what you left behind. We have a few things to talk about." Flynn focused on the duffel bag. They stood no more than a body length apart in that tiny room. Still, he managed to avoid eye contact. The lack of response ignited in Mia a well of emotions, a bottomless mix of dormant energy. "I'd like a reason, Flynn. I think I deserve that much." He seemed at an inexplicable loss for words, as if the answer completely escaped him. "Will you just say it? It can't be worse than anything I've imagined." That registered some solid eye contact, and it was Mia who looked away. Bracing for the revelation, the possibilities spilled from her mouth. "You were taken hostage by some Hells Angels? You hit your head, had amnesia?" When he didn't jump at those, Mia's gaze ticked back and she was forced to move on to less forgivable theories. "You got bored. You found someone else," she said, the bitterness rising with each suggestion. "You decided that you loved me, but not in a forever sort of way. Damn it, Flynn! Why won't you tell me?"

"Because it's not going to be anything you'll want to hear."

"Try me. I'm tougher than you think—thanks to you."

"I'll just bet," came his hard, husky reply. And for a split second she heard it, that undeniable tone. She wanted to grab it, hang on to it, but it was gone. "You were about to graduate, move on. I figured I would too. I . . . I didn't want a scene. It's not like I planned it—not so different from the way I turned up. Remember what I was running from, Mia." He paused, as if to let the dark little reminder sink in. "Did you really think walking out on you was so beyond me?"

She backed up half a step. "Yes, I did." She stared, unsure who she was looking at. Never, not even the night he confessed everything about Alena, could Mia recall seeing Flynn so uncomfortable in his own skin.

"Well," he said dully, "that's where you're wrong. If it gives you some long-overdue closure for me to say I'm sorry, then fine. I am sorry. I didn't mean to hurt you like that."

"Hurt me?" she stammered, wide-eyed and incredulous. "You didn't mean to—"

"You shouldn't have gotten involved with me in the first place. You should have listened to Roxanne. Letting it happen was my mistake, Mia, not leaving you like I did."

She couldn't get past the incidental apology, as if he'd

stepped on her toe. "Hurt me?" She came toward him, only an arm's length between them. "You didn't hurt me. Do you have the slightest idea what you did to me?" He remained a shadowy rendering of himself, silent and removed. "Look at me!" she demanded. His head ticked around, his throat bobbing with a tremendous swallow.

"If you've got a minute, I'll tell you the beginning. It underscores the years. At first I didn't even cry, couldn't get any tears out. I was just weird," she said, her voice bearing every frayed nerve. "But then it started raining, poured all through that first night and I thought, 'Oh, there they are.'" Flynn looked at her, unaffected, until an almost undetectable shudder crossed the solid line of his chin. "I didn't hope because you didn't leave any. It was like you were dead or never existed—and I had no idea which was worse." Mia pushed past the tightness in her throat. It was like a needle under her skin and she had to get it out, reliving the most pointed moment. "I slept—" Her voice pinched and she started again. "I slept on the same damn dirty sheets for months because they smelled like you. Then my mother came to visit. I nearly killed her when I caught her washing them— she thought I'd gone insane. I managed to grab the pillowcase. I slept with it for the next four years and I still haven't washed it! Nothing's allowed to touch it. It sits on a top shelf in my closet, preserved like some bloody shroud, a testament to your existence. Does that give you the slightest clue about how you *hurt* me?"

His jaw shuddered again, almost a gag. If she hadn't known better, she would have sworn he was going to be sick. He shook his head, but it was more like he was grasping at the chance to look away. "I . . . It was for the best, Mia." His voice was nearly nonexistent. "I never said that I loved you. I never promised you anything."

It was as if he had physically shoved her, and Mia staggered back. Her reflexes replied, offering up the slap she'd threatened all those years ago. "Liar," she hissed, knowing the sting to his face couldn't sum up the fury she felt. "You know damn well what you promised." There was a jagged pause, and Mia was unsure if she regretted what she'd just done, or if she should have slapped him harder.

If anything, he appeared grateful for the excuse, a reason to keep his head turned, his eyes focused out the window. "Well," he said softly, "can't say I didn't have that coming. It's not what you think, Mia. Whatever mangled fate put us back in the same place . . . You have a fantastic career, a terrific life. Go back to it."

"Back to what?" she asked, stupefied by the prospect. "For the first six years I made the best of what I could. For the last six I did my damnedest to put you behind me. Just so we're clear, I failed—miserably. And I don't even want to know what I'm going to owe for that!"

He abruptly turned toward her. "You have nothing to feel guilty about. I walked out—you did your best. You don't owe anybody a goddamn thing!" There was a low growl, all the way from his gut, his frustration more obvious than his injuries.

Confused, Mia shook her head, unsure why that of all things registered a reaction. Nothing was making sense and she stepped closer. It was only to clear things up, a simple clarification of facts. But the sheer proximity of him was intoxicating. Mia's fingertips moved fluidly down Flynn's arm, skimming over the edge of the tattoo that peeked out from beneath his shirtsleeve. She felt the fresh scars that bore more recent signs of life. He didn't pull away. An achy sigh, heavy with desire and regret, pulsed from Mia's throat. She could almost taste him, his mouth, his body, coming within a breath of hers. The space left between them smoldered. It was like that first night in the seedy motel when a look between them singed whatever was in their common path. Reaching toward the sharp line of his cheekbone, the side she'd slapped, Mia wanted desperately to take it back. Flynn grasped her hand and gently drew it away. But he held on—as if it was all he dare offer.

"Don't . . . don't confuse this," Flynn said. "I'm not . . . I can't—"

Without a knock the door swung open, the nurse's candy-coated voice oozing in. "Flynn, you got lucky. I caught a taxi just as it was leaving. But you'll have to hurry. He said he's in a no-parking zone."

"No," Mia said, her teeth gritted, her hand now clamped to his arm. "Don't do this, don't go—please." His rough fingers dusted through a fine layer of bangs. He seemed unable to stop, touching the smooth skin of her face. Their gaze bound, twined tight as the wild vines of Athens.

There was another interruption, Dr. Logan squeezing past the nurse. "Wonderful, you haven't left yet. These meds just came up from the pharmacy. You know," he said, "I never did determine what you're made of, Flynn—part titanium, that's for sure. But I do know that without these, even you won't be able to handle the pain."

Still staring at Mia, he answered, "Honestly, Doc, it won't help a damn thing."

"Listen, your insistent departure is bad enough. Humor me. I spent a good deal of time ensuring your recovery, almost as much as Mia. The least you can do is follow some discharge instructions."

"Yeah, sure. You're right," Flynn said, turning away. "What

do I need to know?" Both Dr. Logan and Flynn moved toward the window, forcing Mia out of the small space. She blatantly eavesdropped, catching cautionary words about dizziness and seizures. After a few moments, Dr. Logan finished and Flynn packed up the medication.

"Mia," Dr. Logan said. "There's something else I need to speak with you about . . ." He stopped, hesitating at the door. From the day he'd taken Flynn's case, the kindly doctor seemed oblivious to any personal turmoil. Now he bent his careworn brow, looking thoughtfully between Flynn and Mia. And she realized that he'd been well aware all along. "I'm guessing this isn't a good time. Perhaps I can phone you?"

"Anytime," Mia managed, clinging to the edge of self-possession.

"Good, I'll be in touch. Take care—both of you." Opening the door, he glanced over his shoulder. "Suzie?" She obediently followed, pasting a last look on Flynn.

"These are yours," Flynn said, holding out a neatly arranged stack of drawings, the ones she'd posted around his room. "I . . . I think they're incredible." Mia absently took them, holding them tight to her chest. "I, um, I shouldn't have come back here. Let it go, sweetheart. It . . . it was never anything more than a beautiful disaster." He picked up the duffel bag, and in one sweeping turn, headed out the door.

* *

Mia's physical reaction was a step behind. Real time moved ahead of her brain, which was taking a moment to hold the rest of her together. It all raced through her head like a flash fire, charred ruins, the wind scattering gray sooty ashes. This, she imagined, was how a person felt when everything they had, everything they loved, burned to the ground. She could feel the singe, hot on her face, worse on her heart. Amidst the smoky aftermath, she didn't notice that Roxanne had come into the room.

"Mia, answer me. Where's Flynn?"

Her head ticked around, responding more to a sense of déjà vu than Roxanne's question. She'd had this conversation, lived this moment before. "Gone," she said, dropping the drawings onto the bed. "Everything's gone. Flynn . . . he said that he shouldn't have come back. That what we had was just a . . . that it wasn't real. I don't even know how to—"

"He's lying."

At first she only nodded. Roxanne accusing Flynn of deception was an everyday event, no need to react. Then Mia did a double take, realizing it was all backward. In her hand, Roxanne held out a dirty lavender envelope with Mia's name across the front in Flynn's handwriting.

"This is what I owed you."

"What you . . ."

"Flynn left this for you."

"Today?"

"Twelve years ago," Roxanne said, clear and calm—as if Mia might not notice the gap.

Her gaze jerked between Roxanne and the envelope. There was an audible gasp, and Mia retreated back a step. "Twelve— How? Oh, Roxanne, not even you would . . ." But she was nodding, her chin tipping high as if balancing on a fine line between right and wrong.

"There isn't any excuse—not anymore. No reason that makes what I did forgivable." She extended her arm farther, offering up the coveted contents of the past. "I swear to you, Mia, I thought I was doing the right thing."

Mia's hands flew to her face, the heat in her cheeks nearly burning through her fingertips. "For twelve years you kept that from me? You've known why he left me? My God, Roxanne, what kind of person . . . How could you do that to me?" For the first time in as many years as they'd known each other, Roxanne was speechless. Mia didn't let another second pass, snatching the envelope away and taking what was hers. Turning away, she walked to the window, pulling two sheets of neatly creased paper from inside.

Mia,

By the time this letter is in your hands, the hardest part will be over. There won't be anything you can do to change it. This morning I turned myself in. If I ever get the chance to explain, you'll understand why I didn't have time for the argument. And believe me, Mia, I wanted that argument. I wanted you to say anything, do anything, to stop me. Watching you, all I really want is to wake you up and explain. But I can't. Right now, I don't have answers you'll need. And I won't ask you for any more faith. You already have way too much in a man who hasn't done a damn thing to earn it.

It was always my intention, my plan, that come June I'd go through with this. But I came across some information today, and it fast-forwards everything. This is the only move I have left. Running, especially running with you—it won't fix this. With this letter you'll find a business card. Angela Whittaker is my attorney. She'll explain why I had to do things this way. If, after reading this, you still want us, if you're willing to wait, contact her. A while back we talked about what was too much, and if this is, I understand. Think about your future. Because with or, maybe more to the point, without me, it will be exceptional.

I'd be a fool not to fear what time will do to us. But a life is a long thing when you can't marry someone, can't have a real

*job, can't put the father's name on a birth certificate. I want
all those things, Mia. No matter what you say now, eventually
you'll want them too. There isn't any reason you shouldn't have
them, certainly not because you fell in love with somebody who
can't give them to you. And right now, that's who I am. Do one
thing for me: If you don't want to wait, let it be finished this
way. I don't want any good-bye letters, any messages telling me
you're sorry . . . You have nothing to be sorry for. But, Mia, you
need to understand. From the moment you crossed that street,
every time I made love to you, for the days to come when I'm
living on memories, know that I love you.*

Flynn

Breathing required instruction. Mia looked out the window
where a single star glowed. She told herself to let it out; breathing wouldn't hurt anymore. Turning the envelope over, a crisp
new business card fell onto the windowsill. It should have been
bent and frayed with twelve years of wear. Doubt was replaced
with what might have been. *He loves me. He always loved me.*
And suddenly, Mia felt as if she'd cheated on him. No wonder
he left—again. Her hand gripped her forehead, thinking how
the casual flirtation of an insignificant nurse had agitated her.
"Oh my God, he must have wanted to die when he found out
about Michael." Mia spun around. "Wait!" she gasped, the obvious making its way through the tangled past. "He's not . . . he's
not going back to prison! That's why the police haven't come for
him. Flynn's free!"

"Appears that way," Roxanne offered from behind. "Not only
is he free, but he had nothing to do with the murders . . . with
those girls."

Mia stared, her head cocking to one side. "I see. Your DNA

must have come back. That explains a lot, hard scientific evidence over my word. It's a shame you couldn't have trusted me back then, believed that someone knew more than you. I can't even begin to think the hell it would have saved us all—Michael especially. And you might have hung on to the only friend you've ever really had."

It was a glacial melt, tears streaming down Roxanne's face. "I . . . I understand. I wouldn't expect either of you to forgive me. But, Mia, it's not too late—"

"Isn't it?" she said. "Had you given me the damn letter," she said, thrusting the stationery toward Roxanne, "at least Flynn wouldn't have gone through all that just to find me married to somebody else."

"I don't think that's why he left—not entirely."

"Oh please, we've just proven what you know."

"I know Michael was here."

"Michael?" she said, suddenly willing to listen. "He was here . . . to see Flynn?"

"I overheard the nurses talking. From the amount of shouting going on, I'm guessing it wasn't a pleasant conversation."

A last stand. If there was no persuading Mia, Michael would appeal to Flynn. She could imagine the conversation, one man prepared to do anything to win, the other willing to bow out if he believed it was the right thing.

"Not long after Michael left, Flynn asked to be discharged."

"He did, didn't he?" Mia turned back to the drawings. She saw the news clipping that would have told him everything. Flynn would do anything to protect her dream—including giving up his own. "Keep going, Roxanne. I want you to tell me everything you know."

Roxanne nodded, but before she could comply, there was a

knock at the door. "Excuse me, ladies. I'm, um, I'm looking for Serg—Mr. McDermott."

"He's gone," Roxanne said, barely turning to answer. "Mia, I'll help you in any—"

"Just a second, Roxanne," Mia said, brushing past her. "Can I help you with something, Mr. . . ."

"Jensen. My name's Kirby Jensen." Mia's breath caught on his reply, her fingertips flying to her chest. "I wanted to talk to Mr. McDermott about . . . You see, I—" His gray gaze stared at a point between his worn work boots and Mia. "It's complicated."

"Roxanne," Mia instructed, "would you excuse Mr. Jensen and me. But don't go far, we're not finished." Roxanne offered a curious glance, but no argument as she left the room. Mia turned to Kirby. "She's right, Flynn's gone."

"I see. Damn . . . I guess I came a long way for nothing. His sister called yesterday. She sounded as surprised as me to learn he was here, in Maryland. Would, um . . . would you have any idea how I can get in touch? There's something I owe him."

"Owe him?" Mia questioned. She looked steadily into his face. It was dark, haggard, as if time had had its way with him. It looked as if he hadn't slept in about twenty years.

"Yes, I owe him my life. To be honest, ma'am, a lot of guys owe their lives to Sergeant McDermott," he said, a shaky breath blowing out of him. "But not like I do. We were stationed together, years ago, in Northern Africa. There was something he did back then. Something I wasn't man enough to take the blame for—and believe me when I tell you, the blame was mine. What Sergeant McDermott did allowed me to have a life. It's about time; it's years too late—probably both, but I had to come." He continued, purging his soul. "I wanted to tell him that maybe I didn't find a miracle cure for cancer or go on to save the world.

But I did my best. I got five of the greatest kids you could ask for. The oldest, twins, Kirby Jr. and Anna Claire, they're good kids, starting their second year of college. I don't know, maybe they're the ones who'll leave a real mark. I like to think my being there helped. And I wouldn't have been if it weren't for Sergeant McDermott. I can't ever repay him, but I wanted him to understand that I know what I owe."

Moments later Kirby Jensen left, leaving Mia alone in the room, holding tight to the past and a dirty lavender envelope.

Chapter 31

It was an unlikely scene—a snow day in Maryland, Michael home during daylight hours. Icy water ran like tears as Mia glanced out the window, watching her husband try to dig his way out. The neighbor's snowman fought the weather, the afternoon sun making a serious attempt at murder. A teakettle whistled and Mia hurried to the kitchen, not wanting to wake a baby that she seemed unable to comfort. Pouring the water, the steam penetrated her face. She backed up fast. Like the snowman, it wouldn't take much to melt the façade, leaving a puddle of nothing. Her reflection caught in a stainless steel pot, one of several waiting to be washed from last night's supper. Good thing it was only a pot. Surely the image was distorted, the face not looking like anyone she recognized. As she sat at the breakfast table, the sleeve of her faded flannel shirt grazed through a smear of maple syrup. She rolled it up, weaving her hand past a scattering of mail and crumbs. Underneath the *Wall Street Journal* was yesterday's *USA Today*—or maybe it was from the day before. She opened it, scanning the state-by-state highlights. It was a bad habit, worse than hunting for him on busy sidewalks, less likely than discovering he was a contestant on *Survivor*. Mia looked through the bulleted blips. She was relieved to see that there hadn't been a natural disaster in any of the places he might be—Texas, Indiana, Georgia—thinking that it was too bad there was no such tracking system on the moon. She heard a door open and shut, Michael calling her name.

"Mia?" She felt a firm hand on her shoulder. "Mia, wake up."

She was quick to welcome wide-awake, wanting out of that sticky flannel shirt and the dirty kitchen. More than that, she wanted to escape the feeling that came with it, the unhappy people who lived in that house.

"What are you doing down here?"

She sat up, blinking at her own orderly living room. "I guess I fell asleep. Where . . . where were you all night?" she asked, unsure if it was any of her business.

"After I finished at work, I decided to stay downtown," he said. "I . . . I didn't want to come home and find you packing."

Mia pushed herself to a sitting position. "You wouldn't have—not last night."

He nodded, his gaze traveling the bare walls. "There's, um, there's something I need to ask you."

"Something about yesterday?" she said, wondering how best to fill in those details. His demeanor was different, though; his tone heavy—burdened.

"No," he said, sitting across from her, hesitating, as if the question carried with it a furious weight. "It's something I've wanted to know for the last six years. Something I was never man enough to ask." Mia sat up taller, unable to imagine Michael fitting into such a category. "Do you remember Sacred Grounds?"

She pulled back, her brow knitting. "The coffee shop in Athens?"

"Yes."

"Sure. I probably had a thousand cups there. The place was always packed."

"Do you remember having coffee there with me?"

"With you?" she said. "Except for Roxanne, we didn't exactly travel the same circle."

"I came in once, you were there—alone. I wanted to buy you a cup of coffee, but you already had one. I helped myself to a seat anyway. I commented on the number of empty sugar packets." There was a hum of agreement from Mia. It was a likely scene, but she didn't recall Michael being present in any one of them. "You laughed, said it was habit; that your boyfriend drank seriously strong coffee and the sugar counteracted it." Her gaze tied with his trying to recall the moment. "You don't remember?"

"I'm sorry, Michael, I don't."

He nodded. "I said I was sorry to hear that, about your boyfriend, because I would have liked to ask you out."

"That's not true," she said, a smile curving around her mouth. "I'd remember, Michael, if we'd had that conversation or a cup of coffee."

"No, Mia, you don't. And it's the reason I've never asked. But I remember," he said, offering a level of detail she couldn't fathom. "You were wearing a pale blue sweater; it went with your eyes. You hardly had any makeup on—your hair was damp, you had it piled up in a clip . . . so incredibly pretty," he said, shaking his head. "It had rained earlier that day, and you had on bright yellow rain boots. After I sat, your leg kept kicking, like I was making you uncomfortable, like I didn't belong there."

I remember the sweater; I threw it out after I dripped mustard down the front . . . I remember the rain boots—Flynn found them provocatively amusing . . . I remember that on Tuesdays they gave away free refills. But I don't . . . God, I am so horrifically sorry,

Michael . . . I don't remember you. They traded awkward stares, Mia at a loss for a comforting remark.

"The next thing I knew, you were thanking me for coffee I didn't buy you, then disappearing into the crowd." There was another low hum from her throat. She guessed she'd been waiting for Flynn. Michael leaned forward, his elbows resting on his knees, hands clasped together.

"Michael, I'm sorry—"

"Stop apologizing, Mia. It's . . ." He looked at her, swallowing hard. "It's not your fault." She was surprised by his calm voice. It was something she'd heard during conference calls from his study, wrapping up long negotiations. "And neither are a few other things. I saw Roxanne last night—late. We talked. She told me about the letter, what she'd done." While she kept focused on Michael, Mia's hand inched to the right, her fingers curling around the letter that had spent the night with her. His eyes followed, and he breathed deep as she pulled it close. "He, um . . . he never left you." Mia shook her head, her mouth bending to a frown. "And you would have never left him—no matter what the circumstances." There wasn't even a gesture, just a tear rolling down her cheek.

"I tried to tell you," she said, her voice frayed. "It's complicated. The reason Flynn spent all those years—"

He held up a hand. "I don't need to know. I know you. And you wouldn't fall in love with anyone who wasn't one of the good guys."

She smiled at him. "No, I wouldn't."

"Back then, if you'd read the letter . . ." He stopped, as if searching for a scenario that fit a might-have-been past. "Over the years, I could have seen you at a dozen reunions or hired you to design my entire house—bought you a million cups of coffee. Nothing would have come of it—ever."

"The truth?" she asked, achy and tired from hurting him. "Please."

She nodded, looking around. "The inside of your house would be as beautiful as it was meant to be."

He snickered, a hand scrubbing around the back of his neck. "I often suspected my ambition might cost me. Getting everything you want doesn't necessarily make you the winner, does it?" Mia said nothing, her gaze focused on the letter. "I can't tell you that it's close to anything I wanted to hear—but it'll make a few things easier." Mia looked, watching him suck in a man-up breath, the kind that Michael Wells kept in good supply. He stood, moving toward her. From inside his jacket pocket, he pulled a piece of paper, handing it to her. "This is the name of a good attorney. He'll be fair, reasonable—quick. You're right, Mia. We both deserve something better."

* *

Flynn eased out of a large SUV, partly because he was stiff as hell from two days on a bus, and mostly because he wasn't too sure how to react to white-collar suburbia. Now that he thought about it, he'd never been there. Julia, on the other hand, seemed eager to acquaint him.

"I am just so happy you're here," she said, for at least the tenth time, rushing around to the passenger side. "I would have much preferred putting you on an airplane. The first thing we're doing is getting you a driver's license, some kind of identification." He was only half listening, mesmerized by the sheen on her happy ending. He smiled, looking toward a fine house, a manicured yard. She deserved every bit of it. It sure as hell beat the memory of a paint-peeling bungalow in the middle of Indiana. "Hal will be home in a little while. He's anxious to meet you."

"Are you sure about that?" Flynn asked again. Having your

brother come for an extended stay was one thing. Having a brother with Flynn's past land on your doorstep—well, it might just muck up the finish on that happy life. "Because if it's any problem at all—"

"Nonsense," she insisted. "Hal knows the whole situation, nightmares included."

"About that—the nightmares—you don't have to worry. They're not a problem anymore."

"That's good to know," Julia said, a hand rubbing his arm. "Anyway, you're going to like Hal. He's a good person, no judgments."

Flynn nodded, though he wasn't convinced. "If you say so. It's just that . . . well, who I am—"

"Listen, who you are is my brother." Her hand clasped his as Flynn looked into eyes similar to his own. "Alec and I survived our childhood because of you. Don't think for a second I've forgotten that."

He nodded again, wanting to tell her there was no debt involved. But he was having trouble focusing, organizing any thought that didn't gravitate back to what he'd left behind. It had ridden on that damn bus with him, all the way to Texas, like a bad case of motion sickness. He sighed, a bead of sweat gathering on his brow. The blistering midday sun caused him to squint with his sunglasses on. Christ, he still hated hot places. "Okay, we'll just take it one day at a time, see what happens."

"And I want you to think about what I said. Mom left the insurance policy to all three of us, equally. Spiting yourself with stubbornness isn't the answer. It's not a fortune, but Hal invested your share wisely. Given some time to focus on your future, I can imagine what you'll make of it."

"I told you, Julia. I don't want it—any part of it. Put it in a college trust for your kids."

"Put it in one for yours!" she fired back. He had no response for what he deemed an impossible notion. "You never know," she quietly added.

He started to walk toward the house.

"Oh, did I mention that the apartment is above the garage?" she said, pointing in the opposite direction. "It's cute as a button—Hal fixed it up. He was going to use it as his office, but then his business took off and it was too small. Maybe you want to take your things up, take a nap or a shower before dinner?"

Two days on a bus. Maybe she had a point. "Yeah, sure . . . This way?" he asked, as she headed to the front door.

"Right up those stairs," she said. "You don't mind, do you? I left a roast in the oven and I've got a million things to do before dinner."

"Uh, sure. I'll see you in a while, I guess."

The small apartment was about what Julia had described: brand-new, partially furnished, private, home. The last one would take some getting used to. He had no concept of the word. He only knew the empty ache in his gut was worse than the one he'd carried through prison. Flynn cleared his throat, thinking that he could talk himself into forward motion. If nothing else, for Julia's sake, he would try. On a small table were some framed photographs—Julia's family, the two sons he'd yet to meet, *his nephews*. That sent his mind in a zigzag direction. And Julia had said that Alec's wife was pregnant, due any day. They'd come for a visit just as soon as they could. It was a circle he was supposed to be part of, but really, he couldn't have felt more on the outside. The void was overwhelming, and Flynn turned back, ready to bolt. He could go wherever he wanted, no looking over his shoulder. He could keep moving—if not forward, at least in some direction that led him away from her. He huffed, scrubbing a hand over his face. "Like there's a place on earth," he muttered, moving toward what he guessed was the bedroom.

He pushed the door open. In an instant home and earth collided, crash landing together onto a pin size spot of Texas. On the bed was a satiny cream-colored comforter, begging for someone to fall into it. Propped against a mountain of pillows was a dirty lavender envelope.

"I got your letter."

He turned, staggering back a few steps. The voice, the sight, that powdery scent, it filled him. She stood in the doorway of the bathroom wearing a simple summer dress, pale pink. She looked as astonishing as she did crossing that street all those years ago. "My letter . . . I see," he said, his eyes engaging all brain function, drinking in the curves of her body, the hair tumbling around her shoulders. Her eyes—those sparkling doll's eyes. "Mia, how did you . . . ?"

"I have a couple of ins at the hospital—your billing address, one phone call. That, and your sister's a lovely person. The resemblance is remarkable—same smile."

"You shouldn't be here. When I left—"

"When you left, you lied to me. You've never lied to me. And you know what, Flynn?" He shook his head, wondering if he'd downed one too many pain pills. "You're a horrible liar. Really, didn't you learn anything in prison? So I came for the truth. I came all this way to ask you a few things, to tell you a few things. Face-to-face, no interruptions, no candy-coated nurses . . . and no soon-to-be ex-husband."

"Soon-to-be . . . ?"

"Former husband," she said quietly, as if not to disturb a delicate fact. "Michael's a good man, a dogged fighter when need be. But in the end, he realized that circumstance wasn't any kinder to him than to us." Flynn nodded, listening. "But first things first, I'd like to answer your question."

"My question?"

"The one you asked twelve years ago. The one I haven't had a chance to answer until now. The answer is yes. Yes, I'll wait for you," she stated, firm and determined. "Twelve years, twenty years, whatever it takes. I'll wait until we're both so old and decrepit that all we can do when you get out is hold hands and put our teeth in the same glass."

"That long?" he asked, touched by a prediction she wouldn't have to prove.

"Yes, that's what I would have told you if I'd had the chance. It would have been miserable, and endless, and at first I would have been furious with you for doing it. But now that I've had a little time to mature and think about it . . . Well, like you said, by the time the letter was in my hands, the hardest part would be over. And," she said, a flutter in her voice, "here we are."

"Here we are," he said, just staring, thinking if she took one step closer she was going to be between him and that satiny cream-colored comforter. He edged toward the safety of the door. "Mia, there are a lot of things you need to think about. Your career especially. You don't understand—"

"I understand everything. There are two things I've spent the last twelve years wondering about: One required hard work and perseverance; the other a miracle. Hard work and perseverance I can do, I'll continue to do. Miracles I have no control over. When I first saw you in the hospital, in that bed, really, it was just that much more torture. But the whole time I kept telling myself that miracles don't come gift wrapped. Sometimes they're bloody and beaten and they don't necessarily resemble anything you'd expect. But eventually you'd wake up and tell me . . . well, tell me exactly what you said in that letter."

"But what I said, I had no right to ask you that. I still don't have any right to your future. It was a desperate man's attempt to hang on to the one good thing—the one perfect thing he had."

"You still have it." The sky is blue. It was that kind of a declaration, obvious and understood, a clear disinterest in discussing various interpretations of color. "Now it's my turn to ask a question: What are you going to do with it?"

On occasion there are moments where careful thoughts convey perfect words. After a second, Flynn realized this wasn't one of them. In one fluid motion, she was in his arms, the two of them sinking into that thick comforter. A first kiss was never so sure, as his lips hungrily met with hers. It was an inexhaustible passion that filled sentences and years and the hope for whatever came next. Mia tore at the buttons of Flynn's shirt, her mouth pressed hotly to his neck, his chest. Her fingers fluttered over every unclaimed muscle. He wanted the same, wandering the soft curves, his hands slipping beneath the dress, skimming along her skin, remembering how to touch every part of her. The achy groan from her throat told him he hadn't forgotten a thing. Their bodies twined together, but every few moments he'd pause to look at her.

"What?" she finally asked.

"Get used to it. I am never going to be able to stop looking."

In between the kisses that anxiously met his, she murmured, "Flynn?"

"Yeah," he said, his mouth moving along the line of her throat, breathing her in.

"You should know, if . . . if you keep doing this—just this—for the rest of my life . . ." She kissed him again, her hands moving hard over his body. "I'd die a completely happy woman."

He laughed, his forehead bumping against hers. It was an honest thought but unrealistic. A dozen years of desire couldn't fit into the confines of a kiss. His hand raced along her skin—just touching her for now. "Give me a chance. I have a few things in mind that may make you reconsider. Everything that I've thought about doing to you—with you . . ." He slowed down for a moment, looking hard into her eyes. "Mia, I . . . I need you to know something."

"Right now?" she asked breathlessly.

"It's important. Where I was, that place, all those years. It was very dark, very loud." Her eyes closed, a tear seeping from beneath the lid. "Mia, look at me." She did, and the tears spilled faster. "But the whole time, your voice, it was the loudest, the brightest thing in my head . . . more intense than any of it. Whether you were waiting for me or not. It's the reason I came out on the other side. Every day, for all that time, I'd breathe out and you'd breathe in."

She nodded, her fingertips trailing along. "I know. I know that because I was doing the exact same thing."

His hand reached to her face, brushing the tears away. He shook his head. "This, you're done with. Everything I promised us, Mia. I want to spend every day making you believe, making it happen."

"Well then," she said, pulling him into the kind of kiss that only led to pleasurable forward motion. "I predict a very easy, very happy forever—I'm already there."

Epilogue

"Mia, try to think ahead. It'll be over soon. We can take a vacation. That's it; we'll take a really nice trip—maybe somewhere tropical. Would you like that, sweetheart?"

"You want to go to the beach? Oh, that's just perfect, Flynn! But hey, I'm a little busy right now. Maybe you could pack my bikini for me. On second thought, don't bother. I'm sure I'll never fit into it again." The words trailed off as she grimaced. "I can't do this anymore. I've decided I don't want a baby. I want to go home."

"And disappoint Dr. Logan?" he asked, clearly going for distraction. "He's so looking forward to having the designer of Maryland's first totally green hospital give birth here."

"It seemed like a better idea before we got to this part," she said, squeezing his hand—hard.

"The Lincoln Montgomery Holistic Birthing Center," the nurse calmly added.

"Maybe we can chat about this later . . ." She gulped, glancing between Flynn and the nurse. "But, um, I think right now . . . this is . . ."

"Okay, Mia, one more big push and we'll be there," the doctor instructed.

She tried, but she just couldn't do it, her head flopping back against the pillow. She looked at Flynn. "Are you smiling? The last thing you'd better be doing is smiling!" she said, half laughing, half crying.

"No, of course I'm not smiling," he said, his expression going stone cold sober.

But he couldn't completely hide it; Mia caught the slightest glimmer of a smile beneath the beard. He hadn't stopped smiling since the moment they were married, the second she'd asked him if he'd rather paint the spare room blue or pink. It ended up a soft yellow, as they decided to leave it a surprise. In a few minutes they would find out; that's what the doctor had told them. Three hours ago.

The nurse who appeared tickled at first, managing the care of the hospital's widely acclaimed holistic designer, had transgressed to pushing Mia's leg behind her ear for the last half hour. She patted her shoulder. "Try not to be snappish, dear. He's just trying to help. I'm sure he'd do this for you if he could."

Narrowing her eyes, Mia snapped right back, "He's done quite enough already, thank you!" It was the spark of energy she needed, the final push resulting in the sound of a newborn cry.

The nurse smiled at Flynn. "Gets them every time."

Hours later, afternoon sunlight streamed in but could add nothing more to the happiness that filled the room. Mia, who was tired but content, was sitting up in the bed, holding a tiny bundle of pink blanket. "Flynn, did you see? Did you see her fingers? They're so long like yours. And her eyes, I just know she has your eyes," Mia gushed.

"I see," he whispered, standing over the two of them, kissing the top of his wife's head. "She's perfect."

"No, she's not," Mia said, glancing up at him.

"Huh? What are you talking about?"

"She has no name. We're going to settle this right now. It's not going to drop from the sky, you know, like a sign. Here, you hold her. Maybe it will inspire you."

"Me?"

"Well, yes, you. It was your plan to hold your daughter, wasn't it?"

He didn't reply, carefully scooping the sleeping baby into his arms, cautiously sitting in a rocking chair. "It's . . . it's new territory for me. I'm just a little nervous, I guess." His voice dropped to a whisper, lost in what he saw. "She's so small. I can't believe how tiny . . ."

"Ha! You can have the next one. Then we'll talk about small." She laughed, picking up a well-worn baby name book. "Okay, well you've crossed out, excuse me, blackened out every name that begins with an R. We won't even go there. I, um, I wonder if she's heard?" Since moving back to Maryland and taking on the hospital's massive project to go green, she'd run into Roxanne on occasion. But it would take time before their relationship was repaired, if ever.

"I'm sure it's made it through the grapevine by now. You know the newspaper was downstairs earlier, a reporter. They want to come up and take a picture. With the success of Good Sam going green, and a dozen more hospitals on board, the idea of its designer having her baby here sparked quite an interest. Dr. Logan said it's up to us, but of course they'd love the PR."

"Maybe tomorrow," Mia said, not overly interested in cashing in on her professional success. "I like being the three of us for right now. Her name," she persisted, flipping through the book. "Let's see, you've also eliminated any name or the close proximity to any name of girls you dated, picked up, or played in a sandbox with. I hate to say it, Flynn, but that's a lot of names."

Mia looked over. He wasn't even listening, but was mesmerized, looking down at that tiny face. Wisps of dark hair framed a perfectly round head. Maybe the baby had her nose, but the skin, it looked just like Flynn's and the delicate long lashes, a perfect match. Mia watched in content silence until a nurse wandered in.

"Excuse me, Mrs. McDermott, I have some paperwork for you. I'll just leave it here." She placed it on the tray table, admiring Flynn and the baby before leaving. "Now, if that just doesn't give you faith."

In unison their heads rose up from looking at the baby, and they glanced at one another. Flynn stood, holding his daughter with all the gentleness two hands could manage, and placed her in a nearby bassinet. "I thought you said it wouldn't drop from the sky."

"Well, that's just the thing about a sign. You never know when one will turn up." She glanced at the papers the nurse brought in. "Oh, I've been waiting for this. This is for you." Mia spun the paper around to face him, holding out a pen. "Let's see, you put her name here," she said, pointing. Flynn took the pen and carefully wrote, Faith Georgia McDermott. "And then, here." Mia looked up at him, tears in her eyes. "The father's name goes right here." When he finished, she ran her fingers over the name. Peyton Flynn McDermott. "She couldn't be a luckier little girl to have your name on that birth certificate."

Flynn sat on the edge of the bed, pulling his wife close. "It was a long and broken road, Mia. But I can't imagine it leading me anywhere except back to you."

READERS GUIDE

FOR

Beautiful Disaster

DISCUSSION QUESTIONS

1. Does Mia's wealthy background contribute to her sense of identity? Do you think it has any kind of sway over some of the life choices she makes? What motivates her?

2. How does Mia's father's spirit and legacy animate Mia's life? What pressure does it exert on her, and how do you think he would feel about her life choices—in regard to both her career path and her men?

3. What is Mia's first impression of Flynn? What does Flynn see in Mia? How are these assumptions challenged? Why do you think they are drawn to each other?

4. Why do you think Mia stays after witnessing Flynn's mental collapse at the motel? How does this choice mark a turning point in her life? How might things have been different if she'd left?

5. Does knowing early on about the murders influence your experience of the story—or of Flynn? Did you suspect he was guilty? What clues are offered by Roxanne's research? Were you surprised by the outcome?

6. Do you think Roxanne's protest over Mia's relationship with Flynn was justified? Have you ever had to dissuade a friend from getting involved in a seemingly unhealthy relationship? How might you have reacted in Roxanne's place?

7. Why do you think the author chose to set the story half in the present and half in the past? What effect did this have on your experience of the story?

8. How has Flynn's complex past shaped him? Were you surprised to learn of his military service as a commanding officer? What aftereffects still linger for him? What did the loss of Alena do to him?

9. What influence do Michael and Roxanne have over the course of Mia's life and her decision making? Do you think the control they have over her is healthy? Were any of their actions—hiding the letter, the "sweetheart deal" with Hough—out of line?

10. Do you think Mia ultimately made the right choice between Michael and Flynn? What does each man offer her—especially security- and passionwise?

11. By the end of the novel, how do you feel about Flynn as a character? Were you surprised by all the dramatic revelations in his background—his underlying altruistic nature beneath the gruff, intimidating exterior? Does Mia bring out the best in him?